THE HIDDEN LIGHT OF NORTHERN FIRES

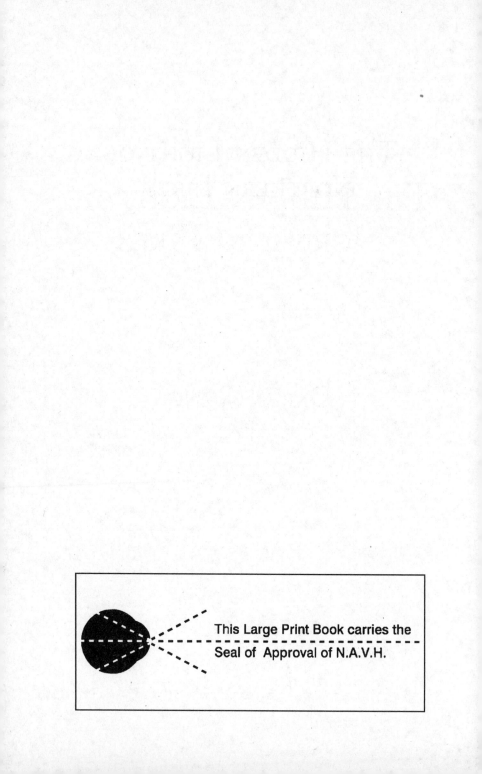

This Large Print Book carries the
Seal of Approval of N.A.V.H.

THE HIDDEN LIGHT OF NORTHERN FIRES

DAREN WANG

THORNDIKE PRESS
A part of Gale, a Cengage Company

Farmington Hills, Mich • San Francisco • New York • Waterville, Maine
Meriden, Conn • Mason, Ohio • Chicago

Copyright © 2017 by Daren Wang.
Thorndike Press, a part of Gale, a Cengage Company.

ALL RIGHTS RESERVED
Thorndike Press® Large Print Historical Fiction.
The text of this Large Print edition is unabridged.
Other aspects of the book may vary from the original edition.
Set in 16 pt. Plantin.

LIBRARY OF CONGRESS CIP DATA ON FILE.
CATALOGUING IN PUBLICATION FOR THIS BOOK
IS AVAILABLE FROM THE LIBRARY OF CONGRESS

ISBN-13: 978-1-4328-4497-4 (hardcover)
ISBN-10: 1-4328-4497-0 (hardcover)

Published in 2018 by arrangement with Macmillan Publishing Group,
LLC/St. Martin's Press

Printed in the United States of America
1 2 3 4 5 6 7 22 21 20 19 18

For my mom and dad

There is no remedy for love but
to love more.

— Henry David Thoreau

PROLOGUE

When I was a child my family moved to Town Line, New York, taking up in an ancient half-converted barn, chock-a-block with the detritus of its hundred and fifty years. There were old farm tools, a huge brass bell in a belfry, a rusted shotgun so old that no shell made today would fit it, and shelves and shelves of books.

My parents took to finishing the conversion with a fever, and the first step was clearing out the mess. Early on they found a book dealer willing to trade out the old books on the study shelves for a recent edition of the *Encyclopedia Britannica* — exactly the thing my three brothers and I would need for our new school.

I remember watching as the old man with rimless glasses took the books off the study shelves and packed them carefully into boxes. One volume made him pause — a diary with a broken clasp. He opened it and showed me the delicate pages. Even then, I thought the handwriting was beautiful.

"That's a lady's hand," he said, as much to himself as to me.

There were other things tipped into the pages: letters and crumbling news clippings and handwritten receipts.

Like most, my childhood home imprinted me. Years later, I went looking for its history and fell down a rabbit hole of wonder. I learned the name of the family that built that old barn and the house attached to it. As I tracked down their descendants and dug through newspaper archives and court records, I saw that lady's handwriting again — signatures on contracts and wills, names on the backs of ancient photos.

I've often imagined the fate of that diary: cared for and revered in some private collection, or buried at the bottom of a stray cardboard box in someone's attic.

I've spent years piecing together the lost story that I had one brief glimpse of as a child.

1861

RAILROAD

$1000 REWARD.
RAN AWAY from the subscriber on the 27 Dec., a negro man, 5'11", medium dark, known by the name of Joe Bell. I will pay $1000 CASH for delivery to me at Walnut Grove Plantation of HARPERS FERRY.

J. YATES BELL
(Newspaper clipping dated January 3, 1861, pasted into Mary Willis's journal)

The shoes had been sound when he set out, but the frozen fields and mountain crossings had worn through the soles, tearing apart the stitching at the heels and toes. Joe had bound them together three nights earlier with a length of rough twine he found by the side of the road and had not taken them off since, afraid they would fall apart and leave him nothing.

Every step broke the crust of snow with a crackling noise and the fine powder beneath sifted into his shoes through the holes and the split seams. The faint sound echoed across the frozen meadow.

He felt as if he'd been hungry forever. He had spent the day hiding in a luggage car under a horse blanket, and the crust of bread he'd eaten had been so dry it had made his gums bleed. The porter, a freedman named Mayfield, had brought it to him along with instructions: "Get off at Alden. The stop after that is Town Line, and the station agent there is a serious one. Checks for stowaways most every night. When we slow down, get yourself off the back of the train so no one will notice you. Stay away from the road. Head west and look for a barn with a white horseshoe. About three miles. Keep your head low. Don't mess around with no one else. There's copperheads in Town Line and they're looking for anyone they can make a reward from, free or slave."

"Is there a sign for Alden?" Joe asked.

"You read?" Mayfield asked, surprise in his voice.

"Yes."

"You don't sound like any fugitive I ever seen before," the porter said. He shifted baggage around to better hide Joe and make himself look busy. "There's a sign, but I don't know what it says. The conductor will call 'Alden station.' Fifteen more miles from there down to Buffalo and the Niagara."

Looking at his shoes Joe asked, "Can't I just stay in here until we get downtown?"

"All this sneaking around you done, you seen any of these fools with a penny pinned to their coat?"

"Copperheads," Joe said.

"They watch the trains down near Buffalo. You see one of them boys, you better run," Mayfield said. "The underground will get you to Canada soon enough."

Joe had been warned about copperheads after he crossed into Pennsylvania. Northerners looking to make reward money on any escaped slaves they could find.

Mayfield straightened up and turned toward the passenger cars.

"What's it like over the border?" Joe asked.

"Shh," Mayfield hissed, his eyes locked on the little round window in the compartment's door. "They see me talking to you, they'll send me back south with you."

He put his hand on the doorknob and looked down at the floor.

"They got no more use for us over there than they do here. There's whole camps of men begging for work, and there ain't nothing about you going to make it any different. But at least you don't have to call them massuh when you beg."

He shook his head.

"Now you stay quiet, cover yourself with that blanket, and don't get old Mayfield in trouble," he said.

When the town was called, Joe jumped from the train and cracked his knees on the frozen ground. Moments later the train came to a rest at a long building on the edge of the field near a clutch of horses tied to a post outside. Joe could see men standing at a bar through the yellow windows of the station and wondered if any were the bounty men Mayfield had talked about.

Joe moved as fast as he could, but the open fields left no place to hide and the full moon lit the field like a calcified sun. He winced as each footstep left a snow-white scar in the gray of the train's coal-ash trail.

He had measured nearly two miles when he heard horses and the bark of a dog on the nearby road. He dropped to his stomach midway through a field, and he turned his head to see the silhouette of two riders making their way up the road, passing a bottle between them. The riders were mismatched, one a skinny boy bundled under a threadbare coat and a knitted skullcap on a mare so swayback the boy's feet were on the verge of touching the ground, the other a giant of a man with an unkempt beard and a shearling coat open to the frigid night air riding a gray-black stallion.

The dog scampered from one side of the road to the other, nose to the ruts in the frozen mud.

Joe had always hated dogs. Whenever there was a runaway at the Bells' plantation, the foreman would take Bell's hounds out and their bays and yaps would echo across the Virginia hills for hours and hours. Afterward, they lazed by the back door of the big house, wrestling over a ham bone given in reward. He'd eye the bone, knowing that in his mother's hands it would have made a week of meals.

One time he raised a stick to his shoulder and sighted along it at one of the hounds, but Yates Bell had clubbed him from behind with a pistol and laughed as he lay sprawled on the ground.

Those Southern hounds seemed puny when he looked at the wolflike thing trailing the riders.

The boy on the swayback held out the bottle, saying, "I don't know why I let you drag me away from the fire to ride this damned road. I'm colder than a witch's teat, and I still ain't never seen a nigger."

17

"They pass through here, come through here near every day," the big one said, a strange accent marking his rumbling voice. "I seen their signs around. Marshal Kidder got eight hundred dollars last year for one, even after he killed it."

"You tell me that story every time, but I still don't have no eight hundred dollars," the boy on the swayback said. "Tomorrow night, I'm staying at the tavern."

"Nein," the other said. "I need the dog."

"Shit. Then I get a share, Jep gets a share, and you get the third. Gimme back that whiskey," the boy said.

The dog stopped downwind from Joe, whined, then barked into the field where he lay.

"Jep?" the boy asked.

The dog snarled in reply.

"She's got a scent," the boy shouted. "I think we got one."

The dog leapt into the field, and Joe jumped to his feet, breaking away from the road toward the looming forest.

The bottle dropped, shattering on the frozen road as the riders brought their horses around for the chase.

"You clumsy son of a bitch," the big rider shouted. "That's coming out of your share."

Joe could feel the hooves pounding the

ground behind him as he ran.

At the forest line, saplings lashed Joe even as he raised his arms to cover his face. Even leafless, the trees closing in above drained all the light from the sky. His feet, numb and aching, slipped awkwardly on fallen limbs, snow, and slick leaves underneath. The ground sloped downward and he could hear the rush of water in front of him. The riders cursed as their horses drove them into the clawing overhead branches.

The frigid air burned Joe's lungs, and the sound of his own gasps drowned out the guttural noises coming from the cur as she closed in on him. He veered away from the moon-soaked flat of a creek bed at the bottom of the incline and ran into an opening cleared by a fallen tree. His shin cracked hard on a limb and he went down, slamming into the frozen ground. He felt the muscles of his left calf tear and snap as the dog ripped into them. Only the sear of teeth kept him from blacking out.

The bitter cold and the tears welling in his eyes clouded his vision as his hands splayed out in front of him. His hand found a thick, jagged branch a few feet long and he grabbed at it like it was his salvation.

Joe twisted around, and flailed toward where the dog gnawed his leg. He felt the

19

limb connect with something. The dog howled and Joe could feel it retreat from him. He rolled onto his back, trying to knuckle vision back into his clouded eyes. The animal was on him again. He could smell the animal's breath, but he saw only the dark brown and the white blur of fangs.

He wrapped his arms around the animal's neck and pulled it to him, even as the teeth clacked at his left ear. Joe squeezed hard until he heard something pop. Sobbing, he let the animal fall to the ground where it lay whining.

He pulled himself up with the branch. He used it to limp out of the clearing, the blood from the gash spilling black on the moonlit snow. His breath came heavily and his teeth chattered. He crouched behind an oak to rest and bit down hard as he packed snow into the open wound.

He watched as the first pursuers stopped over the mewling animal in the clearing, his knuckles whitening on the limb as he took in the great size of the man, towering over the dog, musket in hand.

Joe tried placing weight on his ruined leg and choked off a sob of pain. He shivered, but couldn't tell if it was from the cold, the sharp burning of the wound, or the thought of fighting the man who knelt over the howling dog. He tightened his grip on the limb, measuring its heft, looking for cracks, noting the juttings of broken offshoots, then he pulled himself upright behind the tree and listened to the snow-damped quiet of the night.

"This bitch don't look like she's good for nothing anymore," the man shouted. "Get over here and shoot her. I need my load for the nigger. He's got the jump."

He stood and surveyed the clearing, spotting the blood-marked trail.

"He won't be getting far," he muttered and heaved his bulk forward, breaking to a full stride faster than Joe would have expected.

Joe's hands cramped around the limb. Coiled behind the tree, knees bent, breath slowed, he timed his swing to meet the face of the big man, gritting his teeth as the heavy limb cracked into his pursuer's face. Blood sprayed into the moonlight, and the man dropped to the ground. The impact sent pain humming through his cold-brittled hands and up his wrists and forearms.

Joe released the limb, flexed feeling back into his fingers, and grabbed the musket, noticing the copper pinned to the man's heavy coat. The blood on his hands froze to the cold metal and pulled at his skin. He braced himself using the long weapon and limped twenty paces before kneeling again behind a tree, waiting for the boy with the horses.

He'd never held a gun in his hands before. Back at the plantation, Yates Bell always had a shotgun hanging from his saddle, but putting his hand on it would have brought hellfire down on him.

This one was much longer than that, the end of the muzzle coming up to his chin when he leaned on it. The gun gave Joe a sense of power and he tried to brush away the snow that had frozen in the mechanism above the trigger.

The skinny boy led the horses into the clearing. He knelt down to the whimpering dog. "Ah, Jep. Look what he done to you, girl," he said, his words slurred with whiskey. He scratched the whining animal between its ears then crouched in silence, stroking the animal for a long time before he took up his own musket and backed up a few paces.

"I'll get him for ya, Jep, I swear," he whispered and pulled the trigger.

The shot echoed into the night woods.

Shoulders shaking, he muttered a blessing over the carcass, then stood silently before taking the leads of the two horses and turning to follow the trail. He had taken only a few steps when he came upon his companion lying in the snow and fell next to him.

"Wilhelm," he muttered. "Jesus Christ, look at you."

He dropped his musket and pulled a rag from a pocket to dab at the wound before scooping fresh snow onto it to slow the bleeding. The downed man jerked and moaned.

"Can you stand?" he said. "We gotta get you to Doc Pride."

Another moan.

Joe raised the snow-crusted flintlock to his eye and braced the long barrel against the tree. "I have the musket with a load and a bead on you, and you got nothing. I'm taking the big horse," he growled, pitching his voice low.

The skinny kid scanned the woods. He was little more than a boy, a wispy blond beard poorly masking his pimpled chin. His greasy coat, held together by a lunatic map of patches, was something Joe's mother would have used to stuff a mattress. Joe could see fear in his drunken eyes.

"That dog was the best I ever saw, mister," the boy said loudly. "She's all I cared about in this world. You can go ahead and shoot me, but I sure as shit ain't letting you take the horse."

Joe's hands shook with cold and the weight of the musket. His finger was wrapped tight on the thick trigger, but he could not bring himself to pull it.

"Goddammit," he whispered to himself. He lowered the heavy weapon to his side and limped away from the bloody clearing.

"Why do you come up here anyway?" the voice behind him shouted. "Nobody wants you up here. Why didn't you stay down there where you're from?"

Joe limped toward the sound of the water.

"You'll pay for what you done," he heard shouted into the night behind him, and then nothing more.

"We all do," he whispered to himself as he shimmied out onto the edge of the ice to get to the flow at the center of the creek bed. He plunged his bloodied leg, shoe and all, into the glacial water.

The creek passed in near silence, and he listened for any sign of pursuit as the cold numbed the pain and slowed the bleeding to a trickle.

He stood and followed the flow of the water, first west then north, hopping awkwardly onto the broken segments of sheet ice jutting from the creek bank, avoiding the snow that had settled on the even

24

surfaces. He slipped, and the musket fell into the water. He scrambled to keep from following it. His hands cramped again when he plunged them into the cold water to retrieve it.

As the creek bent, the south bank sloped steeply into a line of trees dangling over the water. He crawled up the embankment and found a black opening to a hollow under the shallow tree roots, washed out by years of spring rushes. He held his breath and listened to the dark of the cave, sniffing at the dank animal smells that wafted up and poking the muzzle of the musket into the darkness. He pushed his fear down, plunged in, and slid into a muddy pocket that smelled of piss and leaf mold.

The cave was about ten feet deep and three feet high at its tallest point, but it was empty and drifted deep with dry leaves.

His leg ached and started to bleed again. He pulled leaves to himself, lay still and tried to sleep, but his shivering kept him in a dazed wakefulness throughout the night.

In the morning, gray light filtered into the cave and he crawled out, desperate for anything to fill his stomach. The wound had scabbed, but his hands and feet were numb and the shivering had turned to fits of uncontrollable quaking. He slid down the embankment and drank at the creek.

He dared not move in the open during the daylight hours, so he climbed back up to the cave and hid again. An early-morning dusting coalesced into a squall, and drifting snow constricted into a halo at the cave mouth.

The den warmed with his breath and he dozed. He tried to recall the warmth of the Virginia sun on his bare shoulders and invoked a memory of a picnic on a bluff overlooking the Shenandoah with his mother and sister. It was his tenth birthday, and somehow his mother had managed half a chicken for the occasion. She spread the treasure out on a cloth, and his sister, Alaura, a six-year-old with her hair tied with blue rags that passed for ribbons, stared at the riches with a look of amazement and joy.

"It's your brother's birthday," their mother said, the joy of putting good food in front of her children shining bright in her face.

His sister reached for the leg from the small pile of pieces, and he remembered thinking that was the piece he wanted, that it was his birthday and that he should get first pick. But then she cupped it in her hands like it was a precious jewel, and offered it to him.

"Happy birthday, Joey," she said, her dimples furrowing into her cheeks.

Joe took the piece of chicken, and bent over to kiss her, because he could not help but kiss her, and she wrapped her arms around him.

"You're my favorite brother." She giggled.

"Not that you have many choices," he said, laughing back at her, and waited until his mother signaled that he could take a bite.

His mother was gone now, sold down to Mississippi, and dead soon after. And now he had left Alaura all alone. He thought of the way that Yates Bell had often eyed her, and he wished as he had a million times that he had taken her with him.

He'd been saving to buy her papers before he ran, had even talked it over with old Mr. Bell, but he couldn't imagine how he could do it now. Not after the money was gone. Not after running. Not after nearly killing Yates.

"I'll get you free, I swear," he said to the thought of her, but he knew the words carried no more weight than the white mist they made in the cold air.

He slipped into a dream of the plantation and of the woods around Harpers Ferry, and the little shack near the sawmill where he used to sleep.

His fever came stronger, and it called other things into his dreams: the crack of the dog's neck jolting through his hands, the sound of the limb breaking on that man's face, the sight of the poor boy down the long barrel.

He woke to the sound of a rider coming down the creek in the late afternoon. Joe peeked out to see the skinny boy, talking to himself as the horse picked its way through the stone creek bed and falling snow, passing within yards of the den.

Terrified, Joe squeezed deeper into the cave and gripped the musket with the ruined load, pulling more of the rotten leaves over himself, trying to make out what he was saying until he had rode on.

Joe's leg throbbed and he sweated and shivered in the cold air. He imagined himself dying in the little hole, his body never to be found; he smiled grimly, thinking how the torment of not ever knowing if he was dead would plague Yates, but then he thought of Alaura and his promise.

When the gray light dimmed, he broke through snow at the mouth of the cave and slid down the embankment to the water's edge. His fever had taken on an edge, and he could not remember where he was, but he understood he would not survive another night in the cave. His leg throbbed and a trickle of blood seeped through the torn pant leg as he set out into the night made darker with clouds.

He came to a road, turned west to put the wind at his back, and stumbled again into the open fields. His thin coat was soaked through with cold sweat. He teetered through a cornfield, and into a line of poplars, upright and gray against the black sky. Squeezing through a gap in the enmeshed trees, he found himself on a hard road rutted with wagon tracks leading past a two-story white house with a wide front porch sitting above the main road. A red barn sat at the foot of the incline and small, neat buildings lined the drive and the barnyard. A white horseshoe was tacked over the wide doors of the barn. He knew that should mean something but could not remember what.

The windows of the house glowed in the night. He could see women in the kitchen, laughing as they washed dishes. Smoke from the chimney perfumed the night, and two men sat together by a fireplace in the parlor. Trembling with cold, Joe stumbled up to the window. The red of the walls, the green of the leather chairs, and the yellow of the fireplace glowed through the glass, a world separate and impossibly far from the black of the clouded sky and the white snow under his feet. He stood, staring, imagining himself in a chair by that fire, warm and full, listening to the men tell stories.

He tried to hear what they were saying through the window.

The old man sat with his fingers tented, his brow furrowed while the one with a serious face and muttonchop sideburns was asking something of him. Joe could hear the plaintive tone, but could not make out the words. They looked like the type of people who would feed a starving stranger, even a fugitive slave.

The sound of laughter shook Joe from his vision. Three men, talking loudly, staggered slowly up the pike. Joe could think of nothing but hiding and slipped away from the highway.

He reached the shadow of the barn and crept down along its rock foundation, leaning hard on the cemented river stone. He followed it to a wooden door and lifted the iron latch. The hinges creaked and he slipped inside and pulled the door closed behind him. A cow lowed in her disturbed sleep. He stepped toward the sound and fell.

MARY

Mary Willis came home to Town Line in May of 1859. She brought with her an Alfred University diploma, a copy of *Uncle Tom's Cabin* by Harriet Beecher Stowe, and a bundle of anti-slavery tracts tied neatly with grocer's string.

The diploma was one of only twenty-six earned by young ladies in New York State that year. The book was both heavily annotated by Mary and inscribed to her by Mrs. Stowe herself. The tracts she carried down to Snyder's General Store the next Saturday afternoon and handed out as she recited a debate-society-perfected jeremiad on the peculiar Southern institution of slavery.

She had lived among the immigrant farmers for all of her life, and should have known that most of them spoke only German and could not read a word in English, but she was encouraged by how quickly her bundle

31

disappeared.

The farmers spent all their worrying hours focused on rainfall, hoeing, and late frost, and had little concern about the issue that was tearing their adopted nation apart. None refused the paper, though, which would serve as a welcome reprieve from the dwindling supply of dried corn husks piled in the corner of their outhouses.

The next night, Nathan Willis sat down for Sunday dinner with Mary and her younger brother, Leander, and delivered his own diatribe.

"When I was your age, I went for months without seeing another white man," he said to Mary, tucking the white linen napkin into his shirt as Katia brought out the roast. "Ten years among the Haudenosaunee. I fought off roaming packs of wolves and once I killed a bear that rammed down the cabin door in the middle of the night. It was so cold in '16 that it snowed in July, and we all nearly starved to death. Poor old Arch Frick had to sell off his own son. The Willises have fought and we have built great things. And despite all that, I find myself embarrassed to walk into the very town I founded. And why? Because the pastor spent his entire sermon this morning condemning my daughter for her uppity, unladylike ways."

Leander, who suffered his father's ire nearly every evening, sat across the table from Mary hanging his head in silence. When she noticed that behind his respectful posture, he was grinning, she had to bite her cheek to stop herself from giggling. As always, her brother brought out the child in her.

"Don't get me wrong," her father said, ignoring his children's antics. "I have no truck with this dealing of human flesh, and when Millard Fillmore was still president, I told him to his face that he set this country on the road to perdition with that Fugitive Slave Act of his. But there's a time and place for politics, and the street corner on a Saturday afternoon is not it. I'll not have you harassing these poor farmers anymore."

There was a long silence as Nathan cut the roast. Mary pursed her lips as she accepted the plate her father handed her.

"I've been thinking," Mary said, finally. "I saw a governess position advertised in *Harper's*. Maybe I could apply."

Nathan scowled.

"Must we discuss this again?" he asked. "You were away long enough. There's plenty for you to do here, or at least there is until your brother starts acting like a young gentleman and gets to work."

"I didn't do anything," Leander said. "Don't bring me into this."

Mary landed the toe of her shoe into his shin and he yipped in pain, while she pinched her lips closed to keep from giggling.

Her father cocked his head toward her, and the urge to giggle disappeared.

"Find something here to occupy that fine mind of yours," he said. "You'll stay here and be the lady of the house."

Mary had always known the term "lady" came with more constraints than privileges. When she and her father sat with the evening paper, she would often read aloud stories of coddled women with fancy dresses, white gloves, and no practical sense. With derision in her voice, she always lingered over the word when she inevitably encountered it.

"It will take more than you requiring my presence here to turn me into the lady of anything," she said.

That summer was a good one for the farm. The rain came and the stalks of rye and wheat grew tall, and the sun shone as the ears of grain swelled.

Her father spent most of his long summer days at his sawmill, leaving his children to navigate their way through the work of the fields. Every few weeks he'd load the wagon full of still-fragrant hardwood lumber and ride the fifteen miles to town. The finest libraries in Buffalo were paneled in Willis oak, and there was always someone waiting on his delivery. He'd check into the American Hotel, where he'd spend the night in his usual room after working through the politics of the day over dinner in the lobby with men he'd known for decades.

By August, it had become clear that Leander believed his sister's duties also included the managing of the field crews for the farm. He spent most of his days that summer playing baseball with his friends while she tried to convince hired men twice her size that they were obliged to take orders from the "lady of the house."

Her only pleasure that summer were her visits with the Websters at the next farm over. Charles Webster had grown up on his own father's farm, and had taken it on twenty years earlier when his father passed. Mary had always admired the tidiness and efficiency of the small homestead and the kindness that Charlie showed to the animals in his care. He seldom spoke, and made it clear that he much preferred the company of his livestock to that of most people, but Mary sensed a quiet wisdom in him. She looked forward to the rare moments when his devastating wit surfaced with some deadpan comment.

His uncle back in Vermont had become concerned for the bachelor farmer, and had arranged for a wife for him. Young Verona had arrived on a canal boat a few summers before. She was a refined and funny woman, perhaps a bit too much for the crudeness of Town Line, but she and Mary became fast friends. She was a sickly woman, and when Doc Pride assigned her to bed rest, as he did often, Charles seemed to welcome the chance to care for her in ways that were easy and straightforward. Still, his sad attempts in the kitchen made Mary wince, and had her carrying meals over to the little farmstead on a nightly basis.

Verona, in turn, lent Mary books from her shelves, and they spent many evenings discussing the latest from Ralph Waldo Emerson or Elisha Kent Kane.

It was during one of those conversations that Verona suggested that as soon as harvest was done, Mary should visit her alma mater and inquire about opportunities at the school.

"Perhaps your father will let you go if you promise to return for the summer."

Mary waited until the wheat had been

harvested and carted to the gristmill before she wrote to her classics teacher, Mrs. Adams, to ask for an appointment.

It had been a leaflet from Mrs. Adams that led her to the weekly meetings where Mary's abolitionist tendencies were nurtured, and it had been in her office that she had met the famous Mrs. Stowe, and had her copy of *Uncle Tom's Cabin* inscribed.

In the weeks leading up to the trip, Mary thought often of the conversations she'd been part of at the school and the sense of shared purpose she'd felt with the others. The thought of being among the like-minded again and perhaps finding work at the school had Mary happier than she had been in months as she rode the sixty miles on the train, but when she arrived in the old widow's office, she found her fidgeting nervously with an old quill and staring out the window. Mary sat across the desk from her for nearly a full minute before the teacher turned her attention to her former pupil.

"To what do I owe such a pleasure?" she asked. "Did you bring some forgotten assignment?"

"I wish that were the case," Mary said. "That there was something I could set my mind to. There's nothing for me to do back home. I feel my mind is wasting."

"You miss school, do you?" the professor asked. Mary could make out dust in the wrinkles of the old woman's face.

"I miss having something to think about other than cow dung and buckwheat harvest," she said. "Are there any positions here? Perhaps I could tutor?"

Mrs. Adams put down the quill, at last turning her full attention to Mary.

"You'd grow bored here soon enough," she said. "You are too much of the world for our little university."

"How can you say that?" Mary asked. "I was so happy here."

Mrs. Adams cocked her head at the statement.

"Ah, poor Mary. You are much too young to be confused by nostalgia," she said, looking over her smudged glasses. "You weren't really happy here. You always seemed to be wishing to be somewhere else. Professor Riepe used to say that she expected you to dash for the station every time the three-ten train whistle blew."

Mary thought of the dour-looking comportment teacher and how she had longed to be anywhere else as she demonstrated the proper use of utensils at tea.

"I wasn't like that in all the classes. Not in

yours," she said, looking out the window at the graying sky. "I miss being here. I'd not take it for granted like I did then."

Mary fell quiet as she felt something she could not name slipping away from her.

"I saw you with that exact same look in your eye nearly every day," her teacher said, interrupting the long silence. "Staring off into the distance. I often wondered where you went in those moments."

Mary looked down at her folded hands to avoid looking into her teacher's eyes.

"Anywhere," she said, hoping to hide the quiver in her voice. "Even now I hear the train roll through our rye field each night and imagine the places the people are all going. They all pass me by and I just stay with everyone old and tired, or too cowardly to do anything that makes a difference."

Mrs. Adams's face darkened.

"I'm sorry, I didn't mean that," Mary whispered through a weak smile, realizing she'd just insulted her friend.

Mrs. Adams followed Mary's gaze out to the wooded hillside.

"The woods, they are mesmerizing, aren't they?" she said. "Especially this time of year. The orange and red of the leaves, the harvested fields."

Mary nodded at her pause, but could not

hide the sadness in her eyes.

"You don't see it, do you?" Mrs. Adams said. "You think you are trapped on your father's farm, held prisoner by acres and acres of fields. But change is all around. The seeds of revolution are planted in those fields. It's your job to tend them."

Mary stared down at her fidgeting hands.

"There's no place for revolution between the house and the barn," she muttered.

Mrs. Adams stood and moved around from behind her desk to stand over her.

"Shame on you," she said. "Your self-pity is unbecoming of a woman in your position."

Mary looked up, surprised by her tone.

"Not twenty leagues from here, my friends Mrs. Stanton and Miss Anthony enrage all the old men of Washington as they fight for our rights as women," she said, wagging a finger in Mary's face. "Elizabeth started the movement when they would not admit her to college, and here you are, a degree in your hand, whining of boredom and cow shit. Just a few miles beyond that, Frederick Douglass risks his life with no defense but his voice and a printing press."

Mrs. Adams lowered her voice to a dismissive whisper.

"I will do you the courtesy of not listing

the advantages you have enjoyed over Mr. Douglass."

Mary dropped her eyes.

"Are you so wound up in yourself that you do not read the papers?" Mrs. Adams asked. "Did you not see that just yesterday they captured John Brown at Harpers Ferry. He will surely be hanged, and it was not so long ago he sat in that same chair as you, asking for help with his cause. I will admit that I threw what coins I could spare into that wishing well. A pittance, certainly, but it was what I could do. And when they torture him, as those scoundrels most surely will, they will ask him for a list of those that aided him, and then they will come for me."

Mary could see that what she had taken as distraction when she first arrived was actually fear, an emotion she'd never imagined in this woman before.

"I sit in this little office, so close to my own end that I'm surprised each morning when I wake up," she said. "Old and tired, as you say, and still I fight. And here you are, a quiver of arrows on your back, without the imagination to take up your own bow, and you fret over trains in the night."

She turned and faced Mary full-on.

"Are you waiting for someone to give you permission? Are you waiting for someone to tell you to take a stand? That is not how revolutions work!" she growled. "But if it will help you, then here I am. Get up! March!"

Mary sat stone still in the ensuing silence until there was nothing more for her to do but rise and leave.

She had nearly closed the door behind her when Mrs. Adams's face appeared at the slim opening, a hint of its old kindness returned.

"It is painful for the fledgling to be chased from the nest, but don't think the mother bird's task easy," she said, and pulled the door closed.

Mary stumbled backward, nearly falling down. She had imagined an afternoon spent with a kind old friend, discussing a way forward for her, but now she found herself alone and rejected in this place she had imagined as some kind of sanctuary. She took a moment to gather herself before walking out of the building into the daylight.

Clouds had moved in, the iron sky to the west promising rain.

She walked the wooden sidewalks of the little town, hoping to see a familiar face. At the St. Agnes Tea Room, two girls had taken her favorite table and tittered into their white gloves about some boy. Even when she went into Saxon Street Booksellers she found that she could not focus on the titles before her. When the clerk offered to help her find something, she couldn't remember the names of any of the books she wanted to read.

As the sky dimmed, she stopped at the train station. She thought of the money she had brought with her and scanned the schedule and maps posted on the wall, wondering how far away she could go.

She imagined herself climbing off the train in Manhattan, checking into a clean little room near a park, and taking a position writing about the evils of slavery and other great wrongs in the world. Or she could ride west into the territories, getting off someplace where the money in her little bank account in Buffalo could buy her her own life. She would claim a plot and make it her own. It would be a place where the people around her were kind and thoughtful, and all she'd need would be a little garden for vegetables and a couple chickens.

But of course, only men could stake a claim in the territories.

Lost was the excitement from earlier in the day. The prospect of a night on the campus now made her feel lonely and she found herself considering an early train home, but she pictured the look on her father's face as she returned from her failed venture toward independence, and she knew that it would be a defeat from which she would never recover.

She walked back onto campus for dinner and sat by herself, a stranger to the girls around her, eavesdropping on their talk of romance and classes.

Mrs. Adams intercepted her as she left for the alumni house.

"Don't worry, the fledgling will vacate the nest at dawn," Mary said, but Mrs. Adams shook her head.

"Mary, we find ourselves with some, ah, surprise visitors at the guesthouse this evening," she said. "I'm afraid there's no longer room for you there. You'll have to spend the night with me in my room."

"What do you mean?" Mary snapped. "I arranged for this stay weeks ago, paid in advance. I dropped my things there this morning."

She started again for the guesthouse, her posture stiff, her stride quick.

"Please, my dear," Mrs. Adams said, struggling to keep pace as they crossed the quad. "I've moved your bag already. Just come with me, and we'll have a nice tea by the fire."

"Who is so important they preempt my arrangements? Some rich patron no doubt, too important to respect others' arrangements," Mary said, climbing the steps and opening the alumni house's front door. "I'll not surrender my place so easily. Didn't you just tell me that I should fight for what is right?"

"This is not what I meant, my dear," the matron said, biting her lip. Mary rapped sharply on the door to her rented room and took the key from her bag. Mrs. Adams put her hand on Mary's.

"Please, you mustn't," she said, but Mary pushed the key into the door and opened it into blackness.

There were no candles and the curtains were drawn to the night. She smelled the stink of the unwashed occupants, felt their fear and breathlessness, and heard the movements of a small space overcrowded with too many bodies. As her eyes adjusted, she made out two men sitting on the bed, the fear-limned whites of eyes offset by faces made a uniform black by the darkness. In the corner, a woman sat in a chair and tried to nurse an infant now fussing with the intrusion.

Mary's face flushed crimson and she

backed out of the room, pulling the door closed.

"Pardon," she stuttered to the closed door and turned away, leaving the key dangling in the lock.

"I did not want you to see them," her teacher said, retrieving the key and taking her by the elbow. "It makes you vulnerable."

Mary looked at her, blinking.

"Legally, I mean," Mrs. Adams said. "If you see them and don't report them, it makes you an accessory."

She led Mary out of the building and into the night. They were halfway across the quad when Mary stopped in her tracks.

"Who are they?" she asked. "How did they get here?"

"Sophie is the mother," Mrs. Adams said. "Palmer is her husband, and Malcolm is his brother. There were two others when they set out, but they've been lost."

She paused, her eyes darting around past Mary at two students walking in the night.

"A hunter was spotted in town this afternoon. If they're caught here, the scandal will be the school's undoing, and all that we've worked to build will be gone. I know I should send them away, but I cannot bring myself to. I cannot imagine what fate awaits them when their master gets them back."

46

"You've done this before?" Mary asked.

Mrs. Adams barely nodded.

Mary looked at the blackness of the clouded sky for a long moment.

"Can they be ready to travel quickly?" she asked. "There's a train leaving for Buffalo in two hours."

When they got to the station, Mary bought two tickets in third class, and two in first. The conductor balked when she insisted that Sophie and her infant ride with her, but Mary looked down her nose and attempted a Southern drawl. "I may need my girl during the trip. And even with a child in her arms, she does me better than the servants you have on these horrid Yankee trains."

Mary tried to focus on a book of poems as rain pounded on the train's metal roof. She eyed the other riders on the half-empty train, knowing that she risked everything if she were found out. For the first time since she graduated, she felt as if she were part of something bigger than her.

She wanted to ask questions of the fugitive woman, of life on the plantation and of her escape, but the ruse allowed no such thing. Mary bought something each time the food vendor passed, then made a show

47

of trying a small morsel before voicing her disgust and passing the remainder to the gaunt-looking woman beside her.

When the train arrived in Buffalo, they had to wait for an old gentleman with a cane to disembark before exiting onto the platform. Sophie pointed to where Palmer and Malcolm stood together as a fat man with a star on his coat waddled toward them.

"Quick," Mary whispered to Sophie, motioning for her to follow.

She stepped in front of the marshal before plying her poor imitation of a Southern accent in front of the frightened black faces.

"What are you two waiting for? Palmer, get my luggage. And Malcolm, find us a cab. Don't you dare look at me like that, it's just rain. Lord knows the two of you could use a bath. Get out there. Your laziness is breathtaking, I swear. After all these weeks on these wretched trains, you still have to be told what to do? I should sell the pair of you down the river."

She clapped her hands together.

"And Sophie, shut that brat up. It has squalled at me the whole trip."

The three of them shuffled to their duties.

The lawman stood over her, smelling of whiskey and looking like he had not had a change of clothes in weeks. "Are these yours?"

"Why? Do you want them?" she asked. "I'll give you a good price."

"Dwight Kidder," he introduced himself. "Federal marshal. Where are their papers?"

"They are somewhere in one of my bags, and I'll not pull out all my private things just for your benefit," she said, indignant. "Go harangue one of these scofflaw Yankees. Just this afternoon I saw some urchin picking pockets in broad daylight. Go hang that wretch instead of wasting my time."

She turned sharply and headed into the rain.

"I'll never understand why my sister would choose to live up here among you heathens," she said loudly.

The cold wind off the lake hit her and her feet splashed in the mud as she left the station, but she felt nothing other than the racing of her heart. The marshal called out for her to stop, but she did not slow, did not acknowledge the voice behind her.

She had never been more afraid.

Or alive.

Palmer hailed a cab and helped her in before Sophie and Malcolm came on board. Mary gave the driver the address Mrs. Adams had made her memorize.

They rode to a little brick church on Michigan Street and a tiny black priest came out and ushered the fugitives into the church basement with nothing more than a nod to Mary.

She wrote Mrs. Adams the next day, telling her of the successful trip and offering herself to the cause.

The next runaway arrived at the house a month later, tapping at the window as Mary sat darning socks by candlelight. She fed him leftover cornbread and hid him in the hayloft. The next morning, she drove him down to the same church, hidden under a tarp in the back of the wagon.

The cotton-haired priest motioned her down when she pulled the wagon into the lot behind the church and introduced himself as Father Thomas.

"You should be more careful when you come here," he said. "This church was built by freedmen, and there are many that are looking for any chance to tear it down. This is the first place the marshal and the hunters look when they come looking for our friends."

She looked up at the redbrick building with worry in her eyes, and he took her hand and smiled.

"Don't you fret," he said. "It's my job to

keep them guessing. Just you be careful. I'll have this one over the river and free by morning."

She knew better than to ask how.

The next time she went down to the church, she timed the trip so she'd arrive just as the winter night was setting in, pulling in under the cover of darkness.

"It'll be a cold ride home for you," Father Thomas said. "Spend the night."

"No, I have my blankets," she said.

"They'll be over the river and free by morning," he said again, as he would each time she made the trip.

Although her father was most certainly aware of the fugitives that continued to arrive over that winter and into the spring, he managed to avoid acknowledging them until the hunter arrived.

Smelling of stale sweat, his beard slimed with tobacco juice, he tore through the barn, knocking over barrels of seed corn in search of a couple that Mary had delivered to the church days before.

"That's not a badge," her father said, using the tip of his hoe to prod the copperhead penny the hunter had pinned to his filthy coat. "You need a warrant to be here."

The hunter sneered and threatened him with a cocked pistol.

"Let's have a look in your barn," he said.

While he was poking a pitchfork through the hayloft, Mary slipped away and rang the big brass farm bell, a signal for the field hands to come in. Scythes on their shoulders, six strong boys arrived to block the hunter's way to the house.

He promised to return with the marshal the next day, but was never heard from again.

At the dinner table that night, her father said, "There are pistols made for ladies to handle."

"I know nothing of guns," she said.

"You're a smart girl," he replied, "make a study of it."

The idea intrigued her. For months, whenever Leander's friends came to visit, she asked their opinions on which guns were best. They laughed when she asked to test their weapons. Eventually she ordered one of the new Colt revolvers from Snyder's General Store, cementing her reputation as some kind of dangerous, lunatic shrew.

Leander was happy to take her out to the woods and show her how to use the pistol, laughing at her the first time she fired it and was knocked to the ground. She climbed to her feet, looked at him sideways, and fired off the remaining five bullets rapidly.

She was surprised by how much she enjoyed shooting, and that summer she spent hours deep in the forest firing into the trunk of a dead oak at ever-increasing distances. After each practice, she carefully cleaned and reloaded the pistol and hung it on a peg next to the front door, a display her father complained was in direct contradiction to the reputation of hospitality he had spent years cultivating.

The summer and fall passed without incident, but when a December blizzard left her housebound, she took a pickax to the cellar wall, hollowing out a hiding hole.

After spending the week snowed in at the American Hotel in Buffalo, her father arrived home to find her hauling a tin bucket of dirt up the back stairs.

"No more!" he said. "You are not preparing for an armed siege. What do other ladies do when they are snowed in?"

"Every godforsaken bounty hunter in this county drinks at Wilhelm's Corner House, less than half a mile down the road," she said. "You are the one that told me I should have a plan."

"Enough," he said.

He grabbed the loop handle, but she held the tin pail of dirt as if it were a lifeline in a stormy sea.

"No more digging," he growled. "I've not stopped you from helping the occasional wretched soul, but there are limits. The barn, not the house. And for only one night. No more."

She nodded, but did not release the bucket.

"I'll finish cleaning up, then set myself to stitching a sampler," she said.

He glared at her, but released the handle.

She finished spreading the dirt and clay in the tomato patch, then returned to the cellar to push her mother's old broken wardrobe in front of the hole.

Charlie Webster came to their door soon afterward, his face a crush of pain, to tell that Verona had passed. And Mary suddenly found herself struggling to keep him from fading into nothingness.

Mrs. Adams continued to send a fugitive her way every month or so.

There was no more mention of the hole, but she felt connected to the dank little space somehow. Once, when the house was empty, she pushed the wardrobe aside and crawled into the space, just sitting on the cool earth, her hands outstretched to the rough clay walls.

Leander considered the fugitives another of his sister's oddities, like her bookishness and impatience with all the local boys.

Although Mary did her best to keep what she was doing hidden from the farmworkers, it did not take long before Katia found one of the runaways in the barn and raised a ruckus in the house. Nathan explained that it was not so long ago that he had taken her in from a passing orphan train, and that extending such charity again was only right. Nathan elicited a solemn pledge from her that she would not tell anyone of the runaways. She said nothing to him about the matter again, though she was happy to make her displeasure clear to Mary whenever the opportunity arose.

As Mary had settled into her secret efforts, she'd become more amenable to the work the farm required, but Leander had become even less involved. Finally, their father had announced that it was time for a change, and that Leander was to move downtown to take on the business side of the family's dealings. He'd arranged for some of his friends there to watch over him, and had found a good room in a boardinghouse from where he could sell the farm's goods and the lumber coming out of the mill. He hoped that separating him from his friends would help him focus on the work he needed to do.

With each fugitive she carried downtown, Mary felt as if she were sending something of herself into the world. She understood that there were dozens of others like her in the chain of barns and chicken shacks where each fugitive had sheltered, and in that, she felt some kinship, some belonging. She wished there was some way she could send word back to each hand that had helped and let them know that they had been delivered, that their risks had not been in vain.

But she could not, of course. She could know the previous stop, and the next, but nothing more.

The fugitives themselves were almost too much for her. They were suspicious of everything and everyone. The fear of their master back home and the pursuing hunters ran so deep in them that she struggled to fathom where they mustered the strength to run at all.

Whenever she asked them about their trip, they would say as little as they could, instinctively protecting their protectors. As the same caution worked in her favor, she knew she should be grateful, but she longed to know more.

She could not deny that she enjoyed the secrecy of it all, though. She found herself making excuses to go to the crossroads just so she could smirk at the farmers that glared back at her. Part of her wished that she could tell them what she had been doing, though she knew she never could.

She was thinking about walking into town for the mail when she found the body sprawled on the dirt floor of the barn. She put down the milking pails and rolled the body onto its back. The man grunted and she thought, *Doctor, not gravedigger.*

The man's skin, the color of squall clouds, hung loose on him, and the stubble of beard was matted with flecks of leaf mold. She covered him with a horse blanket and went back to the house.

Leander's room was still cold from the night, and he groaned when Mary pulled the blankets off his bed.

"What did I ever do to you to deserve such abuse?" he moaned.

"I need you to take the buggy to Alden and get Doc Pride," Mary said.

He looked at her with a bloodshot eye, and turned his head toward the wall.

"Have something to eat," he mumbled. "You'll feel better by the afternoon."

"There's a runaway in the barn, nearly dead," she said.

He pulled himself up and sat on the edge

of the bed, rubbing his face with his hands.

"You want Doc Pride to know about your business?"

She pursed her lips.

"He's going to die without help."

Leander stood and reached for the clothes he'd thrown to the floor the night before.

"He's sick?"

"Passed out," she said. "He's all bloody, looks like a corpse."

She followed him down the stairs and into the kitchen where he pulled his coat on.

"This isn't good," he said. "Even if Doc can save him, what are you going to do with him? He can't stay here. If the marshal finds him out here . . ."

He trailed off as Katia came in with a basket of eggs.

"I know," Mary said.

Mary boiled some rags and took them back to the barn. She dug through her apron's cluttered pocket, found her slaughtering knife, and cut away the rags that covered the fugitive. The smell that rose when she cut the ruined shoes from his feet reminded her of cutting into a hog's entrails.

She bathed him with a kitchen rag, tentative around his swollen and split feet and the festering wound in his left calf.

Wincing, she ran her fingertips over the

whip scars on his back.

She doubted herself for sending for the doctor. It was unlikely the fugitive would survive, but she'd turned the frail old Quaker into an accomplice in her felony.

She straightened up and opened the door when she heard the buggy in the barnyard.

Doc Pride greeted her with his usual nod, but grimaced when he saw the black body on the ground. She raised her hands, palms up, a wordless act of supplication and apology.

"Nearly froze to death," he said. "Are there dog bites as well?"

Mary pulled the blanket back to reveal the bleeding leg.

"I thought it was a wolf," she said. "How did you know?"

He didn't answer, but set to examining the body. He was cleaning the wound when Mary's father came in from his morning walk of the pastures.

"You've turned the family doctor into a felon before breakfast," he said, looking down at the fugitive and propping his shotgun against the rough plank wall. "What next? Dig up John Brown's grave and mount an insurrection?"

Mary straightened up and wiped her hands on her coat.

"I couldn't just leave him to die on the barn floor," she said, pursing her lips.

"This must be the one that nearly killed Karl Wilhelm night before last." Doc Pride grimaced.

"He attacked Wilhelm?" Leander asked.

"Harry Strauss showed up at my door in the middle of the night begging me to save him and gibbering over his dead dog. Made it sound like a black Goliath was wandering the woods."

"Now you are telling stories," Nathan said, raising his eyebrows. "This dust rag doesn't look like he could put down a woodchuck, much less that ogre. Will Wilhelm survive?"

"He'll live," the doctor said. "But I'm not proud of the job I did stitching his face back together. He won't be a pretty sight."

"Poor Harry," Leander said. "I can't picture him without old Jep trailing along."

"Riling up Karl is about the worst thing this one could do," Nathan said. "He's as mean a son of a bitch as I ever seen, and now he's got cause."

"Ever since you caught him stealing that pig ten years ago, he's had it out for you," Pride said. "I hear him griping about you every chance he gets."

"Gives me the stink eye every time I go

into the Corner House," Leander said. "I think he sometimes spits in my beer when I'm not looking."

"Maybe you should stay home and do some work instead of giving him the chance," Nathan said.

"I guess I'll be working plenty once I'm down in Buffalo," Leander said.

"We don't need to discuss this again," Nathan scolded. "And we most certainly don't need to involve Doc Pride in it."

The doctor straightened up.

"He's starved to death, frostbit, and dog-bit just for the hell of it," he said. "He used every bit of himself to get this far. Go ahead and kill one of those fine Rhode Island chickens of yours and make him some broth. If you can manage a decent cup of tea with the sulfur water from that infernal well of yours, see if you can get him to swallow that, too. Even if he gets better, I doubt the leg will. It's festering already. Chances are it'll have to come off, but the amputation would kill him now. I'll send a poultice back and come check on him tomorrow."

"Leander will take you back to town," Nathan offered.

The doctor looked grave as he pulled on his coat. "I saw Harry again yesterday," he said. "He's got revenge for Jep on his mind."

He followed Leander out into the yard, leaving Mary to wring her hands.

"We should move him to the cellar," she said to her father.

Her father grunted and bent down to help her lift the body.

They carried him across the barnyard, up the slope to the big house, and down the back steps. Nathan could not fit into the tunnel and watched as Mary made a pallet, crawled into the hole, and pulled the fugitive in. By then Leander was back with the poultice, and Mary applied it before pushing the wardrobe back into place, entombing the fugitive.

LEANDER

The hamlet of Town Line had formed at the crossroads of an ancient Seneca highway and the surveyor-straight road that marked the border between the fledgling towns of Lancaster and Alden. There wasn't much to it until Nathan Willis sold passage through his rye fields to the New York and Erie line on condition that they install a station at Town Line Road. The narrow three-room building was identical to a dozen others along the line and like them it served as a water stop, telegraph, and post office all in one. The settlers and their mules came soon after, then Snyder's General Store, then the preacher.

Leander Willis had been seven years old when the Zubrichs came, built the parsonage, and brought the gift that all his father's money and influence could not supply: a playmate.

Soon, there would be other boys, but

Hans Zubrich was always first.

The first time they met was at the general store, both boys hiding behind their fathers' legs, but the moment they became friends for life was still vivid in Leander's memory twelve years later.

They had been sitting under the lonely elm waiting to greet the five-fifteen train when Hans told him of the war back in Bavaria. He talked about his brother, ten years older than him, and the night he was dragged out of their house by the soldiers, never to be heard from again.

The train had rattled by, the engineer tooting his whistle and waving at the boys, but Hans, his new friend's arm on his shoulder, did not raise his tear-covered face in response.

The small crossroads hamlet offered little for the boys to do, but the two friends hiked in the woods, they fished and swam, and they built a fort of scrap wood held together by rope and bailing wire, a last outpost fortified against a looming invasion of redcoats and big sisters.

It didn't take long for Leander's father to find the dilapidated hovel. One morning he followed Leander to the clearing with his toolbox and sack of nails and announced he was going to give the two boys a lesson in how to raise a building. Hans took the well-worn level in his hands and made a game of settling the bubble between the scored marks on the glass tube, but Leander snatched the tool from his friend and handed it back to his father.

"This is my place," he'd declared.

And it had been ever since.

There the two boys whiled away the summer, plotting elaborate tricks on Leander's sister, and hiding from Hans's father, Town Line's resident master of the hickory switch.

The roof collapsed onto them while they were waiting out a late summer thunderstorm, and a board opened a cut on Hans's forehead. The scar eventually faded to a faint white trace, but Leander knew it pulsed red whenever his friend was angry.

They rebuilt the shack using the same sack of nails that Leander had previously refused, this time made acceptable by the act of pilfering them from Nathan's workbench.

They abandoned the cabin over winter, and when they returned in the spring, they found a boy living in the little hut with only a mottled orange pup named Jep for company.

Just a year older than they were, Harry Strauss had jumped off the back of the same orphan train that had brought the Willises' new ward, Katia, to town. He had presented himself to her at the back door of the Willises' kitchen soon afterward, professing his love as only a ten-year-old boy could. Flattered by the attention, she pointed him toward the boys' fort and snuck him food throughout the winter.

Nathan Willis watched them tear through his fields that summer and called the orphan a third to their pair. He was fond of the boy, and in the following years welcomed him to his table many times, but Harry Strauss would not be domesticated.

He and Jep soon moved out of the fort, taking up for a while in the workers' cabin on the Willis farm, then into a room over Wilhelm's tavern. When the weather was fair, he'd camp by the creek or under the Town Line Road bridge, and sometimes he'd go back to Leander's shack.

Leander had always admired the way Harry was the master of his own fate, but now that his father insisted he move to downtown Buffalo, Leander sometimes dreamed of moving into the little shack himself, leaving behind his father's many demands on his time to instead spend his days hunting, fishing, and playing baseball.

But he knew he could never do it. And maybe Buffalo wouldn't be so bad.

And he would have his going-away party there, back in the snow-covered woods, by the pond, under the stars, away from everything that was expected of him.

He climbed down from the sleigh and surveyed his domain. The little shack, sitting in the clearing above the frozen pond, looked like it had been assembled by a blind, drunk carpenter.

He opened the door, and chased a family of raccoons out. As he was setting up a cask of ale on the table, Hans arrived and set to clearing a place for a fire.

Leander filled two tankards that he'd pilfered from Wilhelm's Corner House and handed one to his friend as he looked at the wood that Hans had carried over from Nathan's sawmill.

"Couldn't you find any clear scrap?" he asked. "Those knots are going to pop all night."

Hans took a long draught and grinned.

"Susie Munn squeals whenever the fire pops," he said.

The two friends chuckled and clinked the pewter of their tankards together.

"Have you confessed your sinful thoughts to your father?" Leander asked. "All these years of praying for the end of the world so he could see the sinners burn, he's not going to be too happy to see his son first in line."

Hans snorted. "On the contrary, I'm sure he'd enjoy that 'I told you so' more than any of the others," Hans said. "Anyway, if I were to start confessing, it'd be a long time before I got to those particular sinful thoughts."

"I'd like to eavesdrop on that conversation," Leander said.

"I'm sure you would," Hans said. "By the way, are you sure you want to have this little party of yours back here in the woods? It's going to be a cold night. Everyone would have a better time at Wilhelm's, or even in your barn. Your father told me he'd pay the tab at the Corner House if you'd have it there."

"No," Leander said. "We'll have it here."

They set to getting the place ready. Leander shoveled the snow from the frozen pond, swept out the shack, and put out the array of shoddy chairs and stools that had collected there over the years. Hans spit a side of venison and set it over the fire.

The first guests to arrive were a half-dozen Town Line farm boys. Along with Leander, Hans, and Harry, they made up the Forty-Eighters, Town Line's baseball team. They embraced Leander, slapping their star outfielder on the back like he'd scored the winning run.

"How in hell did you convince your father to ship you downtown?" Vaness Weber asked. "My old man won't let me go no farther west than Lancaster, and that's only one station over."

"You're a lucky son of a bitch, I'll tell ya," Edward Eels said. "I'd do just about anything to get out of this town. There's nothing but cows, barley, and slush as far as I can see."

"It isn't so bad here," Leander said. "Better than some office. After tomorrow, it'll be old men and ledgers for me, boys, while come springtime, you'll be playing ball in the golden light of the sun."

"I wouldn't be so sure," Edward said. "Just before I came out tonight, my father sat me down and told me no more baseball. You guys will probably have to find someone else to catch."

Word of Leander's move had brought a collective sigh of relief from the farmers of Town Line. Nathan Willis's status as the founder of the crossroads hamlet and as a county commissioner brought the family moral authority, and Leander's presence on the team gave the other boys cover. But now that he'd been told it was time to put away childish things, the others were also expected to get behind the mule and plow.

The team all stood together in the fading February sun warming their hands on the fire and sipping ale.

A clutch of girls arrived, and the mood lifted. Susie Munn put a cherry pie on the table next to the cask of ale, brushed past Hans, and put a lingering kiss on Leander's cheek as the boys collectively hooted.

"Don't forget me when you're down in the big city, Lelo," she said, her red hair spilling out from her knitted cap.

"How could I?" he asked. "I'm sure Hans will fill me in on all your adventures whenever he has the chance."

She stuck out her plump lip at Leander's reaction.

"Is this a party or a funeral?" another one of the other girls shouted. She had donned ice skates and was gliding on the frozen pond. "Didn't any of you boys bring a fiddle? Do I have to dance by myself?"

She spun herself into a pirouette, eliciting loud shouts from the boys. Hans stepped out onto the ice, took the girl's hand, and mocked a princely bow before twirling her to the rhythm of Edward Eels's fiddle.

Hunks of venison were carved off the side and passed around, and a second cask was tapped. The boys told stories of the day Leander went six for six with three triples, or the time he made a diving catch for the final out only to come up with strands of poison ivy tangled in his hair.

The snow came down then in soft flurries and the girls chased the flakes with outstretched tongues as the boys jockeyed for kisses.

"My father used to stand in the pulpit and call down the wrath of God on Leander Willis and the pack of feral boys that he led through the crossroads," Hans said. "He'll finally have his way now that the scourge of Town Line is leaving."

Leander guffawed.

"Little did he know his own son was climbing out his bedroom window to help lead the pack," he said. "You remember when you, me, and Harry switched up every mule in town?"

They'd traded the story a dozen times in the years since the prank, but Hans doubled over laughing, just for the joy of it.

"It took two days for everyone to get it all straightened out," he said. "And then Olaf Simke liked Alois Bohner's more than he liked his own and wouldn't give it back."

"You remember how we used to play chicken on the train tracks?" Leander asked.

"Yeah, you'd go running at the first sound, even though the damn thing was still a mile away," Hans said. "You could have run five minutes, stopped to piss in the woods, run back, and still gotten out of there in time."

"You weren't much better," Leander said. "But Harry, damn that kid scared the shit out of me. I'd end up screaming myself raw thinking he was about to be hit, and he'd stroll up afterward with that shit-eating grin of his and demand his wager money. I wanted to pop him in the nose."

"Yeah," Hans said. "That kid is the best first baseman I ever saw and he'll waltz around a racing train, but he can't work up the gumption to ask Katia out for a barn dance."

"The poor idiot," Leander said.

Others came, from Alden and Lancaster, and even as far away as Darien. Players arrived to wish Leander well in his move downtown, but were just as glad to not have to face him on the field again. Jugs of rum appeared.

The children of Town Line had spent most of their lives together, and Leander watched as the threads of friendships and flirtations that had been woven and rewoven over the years were loosened momentarily between this or that pair and pulled taut between others.

Katia arrived, looked around, and asked the question that was on Leander's mind also.

"Where's Harry?" she asked.

"He was down at the crossroads early this morning," Ed Eels said. "Some runaway killed Jep two nights ago, nearly killed Karl Wilhelm, too."

Everyone quieted at the news.

"Shit," Hans muttered.

"That dog always smelled bad anyway," Katia said, though there was no missing the sadness in her voice.

"Harry better show up," Leander said. "I won't forgive the son of a bitch if he misses my shindig."

"Then get yourself to not forgiving," Ed said. "He's convinced the escaped nigger is worth a thousand-dollar reward, dead or alive. He'd be on the trail anyway, but you add money in . . . rest assured, money and vengeance are going to outweigh your cask of ale."

"I don't know why the damned niggers don't just stay where they are," Vaness Weber piped in. "We sure as hell don't want them up here, and sure as hell they don't need to come through here messing with old Jep. That runaway better not cross my path, or I'll kill him myself."

Ed Eels started playing his fiddle again, but one of the strings snapped and cut into his finger. He swore in pain, hopping up and down until one of the girls kissed it and wrapped it in a rag.

"It's cold out here," Susie Munn said. "And with all this talk of dead dogs and killing, this isn't much of a party. I don't understand why we're out in the woods like heathens instead of indoors like respectable people? If we were someplace nice, I could have worn a party dress and we could have some real dancing."

She looked Leander in the eye.

"I might have been able to convince you to stay then," she said. "Or take me with you."

Leander laughed nervously.

"Lelo's daddy offered to pay for just that," Vaness said. "Even offered to throw him a grand party at their big house. Was going to invite all kinds of fancy people from the city and . . ."

He stopped short when Leander shot him a hard glance.

"Tomorrow he gets to tell me what to do," Leander muttered. "This is my party. Not his. Now where's that rye?"

Hans produced a bottle, and Leander took a long pull.

"Speaking of your family, isn't Mary coming?" Vaness asked. "At least we'd have our own sermonizer here."

Leander shook his head and drank again, his face harder.

He had pled with his sister to come even as he loaded the sleigh that afternoon.

"I can't leave the runaway," she'd said. "And besides, I have no interest in spending my evening listening to those hateful, copperhead farm boys prattle on about Lincoln the tyrant," she'd said.

"They're my friends," Leander had said. "And there's not a one of them gives a damn about slavery, or who is president. You're the one that starts in on that, every time."

"What else should we talk about, Wordsworth or Melville?" she shot back. "Besides, am I supposed to show interest in the number of points on the buck someone killed last week?"

"That's what the other girls do," Leander said. "That's why they have friends."

She turned her back then and walked into the house.

Mary had never been like the other girls at the crossroads. They all seemed happy for a Saturday night at Wilhelm's Corner House with the boys, but she always wanted something else. His friends all joked that she was hard-hearted, but he knew how much was behind her feined coldness.

He could never shake the image from their childhood of her plunging into the frigid creek trying to rescue a bawling fawn that had been swept into the spring rush. He ran along the creek, chasing the two thrashing figures, shouting and crying in fear. Mary finally caught up to the animal, only to have it kick her in the forehead and flounder out of her reach.

Only when she had lost sight of the lost animal did she turn toward Leander on the creek bank. She was crying for the loss of the creature and blood poured from the gash on her head, but the grief in her eyes turned to fear as the current pulled at her sodden coat and dress. She called out for help, but his own fear froze him where he stood as the water pulled her away from him.

She was under for long seconds and he did nothing but wail her name. The swift water carried her into the shallows where she found footing and pulled herself onto the chunked ice of the bank. Leander ran to her and she took him into her arms even as her body convulsed with the cold. Even now he flinched when he thought of the way he tried to squirm away from the iciness of her embrace.

He'd always been ashamed of that story, and had only told it to Hans. When the others joked about her, he felt like he should tell them, to let them know that in the end, she was the most sentimental of all the girls. But somehow, he never could.

Leander drained the last of the rye and called for another bottle. Edward pulled a flask from his coat pocket. Susie left soon afterward, and the others followed. By midnight, it was down to him and Hans again.

The two of them sat on opposite ends of a log in front of the fire. Leander threw more wood into the blaze and Hans put a small chunk of bacon fat in a long-handled, covered pan and set it over the fire.

Leander smiled when his friend drew a fistful of dried, multicolored corn kernels from his pocket and dropped them into the melted fat.

"Just like my mother used to make," Leander said, as the smell of the popping kernels poured out from the pan.

"I remember," Hans said.

"I'm staying out here tonight," Leander

said. "One last night."

"I'll stay with you," Hans said.

He was pulling the pan from the fire when they heard the voice behind them.

"I thought this thing was going to go all night," Harry said. "I thought there would be dancing girls and fireworks and marching bands."

"Leander chased them away," Hans said as Harry plopped onto the log between them. Leander handed him the bottle and mussed his hair.

"I'm sorry about Jep," he said.

Harry hung his head. Leander wanted to put his arm around his friend, but thoughts of the runaway hidden away in his basement and the guilt of it held him back.

"That dog was the one stuck with me through it all," he said.

"I know," Hans said. "She was a good one."

"She was the best," Leander said.

"You been out tracking the runaway?" Hans asked.

Harry nodded.

"It's pitch black," Leander said. "How are you supposed to track anything?"

"I'm going to find the bastard," Harry said, taking a long pull from the bottle.

"Any sign of him?" Hans asked.

"Found some blood on the creek bank, but the snow's been coming down pretty steady, and I never tracked without Jep before. He's back here somewhere, though. I'll find him."

He paused.

"Wilhelm says your sister's hiding him," Harry said, not looking at Leander.

"Wilhelm blames us for everything that goes wrong in the world," Leander said. "Of course he thinks we're helping."

"She's always going on about abolition this and the South that," Harry said.

"It's all talk," Leander said, trying not to lie to his friend. Harry didn't say anything else and they sat in the firelight, the sky clouded and dark overhead, munching the corn.

"What are you going to do in that big city anyway?" Harry asked.

"Wish I was here," Leander said.

When the corn was gone, the three of them watched as the snowflakes drifted silently into the fading fire. When the bottle was empty, they retreated to the shack and crawled under old blankets and greasy pelts on cots they had built for themselves years before. Their legs dangled above the floorboards and their heads spun from whiskey, but they were together and they slept well.

When Leander woke in the morning, Harry was gone already, back to tracking the runaway. He walked Hans to the parsonage then returned home, where he sat at the kitchen table and drank coffee. Mary never sat still for very long unless she was reading, but she sat with him then for long hours, talking about nothing in particular. He loved how he could make his sister laugh when almost no one else could.

In the afternoon, he went to his room and packed his things into a steamer trunk and then he sat for hours looking out the window of the study while his father ran his fingers over columns of numbers and told him stories of the men he would be meeting in the big gray city to the west.

Underground

We had to take off the fugitive's leg this morning. Father and I held him down while Doc Pride sawed it off. I understand now how he could have bested Karl Wilhelm. He is nothing but sinew, and he fought like a madman, nearly throwing both of us off. Whatever it is that has carried him these many miles is still alive and strong. His fever was down by the evening, and I am expectant that his mind will return to him soon.

Last night Charlie Webster came for dinner, the third time this month my father has invited him. He ate two full bowls of stew and biscuits and it appeared that he declined a third only out of decorum. I don't think he's eaten anything at home but parched corn since Verona died.

I miss her so.

It is good to see him away from that

farm that holds so much heartache for him. He's been reading her books and came loaded with questions. It appears that Mr. Dickens may be the cure for what ails him.

My father announced at the table that he has arranged for all of us to attend the Presidential Ball next month downtown, that he had reserved rooms in the American Hotel where Mr. Lincoln will be staying as well. Even Charlie will join us.

He seems to think that I am somehow willfully unpleasant to the men of Buffalo, and that if I just set my mind to it, I can charm them. He does not understand that I have done my best. I do not understand the rules, I am uncertain of the language these men in fancy clothes speak. I do not have the heart to endure another one of those grand affairs, not even for the chance to meet Mr. Lincoln. I am not sure how I will tell him, but I will not go.

— MARY WILLIS'S JOURNAL,
JANUARY 20, 1861

Joe remembered little of his first days on the farm. There were flashes of the doctor's saw, and screaming himself into oblivion, but nothing more.

The first clear thing he could recall was waking with a pain that felt like animals gnawing at the stump and fearing his teeth would break from the clenching.

He lay there for hours, enveloped in darkness, not knowing where he was, afraid to make a sound, with only the pain to let him know he was alive.

He knew what the future held for a one-legged, fugitive slave. He had seen other castoffs on the streets of Harpers Ferry, husks too used up to be any good, with dirty handkerchiefs spread on the ground in front of them, begging fruitlessly for a stray coin. He found himself wishing that he had not woken up at all, or that there was some way that he could end things right then.

When he thought he might finally go mad, she came to him, pushing away the heavy piece of furniture and letting in the light. She had a lantern and a bowl of broth, and she lay her cool hand on his forehead before she lifted his head and spooned the warm liquid for him.

He could barely croak his thanks, so she talked as she fed him. She told him her name was Mary and where he was and that as soon as he was healthy enough, she would take him down to the river where there were people who would help him cross to Canada.

The broth had a strange flavor to it, but all the food here was strange. The cornbread was blue, and she brought him a bowl of something called sauerkraut, which his mother would have thrown away as spoiled.

He could hear the voices of others in the house and their footfalls above the cellar, but they did not come down the stairs. For him, there was only Mary.

In the morning and then again at midday, she brought porridge and tea and she'd say little before pushing the heavy wardrobe back in place. The porridge had an odd sweetness, the tea had none at all. Sometimes he would sleep through those visits, and he would wake to find the tray next to him.

The evenings were different.

Once he got a little stronger, she would move him to the worktable in the cellar just outside the hole in the wall. There was all kinds of food stored in the cellar, and he loved the smell of them — barrels of apples and cider, and bundles of dried plants hanging from the rafters. He knew some of the herbs, others he did not. There was a snow-covered window at the top of the wall. It was often dark by the time she came, but sometimes there would be daylight and he might glance the blue sky through the bare tree branches.

He tried to ask her about her life, but she said little. She'd sit with him there and ask about the plantation.

He didn't want her to pity him any more than she already did, so he tried to think of good things to tell her about Walnut Grove, but no matter where he started, he always ended up talking about Alaura.

He talked about how smart and beautiful she was, and how the two of them would take long walks after dinner each night and talk about what they'd learned that day, whether it be something Alaura had heard in the master's study or something Joe had read in a discarded newspaper.

"You can read?" Mary asked.

Joe nodded. "We went to church every Sunday, and the preacher would say the chapter and verse before they read it out loud. Momma used to make a game to see how much of it we could remember, but she had something else on her mind. You see, someone had given her a Bible, and we went home and got that book out and we would try to find the passage and work out which words were which. The foreman, he found out, and he hardly left any skin on my mother's back. He started in on me, too, but the old man stopped him before he got too far."

He took a long drink from his glass.

"It nearly got us killed, but it changed everything," he said. "I'd get the old man's newspapers off the trash pile. It didn't take me long to find out what the rest of the world was like. It's against the law to teach a slave to read, but the old master liked to show me and Alaura off like trick ponies. His wife used to threaten to leave him every time I showed up and would stomp out of the room. Eventually, she did go away, though I can't imagine that was the reason. Alaura said she went to Ireland. My sister, she's the one. She's so smart the old master has her take care of him, write letters for him and such. She's pretty, too."

He smiled. "She doesn't look like any person you've ever seen," he said. "She's got different-colored eyes. One brown, one green. The old women back home say there's something magic about her eyes, but to me, they're just pretty."

"What about your parents?" Mary asked.

"The master's wife sent my momma away soon after they found out I could read," he said. "Down to the sugar fields in Louisiana. She didn't last long down there. The old man tried to make it better for me, though. I had my own little place near the sawmill. Alaura, she was just a little girl when Momma went away, and he built a little room for her in the house, where it was cooler than the fields, and she'd come see me at the sawmill in the night and we'd read together. Sometimes the old man would lend me out to other mills, and I'd get some of the money."

"They let you keep it?" Mary asked.

"The old man would. He'd make a good deal for me," Joe said. "I saved up five hundred and twenty-three dollars. I had enough money to buy my sister's paper, but she wouldn't go until there was enough for me, too."

"Where's your sister now?" Mary asked, afraid of the answer. "Did she run with you?"

He shook his head and rubbed his eyes.

"There was no time," he said, going slow, trying not to choke on the words. "She was in the big house, and I couldn't go in there. I was sure I was going to be caught that night, then whipped to death or strung up the next day."

"You didn't plan to run?" she asked.

He shook his head then paused, measuring her against the weight of the rest of his story.

"It was the money. Yates took it. I don't know how he knew about it, but he tore apart my room until he found where I had it hid. Said I had no use for it. Same night he came back and woke me up. He was laughing and smelled like he'd been swimming in a whiskey river. He pulled out the pockets of his fancy trousers, said he lost all the money in a bet. Cockfighting."

Even now, his eyes shone with fury.

"That money was the difference between Alaura being a slave and free woman, and he bet it on a damned chicken." He spat. "I couldn't help myself. I took up a big old rock and bashed him in the head. I ran, then swam, then ran some more. I could hear those dogs even across the Shenandoah. I just kept going."

He looked her in the eyes, hoping she could somehow forgive him for leaving his sister behind.

"How could I take her with me?" he asked. "I was sure they'd get me in no time."

His breath caught and he hesitated. His eyes drifted to the low ceiling and the bundles of herbs hanging there.

"There must be a way to get her free," she said, but the worry on her face made him

88

think she didn't believe what she said.

She helped him back into the tunnel and left him alone to sleep.

He soon found himself wakeful for longer stretches, and she brought him some books. He read a story that started out about wine and ended with a man buried alive behind a wall of bricks. "At least I've got a lamp," he muttered to himself before putting out the light and staring into the dark.

Next she brought him a book about a man who goes alone into the woods and makes a little place for himself to live. He read that one again and again, and the pond, the green meadows, and the little shanty started to show up in his dreams.

He asked for paper to write a letter to Alaura. He knew he could not send it, but he wanted to put his thoughts down. He started over and over again, trying to give her reason to hope, trying to make her feel safe, trying to say that they would see each other again, but the words all felt like lies, and he crumpled the paper and threw it against the back of the wardrobe that blocked him away from the world.

YATES

John Yates Bell gazed with blank eyes out across the plantation's winter-brown fields, his fingernails worrying the scab on his left temple until a bead of blood formed.

The doctor had scolded him, saying that the wound would have healed weeks ago if he would stop picking at it, but his fingers went to the wound whenever he thought of Joe the runaway.

And he could not stop thinking about Joe.

He was imagining him in some northern town, feted by the Yankees as another asset stolen from the rising Confederacy, when the voice of the runaway's sister shook him from his reverie.

"Master Yates, your father wants you in his study."

She was standing on the top step of the veranda, wearing a dark blue dress cut well for her lithe form. And always, there were those eyes. One green, the other brown.

They were unlike any he had ever seen, and they were staring at him.

None of the other slaves dared even look him in the face, but Alaura always glared at him with contempt. He longed to beat the haughtiness out of her, to replace her arrogance with the respect and fear a darkie girl should feel toward her master.

He had tried to long ago, but his father had stayed his hand.

She had been younger then, maybe ten years old, but his father had already moved her into the house and made her his errand girl. Yates's mother had left them just months before, moving back to Ireland.

While the other slaves worked in the fields under the hot sun, Alaura sat in the corner of his father's study as he worked at his desk, fetching him bourbon or a glass of water, or as she had just done again, his son.

He'd been kneeling in the sun, focusing his father's magnifying glass on an ant when she called him to follow her into the paneled study. She went and sat in her chair in the corner while he stood in front of his father's carved desk, and listened as his father berated him for something.

When his father finally fell silent, he was sure he could hear her giggling behind him.

He spun around, but her face was buried in a book.

He could not stand the idea of her laughing, though, and he flew across the room and knocked her to the floor.

He slapped her only once before his father pulled him off. Then it was his turn to be hit, and not just once, and not simply a slap.

"Never touch her," his father screamed over and over.

When the beating finally stopped, Yates rolled over. Behind his father, he could see those different-colored eyes staring down at him. She had covered her mouth with her hands, but he was sure she was laughing behind them.

And he felt like she had been laughing at him ever since. He was sure that whenever he needed to whip a lesson into someone, that Alaura would go tell that darkie afterward of how she saw him beaten, and how she got to laugh at him. And whichever one got whipped, he would laugh at Yates, too.

He sucked cold Virginia air into his lungs. Whatever his father wanted, he was sure it wouldn't be a pleasant conversation. It had always been this way with his father.

He felt his stomach churning like a little boy's as he trod the long Oriental carpet of the hallway that led to the paneled office.

Nothing Yates had ever done was good enough for the old man, and his father had ceased trying to hide his disappointment long ago.

For years, Yates had used the sprawl of the plantation to avoid his father, hiking and riding for days on end, camping in long-forgotten forests, often going weeks without encountering him. And if he rode far enough into the woods, he could forget that both his father and the niggers were nearby.

He'd visited his mother in Ireland only once since she'd left, spending weeks with her in the fallen-down remnants of her family's ancestral manor. The windows rattled in the cold wind and sheep wandered unbidden into the stone kitchen. He could never get her to even mention her husband's name, much less explain the schism that ran through their family. He tried to convince her to come home, but she seemed content to sit by the peat fire and drink her tea with her feet swaddled in wool blankets, tended by a single housemaid. She had one luxury, an elaborate telescope she used to stare out into the dark, finding and naming stars late into the night.

He was able to glean that her paltry upkeep was paid by his father, and that he controlled her as much as he could with the threat of further pauperization.

Another thing he shared with her.

The only part of the trip that brought him any solace was the crossing. He fell in love with the water then, and had decided when Walnut Grove was finally his, he would buy a boat on the Chesapeake where he could sail out of the harbor every fine day, leaving the niggers and cotton behind.

His father was sitting behind his carved desk. He was a slight man, and Yates, at six foot two, felt like he was nearly double his in size. Nonetheless, his father ruled him still in a way that could not be explained by money or size.

The desk's broad top was piled high with books and papers, but the blotter in front of him was empty but for a folded newspaper and a stack of yellow envelopes from the telegraph office.

"What's this?" his father muttered, pushing the paper across the desktop.

"CONFEDERATES FORM PROVISIONAL GOVERNMENT." Yates read the headline out loud, then blinked at his father, mystified.

"Not the story," his father said. "The advertisements, on the back."

Yates turned the paper in his hands, and there was the reward notice he'd posted days after Joe had attacked him and taken

94

off. He'd even paid the extra dollar for the cartoon of a runaway with his swag on a stick over his shoulder.

"Who told you to do that?" his father asked.

Yates furrowed his brow.

"I just figured," Yates said. "How else are you going to catch him?"

"Where's this thousand-dollar reward coming from?" his father asked. "You don't have it, I'm certain of that. Whatever I give you, you spend on whores and liquor."

His father stared at him as if he was expecting a denial, but Yates had been caught so off-guard by the reprisal that he didn't see any point in denying what was true.

"I'm sure as hell not paying," his father growled.

"You're just going to let him get away?" Yates asked.

"He wouldn't have run if you hadn't stolen his money," his father hissed.

"The nigger could have killed me," Yates said, his fingers finding the scab again. "We've got to whip that son of a bitch until he's nothing but a stain on the ground. You've got to show the others, or they'll get ideas."

"You're right about him being able to kill

you." His father sneered. "Did you ever even think about that? Him, standing there with that rock in his hand. You laid out on the ground. What's going on in his head right then? He has to know he's as good as dead anyway, right? No slave ever did anything like that and lived. So what's he got to lose?"

Yates's father paused, waiting for a response, but Yates had nothing to say.

"He could have mashed your skull to jelly, but he didn't. That's what you call mercy."

"You always have taken his side," Yates said. "His sister's, too. Now he's nearly killed your own son, and you blame me for it. What the hell was he doing with that five hundred dollars anyway? Where'd he get that kind of money? If you were half as soft on me as you are on him, I wouldn't have needed to steal from him."

"I wasn't half as soft on him as I should have been," his father said, grimacing as he bit his lower lip. "He's the best sawyer in Virginia. When he wasn't running our mill, there were a half-dozen others lined up to pay me for his services. He made me a lot of money. I paid him because you can't whip someone and expect him to do that kind of work."

"I'm your own son. What do I have to do for five hundred dollars?" Yates muttered.

"Can you run a sawmill?" his father asked, his eyes looking over his glasses. "Because I suddenly find myself with an opening."

"That's nigger work," Yates said.

"And drinking and whoring is a white man's?"

Yates sat silently, his hands clenching into fists behind the chair's back. He imagined ways to make his father suffer for the things he was saying.

"So you are just letting him go?"

"You said it yourself," his father said. "He could have just about bought his own papers with the money he had. You stole it from him. The only right thing to do is let him go. By my figuring, I should be asking you to pay me for my lost sawyer."

"Even Mother hated him," Yates hissed, gnawing at his fingernail.

His father's face flushed, and the muscles in his jaw writhed as he clenched his teeth.

"Yes, she did, and she had her reasons," his father muttered. "But she didn't raise you to steal, not from a white man or a slave. You take his money, then you run this ad with the name of my plantation on it, obliging me to pay this bounty. I know you are waiting for the day they put me in the ground and you can do what you will with this place, but in the meantime, Walnut

Grove is mine, this money is mine. It is not yours to spend."

Yates tried to muster all his hatred into the glare he sent his father's way.

His father looked back, a sadness taking over from the anger of a moment before.

"These niggers as you call them, like everything else on Walnut Grove, they are my responsibility," he said. "Like the house, the tools, the land, I must treat them well if I want them to work properly. I've seen you come back from a quail hunt and spend two hours cleaning your shotgun. We owe at least that kind of care to the slaves in the field."

"Is that what you're doing with Alaura? Or are you taking care of her in some other way?"

His father's eyes blazed.

"She's my secretary," his father said.

"I'll bet," Yates said.

"You're not too old for me to beat," his father snarled.

Yates smiled, wishing the frail old man would try such a thing.

"It seems that Joe's been caught nine times in the last week," his father said, pushing the pile of telegraphs across the desk. "Marion, Ohio. Springfield, Massachusetts. Even a place called Horseheads, New York.

A thousand dollars is a lot of money, and there's more than a few men that'll produce something that looks like a runaway given that kind of incentive."

Yates stared at the stack of envelopes.

"If one of these bounty hunters capture him," his father said. "I'm going to send Joe his papers. Make him a free man."

"Damned if you will!" Yates yelped, jumping to his feet.

His father stared at him until Yates slumped back into his chair.

"He doesn't deserve to be dragged back here in chains. And he sure as hell doesn't deserve to die under your whip. In the meantime, I'll have to honor the ad you placed. I'll dock your allowance until I've recovered the thousand I'll have to pay. You've shamed yourself in this, and you've shamed me. And if you interfere in any of it, any of my trying to make it right, you'll never see another red cent of my money. And neither will your mother."

"Don't you bring her into this," Yates said, his hands gripping the arms of his chair.

His father looked at him over his glasses.

"What am I supposed to do for money?" Yates asked, his voice dripping with hatred.

"Whatever grown men do," his father

replied. "Work. Sweat. Make a man of yourself."

Yates glared at him a long time before standing and leaving the room.

He took dinner in his room that night, reading the last letter his mother had sent, now a month old.

After the house girl had come for the tray, he wrote her back, the first time he'd done so in nearly a year. He apologized for not having gone to see her again, for leaving her alone in that cold place. He wrote many pages of the daily goings-on around the plantation, and how he'd wished his father had not driven her away. He wrote that he loved her, something he could not remember ever saying, though he was sure he had.

By the time he finished, the winter night had fallen, and he sat at his desk listening to the big plantation house — the familiar sounds of the kitchen girls talking as they washed up, the houseboys clanging the brass ash buckets as they cleaned out the fireplaces, Old Walter going from window to window, closing the shutters against the cold of the night. One by one, he listened as the slaves left for their little shacks out past the barn. Then it was just the creak of the old building.

It had always been his home, and he loved

it. But he could not stay.

In the quiet, he rose and packed a bag, then crept down the stairs, avoiding the creaking spots he knew so well. He went to his father's office, opened the safe and took the purse of gold coins his father kept there, then took the stack of telegrams from his father's desk.

While the other slaves slept in run-down shanties downwind from the privies, Alaura had been gifted a pantry that had been converted into a tiny sleeping room so that she could be safe and warm in the house.

Yates stood for a long time outside her door, remembering the layout of the tiny room, where the bed was, where her head would be. Finally, he drew out his knife and shouldered the door until the little hook that held it in place gave way. He fell into the room in a rush, landing on the bed. In an instant, he had his hand over her mouth and the knife at her throat.

"Quiet," he whispered.

Even in the dark he could make out the fine bones of her face, the point of her delicate chin, and those eyes.

"You make any noise," he hissed through clenched teeth, "I'll kill you and drain you like a stuck pig."

The dress she had worn earlier hung on a

peg over the foot of her bed, and he pulled it down and shoved it at her.

"What do you want?" she asked.

"Put this on," he said. "Move."

She stared at him for a moment, then got to her feet and took the dress from him.

"Will massuh turn his back?" she asked, sounding the slave for the first time in her life.

"Why should I?" he asked.

She cast her eyes down to the floor and pulled her sleeping shift over her head.

The starlight that filtered through the tiny window was dim, but his breath came quicker as he took in the curve of her breasts. He held the knife tight, stopping himself from reaching out to touch her skin.

She pulled the dress on quickly. Even as she glared at him, he felt pride in his restraint.

"Let's go," he said, pointing the knife. "You remember, you ain't so special. I can come back for another."

The hollowness of the lie sounded false even to him.

At the stable he shoved her onto a stool.

"It's not too late," she said calmly as he saddled his horse and loaded the saddle-bags. "The old master doesn't need to know about this. Just stop, and everything will go back the way it was."

"Shut your mouth," he said. "I ain't above gagging you."

He mounted, then pulled her up behind him, and rode out the stable doors, pausing to stare at the house before riding down the long drive to the road, turning west.

"Harpers Ferry is to the east," she said. "Where you taking me?"

"There's no fun in Harpers Ferry," he said.

It was less than three miles to Charles Town, but the night was cold and he could feel the tremble of her shivering hands on the cantle behind him. Her silence made him nervous, so he talked.

"Harpers Ferry used to be a little fun, but ever since the zealot attacked two years ago, it's like a convent over there. Watchmen on every corner, the taverns all closed."

"The zealot?" she asked.

Yates spat.

"Surely with all your book learning, you saw in the paper about John Brown and his raiders," he said, contempt in his voice.

"I'm not supposed to read the papers," she said.

Yates had seen her and her brother stealing papers out of the trash heap more than once, but was happy to continue.

"He came down here, him and his band of Yankees," he said. "He was sure he was going to be greeted as the savior by all the niggers. Brought a whole bunch of weapons, thinking you all were going to rise up and join him in a glorious fight. But he didn't understand you all don't have it in you to fight, that God intended the darkies to be slaves, and that's the natural order of things. None of you rose up for him, but me and my friends, we sure did. Hundreds of us, we all rode into town and surrounded that son of a bitch where he was holed up in the armory. We waited him out for a couple days, let him stew in his juice a little bit. Then we all charged in. Those cowards, they folded like nothing, less than it takes to tell the story. I was hoping to kill the zealot myself, but I didn't get the chance.

"I was there when they hung him, though," he said. "We all were. We'd been training the whole time the trial was going on, and we had uniforms and all by then, and they lined us all up pretty just in case some Yankees decided to try something.

"They say you can't hear the neck snap when you hang a man, but I swear I heard his. I surely did."

He turned in the saddle, and tried to smile back at her.

104

"The thing I figured that day, they were only the first. There's more coming. And now, this Lincoln character, he thinks he's going to end the way we do things down here, but there's always been slavery, and there always will. It's God's way, says so in the Bible. And no Illinois bumpkin is going to change that. Since you don't read the papers, you probably don't know that we've already started our own country. Secession, all throughout the South. We'll not have to answer to that fool, and if he tries to stop us, we'll be ready the next time they come."

They were on the outskirts of the town, and music filtered through the cold night air.

"That's where they hung him," he said, nodding. "John Brown, him and what was left of his followers."

"Where?" she asked.

He raised his hand to point at the lawn of a grand house, but as he did Alaura moved quickly, her hands going from the cantle up to his throat. He caught sight of fabric in her hands, the white of her sleeping shift, and then suddenly it was wrapped around his neck.

He tried to pull free, but she'd swung her feet up onto his back so that she was riding him as he rode the horse, the full weight of her pulling at his throat.

"I read it was the Marines that went in," she shouted, yanking harder. "That you cowards all held back, too afraid of that preacher man to go in yourself."

His head swam and he tore at the cloth but could not get his gloved fingers underneath. The horse whinnied under him, and he instinctively fought to stay in the saddle. Finally, the stallion kicked, throwing the two of them. Alaura pushed off him in midair, landing a few feet away from Yates. She climbed to her bare feet and started running. Yates, gasping for air, took after her.

"Bitch," he shouted, jumping her as she slipped in the light snow of the furrowed fields. His gloved hand took in a large swath of her kinky hair. "You're nothing. If I killed you right here, no one would know or care."

She spat in his face and he yanked her hair so hard that she screamed.

He raised his other hand to cuff her, but stopped his hand inches from her face.

"Don't make me damage the goods," he hissed through clenched teeth.

He dragged her through the field, reached into the saddlebag, and pulled out his pistol before yanking her to her feet. He grabbed the horse's reins and shoved the gun in her back.

"Walk," he said. "Up front, where I can see you."

She stumbled, and he pulled back the hammer. She straightened up and moved forward.

"I wish Joe had finished you," she said as she walked. "I wish he had beaten your brains in."

"Don't make me do it," he said.

"They all know the story back at the plantation," she said, goading him. "They all laugh about how Joe took you down with nothing but a rock. You, up in the old house, them all in the back, laughing at you."

"I'm going to kill you," he growled.

"If you were going to kill me, I'd be dead," she said, turning to look at him as she walked. "I don't know what you have in mind, but you still can't touch me."

There were voices and laughter in the distance as he marched her toward the town. Pistol raised, he followed her down the road until they came to a grand house with music seeping out from the windows. A huge man in a floral vest stood guard at the door.

Yates tied the horse to a post and pulled Alaura up onto the porch.

"I'm here to talk to Miss Levant," he said to the doorman.

107

A rush of warm air and the smell of smoke wafted out as the doorman went inside, and soon an elegantly dressed woman stepped out.

"Mr. Bell," she said, running her eyes up and down Alaura. "What a pleasure. Don't you usually join us at the beginning of the month?"

"Yes, well, as you can see, I have a different type of deal to discuss tonight," Yates said, smiling.

"She is a pretty thing," Madame Levant said, running a finger along Alaura's jaw.

"She's been crying, and got a little roughed up on the way over," Yates said. "Cleans up nice, and never been touched."

Levant cocked an eyebrow.

"You're certain?"

"Her brother wouldn't let a soul near her," Yates said.

"Her brother?" she asked. "Sounds like I might have to deal with him."

"He's dead," Yates said.

"What?" Alaura shrieked.

"Strung up, then fed to the hogs. Happened two days ago in a shithole named Horseheads, New York. I only wish I could have seen it."

Alaura fell to her knees and covered her mouth with her hands.

"You are a cold man," Levant said.

"Two thousand," Yates said.

"We don't really deal with her breed here," she said. "And she's not really that pretty."

Yates cocked his head and pulled his lips back in a grin.

"Yes, she is," he said. "Look at those eyes."

"Did you bring papers?" she asked. "Your father's signature."

He shook his head.

"Seven," the madam said. "The lack of documentation complicates the matter considerably."

Yates looked at the crying girl at his feet.

"A specimen like that," he said. "You'll make four on her first customer. Give me eight, and full run of the house tonight."

Levant smiled, and fluttered her eyes.

"Come inside," she said, extending her hand. "Let me get you something to drink."

In the morning, Yates woke alone and nauseous, his head throbbing. The brocade curtains had been drawn, but the bright light of day cut a line between them onto the Oriental carpet. He pulled the velvet cord that hung from the ceiling, and a knock on the door came almost immediately. Still naked, he opened it to the uniformed maid.

He looked her over.

"Do you work here?" he asked.

"I'm just the maid," she said.

"Draw me a bath," he said. "And I'll have someone to scrub my back as well."

In the afternoon, Madame Levant brought him his cash and told him that if he wanted to stay any longer, he'd need to hand some back.

"Keep in touch," she said as he walked out onto the broad porch.

"I will," he said. "You're the only connection I have left in this town."

He went to the saloon, had himself a steak dinner, then retrieved his horse and rode north.

THE BALL

Every attempt was made to keep the crowds out of the depot until Lincoln's train arrived. The main doors were barred, but since the train entrance was open, people walked in by the dozens. As Lincoln's train approached, the mass of people gathered in the depot became alarming. A huge cheer rang out from everyone in attendance as the train slowly came to a halt and Lincoln stepped off the train and onto the platform. The President-elect was met by ex-president Millard Fillmore and acting Buffalo Mayor Bemis.

An artillery brigade began blazing a rapid salute, the people were cheering, and the President-elect's cortege took up its line of march for the carriage between the ranks of military personnel assigned to protect the dignitaries. The rush was tremendous. A squad from Company D threw themselves around Mr. Lincoln and his immediate party and measurably protected them, but it was impossible to protect anyone else. The soldiers pressed bayonets to the crowd, but the pressure from behind was so frightful that it would have been murder to have used them on the unlucky citizens who "had got the best place," and the D Company men had all they could do to recover arms without bloodshed.

The lines were broken and Mr. Lincoln was able to enter his carriage. Women fainted, men were crushed under the mass of bodies, and many others had their bones broken. Once out of the depot every man uttered a brief "Thank God!" for the preservation of his life. More with personal injuries were carried away and the fainted women were recovering under a free use of hydrant water.

The route that Lincoln's carriage took was very brief, being directly to the American Hotel on Main Street. The street was magnificent. The rush and roar and surge of the crowd was its grandest feature, but all the roofs and windows of buildings were filled with people; the gay winter attire of the ladies and the waving of their handkerchiefs as the cortege passed added brilliance to the scene. All the principal buildings were decorated with banners, from every flagstaff waved the stars and stripes — now dearer than ever to the American eye.

The scene from the balcony of the American Hotel was unexampled. From Eagle to Court Street, the mass of humanity was the densest ever witnessed, and the pressure toward the central point was tremendous. Men cheered, looked pale, and perspired.

Mr. Lincoln left his carriage attended by his immediate party and entered the hotel between two files of the escort. He appeared upon the balcony with Mr. Fillmore. His appearance was the signal for the most enthusiastic cheering, helped out by a salute of artillery on Clinton Street.

— *BUFFALO COMMERCIAL ADVERTISER,*
FEBRUARY 19, 1861

"I've paid for the rooms already," Nathan insisted again as he climbed out of the wagon. "You must come. For God's sake, Abraham Lincoln himself will be there. Leander is coming, along with this new friend of his. Charles is expecting you. I moved heaven and earth securing these invitations."

They had been arguing all morning, and he had not stopped even as she drove him to the Town Line station. He took his time fetching his valise from the back of the wagon as he grumbled about her stubbornness.

"I will stand on that platform right there and wave to Mr. Lincoln when he passes through in the morning," Mary said. "The walls of the American Hotel will stand just fine without me helping to prop them up."

She looked up into the gray sky. "There looks to be more than a foot before the morning. More than likely you'll get stuck downtown, and you'll be glad there's someone here to tend to the animals."

Her father stepped onto the platform before turning to her again.

"You've been saying for months that Charles needs to get off that farm," he said. "Well, I finally got him to leave. He's already gone downtown to buy new clothes just for the occasion. I promised him you'd be there, that you'd dance with him. You're making a liar of me. And you know he'll just mope the whole evening away, not saying a word to anyone."

She turned the corners of her mouth down and shook her head.

"Charlie Webster is a handsome man. He'll meet some pretty young thing down there. He has no need of me," she said, shaking her head. "I will not endure another grand ball as a Cinderella with no fairy godmother."

The train whistled its departure.

"You are the most obstinate child any man has ever been cursed with," her father huffed.

The whistle blew and Nathan climbed onto the train, pursing his lips in frustration while she turned the wagon toward home.

Gaslights burned from the columns of the American Hotel, casting a glow on the men gathered on its porch to smoke cigars, talk business, and watch as the squall blew in off Lake Erie.

Since he'd moved to the city, Leander had come to see his father's friends in a different light. He'd remembered them as boring old men with bad breath and too much hair sprouting from their ears, but in the city, their names were in every paper and on everyone's lips. He could see Bill Seward leaning against a white column, unchanged from the days when he brought him sticks of candy and shooed him out of his father's study. Millard Fillmore was there, too. His name had long been banned from the Willis house, but Leander could remember the days before he'd become president when he'd arrive at the farm with a bottle of whiskey and sit on the porch with Nathan all night. Birdsill Holly and Lyman Spalding stood together on the porch and nodded at Leander and Isabel as he drove a buggy to the hotel's entrance.

When Leander went for dinner at this restaurant or that, there would always be one or two of these men there to clap him on the back and remark how much he looked like his father, and to buy him a steak dinner and a snifter of brandy. He'd smile and thank them, all the time gritting his teeth that here he was just Nathan Willis's son.

It wasn't that he was unhappy downtown. In a way, he enjoyed the work. The dealers were happy to see him and would say how the finest rooms in the city were paneled in Willis oak. They'd joke with him and offer him pours of whiskey from the bottles in their desk drawers and pay top dollar. But all they wanted to talk about was how much they admired Nathan Willis.

He could not help but think that tonight, instead of talking about his father, they would notice him and Isabel.

"Pay attention," Isabel scolded him, as he narrowly missed running down one of the soggy onlookers in the street.

He guided the buggy into the valet station, but stole a glance at her as she checked the intricacies of her makeup in a pocket mirror and patted her hair. He found her beautiful on most days, but the gown she wore tonight left him breathless.

He was in awe of her in other ways as well. She was only a few years his senior but had already lived in ways he could not imagine. She'd grown up in New York, married one of the richest men in the city, and been widowed young. She'd spent years traveling through Europe and into the Far East. Her husband had been a trader of bonds and businesses, but she offered few details other than that the wealth he'd built up was now hers and that she had come to Buffalo to sell his interests in several businesses in the city.

Leander had met Isabel Fitch at a soiree at one of the grand houses on Delaware Avenue. Even now it was unclear how she had come to be there. While the ladies and married men sat in the parlor and talked of the theater season, she wandered into the billiard room where the single men had gathered. Before long, the game fell away as the players gathered around to hear tales of her just-completed tour through Europe. She drew them in with her ice-blue eyes and tales of Roman catacombs and the filth of London's alleys. As the evening wore on, she spoke of her long nights spent in the salons of Paris, offering lurid details of famous men hopping into bed with ladies and men and young boys.

Susie Munn in her gingham dresses seemed a silly schoolgirl compared to this silk-draped creature. He had stood at the back of the gathering, unable to take his eyes from her, his overly loud laughter poorly masking his shock.

At the end of the evening she singled him out, seemingly at random, and asked him to see her home through the cold streets to her mansion on Chippewa Street. He had nearly bolted when she explained that her servant was away and she needed his help lighting the stove.

She brought out a silver tray of cut glass and poured a bitter green liqueur over lumped sugar while telling him of the secret places she'd been, chambers draped in silk and incense. She brought out an elaborate device with colored hoses and showed him how to suck the acrid smoke of a blackish-yellow paste through it. His head was swimming and his vision blurred when she put one hand on his crotch and popped the buttons from his trousers with a quick, sharp yank.

She'd left him there during the following day, just him and the manservant, Fuller, and then the next day, too. His days with her blurred after that. Leander would lounge in the parlor with the hookah or sleep in the bedroom. Once he asked Fuller to make him a sandwich, but the only acknowledgment of the request was a barely discernible twitch of the man's mustache.

After a day or two, Leander came to wonder what Fuller did all day and explored the rest of the house looking for signs of his work. He heard grunting at the entrance to the basement stairs, and crept down only to see the servant stripped to the waist, lifting massive barbells overhead in an improvised gymnasium.

Whenever Isabel came home, she would bring things to eat and drink and inhale that he'd never imagined. Afterward she would lead him to the bedroom, and hours later, leave him spent and gasping.

Just that morning he had returned to the rooms at Whitney Place for the first time in a week. He found a three-day-old telegram from his father demanding an update on several deals. He had promised Isabel he'd be back in an hour, and he gathered his

119

things and went down to the waterfront to get some orders. The usual buyers were away, preparing for the big night, and he'd stopped into one of the shadier dealers, asked what they needed, and sold cheap, just to have something to show his father.

He patted his pocket, hoping the one order he held there would be enough.

"What imbeciles would voluntarily stand in such weather? What do they hope to see?" Isabel asked, staring back at the gray and homespun onlookers gathered under a streetlamp in the swirling snow.

"A pretty woman in a beautiful gown?" Leander offered.

She snorted.

"Subtle as a flying hammer," she muttered, rolling her eyes.

He helped her out of the buggy, put his hand at the small of her back, and guided her across the wide porch to the hotel entrance where a surge of heat and a top-hatted doorman met them. He took their coats and directed them to a ballroom filled with gaslight and color. Leander speared a pair of champagne glasses from a passing tray and paused at the ballroom entrance, taking in the sea of black suits and silk gowns that dipped and swirled to the rhythm of a minuet. He looked around to see who was looking at Isabel.

"Hello, Lelo," someone said from behind him.

Leander turned and was disappointed to see that it was only Charles Webster. Leander could not remember ever seeing him in anything but the rough clothes of a farmer. His wind-chapped face and thick, callused hands looked out of place with the stiff black and white of his new suit. Mary insisted he was a smart and kind man, but Leander had rarely heard him say more than ten words in a row.

"Lelo?" Isabel asked with a smirk.

Leander squirmed to hear her use the name.

"That's what his friends call him," Webster said.

"Look at you, Charlie, all dressed up," Leander said, changing the subject. "What are you doing down here?"

"I was planning to . . . ah . . . dance with Mary, but she has chosen to stay home instead."

"You live next door, surely you could dance with her anytime you want," Leander said.

"This was going to be special, though . . ." he said.

"Tell me something else embarrassing

about Lelo here," Isabel said, cupping her elbow in the palm of her hand and smiling over her champagne glass.

Charles blinked at her, surprised at the question.

"Leander's the best baseball player in the county," he said. "All the girls come from far and wide to see him play."

"Baseball?" Isabel asked.

"It's a boy's game," Leander said dismissively.

"Leander's the best damned outfielder on the Niagara Frontier," Charles repeated.

"Is that so, Lelo?" Isabel asked, enjoying his embarrassment. "The best on the Niagara Frontier?"

"I can't believe Mary would miss this," Charles said. "I thought she'd want to meet the president."

"Even I want to see him," Isabel said. "I'm curious to see if he's as ugly as he looks in his pictures."

Charles screwed his face up in surprise. "He's a great man that has shouldered a terrible burden."

"A great man?" she asked. "I hear his accent is so ridiculous that the last time he was in New York, they had to hire someone to translate."

"Have they forgotten English in New York

already?" Charles asked with a frown, then pointedly turned toward Leander.

"How do you like living downtown?" he asked him. "Do you like your new apartment?"

Isabel's face flashed anger.

"He doesn't use that squalid little place," she said. "He stays with me."

Leander flushed red, and Charles looked down at his shoes.

"Why would you say such a thing?" Leander asked, turning on her.

"It's true, is it not?" she asked.

"That's not the point," he said, flustered. "Charlie is a family friend. What of your reputation? You'll create a scandal."

"Scandal is exactly what you need," she said with a sweet smile. "You think I don't know when I'm being paraded around? I am only helping your reputation as a man about town. You should thank me."

"Leander," his father's voice boomed from behind him. "I'll have a word with you."

The tone he used made Leander feel like he was being sent into the yard for a switch. Even though Leander was used to being one of the bigger men in any room, his father always seemed larger, like a holdover from a time when giants walked the earth.

"Father, this is Isabel Fitch," Leander

said, drawing her closer.

His father took her offered hand politely, but looked at her with hooded eyes.

"I have prime lumber ready to sell," he said. "I just spoke with a half-dozen buyers, and they tell me they haven't heard from you in over a week. Exactly what have you been doing?"

Nathan looked again at Isabel in her blue gown, the expanse of milk-white skin exposed on her shoulders and powdered breasts.

"I've got an order for some walnut this morning," Leander said, pulling the folded bill of sale from his coat pocket and offering it to his father.

"I don't have any walnut," Nathan said, skeptical. "You know that."

"It's the only order I could manage," Leander said. "There's that stand of them on the other side of the creek."

"That's Ebenezer land," Nathan said. "Do you expect me to poach?"

"They won't care," Leander said. "They are packing up and heading west."

Nathan scanned the paper.

"Your entire life, you've always done what is easiest and then asked forgiveness," Nathan said. "But no more. Take this back and void it."

Leander's face reddened. He wished he had something to calm his nerves and thought of the opium pipe back in Isabel's parlor. He started to sweat in the crowded room. In his father's stony silence, a black-suited attendant stepped to them.

"Mr. Willis, the Lincolns have changed their plans due to the weather. They are retiring soon in order to get an early start in the morning. Mr. Fillmore sends word that if you and your daughter would like to wish them well, you must come now."

Nathan shook his head, and the messenger moved back into the crowd.

"Aren't you going to meet them?" Leander asked.

"I spoke with them earlier," Nathan said, looming over his son. "They will not miss me, I'm sure. Don't try to distract me. You will not get off the hook so easily."

"You shouldn't sell now anyway," Isabel chimed in. "When the war comes, the prices for lumber will triple overnight."

"Excuse me?" Nathan asked, his eyes bulging at the woman.

"The demand for most things will sky-rocket when the war comes," she said. "You'll be able to name your price then."

The color rose in Nathan's face, and Leander stepped back instinctively.

"What do you know of such things?" he asked.

"Before my husband died, I advised him often," Isabel said coolly. "We made a great deal of money knowing what would come next."

"I can think of no worse type of scoundrel than a war profiteer," Nathan growled. "The war is the reason to sell these goods now. Leander will have more important duties if it comes to pass. I expect him to enlist."

The idea came as a surprise to Leander and his stomach clenched at the thought.

"Surely you don't expect your boy to participate in such a folly?" Isabel asked. "A man of your means, you'll most certainly be able to buy him a proxy."

"He most certainly will fight," Nathan said. "There's been a Willis in every war since Hastings. He will fight or I'll have nothing more to do with him."

"Only a fool would take pennies a day to fester in some useless cause," Isabel said. "There are fortunes to be made."

"I am used to hearing such cynicism from the idle barons of Manhattan, but not from a lady," Nathan said. "Your husband must have truly corrupted you."

Isabel smiled.

"Many say that it was I that corrupted him."

Nathan's knuckles whitened around his whiskey glass.

"I've heard all I care to," he said, shoving the bill of sale back at Leander. "Cancel this order, and get to work with some real business."

He turned and walked away, leaving the two of them standing alone.

"He thinks I'm still a child," Leander blurted. "Who does he think he is to order me around? I will not be told what to do. I am my own man."

The declaration made him feel better, but his hands still shook with anger.

"Where did your friend Charles go?" Isabel asked calmly. "He was just getting interesting."

"Would it be okay if we went now?" he asked. "I need some smoke."

TRAIN

Mary was not used to how the big house echoed with everyone gone. Katia had made the short trip to Hydesville to meet the world-famous Fox sisters. The kitchen girl was certain that she shared the spiritualist gift with the famed sisters, and hoped they would help her develop her ability to talk with the dead.

She baked a cornbread and fried some eggs and went into the cellar to eat with Joe.

"I don't hear anyone upstairs," he said as he settled at the table outside the tunnel.

"Father has gone downtown to see Mr. Lincoln at the presidential ball," she said.

She enjoyed the look of joy on his face. She'd done what she could to raise his spirits in the last few weeks, but the pain he was in and his time hidden in the dark tunnel were taking its toll.

"Why didn't you go see him yourself?" he asked.

"He will make a whistle stop here in Town Line tomorrow morning," she said. "I'll be there to see him then. Lord knows, someone should. The copperheads in this town are more likely to shoot at him than cheer."

She smiled.

"After the train leaves the station, it will pass right through our field. I expect my father will get a good price on presidential rye in the fall."

"I remember the day after the election," Joe said. "No one left the big house at all. They didn't send anyone to take us to the fields, stayed quiet all day, like it was a funeral. That's how we knew who won. So in the afternoon, we all got together and we cooked us up a big meal, and danced and sang into the night. They came out onto the porch then, they just stood there with their arms folded and I kept thinking they were going to come out with their whips, or even worse. But they just watched us. They were afraid."

He scratched at his bandaged stump.

"What I wouldn't give to see the man that makes them so afraid."

"I wish you could," she said, shaking her head. "But there will be people there, probably just to jeer at him, but a few will come. And if anyone saw you, they'd drag you down South and have me in the city jail faster than you could count. It would be the end of both of us."

His face turned grim again.

"You're right, I know," he said. "I know. Even here, after all these miles, things are no better, really."

He chewed the last of his dinner silently, and the brightness that had shone at the thought of seeing Lincoln faded from his eyes.

"Can you help me back into the tunnel?" he asked, quietly.

As she brushed the dirt from her skirts where she had kneeled to help him onto his pallet, she worked through the feeling of sadness she felt. Certainly, she wished she didn't have to say no to him, but there was something else, something harder to define.

She stopped on the stairs when she realized that she would have to spend the evening alone after she had been looking forward to spending it with him.

Mary stoked the fireplace in the parlor and sat with her book in her lap, staring into the flames for a long time. Even though the leather chairs smelled of her father's cigars, the room always reminded her of her

mother. The walls were covered in a vermil-
ion paper that her mother had ordered from
Manhattan, and every day Mary polished
the little table she had used to write her letters. Katia claimed her ghost visited when
the wind buffeted the tall poplars. Mary
waved off the girl's prattle of apparitions,
but as the day's flurries turned into the
night's squall, she found a comfort in the
solid walls of the room that reminded her of
her mother's presence.

Storms always reminded her of lying in
her little bed when she was four, quivering
as limb after limb crashed to the ground
under the weight of an ice storm's inch-
thick glaze. She let out a scream when the
house shook from the fall of one of the
grand elms in the front yard. Within seconds, her mother's tired face appeared over
her, softening as she gave assurances.

But tonight, drifting toward sleep, her
finger wedged in the closed book, she
listened to the crackle and the hiss of the
fading fire and heard her mother's voice,
not soothing, but fraught with worry. She
tried to make out the words, but like the
dimming fire, they slipped toward nothingness.

She awoke to a sharp rap at the front door,
and the book fell from her hand. The fire

had died, turning the high-ceilinged room cold. She shivered as she stood and tripped in the dark.

Even as she held a match to a fresh candle, she remembered her mother saying, "Good news waits, but bad will wake you."

The grandfather clock read a few minutes before five. The rapping came again.

She took the pistol in hand before opening the door.

Ruddy faced and shivering, Charles Webster stood at the threshold, his coat damp, his muttonchop beard flecked with ice, heavy snow haloing his formal black bowler.

"Dear God, what are you doing?" she asked. "At this hour? You are frozen half to death. Get in here."

He looked down at the gun in her hand.

"The Willis hospitality is not what it once was," he said. "I prefer it when your father greets me with brandy."

She laughed.

"I was sure you were a federal agent at my doorstep," she said, hanging the pistol back on its peg. "It's only my father's parsimony that stopped me from shooting you through the door. He'd have tanned my hide if he had to make a new one."

The snow on his collar chilled her fingers as she took his coat and hat and led him to one of the chairs. He wore a new suit, and the snow-caked trousers gave off the smell of wet sheep. She brushed him off, covered him with a blanket, and rebuilt the fire from the ash-covered embers.

Mary had always liked Charles. He was a quiet man who worked whenever there was work to be done. She sometimes thought him monk-like. And though he had doted on his wife, sometimes during the months when the winter left him little to do, he would head into the wilderness for days on end. And now that Verona had died, he sometimes disappeared for weeks, coming back gaunt and unwashed, but with a peacefulness and grace in his manner that she envied.

"I don't know if this is the hour for cordials or breakfast, but since you requested brandy . . ." she said, filling a glass for him. She could feel the cold radiating from him.

"What madness brings you half dead to my door at this hour?"

"I went downtown hoping to dance with you at the ball, but your father said you wouldn't come and were planning to see Mr. Lincoln's train at the station." He blurted everything at once, as if he'd been rehearsing. "I didn't want you to be disappointed, but that will be too late. They have decided to leave early, and will come through here in little more than an hour. They won't stop at the station as planned, they'll just pass through."

"You rode all night to tell me this?" she asked in disbelief.

"I know seeing him is important to you," he said. "As soon as I heard of the new arrangements, the thought that you'd miss him broke my heart."

She shook her head, angry that he would do something so dangerous for her.

"You are a fool," she said, pulling the corners of her mouth down. "Verona might have allowed you to spend days and nights wandering the woods, but I won't have you killing yourself over my stubbornness. I didn't ask for it, and I'll not have it."

She downed her glass all at once and glared at him, daring him to argue.

"A damned fool," she repeated.

Like her, he had always seemed out of sorts in social settings, and she wondered how her father had convinced him to go to the ball in the first place. He sat in the chair like a scolded boy, stiff-backed with his hands on his knees and eyes downcast. She could not say if his lower lip quivered or if she had simply imagined it.

"I'm sorry," he said, staring down at his wet boots. "I thought you would be pleased. I never knew how to make Verona happy, and now I make the same mistakes with you."

She looked down at him and realized that she would have enjoyed being at the ball with him, and would have enjoyed seeing so many people out to celebrate the new president and that she was really just angry at herself for denying herself those pleasures. She reached out, touching the back of his hand. He looked up, open faced and vulnerable.

"Thank you, Charlie," she said. "A stupid thing certainly, but also one of the kindest anyone has ever done for me."

He tried to smile at her, but she could see an anxiousness in his eyes.

"I guess I should have gone downtown after all," she said. "I have caused all this fuss, and now, at best, I can see him whizzing by at twenty-five miles an hour. It will be a pitiful showing at the station indeed."

"Why go to the station at all?" Charles asked. "Why not greet him in your own field?"

Her face brightened at the thought.

"That would be something, wouldn't it?" she said.

"Then it's settled," he said. "We should leave soon."

"We will not," Mary said. "You're not going out into that cold again. You'll catch your death."

"I can go out in it and I will," he said. "I didn't ride all night to not be there with you."

She stood and put her hand on his forehead, a mother testing a sick child for fever.

"At least go put on some of my father's dry clothes. I'll make us breakfast," she said.

By the time he came down, the kitchen was warming from the stoked stove.

Even with the sleeves and trouser legs rolled, her tall father's work clothes hung loosely on him, making him look like a little boy. When he saw her looking at him, he made a face and they burst into laughter together.

He sat at the worn kitchen table and she turned back to the cutting board. She wondered what had brought him through the heavy snow of the night to her door, and she thought that maybe, at last, he was shaking off the darkness that had enveloped him since his wife's death. She thought of all the years she'd known Charlie Webster, and could not name a soul she trusted more.

"I'm going to tell you something I

136

shouldn't," she said, her back to him. "Something important to me, something that I've wanted to share with someone but have never been able to."

She turned to look at him.

"You can trust me," he said.

"I do," she said, wrapping her arms around herself and taking a deep breath. "There's a man hiding in the cellar, a runaway."

He looked at her, stunned.

"He's lost his leg," she whispered. "He has been hiding in a horrible little hole behind my mother's broken wardrobe for weeks, and I fear for him. He's losing the will to live. I go down each morning, afraid that he will have found a way to end things.

"He was sick to death and wounded when he arrived," she said, turning to look in his eyes. "His leg was so putrefied that Doc Pride had to take it off. He hasn't been able to travel. But he's up and around a bit now."

She shoved her hands into the pockets of her apron, fidgeting with the detritus there.

"I want to take him to see the train," she said. "It will still be dark when it comes through, and no one will see him if he comes with us into our own empty field. I think it may save his life."

She watched as emotion played over his face.

"You accuse me of foolishness?" he asked. "Your father's business, his position, this house, this farm. All in jeopardy."

"I know," she said.

She turned her back and put a big iron skillet on the hot stove.

"But these people, these 'slaves' — how I hate that word — they are innocents, and they are suffering," she said. "He is suffering."

"You are putting everything your father has built at risk," he said. "You are putting us at risk."

"Us?" she asked, turning to look at him. "You can go home, and nothing more will ever be said. I did not mean to put you in danger, too."

She paused, looking for some sign from him.

"I know I shouldn't involve you in this," she said. "But I fear for him in the same way I did for you in the days after Verona's funeral. There was nothing I wouldn't have done to help you through then. And there's nothing I wouldn't do to help him now."

He sat in silence, taking the top off the honeypot that sat on the table and lifting the dipper out, watching the honey drip back into the pot. Finally, he pushed back from the table, and her heart sank.

He said nothing, but instead of leaving, he went down the cellar stairs.

She could hear the shifting of the wardrobe, and the voices of the two men, then scuffling on the stairs as Joe, leaning heavily on Charlie, climbed, blinking, into the light of the kitchen.

Charles helped him into a chair, then sat across from him. Wordlessly, Mary put plates of food down, poured coffee, and sat next to Charles. She rubbed his arm with the palm of her hand and smiled at him.

"I had coffee once before," Joe said. "My sister saved me some that was left over from breakfast at the big house. It was cold though, not like this. This is real good."

"I like it with a little cream and some maple sugar," Charles said, pushing the pitcher and bowl to him. "You might try it that way."

When the clock chimed six, Charles got up from the table and went to the barn and hitched Timber to the sleigh. Mary gathered blankets, and gave Joe her father's barn coat to wear. They stepped out the back door into the still-dark morning and Mary braced Joe as he hopped out and climbed into the sleigh.

"Where else will our new president be greeted by a such a party?" Mary asked. "A fugitive, a man too foolish to stay out of a snowstorm, and a twenty-three-year-old spinster."

Charles winced as he set the draft horse off across the highway and through the blanched field. They rode across the ruts and furrows of the dormant land, the rails of the sleigh hissing as they passed through the uneven drifts. An ancient, lonely elm stood near the track, and Charles pulled up under it. They sat looking west into the blackness, and even the horse seemed hesitant to disturb the hushed dark. The clouded sky gave no light, but Charles climbed down and lit half a dozen oil lamps hanging from the tree's branches. "Now, perhaps he'll see us," he said, climbing back onto his seat.

"Where did those come from?" she asked.

"I hung them before I came to your door," Charles said.

The snowfall had tapered off, but a thick blanket covered the ground and the wind gusted, stirring the flakes into low, whirling dances. The shadows of the bare limbs shifted across the perfect white land as the lanterns swayed. Except for the twitching of Timber's ears, all else was still.

"I've seen nothing more beautiful," Mary said. Even as the first intimations of the coming train reverberated in the west, she grasped at the fading moment of peace.

They could see the headlamp in the distance, the yellow light reflecting off the snow-dusted twin tracks. The train crested the hill less than a half mile away.

Wordlessly, they climbed out of the sleigh as the chuff and the rumble grew louder. Joe steadied himself on Mary's right arm, and she grasped Charles with the other. Her face, red from the cold, broke into a wide smile and her eyes shone in the lamplight.

"Here he comes," she whispered with excitement, not caring that she sounded like a little girl.

The field trembled under the vault of the wakening sky.

The locomotive was close enough that they could see the red, white, and blue streamers, sodden, limp, and stained by the coal exhaust. The whistle let off three quick blasts, and she laughed at the acknowledgment. The engine passed, heat, steam, snow, and soot blowing in their faces, the engineer waving from his perch high above them. They stood together as five crowded cars passed, but it was the last one, nearly empty, where they saw the distinct silhouette against the window. The light from the swaying lamps shone on his face for an instant, flashing on those deep-set eyes. He had been standing in the moving car, staring into the dark and breaking country.

He tipped his stovepipe hat in their direction before slipping back into the gray of the early morning, leaving them alone, already exhausted before daybreak.

SWEETWATER

Mary felt like she was being watched all the time.

Snowshoe tracks had appeared overnight under the eaves and around the barn, and someone had broken into the vacant worker's cabin. Once, she'd even seen Wilhelm, his face masked by a scarf, riding the highway back and forth in front of the farm.

She'd blocked the little window in the cellar, and each evening before sitting down with Joe, she'd pull on her coat and walk around the house just to check to see if he was there.

She had been slopping the hogs, trying to decide which one she'd lead back to the slaughter shack when he finally arrived with the marshal. It was her first time doing chores since laying up for a week with a cold. Her nose was chapped, her ears plugged, and she shook with bouts of sneezing each time she knuckled her itchy eyes, but she was enjoying the feel of the bright morning light and the sound of the pigs nosing around her boots when she fell under the shadow of the two riders.

The shock of his face, still raw and infected, left her breathless. The wound, trailing from his mouth nearly to his ear, gave him a gruesome death's head grin.

"Mary Willis?" the marshal asked her from atop his draft horse.

She nodded, feeling his eyes on her, turning her attention again to the hogs.

"Do I know you?" he asked.

She upended the bucket and dumped the last of the slops before she spoke.

"I don't think so."

He said nothing, trying to draw her eyes, but she did not look up. If the marshal recognized her from her run-in with him at the train station years ago, he'd tear the place apart until he'd found Joe.

Nathan came up from the coop, an empty feed bucket dangling from his loose fist.

"Commissioner Willis," the marshal said. "I'm Marshal Dwight Kidder."

"I know who you are," Nathan said.

"I'm here to search your farm for a renegade slave. This man claims the trail for the slave that attacked him leads here. Do you understand that if you or your daughter here are caught aiding a fugitive slave, it will entail a thousand-dollar fine and a year in prison?"

"This man is a thief," Nathan said, pointing at Wilhelm. "I caught him stealing some of my livestock many years ago and I sent him to jail for it. He is a vindictive man, with no proof of anything. By what sense should I let him trample through my house?"

"He says he tracked the slave to your farm, and the law says we get to search the premises," the marshal said.

"The Willises are the thieves around here," Wilhelm said, the wound twisting with his grin. "Wouldn't surprise me to find all kinds of stolen things here."

"It's the law," the marshal said.

"I remember when Millard Fillmore signed that bloodstained piece-of-shit treason into law." Nathan spat on the ground. "They say the ninth circle of hell, the deepest part, is reserved for traitors, and when that son of a bitch finally shuffles off this mortal coil, president or not, you'll find him there, along with the so-called Confederates he aligned himself with. My father fought at Saratoga over searches like this."

"Let's get this over with," the marshal said.

Wilhelm demanded to see the house, but Nathan led them first to the chicken coop.

"I think I saw a fugitive crawl in there this morning," he said, pointing to the run covered in droppings. Why don't you crawl in and take a look, Mr. Wilhelm?"

At the smokehouse, he pointed to the grease-covered dirt and said, "I saw one digging a hole in here last week. Might want to get down on all fours and dig around."

"Enough," the marshal said. "Let's see the barn."

"He could be in the apiary," Nathan said. "Are you sure you don't want to check the apiary?"

"The barn," Kidder said.

Nathan led them under the white horseshoe and into the barn. Mary flinched when Kidder walked in and picked up the blood-stained horse blanket she'd covered Joe in.

"That from him?" Wilhelm asked, pointing at the stain.

The marshal turned to look at Mary as she shifted her feet.

"This is a farm," Nathan said. "There's blood near every day."

"He's here somewhere," Wilhelm said, and turned to glare at Mary. "If you give him up, they might let you out of prison early."

Mary pursed her lips but kept quiet,

positioning herself behind stacked barrels of corn to keep her face from Kidder's sight.

After checking the stalls and behind the equipment, the fat marshal struggled to follow Wilhelm up the ladder into the loft. He stood panting while Wilhelm kicked through the hay, sending a rodent scurrying.

"I guess we have to see the house," the marshal said, finally.

"I told you to check there first," Wilhelm said, finally. "They probably squirreled him away by now."

They walked in through the back door and into the kitchen, their muddy boots echoing on the wide plank floors as they stepped past Katia, elbow-deep in bread dough. Mary worried that she might blurt something out, but the girl acted as if lawmen trod through her kitchen every day.

"We'll check the bedrooms," the marshal said. "Up the stairs."

Wilhelm turned into the study, and Nathan followed him in immediately.

"You've got some mighty nice things here," Wilhelm said. "Mighty fine indeed."

"Do as the marshal says," Nathan growled. "Or I'll take matters into my own hands."

"Just being thorough," Wilhelm said, smiling. He toed the black safe behind the desk with his dirty boot.

"What you got in there?" he asked.

Mary remembered her own curiosity around the big iron cabinet, and thought of the disappointment she and Leander felt the first time their father had opened it to reveal a ledger book and a neat stack of contracts.

"There's no need for him to be in here," Nathan said over his shoulder to the marshal.

"Let's go, Mr. Wilhelm," Kidder said.

Wilhelm picked up the pen from the desk and held it up as he turned to leave.

"Very nice," he said. "Do you have a receipt for this?"

Nathan snatched it from his hand.

The three men went from bedroom to bedroom as Mary hung back, her hands plunged deep into the pockets of her apron.

"Check the wardrobe," Wilhelm said when they stood in Mary's small room. "And under the beds."

Kidder cocked an eyebrow at him, but lifted the heavy winter bedclothes so they could peer under the little bed.

They straightened and stood in a circle, and the marshal shrugged.

"There's a cellar, isn't there?" Wilhelm asked. "Let's see the cellar."

Kidder looked at Nathan.

"At the back of the house," her father said, and led the way.

Mary nicked her finger on the knife in her pocket, and brought her hand to her mouth, sucking nervously at the blood.

The two men followed her father down the stairs, Kidder bracing himself against the stone wall of the foundation as the stair planks bent under his weight. Mary listened to him wheeze as she climbed down after them.

The marshal found the oil lamp sitting on the table and struck a match.

The rafters, hung with baskets and dried herbs, crowded down on the four of them as they struggled to fit among the crocks, barrels, and discarded furniture.

Kidder lifted the lamp and held it close to Mary's face.

"I know you from somewhere," he muttered.

He tried to catch her gaze, but she turned her eyes to the floor, only to see the gouges the wardrobe had left in the dirt. She raised her chin to keep his eyes from the ground and granted him the long look he had been wanting. After a long pause, he turned away, swinging the lamp around the cramped space.

"Nothing much here," he said. "Have you seen enough?"

"He's here somewhere," Wilhelm said. "You saw that blood."

He jerked the wardrobe open. As it rocked on the uneven floor, the lamplight shone on the empty space inside. Mary nearly bit through her lip, thinking of Joe listening helplessly behind it.

"If he was here, he was likely gone by the time you found me," Kidder said. "They generally don't wait around to get caught."

"Thanks for the tour," Wilhelm said, the raw wound writhing with his smile. "It was quite enlightening."

After they were sure the riders were gone, Mary went back down the stairs and pushed the wardrobe out of the way.

Joe was sitting on the cot, his face as ashen as the day Mary found him in the barn.

"They're gone," she said and took his shaking hand.

But they did not seem gone to her, and she could not shake the sense of violation. Every time she went to bed, she could feel Wilhelm leering into her wardrobe and under her bed, and she could only imagine the fear Joe had felt in the tunnel.

Charlie arrived one afternoon with a box of

tools, some harness leather, and a burnished hickory limb.

"If he's going to make his way in the world after he leaves, he's going to need a peg," he said.

Charles fitted the piece to Joe's stump, and rigged a piece of rope to the back of the wardrobe, so he could crawl into the tunnel and pull it into place.

After that, Joe spent long hours hobbling around the cellar, at first bracing himself against the wall, then standing free.

Out of the tunnel, he could sit at the table and read, and his dark mood lifted.

She brought him something new every night with his dinner, and Charlie brought over books from Verona's shelves, too. He read through the Emerson and Kane quickly. He even devoured her father's books on the Gallic Wars. But it was Thoreau that he liked most, and he read that one again and again. She brought him a stack of newspaper clippings, essays Thoreau had written when John Brown had been hanged, and he read those and even copied some of them in his blocky handwriting.

She'd sit with him while he ate and they would talk about the books and newspapers he'd read. She found herself staying with him in the cellar, long after his food was all gone, talking about the books he was reading and how the states were peeling off from the Union more and more quickly.

The late winter was a busy time for Mary, but as she worked, she often-times found herself recalling things he'd said the night before, and looking forward to talking to him in the evening. She'd sit at his table, bone tired, but hoping the clock would slow and she could spend a little more time with him. One night he asked about the smell of wood smoke that seemed to trail her wherever she went.

"I'm making sugar," she said.

Worry lines creased his brow.

"The sugar fields," he said. "That's what killed my mother."

"That's not how we make sugar here," she said.

When she came upstairs with the dishes, her father was sitting at the kitchen table, gluing together a broken milking stool.

"This has been one of the longest winters I've ever seen," he said. "But tomorrow will be warm and I think the ground will be soft enough to plant soon. We'll have to push hard to get the fields plowed and the seed in."

He paused, but she knew what was coming next.

"The farmhands will be here next week."

He didn't need to say more. She pushed a loose hair from her face and nodded.

"I'm taking the sugar and syrup to market day after tomorrow," she replied. "I'll take him downtown then."

She knew that keeping Joe as long as she had invited disaster. He had been well enough to travel for weeks, but neither of them had made mention of Canada in that time.

"Leander is coming home tomorrow," Nathan muttered. "Let Katia know. I'm sure you two will want to slaughter the fatted calf, but nothing more than a chicken, please. He has been nothing but a disappointment since he's gone downtown, and I'm in no mood to celebrate his indolence."

She nodded and slipped back to the kitchen to wash the dishes. She stared into the moonlit patch outside the window for a long time thinking that she would have to spend her evenings alone once again.

The next morning, she rose early and filled a picnic basket with sandwiches and pickles. She was nearly out the door when she went back, chuckling, and filled a pontil jar from the crock of rum punch and put it in the basket.

She went down the back stairs and found him already awake.

"Come with me," she said. "Now, before my father gets back from his morning walk and stops us."

He followed her up the stairs and to the barn where she helped him into the sleigh alongside the lashed-in barrels.

They drove into the dawn light and he smiled broadly as the sleigh hissed over the glaze of snow in the pasture and slid past the watering pond into the woods.

Mary stopped at a tall maple and climbed down to empty a tin bucket hanging from a tap pounded into the tree.

Joe gasped as a wolf rose and trotted away from a hollow in the roots of a nearby ancient oak.

"That's just old Shana," Mary said.

"She's got a name? Like a pet?" Joe asked, raising his eyebrows.

"She's no pet, but my father named her," she said. "He likes to have something of the old wildness left. She's too old to do much harm, and the others don't come round much anymore, though they used to steal sheep near every night. Sometimes even worse. The Landers' baby was snatched right through a cabin window. They say you can still hear his ghost squalling in the night. There's many ladies that won't go into the woods."

She climbed back into her seat.

"But I do." She grinned, and patted her pistol that she'd tucked in the seat cushion.

Timber knew the route so well that Mary did little to guide the sleigh. He led them through unseen breaks in the dense forest and onto hidden paths to stop at cluster after cluster of tapped maple trees marked with red rags. The barrels filled with sloshing sweetwater as the morning stretched on and they dodged the clumps of snow sloughing off the branches in the warming air. Deeper into the woods, they heard the creek rushing and churning up its steep bank, flooded by the spring melt. Joe flinched each time one of the ice slabs cracked against the shale embankment, echoing like a gunshot.

Her father's sawmill sat on a jut of land above the dammed creek, surrounded by stacked lumber and cut trees drying under oilcloths and lean-tos. An iron cauldron hung on a tripod over a black firepit. Mary sent Joe to collect a basket of scrap wood while she used a bucket to move the maple sap from a barrel to the cauldron. Joe lingered at the mill a long time, studying the mechanism and running his hands over the rough boards stacked in neat piles on the platform.

Mary fiddled with the fire, shifting the embers until she was satisfied with the temperature, then pulled a rickety table and a pair of three-legged stools from the mill's platform. She brought out the basket and laid the picnic out on a fraying checkered cloth. Soon, a column of smoke and maple steam rose above them into the windless sky.

"When I was a little girl, my mother always made a party of the sugaring," Mary said. "All the families from miles around would come and my father would make maple taffy for all the children."

She looked around at the scrub wood and sumac that threatened to overtake the clearing.

"This used to be an open meadow back then," she said. "There were always so many of us running and playing around here. Now that she's gone and it's just me, no one comes."

"I'm glad to be here," Joe said, biting into a sandwich. "It's just good to feel the sun again, though I'm not much of a party."

"I tend to define party pretty loosely," she said and reached into the basket and brought out the pontil jar. He laughed as he caught wind of the aroma of rum and fruit.

She dug through the basket but found that she had not packed cups.

"Oh well," she said, and tilted her head back for a quick swig from the blue glass jar before passing it over to him.

"I'm going downtown tomorrow," she said, poking at the fire with a stick.

He paused the jar at his lips.

"It's a good chance to get you out of here and over to Canada before Wilhelm tries anything again."

He drank for a long time and winced as he handed it back to her.

"Thank you," he said, but there was a sadness in his voice.

The fire snapped and hissed as she warmed her hands.

"When I was little, everyone would bring instruments and we would dance into the night, or until it got too cold," she said.

"I'll never be much of a dancer again," he said, lifting his peg into the air in front of him.

"I've seen couples too old to stand sit in chairs and dance with their eyes," she said. "You are too quick to say what is and isn't possible."

"I could try to sing you something," he said, and she nodded.

He took up "The Wayfaring Stranger" and

she got up to stir the pot. He had a deep voice, but it slid between notes at random moments, and she could discern no rhythm. It hurt her ears but she tried not to judge him, wondering if he was using some exotic style from the South, or perhaps a manner of singing passed down from Africa. She watched him intently, nodding. At last, he could not maintain the joke, and laughed at her serious face.

"My momma used to beg me to just move my lips in church," he said.

"If you can't sing, then you'll not have the privilege of seeing me dance," she said with a pout as she dropped onto the stool and took another long pull from the jar. When her apparent anger caused him to choke back his laughter, she guffawed the mule-like bray that her father always asked her to suppress.

She stood then, laughing, and swayed to a tune she remembered from her childhood. She closed her eyes and felt the warm sun on her face, and extended her one arm out and put the other on her breast, and the breeze came and pushed the hair into her face, and still she danced, turning herself around, sensing his eyes on her even through her own closed lids.

When she stopped and opened her eyes,

she was taken aback by the look of longing and loss on his face.

The barrels of sap took hours to boil and they sat together in the clearing, munching sandwiches and passing the jar back and forth.

She was laughing and showing him how to make taffy by pouring a dribble of syrup onto a patch of clean snow when Nathan walked into the clearing, a grimy canvas bag over his shoulder. She felt like a child caught at some forbidden game, and bolted straight up and Joe struck a pose much like hers. Her father stepped to the cauldron without offering a greeting and drew up the dipper, sniffed it, then held it high as he poured thick fluid back into the pot. He watched the twist and shade of viscous liquid as it passed in front of his eyes and then gingerly ran his callused finger inside the empty ladle and put it to his tongue.

"This is nearly ready," he announced. "Maybe another half hour."

He looked at the two coconspirators standing like mustered soldiers.

"Not much left," he said, nodding at the jar in Joe's hand.

"No, sir," Joe said.

Nathan drew an engraved metal flask from his coat pocket, twisted off the top, and half emptied it into the jar before clicking it against the blue glass.

"None have freedom until all do," he said.

Joe looked down at the jar uncertainly until Nathan nudged the bottom, pushing it toward Joe's mouth.

"It'd be rude to not drink when the toast is in your honor," he said, and waited for Joe to upend the jar before drinking himself.

Mary stared silently at her father.

"The chunk ice is flowing pretty fast," he said, dropping the flask back into his pocket. "I came to check the mill for damage."

He started toward the creek.

"There's a crack on the bottom board of the flume," Joe offered. "If you've got the tools, I can get that fixed up for you."

Nathan turned and cocked an eyebrow.

"I used to work on a mill back home," he said.

"Then come along," Nathan said.

Nathan waited for him to limp past before turning back to his daughter.

"There's eyes in this forest," he said. "It was foolish to bring him out here."

The two men stayed at the mill for a long time, and Mary could hear their voices and the sounds of the work being done as she finished the last of the boil by herself. On the ride back to the farm, Mary drove the sleigh wordlessly but smiling as Nathan and Joe traded tales of hewing ancient trees.

At the house, she led Joe back down into the cellar and left him there, alone with his books.

Katia was in a frenzy preparing dinner for Leander, and Mary had to spend the rest of the afternoon in the kitchen, trying to calm the girl.

As he always did, her brother arrived in a flourish, flinging the front door open to the cold evening air, shouting hellos, and stomping the mud from his polished shoes. The rush of noise reminded Mary of how the house had always been the point of congregation for Leander's many friends, and how it had grown solemn and quiet since he'd moved downtown.

He lifted Katia off her feet in a bear hug. Mary told him that his bright blue silk waistcoat and matching cravat made him look like a dandy. He kissed her on the cheek and gave her the smile that she always took to mean that he was up to something, but there was a wildness in his eyes she had never seen before.

Her father came and greeted him solemnly and tried to lead his son into his study, but Leander was all motion and nerves, and could not sit still for long.

He found Mary and Katia in the kitchen, and the words spilled from him in an endless stream as he told story after story about his time spent with Isabel. When Mary tried to interject, he plowed over her without stopping, and soon she just stopped talking altogether while the cascade of stories about this woman's wealth and beauty flowed unabated.

When dinner was ready, Nathan called them all to the table.

As they sat, Leander rummaged through his bag and brought out a bottle. Mary could see there were others in the bag.

"I told Isabel how smart you are," he said, handing it to her. "She sent this out."

Mary looked at the bottle skeptically.

"Brain Tonic," she read from the label. "Premium Coca Wine."

"I drink it all the time," Leander said with a big grin on his face. "It's very invigorating."

Mary opened the bottle and offered some to her father.

"I'll stick with buttermilk," Nathan said, shaking his head and holding his hand over his wineglass.

Mary poured some for herself and Leander. She sipped a little and scrunched her face in rejection.

"It's bitter," she said, but it took only a second for the tonic to clear the haze she'd felt since the day's rum punch wore off.

"Isabel says it's the new thing in Europe," Leander said, emptying his glass in one gulp and reaching for the bottle. "She has cases of it sent over from Corsica every month."

"You are spending a lot of time with her, aren't you?" Mary asked.

"Yes. She's convinced me to move to New York when she returns there next month," he said. "She said it's the place to make real money."

"New York!" Mary exclaimed. "I'm so jealous. I'd give anything to go there."

She looked over to see her father's grim face frozen over his motionless knife and fork and knew better than to say more.

Leander scratched at his neck nervously in the silence as Nathan gathered himself.

"And what will you do there?" Nathan asked through a clenched jaw.

"I'm going to be a trader," Leander said. "There's a fortune to be made there."

"A trader," Nathan said. "What good is a trader?"

"Trading is all the rage," Leander said. "It all happens downtown in Manhattan. You buy these little bits of companies, what they call stocks, you buy them when you think the company is going to grow and make money. If you know something before everyone else, let's say that a company's well has struck oil somewhere, then you can buy that stock before everyone else and then sell it after the news is out. You can make a lot of money in no time at all."

"I know what they do," Nathan said. "That wasn't my question."

Leander frowned. "Isabel knows everything about how it works and she gets all kinds of information before everyone else. She'll help me get up and running. I can make more money investing in stocks in one day than this farm has ever made."

He paused, and there was no sound other than the clock in the hallway.

"That's why I came out to talk with you," Leander said, filling the silence. "You told me you wanted me to manage the family's affairs, and that's what I want to do. I've come out here to ask you to let me take our money to New York. I'll double it the first day. Guaranteed. We can be rich, and then you and Mary won't have to grub in the dirt here anymore."

He stopped and dabbed at the sweat on his upper lip.

"Grub in the dirt," Nathan said. "Is that what we do?"

"I don't mean it like that," Leander said. The color was rising in Nathan's face, and Leander scrambled to head off his father's anger. "It's just that there's easier ways to make money. You're getting too old to spend so much time at that mill. Let me take care of you and Mary. You won't have to worry about anything else. You can move off the farm, get a big house downtown, and be near your friends, have a life of leisure."

A vein bulged on Nathan's forehead, and his face flushed. He stared at his plate for a long time before replying.

"No," he said.

He picked up a chicken leg and bit into it, chewing slowly, not looking at his son. Mary could see he was struggling to keep his anger in check.

"You mustn't say no," Leander said, desperation in his voice. "This is the future. I already know where we should put the money. Isabel knows some men in Schenectady who want to build a factory to manufacture punt guns. When the war comes, both sides will be buying them up. We can't miss this chance. Isabel says that this is the future."

Nathan gnawed the meat from the leg and dropped the clean bone onto his plate.

"What do you know about this woman?"

he asked. "This Isabel Fitch."

"She's marvelous," Leander said. "She's circled the globe and seen the most astounding things, been to the most amazing places. Very modern. Very forward thinking."

"Do you know why she went abroad?" Nathan asked.

"She wanted to see the world," Leander said, surprised by the question.

"What do you know of her husband?" Nathan asked.

"He was a trader," Leander said. "That's where I got the idea. Very successful. He had businesses all over the place. That's why Isabel is here. She is selling some of the businesses he had here in Buffalo."

"Do you know how he died?" Nathan asked.

Leander glared at his father over his untouched plate.

"Have you been checking up on her?" he asked. "What gives you the right?"

"It was quite easy," Nathan said. "She's quite famous, you know."

Leander finished his glass and emptied the bottle into it. A sweat stain had developed on his linen collar. He said nothing.

"He was my age, had a grand mansion on Worth Square in Manhattan," Nathan said. "They found him shot on the steps one day."

Mary gasped.

"You might think she'd be bereft at such a thing," he continued. "But in her grief, she managed to pack and be ready to board a steamer for the Far East the very next day. She later said she feared the killers, but the *Herald* guessed she was fleeing the police."

"Surely you don't think she had anything to do with killing her husband?" Leander asked. Sweat beaded on his upper lip, and Mary wanted to dab it away for him. He fidgeted with his silverware.

"I don't like this woman or the notions she's filled you with," Nathan said. His voice rose, the force of it filling the room like a revival preacher's. "Whatever her interest in you, I guarantee it is not to your betterment. You have forgotten where you're from, what this family stands for. I'd rather go blind than leave this place and move into that city. I would not allow you to bet everything I've built in some New York casino, even if it meant a certain hundredfold return. We are Willises. We make things. We grow things. We are not gamblers, traders of scraps of paper and secrets. It's time we put an end to this foolishness. You will ride with your sister to town tomorrow and bring your things back here. You will come home and work hard for the first time in your life. It's time you show yourself to be a man instead of that harlot's lapdog."

"You will not talk that way of the woman I love," Leander hissed. He clenched and unclenched his fists. Mary feared he would launch himself across the table.

"You love her?" Nathan roared. "You are a bigger fool than I thought. Can't you see that she wants you completely dependent on her? Even now she sends you out here with some harebrained scheme knowing I am the kind of man who would never allow my money to be risked on such a thing. She seeks to break you from your family. She uses you. Can you not see it?"

"You make this about you, and your money. You can't stand the idea of me making a name for myself, of doing better than the great Nathan Willis," Leander shouted back. "It is you who would keep me down, demanding that I come back here and shovel shit while the world is my oyster."

"You are nothing but a spoiled brat," Nathan shouted back at him, cocking his hand over his head.

"I've had my fill," Leander said. He stood, nearly knocking the table over, and his shoes echoed hard on the floor as he snatched his coat from the rack, flung open the front door, and walked out into the black night.

Cold air flooded the room and Mary got up and closed the door behind him.

Nathan sat at the table, staring blankly at the china cabinet across the room. Mary poured some more buttermilk in his glass.

He lifted his face to her, and there was a glistening in his eyes.

"He'll be okay," she offered.

He shook his head.

"I raised you both up like we were still pioneers, but the world around us has changed," he said after a long pause. "You're not on the frontier, but I don't know how to give you that city polish, either."

He reached for her hand and attempted a smile.

"I fear I've situated you such that you'll never find a husband acceptable to you," he said. "It was no secret that I hoped you might find a young man at that school."

She pursed her lips. "What I found at that school was that there should be more than one way for a woman to make her way in the world," she said. "I've leaned against enough cotillion walls to know that I'd be a fool to spend my time and my heart waiting for that mythical creature, that 'suitable husband.' There are many forms of happiness, Father, and from what I have seen, there are none less dependable than love."

He looked up at her, grief in his eyes.

"There's nothing other than love," he said. "All else falls away."

"Look at how you suffered when Mother died," she said.

He shook his head, and looked at her with red-rimmed eyes.

"Is that what you took away from that time?" he asked. "It is my fault. I made you this way."

He pulled the corners of his mouth down. "Do you know why I never married again?"

She shook her head.

"It was you," he whispered. "I saw so much of her in you. Her iron sense of right. Her endless curiosity. Her heart wounded by all that was wrong in the world. I was happy enough just to have you here, to be reminded of the best in her."

He bit his lip.

"It was selfish of me. I see that now. It was too much responsibility to put on such a young girl. And because of that, you would deny yourself so much. Yes, I was ruined for a while. But there's you. And there's Leander. The pain of love is just the chaff against the grain. Would you leave the fields fallow? Of course not. In the end, we are Willises. We are farmers."

HARRY

Harry Strauss knew Town Line better than anyone.

He knew its distances. It was one thousand and twenty-three paces down Town Line Road from the train station to the Seneca highway, but twelve hundred and sixty-seven from the highway down to the creek.

And he knew its secrets. There was a window at the back of Snyder's General Store that could be jimmied with a pocket-knife. Wilhelm sometimes stacked cases of full bottles of beer under an overhang behind the bar. The key to the schoolhouse was under a rock forty paces from the front door.

He had his own secret, too.

When he was a little boy, he'd buried a pickle crock under the cypress windbreak behind the parsonage and that's where his treasure was buried. Sixty-three dollars and forty-eight cents. It wasn't much, but it was a start, and it was all his. Leander and Hans, they were rich, but they didn't really have anything. Everything belonged to their families. They didn't even own their own time. But Harry did. When Leander and Hans were stuck in the little schoolhouse, he and Jep had been out scouting fishing holes. When Leander and Hans were home studying, Harry had been digging up arrowheads.

It was kind of like that now, too. Leander was down in Buffalo doing whatever it was his father told him to do, and now that he was gone Hans's parents kept him reined in pretty well, too. Not Harry, though. He didn't have to answer to anyone.

Though he had to admit it'd been pretty lonely, especially with Jep gone.

Katia had told him he should just get another pup, like every dog was the same, and you could just replace your best friend with some random animal.

She'd also told him that Leander was coming home today, and with that news, he'd been able to pry Hans out of his parents' grip and get him to come out for a drink at Wilhelm's Corner House to wait for their friend's arrival on the train.

The Corner House wasn't much of a tavern. Six stools and five tables, Canadian whiskey and Bavarian Enzian on a shelf behind the bar, and Wilhelm's *hausbrau,* which tended to give Harry the shits.

For entertainment, there was Karl Wilhelm.

When he wasn't telling stories about the whores of München, he complained about the government, taxes, and that arrogant and rich bastard, Nathan Willis.

Harry had learned long ago it was not worth his time to defend the man who had done so much good for him. No argument would sway the barkeep. Lately though, Wilhelm had been telling the story of going through the Willis house with the marshal, and it had been making Harry so mad that he'd been walking the three miles to Oscar Dodge's saloon in Alden when he wanted to drink.

It wasn't that long of a walk, and there wasn't much else to do.

But since Leander would get off at the Town Line station, they waited for him at the Corner House. There was no one else in the bar, and much to Harry's relief, Wilhelm had moved on to a new subject.

"If there's a war, I hope those Southerners put up a big fence to keep their slaves in," he proclaimed. "I'm tired of them darkies coming up here, messing with things.

Killing good dogs and all."

"We sure as hell don't need them here," Harry said, tipping his beer toward the barkeep in salute.

"If there's a war, I'm signing up," Hans said.

"Are you kidding me?" Harry asked. "The army? Why would you do that?"

"It's a chance to get out of this town," Hans said. "Don't you want to see something besides Town Line?"

"I was in Alden just yesterday," Harry said.

"Har har," Hans said. "With Leander gone, there's just not much to do around here. Even if I don't sign up, I'm wondering about moving down to the city. I'm hoping Leander might let me stay with him for a while. I can't take living with my parents much more."

Harry thought of Hans going away and his heart sank.

"They'll never get me in that army," he said. "No way, no how."

"You won't have a choice," Wilhelm said. "They're already drafting every man that they can find down South. Just a matter of time before they do it up here."

"How they going to draft me?" Harry asked. "Nobody knows I'm here."

"What the hell does that mean?" Hans

asked. "Everyone knows you're here."

Harry laughed, shaking his head.

"When I came here, there was a tag on my jacket that said 'Cleveland' on it. I tore it off before I jumped off the train. For all I know, they're still waiting for me over in Ohio. You remember when that census man came through a while back. Everyone lined up to get marked down in his big book, but I wasn't having anything to do with that — went back to Leander's shack and hid out for a month. Hell, they find me, they'll probably want to send me to Cleveland. No way. Everyone else's name might go into the barrel for the draft, but not mine."

"That's pretty good," Wilhelm said. "You might just have them beat."

"Strauss ain't even really my name," Harry said.

"What the hell are you talking about?" Hans asked. "Of course your name is Strauss!"

"They never gave me a last name in the orphanage back in New York, just called me Harry. I think they expected whoever it was in Cleveland to give me a name. I figured I needed one when I got here, and I remembered the conductor on the train that brought us food was named Mr. Strauss. He was a nice man. Even gave me a nickel.

So that's what I called myself."

"Well I'll be damned," Hans said. "I guess if someone put the name Harry Strauss on a draft list, you could change it to something else."

Harry finished his beer and was about to call for another when they heard the train whistle to the west.

"Time to go," Hans said, and they pulled on their coats and walked up Town Line Road and got to the station just as the train pulled in.

The engineer filled the water tank from the tower, the conductor tossed a canvas mail bag onto the platform, but no passengers emerged from the train.

"Did Katia say it was going to be the two-fourteen?" Hans asked.

"She wasn't sure," Harry said. "But I thought this would be the one."

Hans took off his hat and scratched his head.

"Well the next one is after six," he said. "I don't think I want to spend the afternoon listening to Wilhelm, though. Susie said she was going to make a cherry pie today. I think I'm going to go pay her a visit."

"I'll head up to the Willis house, see if Katia's heard anything. Maybe he came in this morning."

He took off his winter coat as he walked up the hill, taking in the first warm day of spring. As he came to the top of the hill, he saw a thin column of smoke and steam rising in the clear blue sky above the tree line.

"Mary's got a sugar fire, I bet that's where Lelo is," he said, thinking for a moment that Jep was there to hear him.

The sugar shack was only a couple hundred yards away through the woods, so he turned into the tree line. The ground was thick with leaves and melting snow, but as he got closer, he took care to be quiet, hoping to catch his friend off guard and jump him.

He could hear laughter, but it didn't sound like Leander. He crouched down behind a clump of sumac on the edge of the clearing, and nearly fell over when he saw a one-legged nigger sitting on a stool, smiling as Mary danced for him.

Then he heard him speak, and he recognized the voice.

It was the one that had killed Jep.

"Son of a bitch," he whispered, twisting his hands around a sumac branch and struggling to keep the beer he'd just finished from coming back up.

He knelt there, looking at the figure sitting on the stool. He'd never seen a nigger before, though he wouldn't admit it to anyone. Even when this one killed Jep, he never really got a look at him. It was dark and everyone was running and hiding and all.

Wilhelm had told him so many stories about them all, how they'd rape any white woman they got near, and how they'd tear a white man apart with their bare hands if they ever got the chance.

But this one, he just sat on the stool, his peg leg stuck out in front of him, laughing as Mary danced.

And Mary. Sure, she was always preaching about the slaves and all, but how could she be messing around with this one? The one that killed his Jep.

He watched as she carried on. She looked happy there with him, like she never was around any of the town boys. She'd always been too good for them.

He looked around for something he could use as a weapon and found a rock the size of a kitten. He hefted it, thinking it would make quick work of the runaway's skull.

Then he remembered how Mary had her fancy pistol. She'd even let him shoot it a few times when he found her practicing in the woods. He'd tried to hit the target she'd pinned up, but it was too far away, and he missed each time. She took the Colt back, reloaded, and hit the bull's-eye four times in a row. And he remembered how she took it with her everywhere.

Feeling like a coward, he let the rock slip from his hand. He'd need help.

He was back at Wilhelm's in less than five minutes.

"Mary's with our nigger at her sugar shack, dancing and carrying on," he said to the barkeep, gasping after running down the hill.

"You sure it's him?" Wilhelm asked, putting down the glass he was washing.

"I know that voice," Harry said.

Wilhelm pulled a new rifle off the wall and handed it to Harry, then reached into a drawer for a pistol.

He was almost out the door when he stopped.

"You're sure?" he asked again.

"He's missing a leg," Harry said. "I'm thinking that's where Jep got him."

"We're not going after them, we're going downtown," he said. "I want that high and mighty marshal to see I was right. I don't want Nathan Willis weaseling out."

"You ain't getting that marshal out here again," Harry said. "Not after last time."

Wilhelm smiled.

"This Southern gentleman came out to see me a few days back, express his sympathy," he said. "Made it sound like he had some connections downtown, and offered to help if anything like this came up. He'll get things moving. You're coming with me — I need you as the witness. Go borrow that nag from the Zubrichs."

Harry didn't move.

"I don't want to get Mr. Willis in trouble," he said. "Let's just go get the runaway."

"Nathan Willis ain't your friend. You think Mary is hiding him without the old man knowing? Of course not. He's been keeping that nigger in his house for months, knowing damned well that he's the one that killed Jep. What kind of friend is that?"

Harry could feel his heart sinking as he realized it was true.

They were on their way down the highway twenty minutes later.

He'd only been to the city a few times before, but Wilhelm came down often to visit the brothels by the canal, and navigated his way down to the waterfront without a problem.

Two men stood guard at the gangplank of the *Abigail,* but they stepped aside when Wilhelm gave Compson's name.

Everything on the boat shone — the dark

wood deck, the little round windows, and the bright brass that seemed to be everywhere. Even the ropes looked impossibly white. Harry had never felt too dirty to be anywhere before, but he did then. While one of the guards went below to get Compson, he rubbed the road dust from his face, kicked the mud from his boots, and spit in his palm and tried to mat down his curly hair.

Compson had gray hair and a dark mustache, neatly trimmed. His piercing eyes looked out from under dark eyebrows. He greeted Wilhelm like an old friend, and gave Harry's hand a firm shake before leading them belowdecks. The cabin's walls were all dark wood with green velvet. The smell of cigars permeated the air. Everything was so nice that Harry was afraid to touch it.

"I seen that nigger," Harry blurted. "I seen him today with Mary Willis on her farm."

"Is that so?" Compson asked. "Have a seat. Tell me your story."

He made a motion with his hands and a black man appeared with two heavy glasses with three fingers of liquor.

Harry looked at it suspiciously, but Wilhelm smiled and nodded.

It was the best whiskey Harry had ever tasted.

Harry told what he'd seen. When Harry mentioned that he'd worked for Mr. Willis, he was asked about everyone's daily routine and the layout of the farm.

Finally, Compson leaned back and stroked his mustache.

"Give me a minute, please," he said, opening a drawer and taking out a sheet of paper. He wrote quickly, folded the paper, and another black man appeared.

"Take this to Marshal Kidder," he said. "He's most likely in one of the taverns by the canal."

He turned back to the two of them.

"You'll ride out in the morning," he said to Wilhelm and Harry. "The marshal will be here at seven, and you need to be ready to go then. Get in and out before the father returns from his morning walk. It'll be just the girl and the slave, and the three of you should be able to handle that. This story can be very useful for the Southern cause — a county commissioner giving harbor to fugitives. It will be ammunition for us. But it must be handled correctly. If one of them is harmed in the capture, the sympathies will be with the abolitionists. So please operate with restraint."

Compson clapped his hands together and told the negro servant to get them some supper and make up beds for them. Harry reached for the decanter of whiskey, but the commander moved it away.

"Get some rest," he said. "Afterward, you can have your fill. Of course, once we have the slave in hand, we will locate its owner and the two of you will certainly be rewarded. You won't be in need of my whiskey, but I'll be happy to pour you as much as you'd like."

After dinner, the negro led Harry to a tiny room. Everything in it was dark wood and bright brass, except for the bed.

The sheets were the softest thing he had ever felt. The boat rocked him like he was in a cradle and he fell asleep almost immediately.

FUGITIVE

Dearest Mary,

Tomorrow morning we will leave for the city, and we will forever be gone from each other's lives.

What can I give to you on such a day as a thank-you? Should I share my grandest dreams? Should I tell you all my deepest fears? Should I bare my soul?

After I cross over into Canada, I will find a pond, and I will build a little cabin on its shore, just like Mr. Thoreau's.

Someday, somehow, I will find Alaura, and I will bring her there, and we will be safe and happy and free.

Maybe someday you will come to visit me there, and we can make sugar. Maybe I can learn to sing, and then I can see you dance again.

And now you know all that this simple, useless man dreams of.

JOE

Joe and Charles were already loading the casks of syrup onto the wagon when Mary came into the barn.

"Your father came by yesterday. He's worried about you taking him downtown alone and asked me to ride down with you two," Charles said. She nodded and smiled, touching his arm in thanks.

She loaded food and blankets under the wagon bench so they could stop and picnic on the way back, and tucked her Colt into the cushion.

"The pistol, again?" Charles asked, cocking an eyebrow.

"Always," she said.

They positioned the barrels of syrup along the outside of the wagon bed, leaving an empty space in the middle for Joe. Charles helped him climb into the space, and Mary handed him a jug of cider and the leftover chicken. She had given him clean clothes, and he'd scrubbed up for the trip. She took a tied handkerchief from her apron pocket and picked lint from it before handing it to him.

Joe untied it and looked at four gold discs emblazoned with Liberty's profile.

"I won't take your money," he said, twisting the coins back into the rag and offering them back to her. "I've taken too much from you already."

"That's not from me. That's from my father," she said. "He's off for his morning walk, but he'll not think kindly of you if you refuse his gift."

Charles looked at her with a cocked eyebrow.

Joe frowned, but tucked the handkerchief into his waistband. Hunkered into the hollow among the barrels, Mary thought he looked like a little boy hiding for a game of kick-the-can.

"Don't make a sound, no matter what you hear," Mary said. "I've brought dozens of folks downtown. I can talk my way out of anything as long as you stay hidden. If they know you are back here, we'll both be in for it."

He nodded.

A shadow cut across the barn floor.

"I need a ride downtown," Leander announced. His face was puffy and pale and his silk waistcoat had a brown stain down the front. He had his bag in one hand, and another bottle of the brain tonic in the other. He took a swallow before he approached them.

"Did you sleep in someone's chicken coop?" Mary asked.

"I swear to God, Wilhelm's whiskey has

gotten worse since I left," he muttered.

"Go clean yourself up if you want to ride with us," she said. "You're a disgrace."

"After he came down on me like that last night, I've got to listen to you now, too?" he snapped at her. "For Christ's sake, my head is pounding. Can't you just be quiet and drive me downtown?"

"Just because you're hungover doesn't mean you have to take it out on me," she said. "I didn't pour that poison down your gullet."

"You could have at least stood up for me," Leander said, his hand on his stomach as he lurched forward a step. He glared at her with bloodshot eyes.

"You want me to defend you, do something I should defend," she said. "You come back here with your head all mush, talking nonsense about a lady you've known for just a few weeks, and you want me to stick up for you? I don't like you this way. You're not right."

"I'm more right than I've ever been," he said. "You don't see how he's holding me back. You don't see how things really are."

He stumbled forward, grasped the wagon wheel, slid to his knees, and vomited on the barn's mud floor.

A sour whiff of rotgut whiskey rose up and

she struggled to keep from wretching herself. She'd seen him hungover many times before, but he'd always been contrite and gentle on such mornings. There was a belligerence in him now, and she wondered whether it had come from this strange woman he'd talked of so much or the potion that he was even then washing his mouth out with as he knelt over his own mess.

"I do," Mary said, looking down at him, a hand over her mouth. "I do see how things are."

He climbed to his feet and stood over her.

"You're no better than he is," he said.

She reached into her coat pocket, took out a handkerchief, and offered it to him.

"Wipe your lips," she said. "You've got sick on your face."

He ignored her offering and ran the back of his hand across his chin.

"Better?" He sneered.

"Not hardly," she replied.

"I'll ride in the back," he said. Without waiting for permission, he started to climb between the barrels, then stopped short when he saw the fugitive nestled among them.

"What in hell?" he demanded angrily.

"He's going downtown with Charles and

me," Mary said.

"Has he been here this whole time?" Leander demanded. "You mean to tell me that while Father refused to risk one red copperhead to help his own son, you were risking everything this family has for some damned slave? This must be some elaborate joke."

"This is none of your business. Get in the house and get yourself cleaned up so we can leave before Father sees you and all this starts again," Mary said, jutting her chin in defiance.

"It is my business," Leander said. "If I am supposed to rot away on this farm, I at least get to say what goes on here. This is my farm."

"How dare you?" Mary snapped. "You've done nothing to deserve this place and last night you made it clear that it means nothing to you."

"Exactly." Leander spat. "But I guess I have to be here anyway."

Charles stepped between the two of them.

"Enough," he said. "Let's just get Joe downtown safe and sound, and then we can work this out."

"Don't get in the middle of family business, Charlie," Leander said. He stood to the side and took another long draft from the bottle. "Let's go before my father gets back from his walk. The last thing I need this morning is to listen to him."

Mary climbed back onto the wagon.

"Don't worry about any of this," she said, looking down at Joe. She offered him her hand and he held it for a moment before she and Charles stretched a stained canvas tarp over the barrels, hiding him from the world.

Mary drove the wagon out of the barn and Charles closed the barn door and climbed onto the bench next to her. Leander climbed onto one of the barrels, sulking.

They got as far as the top of the drive when Harry Strauss, Dwight Kidder, and Karl Wilhelm trotted over from across the highway and forced Mary to brake the wagon hard. Kidder held the reins of a fourth horse, saddled but without a rider. Wilhelm's hand rested across his pommel, gripping a cocked pistol. The riders closed around the wagon. Kidder sidled his horse up next to Mary, and Strauss trotted Pastor Zubrich's old swayback over to sit next to Charles. Wilhelm stayed back, cutting off their exit.

"Me and Hans had us a time last night at the Corner House. Where the hell were you?" Leander asked Harry, then turned to

Wilhelm. "And what the hell is your wife putting in that rotgut? She nearly killed me with that shit last night."

"This ain't a joke," Wilhelm said, glaring at him.

Harry shook his head, a grim look on his face.

"Who's that?" Leander asked, nodding toward Kidder. His face froze when he saw the badge pinned on his coat.

"You bought a marshal out here?" he asked his friend. "What the hell?"

"Enough is enough," Kidder said. "Hand the fugitive over. I'm not leaving without him."

"Again?" Mary cried. "This is absurd. I will file a complaint. Who is your superior? I am on my way downtown right now and I will pay him a visit. You can't continue to rampage through this farm whenever you feel the urge."

"You're not going anywhere today unless it's in chains," Kidder wheezed, shifting on the draft horse. "I'll not be made a fool of again, as you did when you trotted me through the house, or on that day many years ago, playing the Southern belle down at the train station."

She twisted the reins in her fists until the leather carved white furrows in her hands.

"You thought I wouldn't remember?" he asked. "But it all comes back, sooner or later. Bring me the fugitive now, and I might go easy on you and not haul you off to jail."

"Oh, you'll take her in," Wilhelm said. "Or you won't see a penny of the bounty."

"Where is he?" the marshal asked.

"You've been through this farm top to bottom," Mary said, her chin up. "There's no fugitive here."

"I seen him here yesterday," Strauss said. "You with that nigger back at the sugaring fire, laughing and carrying on like a couple of sweethearts."

"Harry, what the hell are you doing?" Leander asked.

"He's the same one killed my dog, and near killed old Wilhelm here. And them two just carrying on." Harry spat. "If I had a gun with me, I'da just kilt him right then and there and hauled the body in for my reward."

"That wouldn't have been any fun," Wilhelm said.

"Leander, why don't you say where he's at?" Strauss asked. "You ain't mixed up in all this."

"You brought a marshal out here?" Leander repeated.

"Shut up, Leander," Mary said. "You're

still drunk."

She turned to Kidder.

"He's not here."

Kidder's fat hand darted out and snatched Mary's wrist. She yelped and tried to pull back, but his grip held. He pulled a pair of shackles from a saddlebag and slipped one onto her forearm.

"Stop this!" Charles protested, lunging across Mary's lap, grappling to free her from the metal.

"Charlie, sit your farmer ass down," Wilhelm shouted.

Webster turned to see the pistol aimed between his eyes, and Wilhelm's scarred face grinning at him over the barrel.

In all the years she'd known him, Mary had never seen Charlie angry, but as he sat back onto the wagon bench streaks of white struck along the lines of his reddening face and his eyes bulged. With her free hand, she reached for his but found an unrelenting, balled fist.

"I'm taking someone downtown today," Kidder said evenly. "The slave or the runner. You can decide on which."

"I've done this to myself, Charles," Mary whispered to him. "Just stay calm and don't get yourself mixed up in it."

There was no change in the rictus of anger

as his glared shifted from Wilhelm to Harry and back.

"You're coming with me," Kidder said, pulling on the shackle. "I've wasted enough time. I've got a witness, and that'll be enough to get you locked up."

The shackle had been sized for a man and Mary wondered if she could slip out of it, but knew the attempt would be pointless. She felt like she might be sick.

"Mount up," he snarled, jerking her toward the riderless paint horse. "Cooperate and I'll take this chain off you and you won't have to ride the whole way like a criminal. If you give me trouble, I'll put it right back."

Her mind raced as she climbed down from the wagon. She looked for a way to signal Charles to get Joe to the church after the marshal had taken her away. Without the fugitive, the marshal would have nothing more than Harry's testimony to convict her, and surely between her brother and her father, they could convince him to back off. Kidder jerked the cuff again.

"Move," he growled.

"What the hell, Harry?" Leander slurred. "Look at all this shit. You didn't need a damned marshal. I was down at Wilhelm's all night. You should have just come to me.

I could have fixed this."

"Shut your mouth," Mary snapped at her brother.

"My goddamned head is pounding like the inside of Urshel's blacksmith shop," Leander said. "If you don't cooperate, they'll send you to jail. Just get this over with. Just give them the damned slave."

"There is no slave," Mary said.

"Oh, for Christ's sake, just get this over with," Leander said, then turned to the marshal. "If I give you the runaway, everyone else goes free? That's the deal?"

"That's the deal." Kidder nodded.

"Leander . . ." Mary growled, but Kidder yanked hard on the shackle and the iron bit into the meat of her twisted hand, drawing blood.

His hands trembling from the effects of the brain tonic and his eyes glazed with the pain of the night's whiskey, Leander climbed from his perch and steadied himself with a hand on the wagon. Mary could see a trace of vomit still on the stubble of his chin.

"He was under your nose the whole time," Leander said as he untied the tarp. When he came around to loosen the bindings near her, Mary kicked his shin hard and he fell to his knees. The riders laughed as her brother scowled at her.

"Judas." She spat as he climbed to his feet, his trousers dripping with mud.

He pulled the tarp off the line of barrels, and there was a long pause before Joe raised himself up to stand above them on the bed of the wagon, his face pained in the morning light as he stared down at them wordlessly.

Kidder dug another pair of manacles from his saddlebag and tossed them on the ground.

"Now get down from there, boy, and put those on," he said.

Joe didn't move.

Kidder yanked on Mary's shackle again and she winced.

"I'll make it harder on her if you give me trouble," he said.

Joe said nothing, but climbed down from the wagon and picked up the manacles from the mud. Mary sobbed as he slipped them onto his wrists.

"Now let her go," Leander said to the marshal.

Kidder grinned, but held the loop of manacle tight.

"What kind of peace officer would I be if I ignored this scofflaw's flagrant disregard of the Fugitive Slave Act?" he asked. "It is my duty to bring both of them downtown.

196

And if you don't behave, I'll take you, too."

"Time to haul off all them Willises," Wilhelm cackled.

"There was a deal," Leander said, looking like he'd been punched. "We had a deal."

"You made a fool of me twice," the marshal said to Mary, yanking on the shackle again. "Now it's my turn."

"You son of a bitch," Mary shouted as she beat her free fist against the marshal's fat thigh.

"Stop," Joe shouted. She looked up to see him staring at her.

His lips pulled into something like a resigned smile even as his eyes welled.

"Just let me go," he said, shaking his head.

He turned to mount the horse, but fell in the mud as his peg slipped out from under him.

"Oh my." Wilhelm laughed.

"Help him up," the marshal said to Strauss.

"No you don't," Wilhelm said, waving the pistol loosely with one hand as he made a show of wiping a tear from his eye. "I'm enjoying this."

"Enough." Nathan's voice boomed as he walked slowly up the driveway, his shotgun level at his waist.

"Take the fugitive if you must," he said.

"We'll deal with that in the courts."

He thumbed back the hammer on the weapon.

"But you'll not have my daughter," he hissed.

He stopped short of the wagon, his feet rooted in the spring mud as he pointed the shotgun at the marshal.

"Leander, help that man," he said, nodding toward Joe.

Before Leander could move toward the kneeling fugitive, a shot rent the morning, sending a flock of ravens screeching from the high branches of the poplars.

Nathan swayed, redness erupting at his right temple. Paralysis overtook Mary, even as she felt the world shifting under her feet. Only the shaking of the ground as he toppled, as if a tree had been felled, released her to move. Screams filled her ears and it was long seconds before she realized they were hers.

Another sound echoed into the morning, this time the familiar pop of her own pistol. She jerked around to see Karl Wilhelm with a ruby bloom at his chest and followed his glare to the wagon bench, where Charles sat, her pistol still leveled. Wilhelm tried to raise his own gun, but Charles fired again, and a rough black hole appeared in the innkeeper's right cheek.

He slumped and fell from his horse, his boot and spur twisting in the stirrup. The horse whinnied and jolted forward at the strange motion, dragging the fallen, face-down body through the mud.

She nearly wrenched her arm from its socket pulling her right hand free from the oversized shackle, and in his surprise, the marshal let go of it altogether. She rushed to her father, knelt over him, and rolled him onto his back. He blinked at her, one eye rolling crazily, the other focused on her face. His lips moved, but no sound came. She cradled his bleeding head in her lap.

"He's still alive," she cried. "Help me, he's still alive."

Charles, holding the pistol on Kidder, climbed down from the wagon. Harry Strauss held his hands over his head in sur-render, but no one paid him any mind.

Paralyzed in horror, Leander stood next to where Joe knelt in the mud, his face buried in his shackled hands.

"Leander! Get him in the wagon, get him to Pride's," Charles ordered.

Leander jerked forward and knelt down to take his father by the legs while Mary raised him by the arms. They struggled to raise him over the sugar barrels and lower him into the hollow where Joe had hidden just minutes before.

"Get these barrels off, they'll slow it down," Leander said, but Mary ignored him and climbed onto the bench and took up the reins. He started to pull himself onto the wagon next to his sister.

She snapped the buggy whip across his knuckles and he pulled his hands back.

"I'll kill you if you come near him again," she screeched then whipped the mule into motion. "I'll kill you."

Strauss moved the horse and corpse out of the way and Mary pulled the wagon onto the highway.

Her father moaned in pain behind her, giving her hope as she lashed at the laboring mule.

The ride to Alden took a lifetime. A crowd of people gathered on Main Street and she drove into their midst shouting, the rattling wheels spattering mud onto their finery. Mothers shooed their children onto the wood plank sidewalks and men shouted at her to slow down, but she continued to flay the animal, its flanks a map of striae bleeding red through white lather.

Mary called out the doctor's name as the mule collapsed onto its knees in his yard. Pride rushed from his office, pulling the hooks of his spectacles around his ears and shouting questions at her. He climbed over the barrels and onto the wagon, gasping as he knelt over his now-unconscious friend.

Mary winced as the doctor prodded the wound with his fingers. Her father did not react.

"I have to trepan," he said, his voice quivering.

They carried the limp body into the office and lay him on a long wooden table.

She could see the tremor in the doctor's hand as he gave her a dropper bottle and an oddly shaped glass, something like a misshapen open-ended hourglass with a cotton rag filling one cup.

"Ether," he said. "If he stirs, you'll have to sedate him. Just a few drops at a time."

Pride said little as the procedure went along, nudging her to apply the liquid to the mask or asking for help holding her father's head still.

He cut into Nathan's skull with a cylindrical saw the size of a pocket knife. Each twist sent a vibration through the bone and into her hands, rattling the shackle.

Mary had taken the slaughtering knife to every kind of animal to be found in those parts without flinching, but the room shifted and spun as she watched Pride work. She caught whiffs of the drug and lost track of time, and had to brace herself against the table to stay upright.

Sometimes the circular blade would jerk and Pride would swear under his breath. He paused a few times to examine his progress and to brush bits from the blade with a stiff-haired brush. He exhaled raggedly when he plucked the dull gray lump from her father's brain and dropped it into the spittoon at his feet.

He paused a long moment, trying to still his trembling hands before proceeding.

He left the hole in the skull open, but sewed the flaps before laying a bandage lightly over the hole and putting the needle down.

"I'll have to drain the suppuration over the next few days," he said. "If all goes well, we can close it then. In the meantime, we pray."

He stood still for a moment, his hands on the table on either side of Nathan's head and his eyes closed. Mary lay her head on her father's chest, taking comfort in the sound of his heart.

"You can come in now," Pride said, opening his eyes and pitching his voice toward the door. Mary had not realized there was anyone there, but Charles Webster, his face a skein of worry, came in and went straight to Mary, enfolding her in his arms.

"The ball had not gone very deep and that is good news indeed," Pride said. "He's a strong old man, but we have to watch for swelling."

Mary buried her face in Charles's chest, and he held her tight. The doctor turned and started to wipe his instruments with a rag.

Charles took a key from his pocket and released her left hand from the shackle.

"I have to go away," he whispered.

She looked at him, trying to understand what he was saying. Everything outside the room had fallen from her thoughts, but now came back to her in a rush. She kissed his cheek, and fought her tears. After a moment, she stepped back and straightened her blood-smeared coat with a tug.

"Kidder took Joe," Charles said, and she nodded. "I don't think he has much heart to bother you."

He moved to the table where Nathan lay and took his limp hand and held it silently.

Pride cleared his throat.

"It's a barbarous day, but I fear there is more to come," he said.

"More? What more could there be?" she snapped at him.

He looked at her, confused.

"You don't know?" He ran his hands through his hair. "Of course, how could you?"

"What else is there?" she demanded, tearing up from exhaustion and worry. "What else?"

He lay a hand on her shoulder, but she couldn't tell if it was in sympathy or to steady himself.

"Sumter has fallen," he whispered. "We are at war."

BELLUM

Joe knelt in the slush and mud, flinching with each snap of the whip, listening to the wagon roll away. He had not looked up at Mary as she had passed. He couldn't bear to see the pain in her face, knowing he was the cause of it.

Only after the wagon's rattle faded did he raise his eyes to see Kidder, Strauss, and Webster still staring east. Leander stared down at the bloody patch of mud where his father had fallen.

Charles Webster stepped between Harry and Wilhelm's body and dug Wilhelm's pistol out of the mud and shoved it into his coat pocket.

"You better get," he said to Leander. "There's no telling what she'll do if you are here when she comes back."

"I need to fix this," Leander said, his eyes a glaze of stunned dismay. "I can help make this right."

Charles stared down at Wilhelm's corpse.

"Just leave," he muttered. "Take Wilhelm's horse. Go."

Leander scanned the faces around him, and Harry nodded at him to go.

"I'm going to make this right," Leander said as he mounted the stallion.

"I killed a man," Charlie said as Leander turned the horse toward Alden. "Nothing's going to be right again."

"Get the nigger on that horse," Kidder said.

"No," Webster said. "Joe's going free."

Harry Strauss spat at Webster's feet.

"Fuck! He's the one that caused all of this," he said. "He killed old Jep. I'll beat him to death right here before I see him go free."

Webster waved the pistol at him.

"You might've done in Wilhelm, and I'm the first to say he had it coming," Harry said. "But I've known you all my life, and you ain't no killer. You're not gonna shoot me."

Webster cocked the pistol, but he couldn't raise his eyes to meet Harry's.

"No more blood," Joe croaked. "No more. I'll go."

Charles looked at him with something like gratitude and helped him to his feet.

Joe grasped at the saddle, but the manacles bit into his wrists and weighed his arms down, and he slipped off as he tried to swing his peg leg over the animal. Charles caught him before he hit the ground and helped him up.

He nodded up at Joe after he mounted then he turned back to the marshal.

"You give her any trouble and I'll hunt you down," Charlie said. "She's got the weight of the world on her already."

"You should be more worried about yourself," Kidder said. "I'm going to see you hang."

"Then I've got nothing to lose," Webster said. "You just stay away from her. I grew up in these woods and that's where I'm heading. You won't see me coming, but I'll be there."

"Big talk," the marshal said.

"Charlie Webster's never been a boastful man," Harry said. "If I were you, Marshal, I'd stay out of Town Line the rest of my days."

Kidder tied a lead to Joe's horse.

"I got everything I could possibly want from this shithole," he said, and turned the horses west toward Buffalo.

The iron manacles hung heavy on Joe's arms. He tried resting them on the saddle, but it made no difference.

"What the hell am I going to do with you?" the marshal muttered as they rode.

Joe stared down at his shackled hands, saying nothing, the sound of the gunshots and Mary's screams still ringing in his ears.

He closed his eyes, listening to the clop of the hooves on the mud.

"Is there anyone stupid enough to offer a reward for a one-legged nigger?" the marshal asked. "You always been one-legged? I guess not, if you were running all over the woods like that. There's probably someone offering money for you. I'll have me a look through the papers and the notices when we get back downtown."

Closer to the city, the streets were flooded with people, some waving flags, others firing their guns in the air. The marshal continued to talk to himself for the rest of the trip, tallying expenses, spending money he didn't have, ignoring the questions children asked as they pointed to the one-legged negro in chains.

At the jail, Kidder yanked him out of the saddle and let him slam onto the ground.

"Don't you get any ideas about taking matters into your own hands. I doubt I can get two bits for a dead one-legged nigger, no matter what you did when you

208

was whole."

Mary's father made a croaking noise that sounded like her name, and she scrambled up from the slipper chair where she drowsed. She went to him, pressing the back of her hand to his forehead, relieved at its coolness.

"Frances?" he asked, saying her mother's name.

"We're at Pride's," she offered. He murmured something in a tongue she could not understand and drifted off again. He hadn't opened his eyes or recognized her voice in the day and the night they'd been there.

She wiped his slack face with a damp cloth, relieved to see it had lost the clenched tightness of the long night. She sat back in the chair, and drowsed in the warmth of the potbellied stove.

She woke to see Pride standing over her father, checking the dressing.

Nathan shouted something in the same strange language.

"Haudenosaunee," Pride said to her. "He's talking with our old friend Jo-no-es-sto-wa. He's been gone nearly forty years."

"Get me my horse," Nathan demanded in English.

"Hasn't lost any of his piss and vinegar,"

Mary said. "Is he in pain?"

Pride frowned, but shook his head.

"Go home," Pride said. "He needs the quiet and the dark, and having a visitor will only work him up, arouse him when he should rest."

"Visitors?" Nathan echoed. "There are scores coming, Frances. Those red-coated bastards have burned Black Rock to the ground. Buffalo is nearly gone. Anyone left alive is heading this way. We'll have a barn full and more. They'll eat us out of everything we've stored up."

He fell quiet.

"Is his mind gone?" she asked, her voice quivering.

"Mount a guard on the highway, Jack," he said, his voice rising to a shout. "Chief Parker is watching the creek. The goddamned redcoats can't be far now. I'll die before I see them on this farm."

"Father," Mary said. "It's 1861. We beat the British fifty years ago."

"Of course we beat them, Frances," Nathan grumbled.

Nathan's eyes opened, and she was grateful to see that they could at least focus on her. She tried to smile for him.

"You do more harm than good here," Pride whispered to her.

"I won't leave him," she said, laying her head on his chest. She closed her eyes and felt the doctor's hand on her back.

"He must rest," Pride said. "You should say your good-byes."

She breathed deep, still able to smell the soap on him. Finally, she stood.

"Good-byes?" Mary asked looking at her father.

"The worst is still ahead," Pride said.

Mary nodded.

"Come back to me," she said, and bent to kiss her father's forehead.

"Watch for the scouts," he shouted, twisting in the bed. "I already got a lobsterback down by the mill this morning."

She nodded silently, pursed her lips, and slipped out the door.

The mule had been hauled to the knacker's overnight, and Charles had seen to having the wagon taken back to the farm.

A crowd had gathered in the center of Alden and Mary could see Lafayette Glass standing on the bandstand, proclaiming his intention to enlist. The widow Slade passed her on the sidewalk, running her eyes up and down Mary's clothes and shaking her head. Mary realized she was still covered in dirt and blood, and turned off the road to walk the rail line instead. At the farm, she went through the barn to check on the animals. Katia trailed her, pointing out the chores she had been forced to do while everyone was gone.

"I made the cabin ready for the new hands," she said. "Mr. Nathan said they would come soon. It is good they come. Soon Mr. Nathan will come home and everything will be proper again. This black man. So much trouble. So much trouble."

Mary gritted her teeth.

The thought of the work of the planting overwhelmed her. Even with her father's authority to back her, it had been a struggle to get the previous year's itinerants to mind her. She doubted she had it in her to fight that battle again.

"Everything will be good again now that the black man is gone," Katia said.

Mary wanted to cuff her across the face.

"I'm going to take the syrup downtown," she said, looking for any reason to be away from the girl. "There won't be time once the workers get here."

She changed her clothes, and drove over the bloody patches in the yard, escaping onto the highway heading west.

In contrast to the crowds of Alden, the Town Line crossroads sat gray and silent, the houses plain and shut to the street.

"Kratzbürste!" A thick-accented old lady shouted from her doorway. It was an old German insult she'd heard muttered more than once before behind her back. "You dare show your face? You sticking your nose where it doesn't belong. This is your fault."

A rock banged off the side of the wagon.

She did not disagree with the old woman's condemnation.

She pushed the old draft horse to an awkward canter for the short length of the little hamlet, watching the Zubrich house, hoping to see Hans's kind face, fearing the pastor would come out and make a scene.

The door stayed shut.

The next town was Lancaster and its opinions were less monochromatic. The declaration of war had brought everybody out, and the street was clogged with boys and men streaming toward the city, some on foot, some in wagons. American flags hung from many of the porches, but copperheads stood on the corners and heckled passersby. "We have no right to make war on these, our brothers," one man shouted from a wheelchair on his porch, shaking his fist at the passing wagons. "Death to the tyrant."

She was grateful to be unknown there. Just days before she would have turned and shouted at the man, welcoming a foil for her argued cause.

She had dreamt for so long of a righteous war to free the enslaved, but now that it was here, the realness of it made her sick. Visions of her father flailing in the doctor's bed came to her and she couldn't help but think of him as the first casualty of the war, and she thought of the pain that would come to so many more. She had been prepared to spend herself completely in this cause, but had never thought that it would be those around her that would suffer the most. She was ashamed that she hadn't considered the real cost.

Closer to the city, there were fewer copperheads, and the Unionists dominated the streets. She found herself a glum addition to an ad hoc parade of flag-waving wagons and carriages filled with men singing "John Brown's Body" or "The Star-Spangled Banner." Ladies in red and blue scarves cheered them on from the plank sidewalk.

A pretty little negro girl in a white dress with a white hat stood alone on a corner, smiling and waving. Mary smiled back, but looked twice when she counted six fingers on each of the waving hands. She wondered if her exhaustion had ruined her eyes.

In Cheektowaga a cluster of abolitionist

matrons uniformed in black dresses and gray hair buns handed out flags to people at the toll gate. She knew a few of their faces from meetings but kept her eyes down and passed without a word.

Farther along, the rumble of nearby trains became constant and coal dust filmed everything in sight. She passed a cluster of four-story buildings and the train yard expanded before her, locomotives and cars spread across the horizon. Clouds of smoke and steam hung low in the hazy sky.

After Depew, wagons clogged the road, slowing progress and the trip stretched longer than Mary had expected. In the city, she had to stop often as thickets of people spilled off the sidewalk and into the streets. The shadows grew long.

A crowd of boys with turkey muskets attempting a soldierly formation brought her to a stop at Genesee Street as they shouted threats to the lives of Jefferson Davis and his kin. She turned to her left to see the redbrick jail and stared at its black windows a long time, imagining Joe locked somewhere in its labyrinth. The driver behind her shouted her out of her reverie and she flicked the whip, moving old Timber forward.

It was nearing dark when she pulled into

the market warehouse by the canal.

"Miss Willis," an old man in a vest and spectacles greeted her. "I'm surprised to see you on a such a day."

"The world goes on," she said.

He climbed onto the wagon, unstoppered one of the barrels, and filled a glass tube. He held it up to a lamp, then downed the little vial of syrup.

"A good amber," he said. "As always."

In past years, she and the clerk had bargained over the price passionately, and there had been few things she enjoyed more than squeezing the last penny out of their dealings, but this time she accepted his insulting offer without comment. He seemed disappointed.

"I have neither the time nor the energy to drive back to the farm today," she said. "Can you board my animal for the night?"

She took her money and went back out on the street.

There were crowds on every corner, and the noise frayed her nerves. She would spend the night at the American Hotel, but before she ran the inevitable gauntlet of her father's friends in its lobby, she wanted nothing more than a place to sit and gather her thoughts. She thought of the little church where just the morning before she'd intended to deliver Joe for the last stage of his trip to freedom.

She moved through the crowds faster on foot, and made her way to Michigan Street just as the lamplighters were passing through.

Most of the modest little houses around the church were empty and dark, but color blazed from the stained-glass windows of the squat little church.

A handful of men standing outside the entrance stared at her as she pushed past them and into the crowded sanctuary.

A white-haired black man stood at the pulpit, his hand raised in the air, his voice filling the crowded room.

"This is not progress," he shouted. "This is more of the same. We pay their taxes, yet we have no representation. Was that not their reason for their rebellion eighty-five years ago?"

A murmur rolled through the room.

"And now, we are deemed worthy of dying in their cane fields, but are unfit to bear arms on their battlefields. Yes, we know the South fights to preserve their 'peculiar institution,'" he spat the words, "but what do our white friends here in the North fight for?"

Another murmur.

"They say it is to preserve the Union."
His voice rose. "But it is their Union, not
ours. They are telling us we have no part to
play. They tell us that we should leave,
should go to Haiti or to Liberia, as if those
places mean anything to us."

She surveyed the room — the front pews
were occupied by black men in fine suits
and their families, the ladies perfectly
coiffed and the children miniatures of their
parents, but those in the rear pews looked
as if they'd come from a day's labor. Mary
had been to many an abolition meeting, and
had even seen Frederick Douglass once in
Rochester, but she'd never been the only
white face in a room of negroes.

Father Thomas, with his shock of white
hair and his labor-warped back, greeted her.

"Miss Willis," he said, surprise in his eyes.
"What brings you down here tonight?"

"I needed a place to be alone," she said.

"This is the wrong place for that." He
chuckled. "Some neighborhood leaders are
using the church for a . . . uh . . . private
meeting this evening."

He cupped her elbow and led her down
the stairs to a cluttered, tiny room with a
crowded desk piled high with papers and
books.

"This is my office. You can stay here as

long as you'd like," he said, lifting a worn Bible from a stack of books and placing it in front of her with a grin. "Here's something to read."

She smiled, and he started to leave.

"Do you think it will make a difference?" she asked.

"The war?" he asked, and she nodded.

"In some ways," the priest said. "But even if the Union wins, defeat will only harden the hearts of the slavers. That is the real war, and this is only the beginning of it."

"My father was shot yesterday," she said. "He was delirious when the doctor sent me away this morning. It was a slave hunter that pulled the trigger, and that man is dead now. My friend killed him. There's still blood in my barnyard."

He sat and put his arm around her.

"You, like us, have been fighting this war for years," he whispered.

"It is too much." She swiped fiercely at her tears. "I cannot bear the cost."

"My poor dear," he said.

She began to sob. She could feel the loss of everyone she loved coming down on her, feel it overwhelming her. The comfort of the priest had cracked something in her. Just as she felt her self-control slipping away, she straightened her back, pushed his hand away.

"No," she said, twisting her face into an angry knot. "I will not allow myself to become some weeping, weakling of a lady."

She stood.

"I will not."

He looked up, confused.

"Father," she said, "thank you for your kindness."

She climbed the stairs, left the church, and started the long walk to the American Hotel. She could not remember when she had last eaten, or really slept. She shook herself, trying to clear her trance of grief, exhaustion, and hunger.

Booming gunfire, wisps of music, and shouting voices echoed off the buildings around her, blending with the remembered sounds of her father's ranting. Men and boys jostled past her on the sidewalk. She came into Ellicott Square, expecting an empty plaza in dimming evening light, but instead there was a throng with torches and lanterns held high overhead.

Carpenters still banged on the supports of a stage even as a stout old man stomped its broad planks, exhorting the young men in the crowd to take up arms to save the Union. The structure wobbled under him. The count of stars on many of the flags waving in the crowd dated them to decades long past. Young men gripping hunting muskets formed ersatz companies around the edges of the square like seedpods clustering on a creek bank.

Mary pushed her way into the crowd, heading across the way to the hotel. Hawkers were everywhere, and the smell of the food made her stomach rumble. An Irishman in a greasy porkpie hat sold her fried perch and potatoes wrapped in a cone rolled from *The Express.*

Cannons had been dragged up from the waterfront, and after each speaker they were fired, echoing into the night as the smoky haze settled onto the crowd.

She felt as if the world around her was falling under a fever that had broken for her the moment her father crumpled to the ground.

Men crowded the platform behind the speaker, and she saw many that she recognized as friends of her father. She wanted to climb onto the stage and tell them that even now as they bravely called for others to march into harm's way, he was raving at death's door.

A jowled man with a tall hat, a severe starched collar, and permanently arched eyes took the stage. His voice boomed out across the crowd as he paced the width of the stage, hands behind his back.

"I know many of you and many of you know me. I grew up here, worked as a clerk not far from this spot before duty called me to Washington and the White House. My name is Millard Fillmore."

The crowd cheered wildly.

"Now just last year, many of you heard me tell you that Stephen Douglas could save our Union. I traveled far and wide in our county telling you to not vote for Mr. Lincoln. But the time for differences ended when we dropped our ballots in the box. We are all Americans!"

The crowd clapped and whooped.

"And now we face the greatest threat to our young nation since we chased the redcoats from this waterfront in 1812. We did not fight then so that we would founder now.

"Not two months ago, President Lincoln took my hand in that building right there," he pointed at the American Hotel. "He asked of me 'Millard, will you help me hold this Union?' I told him then, as I tell you now, that I will give my very life to preserve these United States."

Women banged pots with wooden spoons and the men cheered again.

"Join me, Democrat or Freesoiler, Republican or Whig. Fight, fight with all that you have to save our Republic."

As another cheer went up, a boy in the crowd shouted, "Where do I sign up?"

"A valiant, brave soul!" Fillmore shouted.

One of the men on the stage stepped forward with a scroll.

"I happen to have a roll right here waiting for enlistees," Fillmore said. "Come join me on the platform, young man."

The crowd cheered and cleared a path to the stage. He jumped onto the platform. "Let's go get us some rebs," he shouted.

Like the boys she'd known all her life, he seemed barely old enough to hitch a mule, much less to fight in a war. Leander's friends cared nothing for the politics of North versus South, of Union or Confederate, but she could imagine them signing up in that fever, and it made her despair. As separate as she felt from them, she could not imagine Town Line without them.

And then she thought of Leander, and wondered where he was, and it felt as if her stomach had dropped into a bottomless pit.

"Are you prepared to sign in service of your country while we put this devilish rebellion down?"

"Gasbag," she muttered. "It was you, as

much as anyone else, who brought us here."

"Let me at 'em," the boy shouted, his voice cracking as he raised his fists, an imaginary boxer standing over an imaginary opponent. The crowd egged him on.

"Well, someone get this young man a pen, before he sees a pretty girl in the crowd and changes his mind," Fillmore shouted to laughs.

A pen and pot appeared, and Fillmore stretched the roll out on the rostrum. The youth signed with a flourish, and a cheer rose up under the trees again.

Fillmore reached out and shook the boy's hand. "Welcome to the United States Army, son. Congratulations, good luck, and we'll see you back here for the Fourth of July."

He turned to the crowd, "Who else wants a nice new uniform? The girls love them!"

"Reporting, sir," a chorus of voices shouted from somewhere behind her.

The crowd jostled as a murmur rumbled through the gathering and a group on horses rode slowly into the crowd.

"Let us through, we're here to join," a voice shouted hoarsely.

Mary almost fell to her knees when she saw Leander riding Karl Wilhelm's horse to the front of the stage. Nearly three dozen of his friends flanked him, all faces she recognized. There was Henry Grimes from Alden, a boy she'd danced with once or twice, and Lafayette Glass, whom she'd seen at the rally in Alden earlier. Vaness Weber and Edward Eels followed, muskets on shoulders.

And of course Hans Zubrich, atop his father's old swayback, rode closest.

The former president lifted his hands over his head as the crowd shouted itself raw.

Once the entire company had made its way to the front of the stage, Leander climbed the steps, and Fillmore clapped him on the shoulder and embraced him like a conquering hero.

"The first volunteer cavalry of Alden reporting for duty," Leander said.

The cheering shook the budding trees of the square.

"I know you," Fillmore shouted. "Everybody, this is Leander Willis, son of my good friend Nathan Willis, one of the first men to settle here on the Niagara Frontier. A great man, surely. Tell me, young Willis, how did you come to command this new company?"

"I recruited these men today," Leander said, grinning.

"You formed a company of thirty men in one day?" Fillmore asked, his disbelief theatrical.

"We did," Leander said. "The men of Alden and Town Line stand with the Union."

"Welcome to the fight, Captain Willis," Fillmore said.

"I'm not a captain, sir," Leander said.

"You are now," Fillmore shouted to a laughing crowd. "You men come up and sign this muster roll."

She watched wordlessly as nearly every boy she'd ever known climbed onto the stage and signed themselves over to the Union. The crowd surged to the stage, reaching forward to lay hands on the newly anointed unit, but she turned away, away from the noise and bustle. She crushed the empty, greasy newspaper in her hands and dropped it on the ground where it was soon trampled underfoot.

STATION

Katia always said the dead walked the earth at night. Harry wasn't so sure, but if she was right, Karl Wilhelm's ghost sure as shit knew where to find him.

Ghosts were one thing, then there was Charlie Webster. Harry had known Charlie forever, but he'd never seen him like he'd been when he shot old Wilhelm. Charlie had dug Mary's pistol out from under the bench cushion, aimed it at the innkeeper, and pulled the trigger so quickly that Harry hadn't realized what was happening until Wilhelm was bleeding.

Then there was the look in Charlie's eyes when he'd cocked the pistol and aimed it straight at Harry. If the nigger hadn't spoken up, he'd have been dead right then.

Harry didn't want to think too much about the idea that it was the runaway that he'd been hunting down who probably saved his life by giving himself up. It made him a little dizzy to try and work that out.

So the ghost of Karl Wilhelm might be after him, and Charlie Webster might be after him, too, but what really kept him awake was worrying about Mr. Willis.

Other than Jep, Harry'd never had a better friend than Nathan Willis.

In the months after he'd jumped off the orphan train, Harry had mostly gotten by with stolen apples, poached fish, and whatever Katia brought for him from Nathan Willis's table. When he finally got caught, Harry had expected to get beaten or dragged off to jail, but Mr. Willis had brought him in and sat him down like a proper guest. He had never really had to go hungry since. He'd always been able to count on Nathan Willis.

Of course, Mr. Willis had been helping to hide the runaway, but the runaway had also saved Harry.

He wasn't sure exactly who to be angry with. But he knew for sure it was all his own fault.

As hard as he tried, he couldn't stop seeing the old man, blood pouring out of the side of his head, facedown in the mud.

There wasn't anybody in Town Line that Nathan Willis hadn't helped along in some way. And all those people — they'd be looking for Harry now. Lord knew, he would have hunted himself down for it.

Normally, he'd have hidden out in Leander's shack, but that just seemed wrong now. So he took his old musket and his bedroll and he hid out under the Town Line bridge. He had a bottle of rum hidden there.

He wished he could see Katia, but he was too ashamed. If there was anyone that owed more than him to Nathan Willis, it was Katia. She'd probably kill Harry herself if she had the chance.

That night under the bridge was cold, but a fire would have given him away. He drank the rum and sat up, watching for the ghost of Karl Wilhelm as the creek flowed by.

By sunup, he'd decided to leave Town Line for good. He wasn't sure where he'd go, but he'd start by going downtown. He had business there.

He dug up his crock, pocketed his money, and started the long walk downtown. He could have bought a train ticket, but now was not the time to get all fancy.

In Lancaster, the road was crowded with morons heading downtown to enlist, and he pulled his hat lower on his head.

By the time he got to Depew, the smell of cooking sausages coming out of a crowded gin mill drew him in for something to eat.

The bartender, seeing his swag and musket, took him for a volunteer and told him he was drinking on the house. Saying nothing, Harry settled at the bar and drank what was put in front of him. After a few hours of whiskey, and all the idiots talking about how the South would surrender in a few weeks, he couldn't take it anymore and said how the war was all a fool's errand and he'd sooner eat shit than wear a uniform.

He'd barely finished when three men picked him up and threw him into the gutter outside the front door. The bartender followed them out and emptied the spittoon onto his head.

He got to the waterfront in the early afternoon. He had come looking for the *Abigail,* but at the same time, he'd hoped it was gone. He had been dreading the conversation, fretting how to break the news.

He was led into the same room as before, only now the commander sat alone at a desk with papers spread before him.

Harry hung his head and put his grimy hat over his heart.

"Sir, it's terrible news for sure, but Mr. Wilhelm got killed," he said.

Compson didn't even look up.

"You came a long way for a drink," Compson said, motioning to where the liquor sat on a sideboard. "Just take the bottle and go."

Harry glared at the top of the Southerner's head until the silence caused Compson to lift his face and look him in the eye.

"You can pour that whiskey into that big river for all I care," Harry said, color rising in his face. "I came to tell you about Karl Wilhelm. He was my friend. He treated me alright. And it was my doing that got him killed. I thought he was your friend, too, so I figured I should tell you face-to-face before I moved on. I came to say I'm sorry."

Compson blinked, surprised. "Take a seat, Mr. Strauss," he said, motioning to a chair.

Harry just glared at the Southerner.

Compson stood, and came around the desk. "I'm sorry, that was rude of me," he said, offering his hand. "I'm grateful that you came all this way to tell me. It's far more than most would do, and you've shown yourself to be a man of honor."

Compson's hand did not move for a long moment, and finally Harry took it.

"Please, sit," Compson said again.

It had been a long walk, and he'd bruised his hip when they threw him out of the saloon. He sank into the soft chair.

"The marshal let me know what happened," Compson said, taking the chair next to him. "You shouldn't feel bad. You did just what you said you would, and you did what the law says you should. You've got nothing to be ashamed of. God rest his soul, Karl Wilhelm brought this on himself, and he's to blame for Mr. Willis's fate, too, whatever that might be."

"You can say that all you want," Harry said. "That don't mean it's true."

Compson gave him a rueful grin.

"So what of you? Will you march to war?" the commander asked.

"Hell no," Harry said. "I got no horse in that race. They're all idiots, signing up to get killed."

"You're a prudent man," Compson said with a smile. "So what then?"

"I've left Town Line," he said. "I can't face anyone there. I might try to find some work down here in the city. Maybe over at the canal. I like animals. Maybe I could tend the mules there."

Compson leaned against his heavy desk.

"That's not work for a man of honor like yourself," he said. "Come work for me. I could use someone like you. A man I can trust."

"For what?"

Compson ran his fingers along his thin mustache.

"This or that," he said. "I'm a stranger in a strange land, and I could use a friend like you. Why don't you let me pay you a retainer, and you go back to Town Line and wait for word from me?"

"Nathan Willis is probably going to die if he ain't dead already," Harry said. "The people in that town are as likely as not to string me up if they see me."

"Nonsense," Compson said, furrowing his brow. "It was Wilhelm that shot Mr. Willis. That's not your fault."

He opened a drawer, counted some bills, and stuffed them into an envelope that he pushed across the desk.

"This is fifty dollars. Take it, head back to Town Line, and wait for word from me. It's a first month's pay."

"Fifty dollars?" Harry said. "It takes me a long time to see that kind of money."

"You have done well by me," Compson said. "Stay out in Town Line. I have ideas for that little town."

Harry stared at the envelope. He wasn't sure what a retainer was, but if it meant fifty dollars to do nothing, he couldn't think of a good reason not to take it. He picked it up, shook Compson's hand again, and left.

He rode the train back home and knocked at the Zubrichs' door, hoping he could make Hans understand it wasn't all his doing. Maybe he would let him stay in the barn for a few nights.

The pastor, his blond hair cropped close to his head and his spectacles perched on his nose, answered the door.

"Ah, you are safe," he said. "I read in the paper about the shooting. So bad, this nigger. Praise Jesus you are safe."

Harry scuffed the porch with his boots.

"I was looking for Hans," he said.

"Hans is gone," he said. "Him and the rest of those useless boys. I told him that if he joined the war, I'd never let him back in this house."

He spat.

"You are the only one with sense not to follow that *Hurensohn* Leander Willis to this war. Everyone is gone."

Harry's knees grew weak at the news.

"Who else?" he asked.

"Everyone," Zubrich said. "Thirty boys followed him to this godforsaken war. The Webers. The Glasses. Ach. All ungrateful boys. Only the old men are left to plow the fields."

Harry shook his head in disbelief and turned to leave. He was nearly off the porch when he stopped and turned.

"I was going to ask Hans if I could stay in

your barn tonight," he said.

The old pastor waved his hand.

"Take his room. Stay as long as you want. You can work for it. Help with the garden, other things."

Harry thought of the cold night he'd spent under the Town Line bridge and smiled in gratitude.

After he put his things in Hans's room, he went out again, just to walk around the little crossroads. He felt like a prince with all the money he had in his pocket. He bought some candy at Snyder's, and walked past the train station and the closed blacksmith and the closed school, then turned around and walked past them again before he went back to the parsonage. After dinner, when he was sure no one would see him, he found his way back to the windbreak and reburied his treasure, now almost doubled.

The next morning, he borrowed the Webers' mule and hitched it to the dull plow in the barn and turned the parsonage's little kitchen garden. He helped Mrs. Zubrich plant it the next day.

Pastor Zubrich would often have little projects for him that he'd announce each morning at breakfast, but nothing too hard, and he was usually done by lunch. He hired out for little jobs with the farmers around town and they all told him how smart he was to stay home.

The town was so quiet there was seldom a noise other than the lowing of cows. Wilhelm's widow had returned to Bavaria the day after the innkeeper's funeral, and Harry wouldn't even look at the little black-windowed Corner House when he passed it.

Zubrich wouldn't allow even beer into his house, so the nearest drink was three miles away at Oscar Dodge's saloon in Alden. Harry walked there one evening, but the bar was empty except for a pair of gray-bearded old farmers drinking schnapps and talking in German at a corner table. When Harry ordered a beer, Dodge didn't even look up from his paper as he said that if he wanted to drink, he should have joined the army.

As the spring moved toward summer, Harry sometimes went to watch the younger boys play ball in the same field where he'd played with Hans and Lelo, but it just made him more lonely and sad.

Some mornings he stood under a tree across the street from the Willis place, hoping to see Katia, but he never did. He'd heard that Mr. Willis had survived, and for that he was grateful. But he couldn't imagine facing him or Mary.

Then came the massacre at Bull Run. Hundreds of boys killed on a bright Virginia afternoon.

Up until then, the war had been felt as an absence to the farmers of Town Line. The boys had all gone off and gotten themselves involved in things that weren't their business, but they would be back soon. But now, they were dying.

The mood of Pastor Zubrich's Sunday-morning sermons switched from anger to dread. The girls started organizing sanitary drives, gathering at this house or that to cut old rags into bandage strips and ship them away to field hospitals.

When he saw Susie Munn at Snyder's General Store, he called her by name and reached out for her arm.

"Coward" was all she said, and pulled herself free.

The ball games stopped, and the boys that played them seemed to disappear from sight.

Harry found Mrs. Zubrich crying in the kitchen with the windows shuttered on one warm August afternoon.

"Back in Germany, the soldiers came and stole our boys, took them to their revolution," she explained in her thick accent.

"Brothers. Sons. That's why everyone came to America. Now it will happen here. They hide their boys this time; some they will not let out of the house at all."

Compson came to him soon after that. Harry was sitting on Zubrichs' front porch smoking a pipe, listening to the train rattle out of the station when the commander climbed the steps like he'd been there a dozen times before.

"I need your help," he said.

"I hope it's something good," Harry said. "I'm bored out of my noggin."

Compson smiled under his thin mustache.

"There's a man coming on the late train tomorrow," he said. "The Yankee army will be looking for him. All you have to do is keep him here a while. No one will come looking for him out here, so you shouldn't have any trouble. Bring him down to the *Abigail* after a week."

He gave Harry another envelope of bills.

"Who is he?" Harry asked.

"A man of honor, like yourself," Compson said. "Hold him for a week. The army boys will have forgotten about him by then. Bring him down to the waterfront after."

The next night, the Confederate slid off the roof of the train as it took on water at the station. Harry beckoned him into the shadows from the lighted platform.

His name was Ray, and he was long-bearded, bad smelling, and still wore the stained gray trousers with the black stripe of his Confederate uniform.

"Nobody would guess who you are in a million years." Harry snorted before leading him to the barn behind Zubrich's parsonage and showing him the stack of discarded horse blankets and a mound of straw. He went into the kitchen and brought back the heel of a loaf of pumpernickel.

Ray crawled under a blanket and started in on snoring quicker than Harry would have believed.

In the morning, Harry went to Snyder's General Store and bought a new pair of dungarees. He took the Reb down to the creek where he climbed into the sun-warmed waters and scrubbed himself and shaved off his beard. Harry burned the uniform.

"I'll take you down to the river in a week," he said as he hacked at the man's hair with a knife.

Harry had brought some poles, and they spent the day pulling fat trout out of the creek.

For dinner, Mrs. Zubrich set out a spread under the pear tree and Ray offered to say grace. Pastor Zubrich looked up in surprise as the boy reeled off a long verse from Colossians.

"You didn't tell me we had a Christian guest," he said to Harry.

"The Lord is my savior," the Southerner said, and the pastor clapped him on the back.

Harry found himself longing for a drink for the first time in months as the pastor and the rebel talked scripture for the rest of the meal.

Eventually the conversation turned to Mary Willis.

"This woman," the pastor seethed. "She forgets that it is God's commandment that man is the head of every woman. For that one, there is no one above her. Not her father. Not her godforsaken brother. Not God himself. She must be smitten. That woman needs to know her place."

Mrs. Zubrich just nodded her head.

When they finished dinner, the pastor led the soldier into the living room to kneel and pray, but they were stopped by a knock on the door.

Farmer Eels from down Town Line Road stood at the door, and he looked over the pastor's shoulder and spoke in German.

They talked for a few minutes, then Zubrich closed the door.

"He needs a well dug, and came to hire out Harry here," he said to Harry and Ray. "I signed you both up. Good money."

"I'm supposed to keep you hidden." Harry laughed. "I can't think of a better place to do that than in a hole in the ground."

"Sure," Ray said with a shrug. "I wouldn't mind making a few dollars."

They dug for the next five days, taking the well deep and wide and lining it with river rock. At the end of the fifth day, they collected their wages and Mrs. Zubrich cooked them steak dinners and served them at the table under the pear tree. He and Ray sat on the porch afterward, and the Southerner was rolling a cigarette when Katia walked by on her way to the station for the mail. She shrieked and ran to Harry, nearly knocking him out of his chair.

"*Ja,*" she said. "I thought you'd gone with the rest of the fools. You are here!"

She kissed him full on the lips, something he'd dreamed of many times but had never experienced.

"Why you no come for me?" she demanded, kissing him again. "Why you let me worry so much?"

Ray got her a chair. She asked Harry questions about what he'd been doing, and then finally he asked her about Nathan.

She looked down at her hands.

"The spirits," she said. "They've come for him, but he will not go. All day long, he talks to his dead friends, sometimes in English and sometimes in Indian. They ask him to follow, but he does not go. He is not right. And Mary. All this is her fault. She's the one that brought that bad man here. She is so hard. All the time, she complains that no one will work for her and she has to go find other men. And me, too. I would leave, except for poor Mr. Willis."

In the morning, Harry hitched up the wagon.

"Hop in," he said to the rebel. "They're waiting downtown to get you over the river."

"Are you crazy?" Ray asked. "I'm not riding down there in broad daylight. They'll have me in chains in no time."

"Look at you," Harry said. "You look like every other hayseed in town. Just not so much with the 'y'alls' and the 'ma'ams' and the 'sirs.' Just keep your trap shut, in general. You'll be fine."

In was a fine day and they rode into the city without incident.

Compson was waiting on the deck of the *Abigail* when they arrived and Ray tipped the old worn cap that Mrs. Zubrich had given him.

"Thanks, Harry," he said, his voice low. "You come on down to Virginia anytime. Bring Katia. She'd be pretty in a hoop skirt."

Others came after that, sometimes in twos. Zubrich always found work for them while they were there, and Harry started to think the pastor was getting a cut, but he didn't worry too much about it. The rebs got fed well, and Harry liked most of them just fine.

One Sunday during services, the preacher demanded that the farmers' wives help clothe the good Christian war refugees that were passing through town. Before long, the cabin had piles of worn overalls, patched and clean.

Katia came and sat on the porch with him when she could. He'd never had so much money before, but there was nothing much to spend it on. He started thinking about buying his own place. Someplace with some apple trees, and a creek to fish.

In the fall, Compson started making the payments in Confederate script instead of Union. Harry complained that no one in town would take it, but Compson agreed to double his wage.

BLUE

Leander's head throbbed with each metallic taunt of reveille.

He lurched off his cot and into the dull fog of the Maryland countryside. He scanned the eastern horizon for the sun, but all he saw was a monochrome gray over the wide field of white canvas.

"There's no sunrise," he said, rubbing his face. "I swear if they'd just wait until sunrise to blow that damned horn, I'd be able to get enough sleep."

"Willis," his tent-mate, Lieutenant Corbett, stage-whispered. He nodded his head down the line of uniformed junior officers standing at attention in front of their tents. "The colonel."

Leander snapped to attention, his suspenders still dangling from his waistband. The morning dew soaked through his woolen socks.

Colonel Chapin strutted down the line.

Leander could not understand how a man who lived in a field in the middle of nowhere could keep his uniform so crisp and blue when after just a few weeks, moths had already had their way with his own.

An infantry man trailed the colonel. The officer extended his hand and the subordinate flipped through a sheaf of envelopes.

"Looks like one from your uncle Henry," he said to Corbett, passing it to him. "Send him my best wishes when you write back."

Chapin stopped in front of Leander and looked up and down at his rumpled white tunic, mussed hair, and dangling suspenders. The colonel's face, hidden behind a full beard, was inscrutable to Leander.

"Lieutenant Willis," he said. "Are you capable of doing anything other than trying my patience?"

"Yes, sir," Leander said.

"Perhaps someday you could demonstrate your other skills," Chapin replied. "But in the meantime, could you explain to me why your name continues to come across my desk nearly every day?"

"I don't know, sir."

"You see, I receive mail, also," the colonel said. He put his hand out, and his aide handed him another envelope. "Here's a letter from a Marshal Dwight Kidder. Does that name mean anything to you?"

Leander furrowed his brow.

"Yes, sir."

"You look surprised," the colonel said. "I certainly was. Imagine reading the suggestion that one of my officers joined this fine army as a way to avoid the law. He weaved quite a tale. Fugitive slaves, dead bounty hunters, horse thievery. I'd like some answers myself."

Leander stood at attention and kept his eyes fixed on the dismal horizon. Chapin moved his face close enough that Leander could smell tobacco and coffee on his breath.

"Why are you here, Willis?" he growled.

"I joined to serve my country, sir," Leander said.

"Or did you join so that you could drink and gamble with the enlisted men?" Chapin asked back in a growl. "Because I have reports of you on that side of camp last night with a bottle and a deck of cards."

He paused.

"Yet again."

Leander's eyes landed on the black hairs growing from a mole at the colonel's temple.

"Are those stories true?" Chapin asked, his voice quiet. "Would you like to dispute them? Should I bring men that I trust and respect here to explain to me why they are lying about your nighttime activities?"

"The stories are true, sir," Leander said, grimacing. In fact, he'd lost the last of the money he'd made selling off Wilhelm's horse the night before.

"Do you know the penalty for an officer who fraternizes with enlisted men?" Chapin asked.

"Court-martial, sir," Leander said, the bottom dropping out of his stomach.

"Very good, Lieutenant," the colonel said. "I'm glad that you at least know the rules which you disregard."

Chapin backed up and pitched his voice for his officer corps to hear.

"An army of saints would be the most useless thing in the world, but I do expect fighting men of discipline and character. And you, Lieutenant, have shown me neither. The federal government says that if a man brings two dozen recruits with him, he is awarded a commission. I say that's a hell of a way to build an officer corps. Do you understand me, Lieutenant?"

"Yes, sir," Leander said.

"It is the talk of many that this corps is oversubscribed," he said. "By hook or by crook, we'll get these numbers right. Some will be busted down to private, others will just fade away.

"Payroll will at last be issued in three days. Before then, any of you may request a simple discharge. There are some I would be disappointed to see go and for others, I would be relieved," he said, pulling his long dark beard and looking at Leander.

"After that date, your exit from this army will not go so well. Particularly if it's an involuntary removal. Am I clear?"

"Yes, sir," the gathered men said in unison.

He turned away and moved toward the next group of tents.

Leander's shoulders slumped as he let out a long, slow exhale. He went back into the tent and plopped on his cot, his head in his hands.

"Shit," he said.

"Did you really kill someone?" Corbett asked.

"Shit," Leander repeated, ignoring the question.

"I told you not to go over there last night," Corbett said.

"I know, I know," Leander said. "Another night of sitting around here hanging my laundry just wasn't enough to hold my attention."

"I apologize if my company isn't interesting enough for you," Corbett said.

Dan Corbett had been finishing up his time at divinity school when Sumter fell, and his degree earned him the second lieutenant's brass bar. His talkative nature and complete lack of imagination left Leander praying for the early arrival of sleep most nights, even as the swarming mosquitos kept him swatting and awake.

Leander fixed his suspenders and pulled on the rest of his uniform as the two men headed toward the officer's mess.

"What are you going to do when we're through kicking these rebels back into line?" Leander asked.

"I'm thinking about running for Congress," Corbett said.

"You'd be great," Leander said enthusiastically, slapping him on the shoulder.

Chapin had issued orders for extra drills, and Leander spent the day leading his company through its exercises with all the vigor he could muster with a court-martial and a hangover weighing on him. Despite their dirty looks, he kept his soldiers late and pushed them hard even as the sun fell below the Maryland tree line and a low-hanging bank of clouds rolled in.

After supper, Corbett went to the canvas chapel to lead a prayer meeting, and Leander had the tent to himself. He felt jittery but tired at the same time. He knew that if he could just sit quietly, he could come up with a plan. He'd be able to concentrate after a good night's sleep. He lay down on the cot and closed his eyes.

The clouds of the afternoon had hardened into a thick dark cover, but they brought no relief from the heat, and sweat pooled under his tunic. The wind had shifted, and the smell of the latrines enshrouded the site while a half-dozen bands squawked, pounded, and sawed at each other across the encampment. Leander was certain that his tent was perfectly equidistant to each of them, and the din and smell tormented him, keeping him awake. He rolled over on the lumpy cot and buried his head under his pillow.

As he did each night in bed, he thought of Isabel. It had been forever since he'd heard from her, and he hadn't seen her since the day after his enlistment.

He had tried to be good. He had tried to do what his father would want him to do. That's why he'd joined the army and convinced his friends that they should, too.

But now he wasn't so sure. Katia had written and told him that his father wasn't well. He wasn't doing him any good camping in this field, but he knew he couldn't go home.

If he was with Isabel, he could help by trading and sending money.

He knew his father wouldn't approve, but his father was too old-fashioned sometimes. He'd tried to do things his father's way, and it had gotten him to this damned tent. He'd been so hurt by Mary's anger and the marshal's betrayal, he'd tried too hard to make things right. He should be with Isabel. He'd made a mistake when he enlisted. He knew that now.

After they'd signed the muster roll, he and Hans had found themselves the toast of the town at the Eagle Tavern where every politician in the city fought over the right to buy them drinks. They ended back at Whitney Place in the wee hours, and slept into the afternoon.

Hans had teased him as he got dressed, but even hungover, Leander couldn't hide his enthusiasm at seeing Isabel again. It had been three days, the longest they'd been apart. At the least she would have a bottle for him. He had had the last of his tonic while he'd ridden around Alden recruiting his friends, and his head was pounding and his hands shaking.

He found her in the parlor lounging on the couch with a Celestial lady with a long cascade of perfect black hair. The stove had been stoked and the room was overly warm and close. They both wore thin silk robes, and by the way the fabric draped over their bodies, nothing else. A thin line of smoke rose from the bowl of the hookah, adding to the thick cloud that hovered in the room.

The aroma drew him in, and he breathed deeply, the effect almost allowing him to ignore the way the strange woman's inner thigh bared itself as she shifted position on the couch. She stared at him as she put the embroidered hose to her lips.

Isabel looked at him through hooded eyes and a languid moue.

"Oh," she said. "You'd been gone so long I thought you decided to stay on the farm and herd cows, or whatever it is you do back there."

"I'm a captain in the Union Army," he blurted. "I'm off to Elmira for training tomorrow. Tonight's my last in town. I thought we could do something exciting. Dinner? Dancing?"

"Such timing," Isabel said, bemused.

The Celestial ran her finger across Isabel's cheek, distracting Leander.

"I suppose a send-off is in order," Isabel said, then whispered in Chinese to her companion.

The woman climbed to her feet and

floated by Leander, smiling slyly.

"Who's that?" he asked.

"I guess I should prepare for our big night," Isabel said, ignoring the question. "I'll get dressed."

She stood and went into her chamber, closing the door behind her.

Leander sat on the couch and finished the smudge of opium left in the hookah before going to the cellar to find a bottle of tonic.

Isabel took her time getting ready, but she emerged from her efforts dressed more plainly than he expected.

They went to the dining room at the American Hotel, and he beamed with pride as his father's friends streamed over to the table to congratulate him. He introduced each of them to Isabel, and she smiled at each of them wanly.

"Don't fret, sweetheart," Millard Fillmore said. "This will all be over soon and he'll be back home in your arms."

She nodded, and chewed her steak.

She told him how she had already rented a rail car for her move back to New York and would be leaving the next week. He told her of the shooting at home, but assured her that his father would be okay.

"I stopped to see him at the doctor's, in between rounding up my friends," he said.

"I had to tell him what I was doing. I knew he'd be proud. He was confused about where he was, but I'm sure he'll be better soon. I am doing all this for him, you know. I have to."

"Of course you do," she said.

They went back to her house, and she led him to the bed where he was all energy and enthusiasm. She allowed him to do many of the things she had taught him, but offered nothing new.

When he woke in the morning, she was gone, but the suits she had bought him were neatly folded and packed in a valise by the door.

He'd had to seek out Fuller in his cellar gym just to get the name of her supplier of coca-wine.

He worried about her all the time now. He'd written dozens of times, and had only received two brief notes back. They were impersonal, and cold, and the handwriting looked as if one of her clerks had penned them.

Of course that was more than he had gotten from his sister.

He'd given up after weeks of letters went unanswered. He even had a daguerreotype made of him in his lieutenant's uniform and sent it to his father in care of her, but there was no reply.

He'd begun to resent her anger. Here he was, doing exactly as Father had told him to do and she still wouldn't answer his letters.

After all, it was she who had put everything at risk. It was she who should apologize for putting their father in harm's way. He was the one who was following the law, she was the one breaking it. He thought of her, cool and dry back in their big house, while he festered in this damned camp, listening to the racket of disjointed bands.

Just as the rain started, he took the last bottle from the wooden box under his cot, wrapped it in a rag, and left the tent, heading for the enlisted side of camp.

He wove through the endless rows of white canvas until he reached his familiar destination and pulled back the flap to find Hans sitting on his cot writing a letter. He dug under the cot and found a pair of dirty glasses, uncorked the bottle, and filled them with wine.

"Back for more, Lelo?" Hans asked. "I would have thought you'd want a night off. Do you even have anything left to lose?"

"Not much," Leander said, trying to smile.

"Well, what I won might at least smooth things over with my father back home,"

Hans said. "I promised to send him half of my wages for the church, but they still haven't paid us."

"He'll be especially happy that it's Willis money," Leander said.

"That he will," Hans said with a grin. "I hear he's been using his sermons to condemn that strumpet sister of yours."

"Payroll is at the end of the week," Leander said.

"Did Chapin tell you that when he busted you down for your poor example of drinking with us lowlifes?" he asked.

"I guess you heard," Leander said. "Yes, he said that right before he told me I didn't belong in his army. I'd sure like to know who ratted me out."

"Wasn't me," Hans said. "Probably someone you woke up when you left here in the middle of the night, shouting about how we were all cheats."

Leander paused, gathering himself before he continued.

"I came for a farewell libation," he said. "I will not stay where I am not welcomed."

Hans squinted back at him in disbelief.

"You son of a bitch," he hissed, contempt in his voice. "This was all your idea. I could be home chasing Susie Munn through the apple orchards, and instead I'm stuck here marching up and down that damn field."

Leander downed his glass of wine and pushed the other toward his friend.

"Where do you have left to go?" Hans asked, ignoring the glass. "Sure as shit Mary doesn't want you home."

"I'm sure she doesn't and I've had as much of her as I can take," Leander said. "I'm going to New York. I'm going to be a trader down on Wall Street. I'll be rolling in it."

"Where will you get the money to start?" Hans asked. "They aren't going to bankroll you on good looks."

"I have an idea." Leander grinned.

The rain had started beating hard on the canvas, spattering mud into the leaking tent.

"I'm sure your daddy will be proud," Hans said. "You hightailing to New York and abandoning all of us."

His stared until Leander collapsed into sadness and he hung his head and ran his hands through his grimy hair.

"I don't want to imagine what my father will say," he said in a cracked whisper.

"You don't want to imagine what I'll say when you're gone, either," Hans said. He turned to his letter again, doing his best to ignore Leander.

"You've got nothing to worry about," Leander said. "This whole thing will be over soon. That enlistment contract was only for six months. You can stick the rest of that out. This battalion is dug in so deep it'll never move, and the rebs ain't coming this way. By the time General Winnie Scott figures out where and who to fight, you'll be home eating your mama's succotash and listening to Susie Munn say how handsome you look in your pretty blue uniform."

Hans looked up over the letter.

"I wouldn't bet a plug nickel on that," he said. "They aren't going to let any enlisted men go, no matter what the contracts say. I'm stuck here forever, and you get to go gallivanting. I've had enough of cleaning up your mess."

"What about me?" Leander whined. "You heard Fillmore. They promised me a captain's sash, and instead I end up with butter bars, listening to Chapin break me down over playing some cards."

"Poor Leander," Hans said. "Go ahead, stroll out of here, walking papers in hand. Go get rich and bed that little number of yours, but you better hope you never see me coming your way."

Leander's eyes flashed anger at the mention of Isabel, but he wilted again under his friend's indignant gaze.

"They try to keep you here, you send for me," Leander said, trying to smile. "I'll hire a fancy New York lawyer and get you out in no time."

"I bet," Hans said. "Because I've always been able to count on you."

There was a long silence. Leander pushed the wine toward his friend, but Hans pushed it back.

"You'll not ease your conscience with that swill," he said. "It ain't good stuff. I don't like how it makes me feel, and I don't like you when you drink it."

"I'm sorry," Leander said.

"Make no mistake, I'll never forgive you for this," Hans said, his gaze cold.

Leander tried to push the cork back in the bottle, but it had swelled in the dampness and would not fit. He put the bottle and the misshapen cork on the little camp table.

"I'll be gone in the morning," he said. "So this is good-bye."

Hans's eyes focused back on his letter, and did not look up again as Leander stood and stepped outside.

Leander almost sobbed when the nearly full bottle flew out of the tent and landed at his feet. Still, he picked it up and brushed the mud and grass from it.

The rain poured onto his bare head. It had sent the other soldiers retreating to their tents, but at least it had ended the bands' cacophony. He took in the murmur of chatter and laughter that rose from the rows of soggy canvas, each faintly glowing from candles within. He knew which of them housed the others from home, the boys that had followed him into the army. He knew he should go to each and say his farewells, but he did not have the strength to repeat what he'd just been through. He walked back to his own tent in the downpour.

His civilian clothes had grown moldy in his duffel, but Leander pulled on the least offensive of them and packed a few other pieces in a rucksack. He straightened the bed before laying out the blue uniform on the blanket. It stunk like a wet sheep, but he folded it carefully. Corbett had still not returned when he finished his resignation letter and he left no word for him.

The rain had turned to a light drizzle as he made his way through the bigger tents where the senior officers were housed. He found Colonel Chapin sitting at his lamplit desk, a pair of spectacles on his broad, bearded face.

"Sir, this is for you," Leander said.

260

Chapin looked over his glasses at him, then took the offered envelope and scanned the letter before reading aloud from it.

" '. . . did not appreciate the amount of time and labor it would take to fit me for that responsible position.' "

He leaned back in his chair.

"Well, I can't disagree with that."

He flipped through a stack of documents on his desk, and handed one to Leander.

"I took the liberty of having your discharge papers prepared, Mr. Willis," he said.

"Sir, you knew I would go?" Leander said.

"You're a civilian now. No need for the 'sir,' " Chapin said, and gestured for Leander to sit on the little stool opposite him. He looked out past his tent flap into the blue rain of the night. "Did you know that when I wasn't practicing law back home, I was with the Buffalo Niagaras?"

"The ball team?" Leander asked, impressed. "I didn't know you played."

"I'm a catcher," he said. "Better behind the plate than with a bat, but I've been known to knock a few in."

Leander couldn't help but smile picturing the always-serious captain tossing the ball around in a white woolen Niagaras uniform.

Chapin smiled back.

"I did some scouting, too, looking for

players for the team all around those parts,"
he continued. "Last year, someone, I can't
recall who, told me I needed to see this one
outfielder. He said this one could do it all.
Hit and throw and catch. So I got on the
train and went out to Alden to watch a
game.

"I figured if this boy is the son of Nathan
Willis, he must be something."

He stopped and looked at Leander over
his glasses.

Leander stared back at him, stunned.

"What happened? Did I drop a ball? Miss
an easy pitch? I must have had a bad day."

"I wouldn't say that," Chapin said. "You
went three for four, knocked one over the
fence, and made a diving catch that no one
in their right mind should have."

Leander ran through the games he'd
played the summer before and tried to
single out the one Chapin had come to see.

"Three for four? That wasn't good
enough?" he asked. "You didn't even talk to
me."

Chapin looked at him a long time.

"You could have been one of the best," he
said. "Still could, for all I know. But the
thing I noticed was that when nobody was
watching you, you lost interest. Walked back
to the dugout when everyone else ran,

waved to the girls when you should have been watching the batter."

He paused, scratched at his beard.

"When this battalion was forming, they sent me your paperwork and you were marked down for a captaincy — that President Fillmore himself had said so. I told them I wouldn't have it. Got into quite a fight. I threatened to resign unless they relented."

He nodded, answering an unasked question. "I'm why you were made a second lieutenant."

He leaned back over his desk, and turned his attention back to the paperwork in front of him.

"I knew you'd never last," he said. "I've been waiting for you to resign since the day you arrived in camp. Nobody wants a player like that on his team."

SECESSION

The first mark in the perfect white blanket led from the telegraph shack at the train station to the Weber house up on Town Line Road. The second went farther, up Cary Road to the Glass Farm. The third track was the shortest, but by then, the snow had started to melt, and the mark from the station to the Zubrichs' house was a muddy trample. More came then, a quick shatter of footprints, each another fissure in the ruined pane of snow.

When the farmers and their wives arrived at the parson's house, it was Harry who opened the door and led them into the parlor where the pastor and his wife sat.

Lafayette Glass. Sylvester Glass. Vaness Weber. Hans Zubrich. All of them gone.

The Battle of Ball's Bluff. It sounded like a horrid place to die.

Harry trekked from house to house the next day, spreading the word that there would be no services that Sunday. None blamed the old German pastor, and many said they doubted he would ever have the heart to preach again. In the afternoon, Harry drove the latest Confederate he'd been hiding in the barn down to the *Abigail.*

"My friends are dead," he said to Compson. "All of them, dead. Someone is going to pay for this. Before it's all said and done, someone is going to get strung up in that town. So I brought your man here, just so it ain't him."

Compson sat behind his desk and tented his fingers, nodding.

"I understand," he said. "These people have been friends to my cause. Maybe I should come out for the funeral."

"There's no funeral," Harry said, resisting the urge to spit. "They're all buried somewhere down in Virginia, though no one can say exactly where."

Compson pushed an envelope across his desk.

"I can't do this no more," Harry said, leaving the money on the desk and turning for home.

A week passed and still the preacher did not unlock the church doors. Each morning Harry collected the eggs, milked the cow, and managed the visitors that streamed in and out of the parlor bringing food.

He was expecting Mrs. Weber with her chicken pot pie when he opened the door to find Compson standing there.

"I've come to give my condolences," the commander said.

Harry led him into the parlor.

"Let me speak to these poor people in private," Compson said.

Harry sat on the front porch for a long while, watching the snow twist into tiny funnel clouds in the blustery wind until Compson came and sat next to him.

"Tell the men in Town Line that there will be a meeting at the schoolhouse tomorrow evening. This is civic business, not church. Tell them there will be schnapps," he said. "Even the heathens will come."

Harry spent the next day going door-to-door, and when the appointed time came, Compson greeted the farmers at the door of the mustard-yellow building. He poured them a glass of whiskey and clapped them on the shoulder. Harry had another jug, and circulated around the small schoolroom filling empty glasses.

The farmers' tongues loosened with the alcohol, and talk soon turned to the runaway slave and doings at the Willis place. They spoke of how Old Man Willis was held hostage by his wicked daughter and then they spit on the wide plank floorboards and demanded someone do something, but no one could say what.

Harry had stoked the potbellied stove, but with six score men crowded in, the room became stuffy, and efforts to bank the fire brought no relief. The four tall windows were thrown open, but the cold winter air did little for the men used to open fields and barns.

Compson motioned for the men to take their seats. Those that couldn't find a cramped desk stood in the aisles or against the bright yellow walls.

The pastor stood at the teacher's lectern at the front of the room and gripped its edges like it was his pulpit.

"Citizens of Town Line. *Wilkommen. Warm für November, nicht wahr?*" he said. "Warm for November, no?"

The farmers grumbled.

"We here, we have been through so much together, *nein*?" he asked. "Hard winters and dry summers. But here we are, with our farms, and if you are the lucky ones, your families, too."

Harry could see his blue eyes moisten in the long pause.

"I came here in '48, like many of you, *ja*?"

he asked. "Leaving the troubles of *Deutsch-land* behind. No? *Deutschland.* Do you miss it like me? It will always be my home. Every morning I woke to look at the mountains, and I would know that God watched over me."

He went to the chalkboard behind the desk, and drew an approximation of the German states.

"I had a big congregation there, many hundreds," he said, drawing a lopsided star in the lower right corner. "One day, the soldiers came and they took my son, my Alois. He was gone from us, forever. But praise God, I was able to get away with my wife and my youngest boy."

He drew a squiggly line, the east coast of America, and a childish ship, triangular sail, and waves between the two land masses.

"Like you, I came here. 'Good land for little money' is what everyone said. And all you had to do was plow your fields and milk your cows, and you can make a good farm to leave to your children. Isn't that what you want? Just to be left alone? *Nicht?*"

The farmers, dazed from the liquor and the warmth, seemed to be fading to sleep.

The pastor slammed his fist down on the desk and the farmers jerked awake.

"But then Abraham Lincoln became president!"

He went back to the blackboard and drew a line horizontally across the middle of the map and a flag in the bottom half, an X defining it as Confederate.

"Who here voted for the rail-splitter?" he asked, and his piercing eyes scanned the silent crowd.

Harry looked at a few he knew to be Union men, but they stared down at the wide plank floor in silence.

"No one!" the preacher said, his voice rising. "No one here voted for him. No one in the South voted for him, either, did they?"

He smiled at his own joke.

"How did he become president when so few people voted for him? Did he cheat? Did he steal the election? I don't know, but the question must be asked."

He stood in front of a farmer missing his front teeth. "What do you think, Klaus?"

The farmer looked around, surprised to be addressed.

"Maybe," he said.

"We might never know," the preacher said. "I do not believe he is our real president. He is not my president. Is he yours?"

The men were leaning forward.

"As soon as he is in, Lincoln says to the

269

people down South that they cannot live the way they always have. These people want to be free to live the way they always have, like you, like all Americans used to. But Lincoln says no, so they leave. They secede."

He ran over the horizontal line several times with chalk.

"That's a lie," Old Man Echols muttered from the front row. "That's not how it happened."

A few of the other farmers grumbled at the interruption and Compson stood and glared at him, saying, "Show some respect! This man just lost his son!"

Echols's face clouded. He stood, waved his hand in dismissal at the preacher, and picked his way through the crowded room to the door.

Zubrich waited for him to leave.

"Honest Abe says to those people, 'No, you cannot go,'" he continued. "Then he comes and asks for your sons to fight to keep these states under his power. Most say no, but some say yes. Where's Olaf Simke? Olaf?"

Simke stepped forward from the back wall. He was sweating in the warmth, and had his coat over his one arm and an empty whiskey glass in his hand.

"Olaf, where's your beautiful son, Christian? Where is Christian Simke?"

"*Er ist tot.* Dead."

"I'm so sorry," the preacher said, his voice all compassion. "Let us have a moment of prayer for Christian Simke."

He hung his head, and the farmers followed suit.

"And where? *Wo?*"

"Virginia. Bull Run."

"Bull Run!" Zubrich exploded. "A thousand miles away. They marched Christian Simke a thousand miles away to die! Did you see the pictures of this battle in the papers this summer? I could not believe it. Here they are — look at them."

He took up a ragged copy of *Harper's* magazine and held it aloft.

"Rich people from Washington City had picnics," he said. "They brought their families and had fried chicken and Riesling in fancy glasses and watched this battle, watched and drank wine while Christian Simke died."

He handed the magazine to a man in the front row.

"See for yourself," he grumbled.

Harry watched as the men looked at the magazine and passed it, each one getting angrier than the last at the months-old engravings.

"And now Vaness and Lafayette and Sylvester," he said, then paused, choking on his words.

"And now, Hans," he said, his voice cracking. "My dear boy, gone to God's glory."

Compson moved to support the preacher, but Zubrich pushed him away. Instead, he hung his head and prayed again.

"Through his life here in Town Line, Hans had only one friend he could count on. One boy who was always a good friend. Harry, come up here," he said, and motioned for Harry to join him.

Harry looked around, uncomfortable at being called to the front. The farmers all watched him and their eyes were filled with sadness.

Zubrich put his arm around him.

"Harry, here. He is a good boy. He lost all his friends, but when the news came, who is it that took care of me and my poor wife? Every day it is Harry taking care of us. A good boy."

The farmers nodded.

"Everybody knows, Hans and Harry never went anywhere without each other, at least not until this war. To this, Hans has to go. I told him no, but he has to go. And you, Harry, you told him not to go, yes?"

"Long before things started, I always said

only a fool would go," Harry said. "But he didn't pay no attention to me."

"He didn't listen to his father or his best friend. But who did he listen to? Who convinced him to go off to this war? Who is responsible for getting him killed?"

Zubrich scanned the crowd, as if he expected someone to answer. Finally, Harry spoke up.

"Leander Willis went through town and got all the boys to sign up."

The farmers rumbled their disapproval.

"And where is Leander Willis today?" the preacher asked.

"I hear he went to New York, though he don't dare write to me," Harry said. "Last I heard he was living it up in the big city with a fancy girl."

The murmur turned to anger as Harry left the lectern and sat down behind the preacher.

"Leander Willis sat in my parlor and told my boy they would fight together, him and all the others," Zubrich bellowed. "But they are all dead now while Leander Willis, the son of the rich man, he gets richer every day, and he eats steak every night. Does that remind you of anything?"

The men stirred.

"Is like Berlin in '48, no? The dukes and

273

kings? Don't you think?"

Olaf Simke waved his hand in dismissal.

"Olaf, you say, 'No, Nathan Willis is a good man, Nathan Willis helped me when I come here,' " Zubrich said, his voice reasonable. "But when was the last time any of you saw Nathan Willis? A long time ago, no? He is a sick man. His mind is not right."

Zubrich pantomimed an old man, bent with age, his mouth open and slack-jawed.

"Many of you here have worked for Nathan Willis, no?" the preacher asked. "Olaf, you worked for Nathan Willis, didn't you?"

"Ja," the farmer said.

"Did he pay you fair wages?"

"Ja, good pay," Simke said.

"Who is in charge now at the big farm, eh? Who?"

"Es ist seine Tochter."

"Yes, the daughter. She is quite the lady, no?"

The preacher scrunched his face and waved his finger at each of the men, like a schoolmarm scolding her students.

"All thorn, no rose," he said to the farmers' laughter.

"What is this world coming to? A good man like Nathan Willis lets his daughter run wild like that, to go off to her fancy school. She is so smart, no? The Bible tells us that women should honor their fathers, listen to their men. But that one! No. Not her! She is too smart for that. Too modern. She comes back here, all this talk of freeing the negroes, like that is any business of hers. What did Paul say to the Corinthians? 'Man is the head of a woman.' But not that one. She comes down from her mountain, and she tells us there should be no slaves and that the women, they should not have to listen to their men."

He slammed his fist on the desk again.

"She is godless!" he shouted and his knuckles whitened as they gripped the desk. "She will not hire good, hardworking Germans. No, this lady brings the niggers from the South to take that work away from good German boys."

He drew out the syllables of "lady" into a mocking tone.

"And what happens if King Lincoln wins his war and the slaves are free? What then?" he asked, shrugging his shoulders, scanning the crowd for an answer.

"I'll tell you what will happen. Those niggers will come here and take your jobs, take your farms," he said, his voice menacing.

"I got my gun," Franz Simke muttered. "They won't get mine."

"They'll be sorry, won't they?" Zubrich

replied with a smile. "They won't get you. Right?"

He stared at Simke until he nodded.

"But we know someone who tried to stop the niggers from coming already," he said and gazed across the room, expectantly.

"Our friend, Karl Wilhelm, God rest his soul."

The room went quiet.

"And who is responsible?" Zubrich asked.

A murmur of voices rumbled through the room.

"A nigger!" he shouted. "A runaway slave that he tried to catch, because the government said he should. Where is the justice? Poor Karl is dead, his wife has left us. And who pays for that? No one, that is who!

"What has happened to this country? What? I'll tell you what. The tyrant Lincoln. Abraham Lincoln thinks he is king. Just like Frederick William. Louis Philippe. Just like Napoleon Bonaparte. You came to America to get away from men like these, and now this Lincoln is worse than all of them. He will use the blood of your children to free these niggers and he will give your farms to them. He will give your sons, your farm, your food, your wives. Your wives! Who will sit still for this?"

The ones that were still sitting twisted in

their seats, while those standing shuffled back and forth, their anger feeding off of each other.

"Will you stand still for this?"

Zubrich slammed the desk again. "Not one year ago, Emperor Lincoln came through here on his private train, but he was too mighty, too grand to stop for little people like you and me. He is afraid of people like us, people who work the ground, people who grow things, people who make things. He wants to destroy you, just for his own glory. And how will he do that?"

He paused, his eyes darting across the crowd.

"The draft! The draft!" he shouted, his face crimson, his voice raw. "They will come to your door with guns and take your sons to die while they picnic. Just like they did in Frankfurt and in Baden and Bull Run. What say you? Shall we allow this?"

Their liquor-infused fear and anger had transformed the farmers into a mob that shook the tiny building with its shouting voices and stomping feet.

Harry looked over to see Compson smiling.

Zubrich, his shirt sweated through, gestured with his hands for the few men still sitting to rise as he started a chant of "No!"

The room pulsed in united denial and Compson's smile broadened.

"What do we say?" he repeatedly bellowed to the shouts of "No" and *"Nein"* again.

The preacher led them in a chant of "Hell no," pacing throughout the crowded room, his hands at each man's shoulder or back as the farmers raised their fists and pumped them in rhythm to their shouts.

He wandered slowly back to the front of the room.

"How do we say 'Hell No' to King Abraham? The same way Jefferson Davis did. We leave the Union. Why not us? We leave. Town Line. No country! No king! No governor! No army! Just us, no taxes! No draft! Just us, making our own way. We tell King Abraham to just leave us alone to raise our families."

"We will keep them from our door. We will keep them from our sons, we will keep them from our wives," Compson shouted, standing beside the preacher. "Who is with us?"

The men pounded on the desks and stomped their booted feet.

Compson reached into his coat pocket and pulled out a rolled piece of foolscap tied with a ribbon and handed it to the preacher.

"I have here a decree of secession," Zubrich shouted. "Who will sign with me? Who will tell King Lincoln to go to hell?"

He held the document high over his head, and men rushed to the front of the room while a few of the more sober stood to the back, watching.

1862

LOST

Dear Mary,

I'm writing from a homestead in Iowa. They call this place the town of Amana, though for the life of me I don't see any town. It's flatter here than any place I ever seen, and there isn't much in the way of trees to stop the eye, either.

I hid out in a tree in your woods for a while. When the rain got too much, I crossed over the creek and the Ebenezers let me stay with them. They are a strange little clutch of people. Most of them don't speak English, but when they found me laid up and sick one day, they put me in a room with their holy woman until I got better. They call her a werkzeug. She prayed over me in German for a long time, though I don't know what she said.

She speaks English sometimes, too, and told me that my heart was clouded and I needed to start new. She said I had too much sadness there and I should leave, so I hitched a ride with their next convoy out here. Now I'm here where even the dirt looks different. I should have probably just let the marshal hang me and get this over with, but I ran like a coward.

I think of you often, and your father. I hope he's doing better. I spied him once or twice before I left. I wish there was something I could do to ease your way. I thought long and hard about it when I was still there, and nothing came to mind. Another fugitive would just make your life harder.

I feel like a weed that's been pulled up and tossed in the barrow to be hauled away.

I fear that the marshal has my name posted all over the country, so I'm telling everyone here my name is John Bissell. I'll be moving on soon. Forgive me the evil I've done. I never thought to kill a man. He falls from that saddle every night in my dreams.

It pains me that you see me that way.
YOUR FRIEND,
CHARLIE

Mary stood in the hallway, steeling herself. She could hear Katia and her father inside her father's room, chatting and laughing.

Katia had made it clear that she blamed Nathan's condition on Mary. In fact, she seemed to blame the entire war on her and the fugitives she'd helped. At the same time, she understood it was the girl's constant attention that helped her father mend more than anything Mary had done.

When they had first brought Nathan home, Mary had been convinced that the way to cure him was to break him of his delusions. Each morning she would tell him that his beloved wife, Frances, was long-dead, and each morning she had to comfort him as if the news was fresh. The house would shake with his rage and confusion as he demanded to know what evil trick she was playing since she was, in fact, Frances herself.

It was Katia that convinced her to stop the hellish exercise. Mary relented, as much to relieve herself of the daily anguish as to help him. She felt as if she were giving up, but within days of the change, he stopped confusing her with her long-dead mother, instead calling her by her own name.

Now he lived in a nether world populated by both the living and visions of the long dead. Much to Mary's frustration, Katia took his chatter with the dead as proof of her long-standing claims of spirit visitation. Still, she could not deny that the hours in Katia's care were his most peaceful, whereas Mary's conversations left them both drained and brokenhearted.

Mary closed her eyes, took a deep breath, and opened the door. Katia stopped her prattling in midsentence, put down her needlework, and left without even looking at Mary.

Nathan was sitting in his armchair, staring out the window at the winter twilight. At first glance, he looked much like he always had, but the healthy cast of a man used to work had been supplanted by the sallow gray of someone who spent most of his time sitting. The spark of mischief that had always been in his eye had turned to a dimmed confusion. As she did each morning, Katia had trimmed his mustache, shaved his chin, and dressed him in a clean white shirt with a pressed collar. His white hair had grown back patchy, but Katia had combed it in a way to cover the scar.

"Where's your mother?" he asked.

"She's gone downtown for the day," she said, her heart tightening with the lie.

"Won't be long until we can start planting," he said, nodding out the window at the field. "Who do we have for a spring crew?"

"Nobody," Mary said. "We'll find some men, though. I promise."

"Get Leander to help," he said.

"He's not here, Father," she said.

"Where's he off to?" he asked.

"In the army, Father," she replied.

"Yes, that's right," he said, absently. "I'm proud of him. He's a good son."

Mary nodded. Even in the worst days, she'd hidden the things her brother had done.

She shuffled her feet and bit her lip.

"Father," she asked, "do you have any money hidden around the house?"

"What?" he asked, looking up at her. "What do you need money for?"

"Timber needs shoeing, and I haven't had a chance to get to the bank in a while," she said, her hands fidgeting deep in her apron pockets.

"I think there's thirty dollars in the safe," he said, confused.

"Do you have any hidden anywhere else?" she asked.

"Why would I hide money when I have a safe?"

She bit her lip and tried to smile at him.

"You'll just have to go downtown and take some out," he said.

"Thanks, Father," she said, and turned to leave.

Out in the hall, she bit hard into her lip and wrapped her arms around herself. She rushed down the stairs, past where Katia was working in the kitchen, pulled on her coat and boots, headed out into the snow-covered barnyard, then kept moving, back, back into the woods, each step breaking through the foot-deep cover of snow.

She gasped in the frigid air, taking in the cold, searing her lungs. She found herself at Leander's ramshackle wreck of a hut on the shore of the pond, and she fell to her knees, screaming out all the anger she'd held in for months.

The money was gone. All gone.

It had still been summer when Mary had gone to the downtown bank to draw cash for payroll, only to be told that Leander had cleared it out weeks before.

Struck dumb, she stared at the clerk as he pointed out that their father had given him signing rights at the beginning of the year, and the money was thus legally his. When she asked through gritted teeth how she was to pay the farmworkers, he offered her a loan if she could produce a man as a signatory.

She'd closed out her own little account, taking the meager cash that she'd saved from years of boiling sugar, and had doled it out to the useless workers for the rest of the season, hiding the shortage as best she could.

She'd made it through fall, but there were late rains and the workers had shirked so much work that the harvest was barely enough to keep the farm running, leaving no surplus to sell.

When the spring came, she'd need money to hire hands, but there was little left.

All the time, the letters and telegrams for her father had been coming. The army, among others, offering exorbitant prices for Willis lumber.

She'd even gone back to the mill herself, trying to understand how to jigger the sluice and blade to produce a straight board.

In November, an officer had come to the door, a draft in hand, offering to buy a ten-acre parcel of virgin timber on Town Line Road, but she couldn't bring herself to sell. She'd seen other plots harvested by the army, the trees clear-cut, their stumps left to rot in the ground. She couldn't imagine what her father would say to such a thing.

It was the hiding from him that hurt her the most. She couldn't tell him about Leander's betrayal, or that every penny he'd guarded so carefully all his life had been stolen in such an act of betrayal.

She thought of his raging at the repeated news of her mother's death and the confusion that followed for him, and she couldn't help but think such a thing would be the end of him.

There was so much that she had to keep hidden that she dreaded spending any time with him lest she let something slip.

And that left her completely alone.

She'd gotten a letter from Charlie the week before, and it reminded her of all those she'd lost in the previous months.

She missed the ease and the calm that he always seemed to bring into any room.

She missed her evenings in the cellar talking with Joe as he ate. She had sent dozens of letters and called on her father's friends trying to find a way to free him from the jail, but none had offered help.

There were even moments, fleeting times when his betrayals slipped away from her, when she missed her brother.

And then there was Hans. She liked to picture him laughing at one of Leander's jokes.

Somehow, she'd thought these people would always be here, and that even if she went away, she would be able to come back to a place frozen in time. Instead, she found herself frozen there, and alone.

She screamed her rage into the leafless trees again, but the sound was deadened by the thick blanket of snow, and all that answered her was cold silence.

She dropped her bare hands into the thick snow and stared down at the untouched white, the only sound her own breath.

And in the blank whiteness, she saw Joe's face, and she closed her eyes.

The numbing cold made her hands ache, but she stayed there, on her hands and knees, thinking of him, of how abandoned he must feel in that dark place. And how good it would be to have him back there with her.

She sat back, kneeling in the snow, and stared into the blue sky overhead. A cardinal, brilliant red against the snow, hopped down from a high branch to peck at a fallen pinecone, just feet from her.

She rubbed her nose with the back of her hand, and it cocked its head at her and chirped its song. She nodded to it, and it took flight.

Mary stood then, and stared at the faint

mark the bird had left. She brushed the caked snow from her knees, pulled her hair into place, straightened her back, and turned back to the house, knowing her way forward for the first time in months.

HOLE

**Richmond's *Daily Dispatch,*
February 4, 1862**

THE UNION FRACTURES

A deserter from the Union Army of Western New York reports that the fault lines of the Union have been aggravated by recent defeats, and the disintegration of the North is imminent. Late last year, in the first of what we expect to be many, the city of Town Line, New York, threw off the tyrant's shackles and declared itself an independent and sovereign state.

"We are our own state, with no allegiances beyond our borders," wrote Alois Zubrich, Sr., the local pastor and newly elected president. "Union Blues or Confederate Grays are assured safe passage within our borders, as long as they abide by the laws of Christ."

Even now towns throughout the North

are considering similar breaks from the tyrant.

Rest assured, loyal sons of Dixie, our cause is just, and there are freedom-lovers, even in the furthermost reaches of the Union that rally to us.

When Joe slept, he dreamed of Mary. He tried not to. When he lay down, he would try to think of Alaura or his mother, but Mary would come to him anyway. He dreamed of a little cabin in the woods. She would cook while he fixed the roof, climbing the ladder with both his legs.

There would be whole days in some of the dreams, and they would work together in the day and eat together in the evening and then they would go inside as the light faded. The details were burned into him. The way she danced by the sugar fire, the sidelong glances she sent his way as she shared her whiskey, even the sadness in her eyes whenever she spoke of her mother. Then that sound would come back to him. The wail she made as her father fell to the ground. It rang in his ears, jolting him awake.

In the dark he could hear madmen talking to themselves and petty thieves planning some elaborate and ill-fated scheme. There were lost souls, too, telling of each regret that led them to that place. The murmur permeated the night, making real sleep impossible.

They'd taken his peg, but no one had thought to search him for money. When the morning light came through the barred window, he would take out one of the coins she had given him and look at the profile of Liberty struck in gold.

During the day, his mind would drift to the books she'd lent him. His thoughts would slide to the one where the man was walled up in a dungeon, but again and again he turned back to the little hut by the pond.

The only way for Joe to mark the days was Kemuel, the white-haired black man that brought him his food and cleared the slop bucket. Nonsense words streamed from him like water through a millrace. There were stories about his cat and lists of groceries or people, but sometimes there was news, too, stories of armies amassing in this place or that.

"Hey, Pegleg," Kemuel said to him after he'd been there for a couple weeks. "You training to be a statue or something? You ain't moved an inch since you got here. You a runaway?"

Joe nodded.

"What's your name?"

"Joe," he replied.

"Joe what?" Kemuel demanded.

"Just Joe."

"Who's your owner man?" he asked.

"Old Mr. Bell, I guess," Joe said.

"Well, if that's his name, then that's your name. Bell. Joe Bell. That's what they'll call you when they round us up. That's what I hear they gonna do. Round us all up and send us back down South. Just to stop the war. Hell, I was born in Philadelphia, but they're gonna send me south anyway."

"They can't do that to you," Joe said.

"You ask the Cherokee about what they can do," Kemuel said.

A couple days passed before he said anything directly to Joe again.

"You still here? Usually they ship a runaway out by now. I guess this war has everything gummed up."

"Can you bring me something from the outside if I pay you for it?" Joe asked.

"I ain't bringing you no hooch," Kemuel said, suspicion in his eyes. "You just trying to get old Kemuel in trouble."

"No, nothing like that," Joe said. "Just some paper and pencils. I'll give you a dollar for them."

"A dollar for pencil and papers?" Kemuel

scowled. "What are you going to do with that?"

"There's some letters I want to write," Joe said.

"You probably want me to mail them, too," Kemuel said.

"No," Joe said. "Most of the people I want to write to are dead. I just want to write it down."

"I never seen one negro man in this hole knew how to write," Kemuel said. "I don't believe you."

"I've got a dollar. Gold," Joe said. "Bring me twenty cents' worth of paper and five pencils, and you can keep the rest."

Joe held up one of the gold coins and Kemuel reached for it, but Joe made a fist around it and held it tight.

"You bring me paper first," Joe said.

Kemuel scratched his chin and rubbed his hand under his nose.

"I don't suppose no one will care much about those kinda things," he said.

For three days, the caretaker acted like he'd never had the conversation, talking of nothing but the slaughter at Bull Run. On the fourth day he brought a bundle of blank pages wrapped in butcher paper and twine, along with a handful of pencils.

When Joe gave him the coin, Kemuel bit

it hard and then grinned.

"You need those pencils sharpened, you let me know. I'll take them outside and give them a whittle for you."

His started his letter to his sister warning her that it was hard in the North, maybe harder than back home. But then he wrote to her about Mary, and how this woman had fought for him, and he told her that maybe, somehow, she could find a friend like her, and that even in the worst times, that would make a difference.

He wrote to her of the walks they used to take around the plantation. He thanked her for the things she had brought him from the kitchen when she could. Sweets and sometimes fruit and cheese and meat that the master had left on his plate. He wrote about how she used to cry when they heard the hounds baying after some runaway, and he hoped that she hadn't cried too much when they were after him.

The next letter he wrote was to his mother, now dead fifteen years. He told her of life on the plantation after she'd gone, and how proud she would be to see Alaura.

He wrote to Nathan Willis and told him he was sorry for the trouble he'd caused. He even wrote to Yates Bell and told him how he was glad he didn't die. He wrote a letter to Charles Webster and thanked him for helping Mary.

Then he wrote to Mary, and filled six pages.

The next day he wrote to her again.

After a few days, he took another coin from the rag he'd hidden in his waistband and sent Kemuel for more paper.

The work made him tired in a different way. By the time the daylight would fade from his window, his shoulders and back were so stiff that he could barely move. The caretaker allowed him to keep his tray and he used it for a lap desk, and things got a little better.

At first, he told her of his escape from Walnut Grove, the path through the mountains and rivers. Then he wrote of the good days he'd had with his mother and sister on the plantation, of the fine spring afternoons when there was food to eat and the sun seemed to make his skin glow with warmth.

He wrote of the way his mother smiled when her children found a form of hares and stared in wonder at them.

Sometimes he would start to write the other stories, but he would only write a word or two, then stop himself.

He'd think of those nights when he was little more than a baby himself, and he wondered if maybe they were just a trick of his memory, something false that just seemed true. They were so long ago, he couldn't be sure.

He was certain of some things. The good things.

He could remember the old master bouncing him on his knee in the cool of the evening, laughing as Joe fingered his gold watch.

And he could remember the old man giving his mother the Bible that she would use to teach him to read.

Those he knew. He remembered the smell of the old master's breath, the tobacco and whiskey, and the neat, clipped line of the old man's white mustache as he held the watch aloft for Joe to play with.

He wondered how things were for Alaura back at Walnut Grove, whether she'd been punished for him running off, and whether things were worse or better for her and the rest now that the war had come.

He'd get lost in worry for her, staring at the cell wall, his eyes twisting the patterns of the rough brick into faces in pain.

He found ways to exercise in the tiny cell, pushing himself off the stone floor or hopping on his foot, just so he could feel motion.

The days got shorter, and the wind that came in through the barred window got colder.

He wrote about the books Mary had lent him, and he remembered books she had said he should read but that she didn't own. He wrote a title on a scrap and sent Kemuel out with another gold coin.

When he couldn't think of anything else to tell Mary, he wrote about the jail keeper's ramblings, telling of the cat's adventures and what he needed to buy at the market that day.

"The man in the bookstore laughed when I showed him this name," Kemuel said, holding up a thin brown volume. "What is it about?"

Joe smiled, took it from his hand, and opened to the title page.

"*The Last Day of a Condemned Man*," he read. "Victor Hugo."

"That's not really something to laugh about," Kemuel said.

"No, no, it's not," Joe said.

Snow seeped in the window that night.

He spent the short daylight hours exercising or reading and rereading the book, making notes in the margins. He struggled with some of the words at first, but he read them again and again, and they made sense to him soon.

Before the light faded each evening, he'd write to Mary for a few minutes, and then, after the dark had fallen, he'd finger his one remaining coin, running his fingertip over the woman's face.

The nights had gotten so long and the days so short that he'd begged Kemuel for a candle to read by, but the old man wanted to be paid for it and Joe wouldn't give up his last coin. So he sat for hours before sunrise with his eyes closed, wondering what Mr. Thoreau would be doing then. He was sitting that way when a tall white man appeared at the door to the cell, held up a lantern, and unlocked the door.

The jailer tossed Joe's peg onto his cot.

"Joe Willis," he said.

Joe shook his head.

"That's not me," he said.

"No, it's you, boy. Let's go, don't make me go in that shit hole and get you," he said, standing outside the cell.

Joe strapped the peg back on, picked up his bundled papers and his book, and limped out of the cell.

The guard led him to a concrete room and stripped his filthy clothes from him. The last gold coin fell to the floor and Joe went down on his knee, scrambling for it. The guard heaved a bucketful of water at him and kicked him a cake of soap. Joe covered his eyes with his clutched hands as the rough bristles of a long-handled broom tore at his skin.

"The judge don't want you stinking," the guard said, handing him a tunic and loose pants stitched from burlap. He stumbled through a maze of dark hallways until he was finally pushed into a courtroom.

He was so dazzled by the morning sun streaming in through the high windows that his knee buckled and the guard had to grab him before he fell. The light painted bright white boxes on the dark wood floor and illuminated a woman where she stood in front of the judge's bench. She wore a black dress with her hair covered in a lace bonnet. Her face was powdered white and her hair pulled into a severe bun. The courtroom was empty except for her and the judge, who looked down on the woman in consternation.

"There's thousands of slaves flooding across the battle lines, and no one knows what to do with any of them," the judge growled. "They aren't slaves anymore. The army calls them contraband when they arrive in their camps, but I don't know what that means. We will not send them back to the enemy, and the police now arrest the hunters on the same streets where the slaves were arrested a year ago. What is your interest in this one?"

"He is a sawyer," the woman said.

At the first word, he knew it was Mary.

"The army requisitions lumber from us every month, but my father is too ill to run the mill," she said.

"You take care of him," the judge said. "He is a good man."

"He is not well, but with God's mercy . . ." Mary said. "He cannot run the mill. This man can. He can help the cause."

"She says you're from Virginia," the judge said, turning to Joe. "What plantation?"

"Walnut Grove," Joe said. "Harpers Ferry."

"Harpers Ferry? That area has been overrun so many times, there's nothing there left to fight over."

Joe could feel his heart sinking.

"Alaura," he whispered to himself.

"What?" the judge asked.

"My sister," Joe said. "I left my sister there."

"I hope she's a fast runner," the judge said. "Good luck to her. Maybe she'll end up here."

"Is he free?" Mary asked.

"Take him with you," the judge said. "I don't know what to do with him, but we don't need him in jail for doing last year what hundreds are doing every day now."

He motioned to the bailiff.

"Get him out of here before someone notices."

The bailiff pushed him forward and he stumbled into Mary. She offered an arm, helped him back up.

"Thank you, sir," she said.

She kept her head lowered as she took Joe by the arm and rushed him past the empty tables and gallery, through the oak doors, and into the morning. He shielded his eyes from the brilliant sun reflecting on a fresh landscape of snow.

"Fast, and keep your head down," she said, pulling at him hard as he stumbled down the snow-dusted marble steps. She kept looking left and right even as she helped him into a waiting cab. They rode to the train station where she rushed him through the terminal and into a car. She continued to scan the platform and the ticket booths, shushing him every time he tried to speak.

Only when the train jerked into motion and cleared the platform did she turn to him with a broad smile.

"That wasn't precisely legal," she said as the train gained speed. "I wouldn't want to be there when Kidder catches wind of it."

He could not get his voice to work, could not say anything to meet the measure of the moment, but he looked full into her serious, joyful eyes and she did not look away.

He wanted to take her in his arms, he wanted to throw her in the air and scream at the top of his lungs, but the smattering of other riders were already staring at the odd pairing.

The train whistle blew as they approached the Cheektowaga station.

"I thought they were leading me to the gallows," he said finally.

"They are barbarians," she said. "They wouldn't let me into the jailhouse to see you. I've called on every lawyer or judge that owed my father a debt, but none would do me any favors. Finally, I remembered Judge Tolliver. He used to scold me for being an immodest little girl when I wore Leander's breeches, but he is a Quaker, and sympathetic to the cause.

"I knew I could appeal to him if I did my best to look like a pious young Quaker lady," she said, fidgeting with the front of her plain black dress. "Don't I make a fine-looking widow?"

"I thought you were a messenger from God when I saw you," he said.

She smiled, and through the heavy powder, he made out a sprinkle of girlish freckles on her cheeks that had somehow remained hidden to him until then.

"Of course, I won't hold you. You can go over to Canada anytime you want," she said, looking down and pulling the white gloves from her hands. "But I'll pay you a decent wage if you stay to work the mill. We get telegrams nearly every day asking for lumber and my father can't work anymore."

"He is alive?" Joe said.

She nodded, and it seemed the daylight brightened.

"Somehow," she said. "But he is not himself."

She looked down at her fingers, picking at her thumb nervously.

"I have so much to say to you," he said. "I've written you, but now that I'm here with you, I'm too embarrassed for you to see it."

He held up the filthy ream of paper.

"You must let me see it," she said, reaching for it. He smiled and held it away. She laughed and reached for it, playfully, and he breathed deep, taking in the smell of soap on her skin.

She settled back into her seat and looked him in the eye, serious again, but not fearful, as she had been in the station. He felt dizzy as the train rattled and swayed as the track curved toward Town Line. He wanted to reach for her hand, to hold it as he had before she'd covered him with the tarp a lifetime ago, but he knew that such an act, and the things that could follow were more dangerous than anything else he could imagine.

He set his face grimly, looking back at the smattering of passengers that were watching them.

"You're alone there, aren't you?" he asked.

Her face darkened, first with sadness, then a wave of anger.

"Don't you dare pity me," she snapped. "Not you. Not coming from that place."

The conductor came through the car and she fished the tickets from her bag.

"You must be starving," she said. "You look almost as skinny as the day you first came to me."

"Of course I'll stay," he said.

When the train slowed for the Town Line station, he stood to get off, but she pulled him down.

"Not here," she said. "The wagon is at Doc Pride's in Alden. I won't go through the crossroads if I can avoid it. They spit at me in Town Line."

In Alden, people on the sidewalks stared at them as she drove through the center of the town. She looked ahead, her back straight, ignoring them all.

TERMINUS

Joe's worked the mill nonstop for months. Tomorrow, we'll take the fourth load in as many weeks downtown. Perhaps with that money in hand, this clenching in my chest will finally subside.

My load has already eased so much with him here. It's more than the work he does. I feel now that there's a way forward, that all is not lost.

He helped birth an early lamb today. He held up the squalling thing and suggested we name it Katia. I laughed so hard, I fell to my knees beside him. I can't say how long it's been since I laughed at all.

It's an early spring. Leaves are already opening on the trees. I've been searching high and low for a crew to work the fields, but even if I could find them, no Union men will come to a seceded town.

Joe tells me he's heard there's black men over the border looking for work, so we'll ride over to see what we can find after we make the sale.

— MARY WILLIS'S JOURNAL,
APRIL 14, 1862

A weak sun burned off the last of the morning fog as they drove side by side through the crossroads in the lumber-laden wagon.

In Cheektowaga, they rode through a band of blue-uniformed soldiers marching toward the waterfront, and Mary looked at them closely, scanning for any faces she might know. Though she doubted they'd want anything to do with her, she longed to see any of the old Town Line boys alive.

At the docks, they were able to sell the timber right off the wagon at a price so high that Mary would have felt guilty collecting it if she did not need money so badly.

After the wagon was emptied, they rode onto the ferry for Fort Erie.

As the flatboat left the dock, they both leaned against the wagon, watching the water and chunked ice pass under the high blue sky. Half-frozen Erie stretched out vast on the port side and Mary tried in vain to find the plume of Niagara Falls to the North.

"I stowed away on one of those on the Allegheny," Joe said, pointing to one of the many steamers on the lake. "It's how I got upriver. An old cook hid me below and brought me what food he could. In the middle of the night, he took me up to the deck, and he gave me a little keg. He said, 'I hid a little bit of food in here and it should keep dry. Now, when you can see some lights on the shore, take it with you and jump overboard. It'll keep you floating until you get to shore.'

"It was about New Year's Day," he said, facing into the cold wind coming off the lake. "The water was so cold I thought I'd die. I held on to that keg with everything I had and kicked my feet and came up on that eastern shore. I think if I'd gone off the west side, I might be in California now." He paused. "I always wanted to go to California. I read they have trees there bigger than mountains."

"I have a friend there, a roommate from school," Mary said, looking west for a long moment. "She told me the walruses and seals climb right up and sit next to you on the beach. I'd love to see that someday."

"The railroad will be done soon," he said. "It will take you all the way to San Francisco. You should go see your friend then."

Mary turned and looked at his dark eyes, "Why haven't you gone? You could have left all my troubles behind you."

He looked down.

"You might guess," he said and touched her elbow lightly through her coat. She felt something run through her.

He turned to look at the docks receding behind them, and then back at the oncoming shore. "I think we're past the halfway point, don't you?" he said.

"I think so," she said distractedly, her hand on the place where he had touched her.

"I'm free," he said, almost a whisper.

She looked at him, confused.

"We're in Canada," he said. "I'm a free man."

The boat rocked under her feet, and she stumbled a little as she looked into his face. She had been so caught up in her own worries that she hadn't considered what the trip meant to him. Emotions played across his face, first joy, then sadness, then regret.

"I wish Alaura was here," he said.

He moved to brush away tears, but she reached up and stopped his hand.

"Don't," she said. "They may be the most beautiful thing I've ever seen."

He held her eyes, and put his rough callused fingertips on the back of her hand. She looked down, straightening her coat and her bonnet.

"I should be ashamed of myself. How could I have not considered this occasion?" she said. "I should have planned something, brought a gift or some such thing. I guess I stopped thinking of you as a slave long ago."

He smiled. "That's as much of a gift as I could ask."

When they drove the wagon off the flat-boat, Joe took the reins and turned north. The roadway was overhung by red maples. The new leaves glowed ruby in the spring sun like the stained glass of a cathedral.

They came into the village of St. Catharines and found a pocket of ramshackle buildings where black faces peered out from opened doorways. A woman with a baby in a sling pointed them to the church, a simple brick building with pointed arch windows and a twin staircase.

"I heard there's chicken and slicks to-night," the woman said, her Kentucky accent thick. She looked them over and added, "But y'all don't look like you need food."

"We need workers," Mary said.

"For what?" she said, her eyes lidded.

"Farmwork," Mary said. "Good work for a decent wage back in the States."

The woman's face clouded.

"You pay a good wage and come all the way up here to hire black folks?" she asked. "I'll believe that when I see it."

Eyes watched them from shaded porches and through dark windows.

Behind the church, a clutch of women were gathered around a steaming cauldron under a ragged canvas canopy. Laughing children chased each other through the muddy field behind them.

When Mary and Joe climbed down from the wagon and approached, a black priest with a fringe of snow-white hair and soup-steamed spectacles pushed his way through the women.

"Can I help you?" he asked, wiping his hands on his white apron.

Men filtered over from the houses, some holding knots of wood.

"We've come looking for hands for the season," Mary said. "Back across the border."

"That so?" the priest asked. "Not sure we can help you."

Mary eyed the skinny children. Their mothers followed her gaze and called them to their hips, where they stared silently at the white lady and the one-legged negro.

"I'm offering a good wage, a bunk in a

watertight cabin with a warm stove, and three square," Mary said, defensively. "I would think there'd be men eager for the work."

"There's nobody here going back across that border with you," the priest said. "You might as well turn around and tell that to whoever sent you."

Mary shifted on her feet.

"Nobody sent us," she said.

Slowly, wordlessly, the women in the crowd slipped back while the men stepped in front of them.

"This is a fair offer from a good woman," Joe said. "I've been on this farm for a good while, always been treated good. You can trust her."

"And who are you?" one of the men in the crowd growled. "I don't know you."

"What's going on here?" Mary said. "What have we done to you?"

"You bounty hunters come up here, offering up this or that to get people back across that border," the priest said. "We know your ways. There's always someone waiting on the other side with chains."

The circle of men had closed in and she could see no way past them. The men stared back at them with hard eyes.

Joe pushed his way in front of her.

"If you don't want the work, then we'll just leave," he said.

"Yeah, you will," one of the men growled, but the crowd tightened in on them.

"Is that you, Miss Mary?" a woman's voice shrieked from the back of the crowd. Mary turned toward the sound.

"Lord, it is," the same voice called out.

A woman shoved her way to them, jostling the men out of her way.

It took Mary long seconds to recognize the woman she'd helped come up from Alfred years before.

"Sophie, look at you!" Mary blurted, though she was shocked at how gaunt the woman had grown in the years since they'd ridden side by side in the first-class car of the New York and Erie.

"You get away from her," Sophie said, putting herself between Mary and the line of men. "She ain't gonna hurt you."

She took Mary into her arms.

"You'll have to go through me to get at her," she warned. "She's the one who saved me and my little Abbey. I told you all about her. She's the brave one, faced down that old fat marshal, bought me and my baby a ticket on the train. I told you all before."

Shoulders dropped and eyes softened across the crowded faces.

"Yes, I remember, Sophie," the priest said, motioning the men back as he extended his hand.

"I'm Brother Hiram," he said. "Forgive us our rudeness. You are most welcome here. Times are so that we can't tell our friends from those who would do us harm."

"Who you got here?" Sophie asked, eyeing Joe.

"This is Joe," she said. "He works on the farm."

"You really hiring black folks?" Sophie asked, her voice rising with interest. "I just don't believe it. But if anyone would do it, it'd be you, Miss Mary. You just ask, we'll be there in no time. Me and Palmer and little Abbey. Malcolm will come, too."

Mary hesitated.

"Malcolm and Palmer only," she said. "It's not safe for women and children. The folks out there won't be happy when I show up with a wagon full of negroes."

"These men can hold their own if there's honest work," Brother Hiram said. "How many do you need?"

"I can use a half-dozen men for planting, and come summer, perhaps one or two more to help on the sawmill, and then another four or five for the harvest."

"I think we can come to an agreement,"

Brother Hiram said.

They dickered over arrangements while the priest tended the soup.

"It's one chicken in a pot for thirty people," he said. "A humble meal, but we'll share what we can. The men will all be here, and we can work out who will go with you. They'll be ready in the morning."

Mary asked Sophie if there was a store nearby and Sophie directed her across town.

She and Joe drove the wagon over and Mary spent some of the lumber money. They returned with a sack of cornmeal and another of flour and a bushel of cabbages. A trio of chickens squawked in a wicker cage and Mary plopped a pair of whiskey jugs in front of the pastor.

"If the families have to be apart, then there should be a going-away party," she said.

Word of the feast spread quickly and the women dove into the provisions. The fire had been stoked against the evening dark and the tables were gathered around it against the coolness of the spring night.

Sophie introduced Mary to all her friends like she was a prize she had won while Joe asked everyone he could if they'd seen a girl with different colored eyes, or anyone else from down near Harpers Ferry.

When the food was gone, instruments appeared and the sound of music filled the night air. Couples took to a patch of hard earth and danced. A crock of applejack was passed around with the whiskey, and Mary drank freely. Joe heard a tune he knew and wobbled into the dancing crowd, hopping and jumping on his one leg, clapping in rhythm.

He pulled Mary from the bench and into the crowd, and she laughed as he twirled her around. She slipped and he caught her in his arms, nearly toppling himself, struggling to stay upright as he balanced on his one good leg and his peg. She dangled upside down for a moment and she felt as if she floated in the heavens.

Afterward, the pastor directed them to a farmhouse where the owner, a stern man with a large goiter, looked the two of them over before offering the foreman's room to Mary and blankets and the adjacent hayloft to Joe.

She helped Joe pull together a sleeping pallet in the loft and went into the room and closed the door.

She changed into her nightclothes and lay in the cornhusk bed still humming the tune they'd danced to. The room spun and she wasn't sure if it was the whiskey or the leftover sensation of dancing. She lay there for a long time, hot despite the cool of the room, listening to the farm animals and the wind in the eaves. She could still feel his arm on her back where he had caught her, his fingers on her elbow where he had touched her.

She slept lightly, her dreams tangled with the smell of the animals in the barn below her and thoughts of him nearby. She woke before the dawn, and watched the light come up, feeling free of the weight of the farm, dreading the return to the obligations there.

She opened the door to the loft where he lay.

"We could go," she said. "We could leave from here, never go back. Leave everything to Katia. We are not wanted back there."

"Mmm," he said, sleepily. "Go where?"

"California," she said. "We could go see the trees taller than mountains, see the sun set over the Pacific Ocean."

Joe rubbed his face as he sat up. "California," he said.

He looked at her a long time, hope and sadness playing over his face.

"Each day I feel a hole where the ones I left behind should be," he said softly. "Such a thing would ruin you."

A cow lowed in the morning light and she dropped her eyes.

They rode quietly through the morning to the church where a small crowd had gathered. Palmer held his daughter, while Sophie fussed over a towel full of biscuits. Malcolm chatted with the other men heading for the farm. Mary and Joe watched as one by one, the men stepped away from their families and climbed onto the wagon. Brother Hiram said a short blessing before the wagon rolled out of the little churchyard. While Joe drove, Mary turned and watched as the wives and children stood and waved good-bye.

GRAY

Yates had been in a hotel in Montreal when he finally received Levant's letter telling him that his father was dead. It was three months old by then, but it came just in time. He was almost broke and he wasn't eager to take another winter in the Now, at last, Walnut Grove was his.

It had been a year since he'd been home.

He'd followed up on every one of the telegrams he'd taken from his father's desk so long ago, and he'd been through the hovels of New York's docks and the parlors of Philadelphia. He'd fallen ill in Detroit, and was laid up in a dirty room above a saloon with fever for two months, spending his days staring out over Lake Michigan and dreaming of the nigger.

He'd torn through the fugitive hovels on the outskirts of Montreal the week before and was convinced that Joe wasn't there.

He was ready to concede that Joe had

probably not made it out of the Allegheny River on the night he'd run.

Yates rode south the next morning, crossing into Vermont near St. Albans and then riding down into the Hudson Valley. He camped deep in the woods as a precaution, but no one paid him much mind when they saw him.

Through Pennsylvania, he saw more blue uniforms on the road, but he gritted his teeth and rode on past them.

He was stopped three times near the Maryland border, twice by Yankees and once by Confederates. Each time he showed the madam's letter. The Yankees waved him through, not caring much about an errant Southerner, but eventually a gray-uniformed Confederate took him by gunpoint into his CO's tent.

"What unit are you with?" the officer had asked.

"I'm not with any," he said. "I was with Bott's Greys before the war, but have been in Canada most of the time since then."

The grim-faced man read the letter again, lifted it to his nose.

"Why haven't you enlisted?" he asked. "Surely you've been drafted."

"I've been north," he said. "There was no way to reach me."

"But the whore found you."

"I have my priorities," Yates said with a smile. The officer didn't smile back.

"Go home and get your affairs in order," he replied. "Bott's Greys are under Jackson now — they're camped over near Manassas. I'm sure they're expecting you."

The frost was thick when he rose the next morning and rode on.

The next day, he heard a din in the distance and rode toward it in the dimming light. He was leading the horse through a thicket in the darkening woods when he found himself on the top of a ridge overlooking a broad plain.

White canvas tents stretched as far as the eye could see. Campfires punctuated the night, and countless men in blue uniforms surrounded them, laughing and playing music.

He led the horse away, deep into the woods and slept that night without a fire.

The next day he was into the territory of Kanawha, or West Virginia, or whatever they were calling it in Washington. It had broken off from Virginia the year before by a vote that included none of its citizens, and was putting itself through the machinations to become part of a union it hated to the core. The forest blazed in fall colors, the hills rolled into the horizon and somehow, he felt he was home.

He came into Harpers Ferry the next morning. The streets were abandoned, and he passed three burned-out ruins on his way to the office of his father's lawyer on Washington Street.

He was quickly ushered into Mr. Philips's office.

"Yates?" Philips said, a look of shock on his face. "What are you doing here?"

"I'm here to see about my father's will."

"Of course, of course, have a seat," the lawyer said, motioning to a chair. "It's just that . . . the army has asked me for your whereabouts several times. You've been drafted, as nearly everyone else has been, and they've been looking for you."

"I've been in Montreal," Yates said.

"Looking for Joe?"

Yates nodded. "I only learned last week of my father's death. How did he die?"

The lawyer got up and walked around to lean on the front of his desk.

"The Yankees wanted Walnut Grove," he said. "He made it hard for them, but they took it anyway. We've buried him out at Sandy Hook."

Yates's stomach twisted at the thought of

his father fighting the Union Army on his own.

"I guess if he was going to die, that's how he'd have it," he said. "Fighting to save that place."

"There's the better part of a battalion camped in the west fields," he said.

Yates blinked.

"The Yankees occupied my plantation?" he asked. "Are they paying for it?"

The lawyer cocked a bushy gray eyebrow at him.

"You're not going to collect rent from the Yankees? Not much of a patriot, are you?"

"It's mine. How do I get it back?" Yates asked.

Philips took off his glasses and rubbed his eyes. He went to a cart and poured a glass of bourbon and put it in front of Yates.

"It's complicated," he said.

"Complicated?"

"Your father changed his will after you left," he said.

He went over to a cabinet and pulled out a file folder, sat behind the desk, and opened it in front of him.

"You see, his will frees Joe, accepts him as his lawful son, and splits the estate evenly between the two of you, with a generous stipend for Alaura."

The tumbler of bourbon dropped from Yates's hand and smashed on the floor. He ran his hands through his filthy hair. He gripped the arms of the chair to prevent himself from falling out.

"What?" he croaked.

"Alaura and Joe are your half-siblings," Philips said. "And your father has left half the estate to them."

Yates's knuckles whitened as he gripped the arms of the chair.

"He can't do that," he said.

"You're right, he probably can't," Philips said. "There are remedies. No Southern court would allow it, that I'm certain of. But we're in a territory occupied by a federal force, and the occupying government is trying to attain statehood. Nothing makes much sense here. The irony is that come January first, this damned Emancipation Proclamation is set to take effect. He won't be a slave in the North. And he won't be a slave in the Confederacy, but damned if he wouldn't still be a slave here in the territory of West Virginia."

He got up and poured himself a drink, and filled a second for Yates. He handed it to him, lingering overlong to make sure that Yates's grip would hold.

"I'm not willing to hand the keys to one

of the finest plantations in the South to a nigger," Philips said. "I'll fight this with you. I'll argue that it should be invalidated based on insanity if you'll permit me. I'll do whatever I can."

"Joe's dead," Yates said. "I tore through the better parts of two countries and didn't find a sign of him. I'm sure of it."

"That's helpful," Philips said. "That might help the court move the issue along, but we got another telegram after you left. It'll need to be followed up on."

Philips riffled through the file of papers and found a telegram.

"There's a Marshal Kidder in Buffalo said he's captured him in April of last year," he said. "You been up there?"

"Not Buffalo, no."

"Honestly, I'd hoped the Yankee prison would have ended the need for us to solve this problem. Maybe it has."

"Marshall Kidder?" Yates asked.

"Don't get any ideas," the lawyer said. "You've been drafted. Report for duty. They've already shot a few deserters, and when the winter comes, it's going to get much worse. At the very least, you'll get no sympathy from the court if you are wanted as a deserter," Philips said.

"I'll need money." Yates nodded. "I have

to equip myself."

Philips smiled. "Of course," he said. "However much you want. You're a Bell of Walnut Grove. I can give you a loan against your share of the property."

He provisioned for a long ride at the general store and set out straight north that day.

A Confederate scout found him that night as he made camp south of the Pennsylvania border.

"Seen your fire," he said from atop his horse. "Mind if I share?"

Yates gestured for him to sit, and the man climbed down from his horse.

"Nice animal," Yates said.

"Trey Williams," the scout said, taking off his glove and offering his hand. "Fifty-third."

"Yates Bell. Bott's Greys."

Williams sat on the ground and offered Yates a filigreed flask. When Yates shook his head, he put it back in his coat without drinking.

"Bott's? Out of Harpers?"

Yates nodded.

"I heard they sent you boys over Maryland way. What the hell you doing way up here?"

"I've got business."

The scout waited for more, but Yates offered nothing.

"Is that cornbread?" he asked, pointing at the skillet in the fire.

"Just the way my dear mammy used to make," Yates said, smiling and nodding.

He pulled a plate from his pack and handed it across the fire.

"I was hoping we'd have beaten them Yankees before the winter came down," Williams said.

"We're never going to beat them," Yates said.

Trey looked up from the fire, surprise and anger in his eyes.

"Of course we are," he said. "They're cowards. Look at how we slaughtered them at Manassas. A couple more like that, and we'll be rid of them. We just need to keep at it."

Yates looked at Williams out of the corner of his eye and shook his head.

"I saw a Union encampment two days ago," Yates said. "Probably wasn't a million, but sure looked like it, lined up row to row to row. It was an entire city, just waiting to kill us all. I was in New York City a month ago, and the streets are full of men and boys like there was nothing going on down here."

He poked at the fire.

"We can kill them all we want," he said.

"They'll just keep coming. We have to make them pay some other way. That's what I'm aiming for, just to make them pay."

After they finished their mess, Yates stoked the fired against the cold night and lay out his bedroll while Trey wrote in a little brown notebook. When he was done, the scout climbed to his feet and went into the bushes. He was still buttoning his trousers when he came back into the fire's circle to find Yates pointing a pistol at him.

"I'm not going back," he said.

"I'll not cotton to any deserter," the scout said.

"The Yankees killed my daddy," he said. "There's an entire battalion of them living off my plantation. There's this runaway up north. He's ruined everything. He drove my mother away, and he split me and my father. He nearly killed me, and now I have to kill him. I'm suffering plenty for the cause."

Trey shook his head. "My captain might understand and let you move on," he said. "But it's not for me to decide."

"It's not for him, either," Yates said, and pulled the trigger.

He covered the body with the man's bedroll, took a bottle of bourbon from his own pack, and sat down by the fire.

"I wish I hadn't had to do that," he said,

looking down at the covered corpse. "I know now, there's one thing God put me on this world to do, and I've let too many things get in my way. I won't let anything else."

In the morning, he went through the scout's saddlebags for provisions and packed some jerky and ammunition. He put the Bible he found in Trey's graying hands, and left his horse to stand guard against the circling vultures.

He rode north again, but midway through the day he heard gunfire in the distance, enough for him to guess there was a full-on skirmish. He headed away from the noise, west and south into the mountains.

It snowed during the night, and he sheltered under a tall cedar.

He headed farther up into the Alleghenies to avoid scouts from either side, but the winter found him in the high country. He holed up in a cave for three days with a fever and got snowed into an abandoned cabin in a high pass soon after that. He was there for three weeks and had to shoot the horse. His Christmas and New Year's feasts were both horseflesh carved off the frozen corpse and boiled in melted snow.

After that, he struck straight north again, heading for the big lake. His beard grew thick and scraggly, and he stayed away from roads and little towns.

On the ferry across ice-chunked Erie, there were four other men as rough-looking as he, and they avoided each other's eyes like the wanted men they all were.

The crossing took seven hours, and the rocking of the boat on the inland sea brought him back to an ocean crossing he'd made as a child. The waves and the smell of the air off the water had entranced him then, and did again now.

He stepped off the ferry in Nanticoke. He took a deep breath of the frigid Canadian air, and doubled over with a coughing spasm.

On his second day in Canada he came to a cluster of snow-covered ramshackle houses. Hoping to find a meal, he knocked on a door, only to have a runaway nigger woman open it.

He grabbed her around the throat, and pressed the muzzle of his pistol to her head.

"Where's Joe Bell?" he hissed.

"Joe who?" she asked, terror in her voice.

He dragged her from hovel to hovel, kicking on the doors and threatening to kill her if they didn't produce his slave. Each shack was tiny, with no place to hide, and he could see they held nothing but squalling brats and frightened women. In the last one, he found a haunch of venison spit over a fire and wrapped it in a greasy rag.

He cut pieces from it during the rest of the day's hike and was gnawing the last of the meat from the bone as he came into Fort Erie.

At the waterfront, he could see the Yankee city of Buffalo across the wide river, and visions of it burning flashed before him.

He watched the gaslights go on as night fell, then found two men with a jon boat for hire to carry him over the wide river under the cover of darkness.

He scouted around the city during the night.

Parts of it made him remember the broad avenues of Washington. Well-dressed ladies and gentlemen rode in coaches under the streetlamps. A coughing spasm came over him and he sat on a wooden bench to catch his breath. A gray-whiskered man tossed a coin at his feet and told him to buy a meal.

Near the canal, though, it was Gomorrah.

Liquor was everywhere. Drunks tottered out from the gin mills, past the whores that called to every passing man.

But not to him. He had not bathed since Harpers Ferry and the women that passed him on the street cowered like he was a wild animal. There were many black faces here and each one made his blood boil. The riches of the South, stolen and gone to seed. He scanned the passing faces for signs of Joe, though he doubted the serious boy would ever be in such a place.

He wanted to strike them all down. He fingered the pistol in his coat pocket and imagined himself barging into one of the taverns and taking as many down with him as he could. But like the Yankee tents arrayed in the Maryland field, there were too many.

Eventually, he found a thicket of woods to the north of the city and camped by the river.

He didn't have to ask around much. It was midday when he found the marshal in a tavern, a plate of sausages and a mug of beer in front of him.

"Kidder?" Yates asked, standing above him at the table.

The fat man looked Yates up and down.

"Ten dollars if you want a warrant served," the marshal said. "Another ten if I have to ride out of the city."

"I'm here for my nigger."

The marshal stared at him.

"Joe Bell."

Kidder's eyes narrowed.

"I was expecting a Southern gentleman . . ." he said, wiping grease from his face with his coat sleeve.

"There's no place for a gentleman in this land," Yates said.

"It's close to two damned years since I sent that telegram," the marshal said. "You can't expect me to still have him."

"I'll pay you the thousand when you deliver."

Yates flashed a roll of notes.

The marshal eyed the bundle.

"Let me go check at the jail to see if they still have him," he said. "This might take a while."

Yates told him where he'd camped.

"The river is cold, but it's clean down there," the marshal said. "You might spend a little of that on soap."

Yates went back to his camp, and knelt, waiting silently for any movement around him. When a muskrat climbed out of the river, he shot it and lunged into the water to catch it before the current carried it toward the distant falls. He was kneeling in the water skinning it for his dinner when Kidder finally came around.

"They let them all go, all the runaways," the marshal said. "Because of the war, no need to hold them."

"Where's Joe?" Yates asked, coming out of

337

his crouch, knife still in hand.

"I don't know," the marshal said. "But I have some ideas. He was headed to Canada when I caught him. Maybe he had people up there? I can find him, but we'd have to negotiate a price."

"Negotiate a price?"

"Well, there's the thousand reward, then the board for him for the year we had him, then my time hunting him. I have expenses, you know."

"You let my nigger go, and you want to negotiate a price?" Yates asked.

"I didn't let anyone go," the marshal said, backing away. "The judge did. I don't run the operation."

Yates jabbed the knife with a quick, smooth thrust, cutting through the marshal's coat and piercing his chest. Kidder looked up, cupping the blood that poured from the wound at his heart. His knees buckled as Yates stepped forward and kicked him in the chest. He fell backward and splashed into the cold water. Screaming, he flailed his arms uselessly as the river pulled him away from shore and toward the cataract of Niagara Falls.

"Just another goddamned Yankee trying to bleed us dry." Yates spat. "Shit, I wish I could kill you twice."

He cooked the muskrat over the fire, packed up his swag, then hiked to the suspension bridge over the river, where the guard welcomed him back to Canada.

1863

June 15, 1863, FROM HAVANA AND MEXICO. ARRIVAL OF THE STEAMSHIP *EAGLE.* The French Army Still Before Puebla. CAPTURE ON THE GUERRILLA, CAMACHO.

The steamship *Eagle,* Capt. Adams, from Havana, arrived at this port yesterday. The correspondent of the Associated Press furnishes the following interesting items of news:

The overwater days on the freighter were kept lively by the unexpected company of New Yorker Isabel Fitch and her entourage, absent these shores fourteen months. The ship carried several primitive sculptures she purchased in South America and that she expects to display in her home on Worth Square.

— *NEW YORK CHRONICLE,* JUNE 15, 1863

Leander slipped away from the hovel on

Ann Street in the early morning, before the landlady came for the rent.

There wasn't much in his swag, just a dull razor, a bar of soap, and his remaining suit — robin's-egg blue. There'd been a cravat that matched the rust color of its pinstripe, but it had disappeared a long time ago. He couldn't say when.

Once, he'd had six others, just as fine, but they were all gone now. The ones Isabel had given him back in Buffalo were much too backwoods for New York, and he had given them to the bellhop at the St. James. Image was everything for a trader, so he had invested in some new ones from a Fifth Avenue tailor.

The one he still had was his favorite, but there were moth holes in it now. It would surely get him laughed off the floor at the Gold Exchange even while it would get him knifed on Ann Street. But he hoped that it would at least get him through the front door of the Fitch mansion on Worth Square.

He walked the long blocks to Broadway where the morning's delivery traffic was already rattling on the cobblestones. The predawn streets felt like another city, a different world altogether than the bright days and addled nights where he spent his time. Icemen, fishmongers, and newspaper boys scurried by, oblivious to the unkempt man with the mangy beard. Barnum's American Museum sat on the corner, its garish colors a bizarre contrast to the nearby sternness of City Hall, its windows already lit by ambitious men setting to their work.

He turned north on the wide boulevard.

The army had turned City Hall Park into a deployment station and uniformed men filed through its canvas corridors, tramping hard paths into the former green. Leander moved toward the Croton Fountain and its promise of water, keeping his eyes on the ground as he threaded his way among the soldiers.

He hadn't been able to look at any face under a blue kepi since he'd heard the news about Ball's Bluff.

He had still been living at the St. James Hotel then, though his money was almost all gone and he hadn't paid rent on the room for a month.

The *Tribune*'s small gray print was almost illegible and there were many names on the list. He strained to make out Hans's right above a big ink splotch that obscured several other dead men. He could not be sure, but thought one of them was Lafayette Glass. In another column, Vaness Weber was listed as missing.

He did not leave his room that day, drawing the curtains on his view of Central Park and sitting in the dark. He chased the chambermaid away when she came by in the afternoon and downed a bottle of brain tonic as the day wore on.

Images of the battle came to him then. He saw Hans lying there among strangers, cursing Leander for leading him to such a miserable death. Then he saw him leading a charge, the men around him rallying to the flash of his saber. But the image that settled in to stay was of his friend in pain, dying slowly and alone.

He wished he had been there. He wanted to hold his friend's head in his lap to ease his way, and to tell him it would be alright, to lie to him and say that he could hear the flutter of angel wings overhead and that they were coming for him.

He was in a drunken stupor when the night clerk came to collect on the overdue bill. The raps on the door sounded like gunshots and his name sounded like a dirge as it filtered through the gauze of the drug. Leander wailed like a frightened lamb, fearing the reaper had come to collect a different debt altogether.

The clerk barged in, fearing some violent act was in progress. After Leander calmed down, he tried to make a joke of his fear, but he knew then that it should have been him dying in that ugly-named place. He should have left Hans back home to pull fat trout out of Cayuga Creek alongside Harry while he had gone to fight.

Hans came to him that night, a bloody and silent ghost, and had been with him ever since. He'd been removed from the hotel the next day, and the unheated shack on Ann Street had been the last in a long line of humiliating circumstances since then.

The Croton Fountain's tepid water was strewn with the flotsam of the city, making him long for the cool, clear Cayuga and the smell of the leaf mold of his father's forest.

He stripped off his ragged shirt and bent into the water, scrubbing. Isabel had never hesitated to point out when he smelled bad or did not look his best. He would do what he could not to give her reason to complain today.

The razor needed sharpening but he used the soap to lather his face and hacked away at his grizzled whiskers. He had no mirror, and nicked his face several times, sending little drips of blood down his chin and into the dirt.

He pulled off his cheap shoes and ragged trousers, and sat in his underclothes on the edge of the fountain, scrubbing his feet.

He did his best to clean the used brogans he'd bought on the street. His good shoes were long gone, filched one night while he lay in an opium daze at Mrs. Chiu's.

Others came to the fountain to collect water. He nodded his farewell to a woman he'd seen before, but she paid him no mind. He would not miss washing in public once he was ensconced at Worth Square.

The mustiness of the suit made him sneeze. It was loose where it had once been tight, but as he ran his fingers through his wet hair and took in the morning sun, he began to feel like his old self. Like the world could be his again. He left the rags of his old clothes there at the fountain and walked through the encampment, smiling as he noticed the soldiers who had glared at him before now stepping out of his way.

The street was more crowded now. He crossed Chambers, looking up at the big painted sign proclaiming DELMONICO'S, THE PLACE TO BE.

He'd gone nearly every night during his first months in the city, buying drinks and gleaning tidbits of information he used the next day on the trading floor.

It was also the place he finally found Isabel.

He'd made good on a few small trades, and had almost won back the money he'd spent getting set up. With each small victory, he gained confidence and he knew that if he could find just the right tip, make just one big hit, he'd be able to return the money to the account back in Buffalo and no one would even know it had been gone. He'd have the profit to trade free and clear. On the street, they called it "playing with house money."

That night, he was entertaining a stout man who claimed to be a Pittsburgh banker with many clients on Oil Creek. By the time he had polished off three bottles of French wine and two steaks, Leander had begun to doubt he had even the vaguest knowledge of the oil business.

He had gone to the lobby to walk off his frustration, and seen Isabel there, talking with a couple, glowing under the crystal lights. She threw her head back and laughed at something the woman said and he caught his breath at her beauty. She'd always been a striking woman, but she seemed to blossom in her native city.

He had not been able to get to her until then. He'd hand-delivered four letters to her door and Fuller had taken them, but Leander had become convinced that he had

not delivered them. Leander had even offered him a bribe with the last one, but the
block of a man insisted that the missives
had in fact been delivered and closed the
door in his face.

He tried to step up to her under the
gaslights at Delmonico's, but the brawny
manservant was there again, and stood in
his way.

"Isabel," he had called. "I can't believe
I've finally found you."

It seemed to take a moment for her to
recognize him.

"Oh, Leander," she said. "What a surprise."

"Let me through," Leander demanded,
pushing up against Fuller, but there was not
an inch of yield in the man.

"I've been trying to get to you for months,
but this infernal man refuses to deliver my
letters," he said. "I'm here now, in New
York, trading. When can I see you?"

"How tragic." Isabel pouted theatrically.
"I'm leaving in the morning, and will be
touring for more than a year."

"What? How can you?" Leander blurted.
She shrugged.

"Don't you want company?" he asked.
"Surely you'd like me to come with you?"

The woman with Isabel sniggered and Leander shot her a glance.

"How is your trading going?" Isabel asked.

"It's hard to get things started," he said. "I could use your help."

"You must stay here and work until you get the knack of it," she said. "When I come back, I expect you to be rich beyond your wildest dreams. Come see me then and we'll have a gay time."

"Can I come see you tonight after dinner?" he pleaded.

She pouted again.

"I have far too much to do," she said. "But come see me when I'm back in town."

She waved as the maître d' led the party away to a private dining room.

He'd gone back to the banker distracted and upset. When the bill arrived, he barked at him in frustration, demanding some useful information to offset the outrageous tally. The fat man had leaned over and whispered the name of a company in his ear, then sat back with a smile.

Leander looked askance at him, but the man nodded, his jowls jiggling reassuringly.

The next morning, Leander placed a buy order for five thousand shares of the company. By the end of the following week, it had gone bankrupt.

He'd not had a good buy in the year since.

The scraps of his last trade had paid the rent on the room on Ann Street the month before, but last week he'd read the notice in a discarded paper of Isabel's return to the city on a ship.

A crowded trolley rolled past, and he considered hopping on. When there were so many on board, it was not hard to jump on and off without the fare. He decided not to risk it, though. There was no rush. Isabel had never been an early riser, and he didn't want to knock on her door too early.

As he walked, he daydreamed of the exotic things she would have brought back from her tour, and it wasn't until he stood at the battered red door at Mrs. Chiu's that he realized he'd turned up Canal Street out of habit.

He did not dare open the door, but imagined he could smell opium smoke seeping through the jamb.

Smoke was the only thing that had helped him through the past year.

The brain tonic brought out the worst in Hans, so Leander had sought out other methods to calm the ghost. Wine and whiskey did not help, but the memory of slow days on Isabel's couch had sent him searching for a den. In the dim light and the languid movement of the opium smokers, he could drowse through the night. When the opium was just right, he would see other scenes in the candlelight, visions of Hans and the others, not dead and lost, but running through the Maryland woods, stripping off the heavy Union-blue wool and plunging into a pond, free of the war, free to go home.

He would stay for days in the sweet, acrid smoke, watching the Chinese girls with their pots of tea, leaving only when Mrs. Chiu ushered him out after his roll of currency had been exhausted.

He'd given the Chinese woman forged notes just two days before, amazed that she'd been fooled by them. She'd surely discovered her mistake by now, and even as he stood at the door, he knew if he was spotted there, he risked a beating if not worse.

There were other dens. Better ones. Isabel would know where to get the best.

He turned back toward Broadway, stopping along the way to rest. His legs cramped from walking, and he was short of breath, and when he passed a bakery, the smell of fresh bread brought tears of hunger to his eyes. In the university district, he found a bench and sat for a while, watching the midmorning crush of buggies and walkers on the streets.

"Agenbite of Inwyt," one of the bespectacled professors announced in a stentorian voice as he walked by. "That's at the heart of the matter."

Leander chuckled to himself at the man's pompous tone, but the air of scholars reminded him of Mary, and visions of home flooded him. To think of his father, Katia, and the others brought him too much pain, but remembering simple things calmed him — the hand-hewn beams in the barn, the pattern that Katia pricked in the crust of her pies, and Mary's apron hanging on a hook, its pockets weighted with all the useless things she accumulated there.

He had not gone three days without smoke in months, and his nerves were terrible as he walked the last few blocks to Worth Square.

He tried to imagine a way back into Mrs. Chiu's. Maybe she would give him credit, just this once. He'd spent enough with her that he was entitled to at least that. Or maybe he could trade his suit. Suddenly, he regretted leaving his old clothes at the fountain.

The Fitch mansion, an entire block of shining windows three stories tall, dominated the green patch that was Worth Square park.

Leander stood in the street trying to calm himself. Even a belt of rum would help, but he didn't even have pennies for a tavern.

When he had at last worked up the nerve, he knocked on the door only to have Fuller open the door with a white-gloved hand.

"I'm here to see Mrs. Fitch," he said.

"Who may I say is calling?" Fuller asked, a smug look on his face.

"You know who, dammit. Lieutenant Leander Willis," he replied, puffing out his chest with the lie.

"Wait here," the butler said.

Leander stood for a long time, sweating as his back warmed in the morning sun.

"She is not available." Fuller sneered upon returning.

"Let me in," Leander demanded, shoving his brogan into the crack in the door.

The butler kicked his foot out of the way and slammed the door shut. Leander could hear the bolt of the lock fall into place.

"I will wait for her to become available," Leander shouted at the door. "I will not leave the park until she sees me. Go tell her, or I'll throttle you the next chance I get."

He was shaking as he went to the park and found a bench under an elm. He took off his suit coat in the warm sun, but the breeze chilled his sweat and caused him to shiver. He became groggy and his hunger turned to a clenching pain in his stomach.

Old men played chess in the afternoon sun at the nearby tables. A pair of teenage boys came with gloves and tossed a baseball between them. He listened to the perfect rhythm of the ball striking the leather pocket of their gloves as they chattered about school, girls, and their team.

The shivers turned to spasms as he sat out the day in the shade of the tree.

Hans came to him then, but not the rotting corpse of his tonic nightmares or the ethereal vision of the opium, but as his friend from home. He had a mitt tucked under his arm and leaned on his bat the way he always had.

"Bases are loaded, Lelo," he said. "We don't need a home run. Just drop a bunt is all."

"You watch, I'm going to put it over the fence," Leander said through quivering lips.

"Not this time, Lelo," Hans said, frowning back at him. "Man at third is coming home."

"It has to be me," Leander mumbled. "It has to be me."

Isabel shook him awake.

"What is it you want, Leander?" she asked impatiently.

"Isabel," he said, relieved to see her finally. "You've come."

"I'm very busy," she said. "What do you want?"

"I'm here to see you," he said. "It's been so long. I've come so we can be together."

She stood straight and folded her arms.

"I have no time for this nonsense," she said. "I need you to leave. I can't have you lollygagging around my front door in this condition. This park is for children. You are frightening the neighbors."

His hands quivered as he reached for hers, but she drew away and pursed her lips. He climbed to his feet, shaking.

"Leave?" he said. "You told me to come as soon as you returned. You told me you'd help me. I gave up everything to come here for you. I can't just leave."

She shifted on her feet.

"That was so long ago," she said. "Certainly you don't expect me to repeat our little trifle?"

"Trifle?" he said. "I love you."

"Love?" she said. "For Christ's sake, I hope not."

His knees gave out and he slipped back onto the bench. She stood over him with folded arms as he buried his face in his hands.

"I have nothing," he said. "It's all gone."

She reached out her hand and touched the back of his head gently.

"You are a fool," she said, softly. "A handsome fool, but a fool like I've never known. I guess we must send you home then. Where is that place you are from? Where's your little farm?"

He looked up at her, confused.

"But I can't go back there. I can't."

"Town Line," she said. "I remember now."

She waved her hand and Fuller stepped into view.

"Take him to Pennsylvania Station and buy him a ticket to Town Line. It's back near Buffalo somewhere," she said, waving her hand vaguely west. Leander watched her dismissing the place as nothing, dismissing him as nothing.

He lunged at her, but she stepped away from his attack and instantly Fuller was there, punching him hard in the stomach.

He fell to his knees, seeing nothing but red.

"This is good-bye," he heard her say.

His eyes focused again and he watched as she walked across the street and opened the door to her mansion.

"Buy him something to eat before you put him on the train," she shouted over her shoulder. "He looks like death warmed over."

SUMMER

The men had come back different this year.

In some ways, it felt the same way it always had, even like the days before the war. On fine summer evenings, Mary and her father sat on the front porch and listened to the voices of the men gathered around the bonfire down by the barn. Field workers sitting together after dinner and a long day's work. Sometimes there would be singing and music, sometimes there would just be the talk of bone-tired men content in their hard work.

But if she listened closely, she could hear the difference, a cadence to the voices unlike the usual talk of men. Sometimes there was the stilted staccato of a phrase, then the same phrase, again, quicker, and with relief and laughter.

They were teaching themselves to read.

When they had first come to the farm, there was a tentativeness, an uncertainty.

Palmer took charge early, asking Mary each evening what they should work on the next day, then leading the men out to the fields, but it seemed like she had to tell him each detail, each little thing that she thought the field hands would already know.

And no matter what she did, there was always fear in the eyes of the men.

It had been during harvest the year before, the busiest time, when the news came. She read it to them that evening as they all sat down to dinner.

"And by virtue of the power, and for the purpose aforesaid, I do order and declare that all persons held as slaves within said designated States, and parts of States, are, and henceforward shall be free; and that the Executive government of the United States, including the military and naval authorities thereof, will recognize and maintain the freedom of said persons."

They stared at her blankly.

"What does it mean?"

"You're free," she'd said. "Or you will be on the first of January."

"Are we in a designated state?" Malcolm had asked.

"No, but if they took you back to one, they

couldn't keep you."

"That don't sound like it'll make a difference."

The men had gone back to their food, acting as if she'd just read them a review of an Elisha Kane book. The harvest was done soon after, and she'd loaded them in the wagon and taken them back across the border. They'd nodded their heads, hats clutched in front of them when she thanked them for the work they'd done, and asked them all to come back.

Not all did come back in the spring. Chauncey and his family had taken their little savings and headed west to claim a farm in Kansas. Lonnie had gotten work at the commercial slip in downtown Buffalo.

Malcolm, Palmer, and the others, though, they seemed happy to be back on the farm, but it wasn't like the year before.

Palmer still came to her each evening, but now it was to tell her of his plans.

"We'll plow the west field tomorrow," he'd say. "You want alfalfa there, right?"

She'd nod, and not have to worry herself about the west field again.

The men talked more at the table. And laughed more.

They told their stories, too. Malcolm told of how his sister had been taken from his mother's arms, and how she'd been sold down the river, and how he'd been beaten to an inch of his life for the fighting of it. Mary watched Katia as she listened, her fork held still over her plate, her mouth agape. When the kitchen girl brought out plates of cobbler for dessert, Malcolm's bowl was piled impossibly high.

But the biggest difference was for the families.

When the men came to Town Line, the families crossed back over the border with them, moving into rooms downtown. The women took in piecework and laundry, and early in the day each Saturday the men would pile into the wagon and drive down to the church on Michigan Street where their families would be waiting. There'd be long Saturday-night meals and then Sunday-morning services, a picnic, and then the ride back to Town Line for work the next morning.

One evening after Mary read them news of a battle down South, Palmer spoke up.

"I want my little Abbey to be able to read," he said. "They're teaching her a little at the church, but they don't have a real school. If I learn here, I can help when I see her on Sundays."

Mary tried to help at first. As the men

gathered for lunch one day, she brought out the primers she and Leander had used when they were little. The men all nodded their heads and listened close as she tried to teach them, but they did not ask any questions. They all thanked her solemnly and went back to the fields. That night, Joe came to the house and asked for the books. She gave them to him, and after a few minutes, followed him to the fire pit and watched from the shadows as the men joked with him while he sounded out the words, asking him to repeat the harder ones.

For all the tragedy that she had heard in their stories, there was a part of her that was jealous of them. She listened to their voices and the loud peals of laughter and she'd wonder how they could be so at home there while she felt like a stranger in the house where she'd been born.

She longed to be welcomed in such a circle. She knew if she went back to the fire, Joe would make a place for her to sit next to him and Malcolm would find a clean glass and pour her some rum, and Palmer would offer her some of the corn he loved to pop. There'd be kindness, but the only laughter would be the polite kind, not the loud, rude cackling she so often heard from a distance.

She was grateful to them, not only for the work they did, but also for bringing the farm back to life.

And it had never produced so well. There'd been plenty of rain after the seed was in the ground, and June and July had brought long days of high blue skies punctuated by brief, soaking showers. The apples and pears in the orchard were swollen and plentiful and the fields waved emerald green in the summer sun. Joe was working his way through their acres of forest, culling trees here and there to supply the army's constant demands.

The men were happiest as they cleaned themselves up and piled into the wagon on Saturday mornings. They knew they had done good work, and they knew the pay they would deliver downtown was making things better for their families there.

Joe would go with them sometimes, and he would scour the city for newly arrived refugees, asking after Alaura. Once, he heard tell of a girl with different-colored eyes over in St. Catharines, and went over the border, but he came back four days later, forlorn.

On those weeks when he stayed on the farm, the others always asked after her, and the wives were even more diligent during the week.

Mary asked him once why he didn't go with them, and he said that seeing all the other families made him too lonely.

After the wagon rolled out of the yard, he would disappear into the woods.

Mary told him that he was welcome at the table for dinner as always, but he never came.

She would wonder about him through the rest of the evening and into the next day, but when she asked, he'd only shrug. After much of the summer had passed, she gave in to her curiosity. She pulled on the old pair of her father's trousers she wore to hike the woods, packed a lunch, and followed him into the woods.

She seldom went into the forest anymore, but the stillness of dappled green light and the rich smell of the humus underfoot brought her back to long days she had spent with her mother gathering blackberries. Though she knew the land far too well to ever be truly lost there, she meandered among the ancient trees as if she were.

The day was stretching into afternoon, and a bank of clouds had intruded into the blue sky when she found Joe in Leander's clearing next to the spring pond.

He was sitting on a log stump, trimming

roof shakes with a hatchet.

The building that stood in the clearing had little in common with the ramshackle wreck her brother had left. The walls had been trued, and the beginnings of a roof were in place.

"I hope you don't mind," he said when he saw her. "Someone tried to build something, but it was just a pile of scrap when I found it. I decided to make it right."

"This is where you come?"

He nodded. "When I saw this place I thought of the book, and I wanted to make a place like that," he said.

"Thoreau," she said, putting the basket of food down and sitting next to him.

"When they had me in that cell, I used to keep myself sane by planning each little part of the cabin I would build," he said.

He laughed, keeping his eyes on his work.

"The way he describes it, being alone out in the woods," he said. "It made me think that maybe there could be a place for me somewhere."

He waved at the half-finished building.

"This is your father's land, I know it could never be mine," he said. "But I wanted to know what it was like to build something. Maybe someday I could do it for myself."

"The deed might say it's my father's," she

said. "But you've made it yours."

He held a shake up, checking it for cracks.

"That's the way with me," he said, a hint of bitterness in his voice. "Free, but not."

"You're free," she said. "Even the president says so."

"Not really," he said. "Walnut Grove is in West Virginia. That's a border state. He freed the slaves just about everywhere else, but not there. Alaura is still there. Alaura is still a slave."

He swung his dark eyes over to her.

"In the book he had visitors that would come," he said. "I thought maybe you would come visit me."

"I remember," she said. "They'd bring him food."

She lifted the basket she'd carried all morning.

"And here I am," she said, smiling.

A raindrop fell onto the still, mirror-gray surface of the pond and Joe held his hand out into the air.

"We should get back," he said.

"It's just a summer sprinkle," she said. "Let's stay."

The sky opened all at once, pouring buckets in a flash. Joe grabbed the basket and together they ran into the cabin for cover.

Most of the roof was open, but one corner was solid enough and they crowded under it, laughing at the futility of the effort. The downpour lasted only a few minutes, but they were soaked through.

The rain stopped as quickly as it started, but fat drops fell from the leaves all around them, so Mary stepped back into the clearing under quickly moving clouds. Steam rose around her as she squeezed water from her hair.

Joe dashed past her, faster than she would have believed he could on one leg, and dove into the pond. When he surfaced, he was smiling from ear to ear.

"It is warm and glorious," he said, motioning for her to follow.

"I can't." She giggled, even as she pulled off her shoes and followed him headfirst into the little pond.

The surface was sun-warmed, but the spring below fed ice-cold water up from the bottom, and the thrill of the shifting temperature on her legs gave her goose bumps. She dove to the bottom and her bare feet broke the surface for an instant before slipping again into the dappled water.

She ran her finger along the sole of his foot and laughed a storm of bubbles as he yelled in surprise.

The pond was shallow and calm, but the tug of the water on her clothes reminded her of her time in the creek long before, and brought her chills.

The rain had churned the water murky and she couldn't even see her hands a few inches below the surface. She reached down and pulled the trousers from her legs and slung them onto the shore.

Joe looked at her wide-eyed.

"Don't tell," she said and splashed water in his face.

As the sky cleared above them, they swam together until her hunger got the best of her and she said they should spread the picnic on the bank of the pond.

She made him go into the cabin and turn his back before she climbed out of the water and pulled the wet, heavy trousers on again.

He brought the basket out and she put some dishes on a blanket. They lay themselves side by side on the grass to dry in the sun.

"The book," he said, staring into the shifting clouds and chewing on a grape. "The part I got caught up in first was as a place to escape to. But that's not the best part of it, really. The part that I love is how he sees every little thing, the ways the leaves change and the different sounds the birds make."

"He went to jail, too," she said. "Though just a single night, and as much by choice as anything."

He was quiet for a while.

"I can't imagine anyone that could live in a place like this going into a cell like that by choice," Joe said.

They lay that way for a long time, dozing in the afternoon sun as dragonflies flitted over the still pond.

The western sky was turning orange and the bats had come out and were chittering over the treetops when they walked back into the barnyard. The men had returned and were gathering at the table under the elm while Katia brought out dinner.

It was Palmer who shared the news.

"They found that marshal dead," he said. "Down in the pool under Niagara Falls. At least they think it was him. The star was on his coat, but he was a mess."

Mary shivered, her left hand unconsciously rubbing the scar where Kidder's shackle had cut into her. She looked at Joe, expecting to see relief in his face, but instead there was fear.

"It was Yates Bell," he said. "He's here."

"How can you say that?" she scoffed. "That marshal had enemies everywhere he went."

"He's come for me," he said. "He's down there somewhere."

ERIE

As Yates Bell left the clutch of nigger hovels at St. Catharines, his mind kept circling back to the old priest. Something in his eyes had flashed when he had mentioned Joe.

He was sure Joe wasn't there, but that old priest didn't look right.

Even back at Walnut Grove he'd always known when a darkie had something to hide.

He'd perfected the art of ransacking the encampments. He liked to surprise them. He'd sneak in when they had all gathered for dinner. He'd circle around, looking for a woman on the edge, or even better, one of the countless brats underfoot. He'd grab it, put his pistol to the squaller's head, and swear that he was ready to pull the trigger. The whole village would come to heel.

He also knew that it was never a good idea to go back. They'd all be angry and alert.

But that priest knew something.

He turned, looking back west toward the village, took his pistol from its holster, and started walking. He was nearly at the church steps when something came down on the back of his head.

He woke up in the back of a donkey cart, his feet and hands bound, his head throbbing. He was relieved to look up and see a white man driving.

"Let me lose, goddammit," Yates shouted. "Where are you taking me?"

"Shut the hell up, or I'll gag you," the man said.

Yates glowered, but kept quiet.

It wasn't long before the cart pulled onto a dock, and the driver climbed down and pulled Yates out of the back. He motioned, and two men took his arms and dragged him across the planks toward a sleek-hulled steamer with the name *Abigail* painted in gold on its bow.

"Mr. Compson is doing you a favor," the driver said as Yates struggled. "There's no one that will give a damn if these men kill you, so you best not give them reason."

They carried him into a dark-paneled cabin with a round table in the middle and a heavy wooden desk to the side. The first well-groomed man he had seen in nearly a year sat behind the desk and motioned for

Yates to be put in the chair across from him.

"More of the same," the driver said, dropping Yates's pistol and holster on the desk.

"Untie Mr. Bell," the man behind the desk drawled.

He waited for the men to finish and leave before continuing.

"At least you weren't fool enough to wear a Confederate uniform," he said. "Other than that, I can't imagine you making a bigger mess of yourself."

"Who are you?" he asked.

"Jacob Compson," the man replied.

"You're from Richmond, aren't you?" Yates said. "I heard your name a few times."

"I'm from Oxford, Mississippi, to tell the truth," he said. "But I've spent a good amount of time around Richmond."

"What are you doing up here?"

"I'm running the Confederate Secret Service."

Yates flexed his arms, loosening his joints after being bound.

"I've never heard of such a thing," he said.

"The middle word is 'secret,'" Compson said. "It has a very clear meaning, and you'd make my life easier if you learned it. The better part of valor is discretion."

"What do you want with me?" Yates asked.

"This is not the Old Dominion. You can't

just terrorize the niggers without conse-
quences," Compson said. "Your effort to
find this slave of yours is causing difficulties
for the local authorities and they've asked
me to deal with you."

Compson pulled his sleeves and adjusted
his silk tie.

"You have a choice. I can take you to the
quaint little jail they have here or I can take
you to the Riley Hotel. At the jail, you'll
serve a month or two for this latest adventure. After that, if you have another run-in
and my friends on Her Majesty's government ask what should be done with you, I
will suggest hanging. The Confederacy's
relationship with Canada, the queen, and
England are delicate and vital to the cause.
Do you understand?"

Yates grunted.

"I expect better manners from you,"
Compson said. "I knew your father, and I
know you were raised better than that. Sit
up, son."

Yates found himself straightening in his
seat without thinking.

"And what if you take me to the hotel?"
he asked.

"The hotel is a simple place. Perhaps not
up to the standards of the Bells of Walnut
Grove, but it is discrete. Many of our

countrymen are there. Some have escaped the prisons of the North and are on their way back to the good fight. The others are my operatives. We have opened a stealth front on the Yankees' northern border. It is a quiet thing, as it must be to accommodate our British friends. You would be part of that."

"How?"

"You are a clumsy fool, but your name carries weight in Richmond," he said.

Yates stirred at the insult.

"Calm down," Compson said. "Yes, you are a fool. One does not stomp around Canada pillaging nigger villages. One does not murder Union marshals who have gone around asking after your fugitive."

"He had it coming," Yates said.

". . . and one does not murder Confederate scouts."

"You're lying," Yates barked.

"Do you deny it?" Compson asked. "I have it all, you know. A nice file on you. Richmond told me you would be my problem. Mr. Philips, your lawyer back in Harpers Ferry, sent a note that you would be coming this way when you didn't report to camp. He told me you'd be looking for Marshal Kidder, as well. It doesn't take much to connect you to him. And the scout.

How foolish a man are you? You murder a man after he writes your name in his journal? And you leave it laying next to his moldering corpse? I could survey all the generals in the Yankee army, and I still couldn't find a fool as big as you."

"Philips, that bastard. He betrayed me," Yates hissed.

"You betrayed yourself," Compson said. "You betrayed your country. You shot a good man, left him laying out in the open for the vultures."

Compson was standing over him now, looking down.

"But as I was saying, we value bloodlines down South," he said. "Richmond will be happy to know that along with the fodder we use for this or that task, there's a Bell of Walnut Grove up here. It will reassure them, make them more likely to open the purse strings."

"What would you have me do while you raise funds off my name?" Yates asked.

Compson looked at him across the desk.

"Be a leader of men," he said. "I am finalizing plans for several . . . operations that would be well suited for you. Situations where having the name Captain John Yates Bell attached to the venture might be helpful."

"Captain?" Yates raised his eyebrows.

"Don't get ahead of yourself," Compson said. "And by the way, your nigger is dead."

"Dead?" Yates said. "How would you know?"

"The same way I know all about you," Compson said. "It is my job. He died in the Yankee jail years ago. You've been chasing a ghost."

"Kidder said they freed him," Yates said. "That he was heading here."

"They did indeed free all the contrabands," Compson said. "But he wasn't among them. There's no record of Joe Bell being released at all. They must have tossed him in the potter's field."

"He's still alive," Yates said.

"He's not," Compson said. "And I'll not let you tear this escarpment up trying to find your ghost."

Yates looked down at his filthy hands. "Take me to the hotel," he said.

The Riley Hotel sat on a dirt road half a mile up from the Niagara River. The rooms were small and shabby, but the castoffs spent all their time in the lobby.

The two camps of men segregated themselves. The escapees, gaunt and hollow-eyed, stayed for a night or two before boarding a barge up the Welland Canal to Lake Ontario where they'd get passage through the Saint Lawrence and back down to the Confederacy.

Then there were the operatives. Like him, they could not go home. They shuffled through their days like shades on the shores of Styx waiting for a way to move on.

Some told of their heroic acts and the bad luck that had landed them there, and in those Yates recognized the smooth, re-hearsed ways of liars. Those men he knew to be cowards. They meant nothing to him.

It was the other ones that weighed on his mind. Most days they sulked in corners smoking. But when they had too little or too much to drink, their mood would change, and they'd join in the storytelling. And the stories they told had Yates propping a chair under his doorknob each night just to sleep.

Yates learned that Compson had been sent north by Jefferson Davis himself to wreak as much havoc on the northern fringe of the Union as he could manage. The *Abigail* steamed around the Great Lakes, going as far west as Windsor or north to Toronto or Montreal. It had a reserved berth at Fort Erie in Canada and at the Buffalo marina where Compson had paid off enough officials to have it deemed a pleasure boat.

If there was a leader, it was Erastus Dratch. He was a burly man, barrel chested with a bushy beard who sat at the same table in the lobby all day long.

Compson came to the hotel once a week to pay the bills and sit with Dratch as they doled out assignments. They would gather a selection of the deserters around the little table in the corner of the lobby and distribute gold pieces and the men would be gone the next day. The ones who came back bragged of slipping across the border and blowing up rail lines or scuttling boats on the Union docks.

For the ones that didn't return, Dratch would open their rooms and take anything of monetary value before letting the rest of the men scavenge the rest. Letters and photos and other useless things were burned in the lobby fireplace.

Dratch made it clear that he had taken a disliking to Yates. Compson introduced them by saying that given his family name, he was to be treated with respect, but the privateer was not of the same mind, and his opinion held sway over the others.

When the men gathered for their rotgut in the evening, they would all move away from wherever he sat. Every time Yates asked for an assignment, Dratch would tell him that it was beneath His Highness's status and the others would laugh.

When boredom set in and too many of operatives talked of leaving, Dratch would gather a hunting party and send them over the suspension bridge into Buffalo to hunt down fugitives. There were always easy pickings around Dug's Dive by the canal.

Dratch claimed that he'd seen a description of Yates hanging on the guardhouse at the border, and disqualified Yates from such pleasure trips.

That was fine with Yates. If Joe was over there, the marshal would have offered him up. There was nothing left for him over the border.

No, Joe wasn't in the city. But he wasn't dead, either. Everything Compson said stank of deceit. Yates could feel Joe in his bones, and he knew he wasn't dead.

When the others went across the border, Yates would strap on his pistol and wander the back roads around Fort Erie. He'd been through nearly all the settlements by then, but there were a few he'd check again.

It was in a little town called Pelham that he thought he'd caught up with Joe.

The buck had the same straight-backed arrogant walk, the same quick stride. Yates jumped him from behind, rolled him over, and shoved a knife tip up to his chin.

When the face wasn't Joe's, Yates hesitated, and in that hesitation, the darkie's hands were on Yates's throat. Yates barely had time to get his gun from the holster and shoot the mongrel.

He was swarmed before he could get to his feet, and he was bloodied by the time the sheriff arrived and took him to jail.

It was weeks before Compson came for him.

"You have managed to become eligible for hanging in three nations in the course of two years," Compson said. "That is a rare accomplishment."

"Why'd you leave me here so long?" Yates asked.

"Dratch didn't mention you were missing," Compson said through the bars. "Nobody there seems to like you much."

"I didn't know it was required that I make friends," Yates said.

"It would have been . . . helpful if you'd made the effort," Compson said. "They're not obliged to take orders like slaves."

"Aren't soldiers required to take orders?" Yates asked.

Compson cocked an eyebrow.

"Given your current circumstances that's

quite the thing to say," Compson said.

"It was self-defense," Yates said. "He would have killed me."

"And what were you doing there in the first place?" Compson asked.

Yates shrugged.

"I have a mission for you," Compson said. "You can rot in here or take it."

"If I must," Yates said.

Compson called for the guard.

As they rode down to the waterfront in a black-lacquered carriage, the commander pulled a few British notes from a roll in his pocket and handed them to him.

"You'll need to buy provisions," he said.

Tied up next to the *Abigail* was a sail canoe with the word "Swan" painted on her scuffed hull.

"We have people at Windsor in Ontario. Over on the west end of Erie," Compson said. "Go there. You'll be using the *Swan* to run escapees over from Sandusky."

"Have you lost your mind?" Yates asked, looking at the broad expanse of Lake Erie. "I don't know how to sail."

"If you don't make it, I'll make sure the report says you died bravely, in the line of duty," Compson said.

"I'd rather stay here and fight," Yates said.

"If you stay, the only fighting you'll be

doing is with the others," Compson said. "I'm surprised you haven't been knifed yet."

"I don't know how to sail this," Yates repeated.

"Buy a compass," Compson said. "Just go west, you'll find it. Windsor, across from Detroit. Hard to miss. And don't get any ideas about staying around here. I'll set those boys on you for sport."

Yates watched as Compson boarded the *Abigail* and gave the order to set sail.

He knew he should be angry, but instead there was lightness in his step as he spent the morning at the general store buying provisions for the trip. He was on the water by noon.

He struggled to make the sail work, trying to remember how the sailors on his childhood trip had driven the ship into the wind by angling the sail just so.

The waves of Erie were tiny compared to the ocean, but the little boat nearly capsized several times, and he was perpetually soaked from the spray. Eventually, he stowed the sail and paddled, but the wind pushed him back as quickly as he could move forward.

He'd covered no more than two miles of shoreline by the time the sun went down, and he could still see the lights of Buffalo across the water. He didn't have the strength to put up the tent or start a fire, and huddled under his blankets eating a cold can of beans.

In the morning, he could barely move his arms and his hands had blistered, but the wind had shifted and he was able to make progress with the sail. The morning was rainy, and he huddled under an oilcloth as the boat rocked slowly west. The afternoon cleared and the wind came up stronger. He stayed on the water later, trying to make up for lost time. As the sun went down, he spotted a fire in the dense woods of the north shore.

There was another boat on the rocky beach, and Yates could make out a man and woman in the camp. She was hanging a line of gutted fish over a smoking fire and he was stretching a raccoon hide on a rack.

"What the hell are you?" the man asked with a laugh as Yates pulled the *Swan* up onto the shore. "You look as lost as lost could be."

He was wiry and balding with sideburns that extended to his jawline.

"Can I warm myself?" Yates asked, his voice cracking.

"Oh, for God's sake," the man said. "Nelda, we got us a Southern boy here so lost he's sailed himself to Canada. Can you get this deserting fool some food?"

"I'm busy here," the woman shouted back at him. "You know where the bowls are. Feed him yourself."

"I thought you'd be happy to see a fellow Confederate," the man said.

"Just because I'm from Georgia don't mean I want anything to do with that nonsense," Nelda said.

The trapper stood and offered his hand.

"I'm Scott," he said, and led Yates to the fire, dug a bowl out of a pack, and ladled it full from an iron pot hanging over the campfire.

"I'm not a deserter," Yates said.

"Then what are you doing here?" Scott asked.

"I am on a mission."

"What kind of mission has you here?" Scott asked. "There's nothing up here but fish, bears, and beavers."

He handed Yates a mug of rum. "You handle that boat like you're infantry." He grinned as he turned back to stretching the hide. "That little yawl of yours should move like a dream. I'll give you a few pointers in the morning."

Yates gulped the warm stew and sipped the rum. Nelda finished with the fish and helped him pull his gear out of the boat and put up his little tent.

"You surely are a lost little thing, ain't you," she said. She mussed his hair like he was a ten-year-old. Yates took off his boots and propped them to dry by the fire while she draped him in a coarse blanket. The night fell quickly, and the couple came and sat around the fire and ate.

Scott told stories of their life in the woods. Nelda interrupted often, and the two of them argued about the details he gave.

"That wasn't a grizzly," she insisted at one point. "There's no grizzlies this far east."

"That's my point though — it was a grizzly. Why would I tell this story if it was just another black bear?"

"Come on, poppy, I was right there, pointing a shotgun at her and it wasn't a grizzly."

"Then it must have been High Hat, 'cause that wasn't no black bear."

She punched him in the arm.

"Poppy, you are an idiot. High Hat is just Haudenosanee nonsense. There ain't no ten-foot wild creature with Abe Lincoln's stovepipe hat roaming the woods."

The eyes of wild things reflected firelight from under the low hanging trees, and Yates worried about what a High Hat was, but he said nothing as he sipped his rum and listened with a smile on his face.

"Those Haudenosaunee have been here a lot longer than us. I tend to believe what they say," Scott said.

"Okay, then it was a grizzly," Nelda said, but her tone made it clear that the issue was not resolved.

In the morning, Scott woke Yates by nudging the bottom of his foot with a muddy boot.

"I don't have all day," he said. "Let's get out there."

The sun filtered through the mist on the water as Nelda handed him a mug of the best coffee Yates had ever had. He took three biscuits with him and climbed into the boat. Scott pushed off with the paddle and the *Swan* glided onto the glassy water. The air seemed dead still to Yates, but Scott lifted his nose to the wind, raised the white canvas sail, and caught a phantom breeze. The boat jerked to life and headed out into the bronze-tinged expanse of Erie.

Away from shore, the wind was stronger and the mist cleared in the sun. The *Swan* picked up speed and it seemed the hull barely touched the water. Scott showed him how to tack and gybe and pushed Yates's head down as he brought the boom around each time. He showed him how to set the sails and tie them into place, how to set a course, and how to make knots that slipped off easily when pulled one way but held firm when pulled the other. They made their way out to the middle of the lake, and he had to squint to make out any sign of either shore. The boat slowed and Scott furled the sail, reached into his pocket for a flask, and settled into the bow, his arms resting on the gunwale.

"Now you get us back," he said.

Yates pulled the sail back up, eyed the telltales, and pulled the boom into place. The wind caught in the canvas, pushing them back toward the north shore.

"There you go," Scott said. He offered the flask, and frowned when Yates shook his head.

The *Swan* moved much more slowly under Yates's hand than Scott's, but it made steady progress, and the trapper pointed out this fix or that as the Confederate shifted around the boat.

Yates was beaming when he jumped into the shallow water and pulled the boat back onto the beach. Nelda was splitting limbs into kindling with a hand axe. His tent and blankets were bound up tight and waiting to be loaded.

"Well, you didn't get yourself killed," she said. "That's a start."

She shaded her eyes with her hand and looked at Scott.

"Poppy, you better check those traps on the east line," she said. "If there's any creature in them, they're most surely dying in misery."

Scott hopped out of the boat and grabbed the packed tent and stowed it in the bow under an oilcloth.

"The key to a happy marriage is to know when to listen," he said.

"That'd be true if you'd ever married me," Nelda said.

"Of course I married you," Scott said. "We stood under a starry sky and I declared myself to you."

"But there wasn't no preacher," she said. "How's it a wedding without a preacher?"

Scott rolled his eyes and Yates couldn't help but smile.

"I got a couple old nets I could sell you cheap," Scott said, inspecting the *Swan* one last time. "I suppose I'd have to show you how to fix them up. This little boat wasn't meant for war. There ain't even a place to hang a flag on it. But you could have a nice life hauling fish out of this lake."

Yates surveyed the neat little camp, and the redheaded woman waved and smiled back at him.

"Anybody sets a man out into this lake and doesn't show him how to sail ain't expecting him to live," she said. "You should just skip out. They'll think you drowned or got et by High Hat or something."

"I have orders," Yates said and climbed into the boat.

Scott pushed it into the water.

"You used to be a fool who couldn't handle a boat," Scott said with a laugh. "Now you're just a fool."

EXILE

June 23, 1863
To: Jefferson Davis
Richmond, Virginia

Dear Jefferson,
Mr. Bell is cocked and loaded and of significant enough caliber to inflict real damage. But like so many ordnances at our disposal, he will be difficult to aim, and as likely to cause harm to us as to the Union.

I have tried to find a way to save him up for the appropriate task when it comes.

Our plans for Buffalo unfold as hoped, and I expect it will come to fruition just as the campaign in southern Pennsylvania comes to a head. The twin defeats may be the dagger in the heart we hope for.

MY BEST TO WINNIE AND THE

CHILDREN,
JACOB COMPSON,
FORT ERIE, ONTARIO

Leander shivered in the cool night air as the width of New York State passed under the train's steel wheels. Even the Union soldiers who crowded the aisle refused to take the seat next to him.

The fifteen-hour trip had taken him a week.

Three times his dry heaving and fever had convinced the other passengers that he had typhoid and he'd been forcibly removed from the train. And once, outside of Ithaca, the conductor shook him awake for screaming himself raw and left him on the platform.

He stopped in Attica, a little town twenty miles east of Alden. In a surprising act of mercy, Fuller had shoved a few notes in his pocket when he dumped him on the train. He fingered their remnants in his jacket pocket as he walked the town looking for a barber. He hoped a shave would steady his nerves before he rode into Town Line.

"Did they pick your number?" the barber asked as he lathered his face.

"I've been in already," Leander said. "They don't want me back."

"Aren't you the lucky one?" the barber replied. "They're going door-to-door around here, rounding up our boys at gunpoint. It's not going over too well, though, I tell you. There's pamphlets floating around."

Leander grunted.

"It's ugly here but nothing like it is down in the city. People are learning what this war's all about. I wouldn't go to downtown Buffalo right now for all the tea in China. A powder keg, I tell ya."

"What this war's about?" Leander repeated.

"Yeah, the real story. Not what the politicians say. It's all those negroes down there in the city. Where'd they come from? They brought them up here to take honest men's jobs is what. The papers say it's all about freeing the slaves, but that ain't it. They don't want to be free. Hell, I hear there's even an island down near Cuba set aside for them all to move to if that's what they want. Why don't they go there instead of coming here? No, they want our jobs. That's what's going on. Send the white man off to die, get the negroes to do the job for half the price."

Leander said nothing as the man ran a straight razor over his stubbled throat. He nearly fell when he got up from the chair, so the barber took the last of his money and gave him a fancy walking stick another customer had left behind.

Leander made his way back to the train station and waited for hours before he caught the local. It was only twenty miles to Town Line and he sat in the hard wooden seats watching the silvered summer fields under the full moon.

Hans came to him just as the train passed through his own rye field. His friend stood in front of him, shaking his head and staring at the ground. Leander's knuckles whitened on the silver-topped stick as the brakes squealed and the train lurched to a stop at the Town Line station. He mopped sweat from his face and straightened himself.

The engineer called for water, and as Leander walked up the aisle, he could see a crewman climb onto the tower to fill the engine's reservoir.

On the platform, he watched as a man in the shadow of the ticket booth gestured silently toward another slipping from the baggage car. Leander recognized his old friend and smiled broadly.

"Harry, it's me," he shouted.

For a long moment, nothing answered his

call other than the summer cicadas.

"Son of a bitch," Harry bellowed and broke from the shadows. Before Leander knew what was happening, Harry was on him, knocking him to the ground, slamming his head onto the platform. Bursts of light flashed in Leander's eyes and he felt like he was going to black out. A skein of hatred flashed across Harry's face as he landed punch after punch. Leander rolled onto his side, curled into a ball, and brought his hands up to shield his face. He let out a wail when Harry's knee slammed into his lower back.

"Leave him alone," a voice shouted. Through the grunting of the men around him, Leander could hear the cocking of guns.

Leander uncovered his face to see half a dozen Union soldiers with pistols standing on the platform.

"This ain't your business," Harry said, still straddling Leander.

"Can't you see the man's dying?" the officer asked.

"It's about goddamned time." Harry spat. "That uniform don't mean shit around here. Get the hell back on that train. This is Town Line. We quit the Union long ago."

The officer laughed. "This is that seceded

little jerkwater?" he said. "I've been meaning to come out here and burn you sons of bitches to the ground."

He turned and looked at the soldiers standing in line, pistols at the ready.

"What do you think, boys, can we find some kerosene in this shithole full of traitors?"

"Yes, sir," said one of the men.

The officer smiled as he swung his boot and caught Harry in the chin, knocking him backward.

Harry scrambled off the platform and ran into the night.

"Draft-dodging hayseeds," the officer said, helping Leander to his feet and brushing him off. "Goddamned cowards, attacking a gentleman like that."

"I'm not dying," Leander said, pushing the soldier away with shaking hands.

"If you say so," the officer said as he brushed the dirt from Leander's rumpled suit.

"All aboard," the conductor shouted at the soldiers.

The soldiers piled back on, leaving Leander standing on the platform alone.

He gripped the silver of the walking stick and hobbled through the quiet crossroads and up the highway to the farm. The walk, less than a mile, left him exhausted.

The house was dark except for an orange glow in Mary's room. He stopped at the foot of the steps and gathered himself, straightening his suit and running his fingers through his pomaded hair. He spat into his handkerchief, wiped the blood from his split lip, and climbed onto the porch. The door was locked.

He knocked, softly at first, and then, as if it was Fuller himself standing before him, he began to pound the smooth red surface with his shaking hands.

It felt like hours before Mary opened the door, and when she did, he hardly recognized her. Her face had taken on a sternness, and her eyes had hardened. Even in the lamplight, he could see a few strands of gray in her straw-colored hair, but she stood taller with a confidence that reminded him of their father.

"Let me in," he said. "This is my house."

A look of recognition played across her face, and her eyes welled. He moved toward her, but she backed away and the hardness in her face returned. He could see the muscles twist as she clenched her jaw, and then the door was closed again.

He pounded on the unyielding wood, and then, in a moment of fury, he wound up like a batsman and struck the door, splintering the stick and leaving a dent in the wood his father had milled fifty years before.

"Mine!" he screamed into the night.

Something in his chest collapsed and he fell against the door. He slid down until his face pressed against the cool, wide planks of the porch. The world spun and he felt like his blood and breath was draining from him, seeping through the cracks in the wood and into the soil below. His body convulsed.

"Mercy," he whispered as he fell still at last. "Dear God, have mercy on me."

He lay that way for a long time before he pulled himself to his feet. His legs felt rubbery, and he held the railing of the porch tightly as he slid down to sit on the steps. He leaned into the post, his fingers finding the place he'd scratched his name as a little boy. He stared through the dark into the familiar landscape.

Voices came to him through the night air, the sound of men together, laughing and joking. Somewhere behind the house. He gathered himself and tottered down the driveway.

A group of black men sat around the firepit that he'd shared with his family so many times. He braced himself against the river stone foundation of the barn as his knees nearly buckled under him. He recognized the runaway that he had betrayed so long before, and stifled a gasp, afraid they would hear him, afraid of what they'd do to him.

Leander wondered how he could still be here when so much else had changed.

"So this book with the shed by the pond?" one of the others was asking. "Why is it I'm supposed to live in the middle of the woods?"

"No, no, it's not about the shed itself," Joe answered.

He had his finger on a page in a book, and another man, shoulder to shoulder with him, was trying to read it in the firelight.

"This man that built this little place," Joe said. "He says it's about being your own man, being free. If the people around you aren't doing things right, you should just leave, and do right for yourself. He is saying that when things aren't just, aren't the way they're supposed to be, you should fight them by not being part of it."

"He was living in the woods," the first one said. "He probably didn't have any money."

"No, he had the money," Joe said. "His family owned a pencil factory. It wasn't about the money."

"It's always about the money," the other

one said, and the others laughed. "Isn't there an easier book to learn from?"

The men fell silent then. One was popping corn in a metal basket over the fire and the aroma intertwined with the sweet smoke of applewood.

The cook withdrew the long-handled basket from the fire, and opened the metal lid with his bare fingers. He offered the snow-white kernels to each man around the fire, then turned and extended it toward where Leander leaned against the barn.

"You can come out," he said. "Come sit by the fire."

Leander tried to raise the strength to run, but the cook smiled and said, "Go ahead, while it's still hot."

He stepped forward, reaching out for a handful of the warm, fragrant kernels. He cupped them to his face, drawing the sweet smell deep into his lungs.

Hans was there again, and Leander felt his friend's hand on his back.

At first, he simply wept as a kernel melted to nothing on his tongue. He struggled to hide his tears, but a wave broke over him, and he fell to his knees, sobbing again.

Somebody draped a blanket over his shoulders, and one of the men helped him stand and led him to the cabin, where they took his coat and shoes off before putting him on a cornhusk cot. He tried to stop shaking and crying, but he could not control his body.

"I've seen this before," said the one who'd helped him. "He put that poison in his blood. He's got it bad."

"Do we need to get the doctor?" another asked.

"There's only three ways to get through this: more of the same; just dying; or, if he's lucky, a week or so of sicking it out."

"Who is he? What's he doing here?"

"That's Leander," Joe said. "Mary's brother."

"He's that one?" the first said. "Son of a bitch, let's leave him to that wolf."

"No," Joe said. "Do what you can for him. I don't want him on my soul."

The men all filed into the long cabin and climbed into their bunks.

Leander slipped into a fitful sleep, waking briefly the next morning to the noise of the men readying to head out into the fields.

When he woke again, it was Katia sitting near him.

"You can't be here," she said.

He reached for her, but she backed away.

"You can't be here," she repeated. "If Harry finds you, he'll kill you."

"Harry already got his licks in," Leander said. "Where's my father? Can you bring him to me? He will make Mary listen."

She twisted her hands.

"I will try," she said. "But you have to go."

He slipped back into sleep.

His father was sitting on the stool next to him when he woke next. His face was papery white, and his hands were nearly translucent. Katia sat on a bunk behind him.

"Leander, my boy," Nathan said, his brow furrowed in worry. "Where did they get you? Where's the bullet?"

"I'm sick, Father," Leander said.

"Let's get you fixed up and back out there," Nathan said. "There's a mess brewing down there in Pennsylvania. They need you."

"They don't want me," Leander said.

"Want you?" his father said. "What's that have to do with anything? You're a lieutenant. You have a duty."

"That was a long time ago, Father," Leander said.

"Mary gave me the picture of you in your uniform just the other day," Nathan said. "When was that, Frances?"

He cocked his head toward an empty bunk.

"You see, not that long ago," he said.

Leander looked past his father to where Katia sat.

"He has the gift now, too," Katia whispered. "He hears the voices of those gone."

Leander stared at the empty bunk, worried that perhaps his own ghosts would appear. There was nothing but dust motes floating in the afternoon sun.

"I've come home to run the farm," Leander said. "Like you told me to. But Mary won't let me in."

Nathan's face clouded.

"Mary's in charge now," he said.

"But you always said the farm would be mine," Leander said.

Nathan patted him on the shoulder.

"Don't you worry about that," he said. "I've never seen the farm run better. I know your heart was never in it. Lord knows I could tell. I shouldn't have forced you like I did. Now Mary has it running like it never did before. You just need to get yourself back with your friends. Mary told me how you all rode downtown together, you in front of them all. I wish I'd been there to see it."

"It was a mistake, Pa," Leander said, starting to sob. "I shouldn't have done it. I shouldn't have done any of it. They all died."

Leander's face collapsed in pain and he

struggled to get the words out. His father stared at him in confusion, but his eyes were soft.

"Hans died. Because of me. They're all gone. Hans is gone."

He reached a quivering hand toward his father.

Nathan went to his knees next to the bed and took his son in his arms.

"I've been so wrong." Leander wept. "I've been so wrong. You've got to forgive me. Someone has got to forgive me. Someone has to. Something has to."

Leander held onto his father. Even now, he could feel the strength that had always been there. Nathan patted him on the back, whispering, "You're a good boy," over and over again until Leander had cried himself to exhaustion.

Katia and his father helped him lie down in the bed again and his father straightened his blanket, tucking him in like he was a little boy, then he straightened up and ran his fingertips over the rough wood of an overhead beam.

"I still have the old adze I used to cut this," he said. "When I came west, this cabin was the first thing I built. I was your age. That's when my life started. I forget just about everything before that. None of it seems to matter."

He opened the door and stepped into the daylight.

Katia had left a tray of food for him on the bedside table and he emptied the bowl of succotash quickly, then wolfed down the square of cornbread. It was different than any he'd had since he'd left home. There was maple sugar instead of cane, and less of it than others would use. He knew that his sister's hand had made it. He licked the crumbs from his fingertips.

The milk tasted of the farm's rich black earth and he savored it as if it were a Margaux.

The food stayed in him, the first since New York. He dozed again and woke to the sound of the house bell tolling three times, signaling the workers to come out of the fields for dinner.

Leander could hear men in the barnyard joking as they washed off the day's grime in the rain barrel. When two men came in and saw him there, they became as quiet as visitors at a wake and left quickly.

Eventually, the yard outside the cabin hushed as the men left together for the evening meal.

Leander gathered himself. He was weak, but his legs didn't wobble like they had before. He stood, hands on the doorway, and looked up into the front yard.

Two crowded tables sat in the red light of the evening sun. As he watched, Mary came out of the house and added a bowl mounded with potato salad to the ample food. Even so far away, Leander could smell the fried chicken and boiled corncobs. After Mary sat, his father motioned with his hand and the food began to be passed.

Leander stepped into the yard and leaned on the barn as he watched the whole meal. His belly was still full from the food Katia had left, but he felt hungry in a way he hadn't in years.

Even after the pie dishes were cleared, the men lingered, talking of their plans for going downtown the next day.

His father spoke little, but laughed with them sometimes.

As each man stood to leave, he would first nod to Mary, then stop at the head of the table and lay a gentle hand on their father's shoulder or arm, as if the contact was some form of mutual blessing.

As the men headed in Leander's direction, he slipped into the barn to avoid them.

Inside, there was little light, but he knew his way through the old building by feel. He ran his hands along the worn places and listened to the familiar creak of old planks underfoot and the rustle of the animals settled in for the night.

He remembered a childhood adventure and dug in a corner by the pigsty, unearthing the treasure of a quarter he'd buried there as a little boy. As then, it was all the money to his name.

He found a barrel of apples and took one for himself and gave another to Timber.

He climbed up the ladder to the loft, piled high with the summer's hay.

Another ladder led to a hatch and he climbed through it out onto the roof. He settled into the little notch at the peak where he'd sat so many times before, and remembered so many conversations he'd had there with Hans and Harry.

The moon had come up full, and he could see the fireflies floating above the summer fields. He took the apple from his pocket and bit into it. From the rooftop, he could look at the velvet black of the forest stretching to the south and map every path, gully, and spring. Even the rhythm of the crickets sounded right in a way they did nowhere else.

Finally, he climbed down and walked toward the men at the fire.

When Joe saw him approach, he stood and

left. The others turned quiet.

"He doesn't like me much," Leander said.

"No, he doesn't," the popcorn man said. "But that didn't stop him from giving up his bed for you to sleep in. I'm Palmer."

Leander felt the weight of the moment he'd betrayed the man, pulling the tarp off the wagon and setting so much in motion, and wondered if he would ever be able to atone.

"Sit," Palmer said. "He's just gone for a walk before turning in. He does that a lot."

Leander took a spot near the fire and stared into the flames.

"I'm Macolm, and you can have my bunk after tonight," another said. "I'm leaving."

"Where you going?" Leander asked.

"I'm a private in the Corps de Afrique. The 78th You Ess Cee Tee," Malcolm said, stretching out each letter. "Riding downtown tomorrow to muster."

"Don't get him started," Palmer said. "It's like he's a general or something."

"I was in the army," Leander said. "It was the hardest thing I ever did."

"I was a slave," Malcolm said. "That wasn't much fun, either."

The other men laughed and Leander turned red-faced in embarrassment.

"After Old Man Goggins and his whip,

there ain't nothing the U.S. Army can throw at me that I can't handle," Malcolm said with a smile. "I know most of them soldiers don't give a damn about us. They're fighting for God and country, whatever the hell that's supposed to mean. I just know that I seen my family sold off piece by piece. Me and Palmer, we were the lucky ones. Goggins bought us together, but my momma was sold down the river. God or country don't mean a lick when you watch your baby sister yanked away from your mama. All these boys on either side can fight for whatever they think they're fighting for, but the ones fighting on the side of Goggins, those are the ones I'm joining up against. Whatever they want me to do in that cause, I'll do."

Leander didn't say anything.

"I'm sorry the army was hard for you, though," Malcolm finished.

There was a long silence after that until Leander stood and walked away.

He headed back into the dark woods and turned toward his shack.

When he heard voices, he slowed, thinking it might be Harry and the train stowaway. He crept behind some scrub brush at the clearing's edge.

It was his sister and Joe sitting by a fire on

the bank of the pond. Behind them was a neat little cabin where he'd built his shack so many times.

Mary was resting her head in Joe's lap, crying.

"I can't save him, I can't save him," she said over and over as he stroked her hair. "I don't know how. I can't save him."

Each sob that floated over the pond felt like a blow to his stomach. He knew how hard his sister worked to hide her vulnerability. He stared in wonder at the way she shared her pain with this man, and the way she seemed to take comfort in his tenderness. Leander understood that somehow to spy on her then was as much a wrong as any he had ever done. Ashamed, he turned away, moving deeper into the woods.

His father's mill stood on the bank of the dammed creek, black against the starry night sky. Leander climbed onto the platform and ran his hand over the well-worn saws and the iron tools hanging neatly on the wall.

There was little lumber in the clearing, but the mound of fresh sawdust testified to the work done.

He picked up a piece of fine walnut from the scrap pile, running his fingers on the smooth, planed side, admiring the straightness of the cut.

He sat in the dark, listening to the gurgle of the creek, remembering the times when he had swam with Harry and Hans in the mill pond.

He sat there for a long time before climbing to his feet.

Mary and Joe had left the clearing, but the cabin drew him back.

The neat little building he found had little in common with the shack he'd left behind. Even in the moonlight, he could tell it was perfect of line, with a tight roof and a little porch extending toward the pond.

The door was closed, but there was no lock. Inside he found a few pieces of simple furniture and a small bed.

He lay down, thinking of the night he'd spent there with his friends in the cold winter before he'd gone away and he fell into a deep sleep.

The sun was high when he woke. He stripped off his clothes and plunged into the pond and swam to the bottom. He opened his mouth, taking in the clear, cold water from the spring.

He dressed, feeling better than he had in years. Before he left, he took the quarter from his pocket and lay it on the bed, the only payment he could make.

In the barnyard, the men were loading into the wagon for their trip downtown.

He went to where Malcolm stood among the men.

"May I go with you to the enlistment office, please?" Leander asked.

The cart was nearly out the driveway when Joe followed them, hopping to climb into the wagon bed.

**Riot in Buffalo: Furious Outbreak
between the Irish and Negroes.**
Our city yesterday was again the scene of
a terrible riot, instigated by some of the
laborers on the dock. There has for some
time past been a growing antipathy between a portion of the Irish laborers and
the negroes, the former being unwilling to
allow the latter the privilege of working
along the wharves. . . .

The appearance of the negroes was the
signal for another onset, and the crowd,
yelling like so many demons, and armed
with clubs and stones, made a rush for
the terrified victims. . . .

— *BUFFALO COMMERCIAL,* JULY 7, 1863

Since the secession, Harry had helped
plenty of Confederates pass through Town
Line, but this one was different.

The ones from the Elmira prison camp

showed up closer to dead than alive, and stared at him with eyes like accusations. He always thought they were sizing him up for a meal.

They didn't speak much, and he was fine with that.

One had come through the summer before and talked his ear off. He told stories about his heroics at this battle or that. Harry tried to ignore him, but when he said something about shooting Union boys at Ball's Bluff, Harry had knocked him flat with one punch to the face. It had taken everything he had not to skin him right then. He had put him on the next train, and Compson told him later he'd been caught in Lancaster. Harry was fine with that.

This new one was named Keith, and he talked a lot, but mainly asked questions. He asked why Harry had attacked Leander and what kind of oats were in the field they were walking through on their way to the parsonage. When Harry showed him the loft in the parsonage barn where he would sleep, he asked what denomination the pastor was.

Before Harry left him there, Keith offered him an apple out of the haversack he had slung on his shoulder.

The others barely had clothes, much less a bag. Much, much less an apple.

Harry gave short answers.

"He had it coming."

"I don't know."

"The preachy kind."

He felt kind of bad for not talking much, but he wasn't in the mood. He kept thinking about Leander, about the way he'd called his name, like he was glad to see him. The nerve of him to come back here. How could he not know Harry wanted to kill him?

The sound of his old friend's whimpering made him feel sick and he hardly slept that night.

In the morning, Harry looked for the Confederate in the barn, but instead found him, shaved and scrub-faced, sitting at the breakfast table with the Zubrichs. He was wearing a pair of patched overalls.

"Your friend here was just telling us about his time in seminary," the pastor said as Mrs. Zubrich poured him a glass of buttermilk.

"It's true," Keith said. "I thought I had the calling in my youth, but I found myself too susceptible to worldly things to take the vows."

"Nonsense," the pastor said. "We all feel that pull away from the blessed life. You'll be a fine preacher some day."

Harry reached for the plate of flapjacks.

"You have work for us?" he asked.

"Mr. Weber needed help with his chicken coop," the preacher said. "But that can wait. Why don't you boys have a day and go down to the creek and do some fishing?"

"What did you say to him?" he asked the Confederate, laughing.

"I think a man of the cloth should enjoy God's grace on a beautiful day like today," Zubrich said. "It would be wrong to have a man of such a fine intellect digging in the mud."

While Harry finished his breakfast, Mrs. Zubrich packed them a basket and they set off into the summer morning.

They settled around one of Harry's favorite holes, but the sun was warm and bright and the fish stayed down. Harry pulled his hat over his face and napped in the sun until Keith woke him by digging into the basket.

"You people drink around here?" he asked, a chicken leg between his teeth.

"I thought you were one of those preacher folks," Harry said, rubbing his face.

"I dropped out," Keith said, pulling a bottle out of his bag and taking a swallow. "Best bourbon in Kentucky," he said.

He passed it over to Harry.

"Anyway, Christ's first miracle was at the

wedding at Cana," Keith said. "He turned water into wine. The temperance folks say it was grape juice, but that just don't make sense. Those temperance preachers, they tell you that you've got to follow the rules exactly like the Bible says. Exactly like it says. Then you ask them about the wine at Cana, and they say everyone at the wedding got themselves worked up over really good grape juice. Something's got to give in all that."

Harry took a swig and it was as good as the stuff on Compson's boat.

Keith chewed on the chicken and looked at the dragonflies darting across the slow, rippling creek.

"Over there." He pointed.

"What? Is there someone there?" Harry said, staring into the reeds near the bed.

"That's where they'll be biting," Keith said.

Harry stared across the creek.

"I fished up and down this creek my whole danged life," he said, laughing. "There ain't a fish within five rod of that spot."

"There's none here," Keith said. "Indulge me. It's the price of the bourbon."

"Ah, what the hell," Harry said, climbing to his feet. "There's shade over that side anyway."

They had their lines in the water for less than ten minutes before Harry pulled out a fourteen-inch brown trout.

"Son of a bitch," he said, laughing, pulling the hook from the squirming fish.

"Did you really quit the Union?" Keith said.

"Yes sir," Harry said. "It's been a year and a half now."

The Confederate nearly doubled over laughing.

"Well, since you're a fellow Confederate, I'll even clean that thing for you," Keith said, pulling a huge bowie knife from his bag and reaching for the fish.

"How's that work?" Keith asked as he lay the wriggling fish on a rock and crushed its head with the butt end of the knife. "You stop the Yankees from coming in and all?"

"They don't really bother us," Harry said. "Not much has changed, except the pastor runs the town now."

The knife was so sharp that he barely touched the fish's belly with its tip before guts blossomed out of the silver skin.

"They say you should wait and do this when you're ready to cook," Keith said as he pulled the innards out of the fish's cavity. "But I like to do it right then. Feels better to me."

He submerged the fish until the water ran clear.

"Something took my bait," he said, pulling his own bare hook from the water. He squeezed another worm onto it and dropped the line again.

"Pastor Zubrich?" he asked as he settled back onto the bank. "He said you're the sheriff, you're in charge."

Harry laughed as he re-baited his own hook.

"He says that so if someone doesn't like something, they can blame me," Harry said. "But he makes all the rules, collects most of the fine money."

Keith turned to look at him.

"That so?" he said. "The pastor takes all the money. What's he spend it on? Girls?"

"Not many girls around here," Harry said. "Not since Wilhelm got killed and the Corner House closed down. As far as I can tell, he's got it all saved up somewhere. He collects all the money in the plate each Sunday, but damned if I ever seen him part with a red cent. He's got a decent-sized vegetable patch behind the barn and he makes all the runners like you do the work."

Harry took another swig of the bottle. "Except for men of the cloth, of course." He laughed.

"So what do you all do for fun around here then?" Keith asked.

"Fun?" Harry said. "Shit, we don't have no fun around here. All the fun people are dead. Nothing but a bunch of old farmers in this town now."

"Shh," Keith's said, sitting up as his line tightened. He studied the rippling water for a few seconds before yanking the rod hard. The surface of the water exploded as a fish struggled against the line.

Harry watched as the Southerner pulled in a monster, nearly two feet long.

"Katia would fry that up fine," Harry said.

"Katia?" Keith said, setting about to gut the second fish.

"Don't get any ideas," Harry said, laughing. "She's taken. We're going to get married and move down South and I'm going to buy a big house like those plantation people."

Keith feigned shock.

"You really are a Confederate," he said. "I'm not going to go messing with your woman. How could I? We're practically brothers in arms. Why don't you get her down here tonight? We'll build us a fire and fry up some fish, drink whiskey, and howl like wolves."

"It's been a long time since I done something like that," Harry said. "I'd like that."

He pulled his hat back over his eyes and lay back for another nap.

They built the fire in the dry stones of the low creek.

Before long, Katia arrived, directed there by Mrs. Zubrich. She brought strawberry pie and a half-dozen ears of corn to roast in the fire. Keith asked her about her childhood in Germany, and about her work at the farm.

"The place sounds like a plantation, what with all the niggers and all," Keith said. "They rich like the plantation folks down South?"

"There's a big safe in Mr. Nathan's study," she said. "I'm sure it is full of money, though even his children don't get to see it."

They passed the bottle until it was empty.

"You ain't said nothing about yourself," Harry said to Keith. "How long you been in the army? Where you from?"

"I ain't never been in the army," the Southerner said. "I'm kind of a hired hand, more than anything. Mr. Compson hired me on for some work down in Buffalo. I'll be on my way there tomorrow."

"You already talked to Commander Compson?" Harry said. "I didn't know I was supposed to take you downtown tomorrow."

"Commander? Is that what he calls himself up here?" Keith said. "As good as anything else, I guess."

It was a fair evening, and they slept under the stars.

Keith was gone in the morning, and Katia and Harry stripped and bathed in the warm water. She scrubbed his back with the silt of the creek and he washed her hair with a piece of soap she had brought.

"We should leave here," she said. "It's time to go. How much money do you have?"

He thought of the pickle crock full of notes he'd buried in a pine grove behind the parsonage.

"I think there's about five thousand," he said.

She gasped.

"I know," he said. "Every time I tell Compson I want to quit, he just gives me a bigger wad of cash."

"I don't want to wait anymore," she said. "Mr. Willis says bad things are coming."

"Hold on for just a while longer," he said. "I almost have enough."

"We are rich, no reason to wait," she said.

She moved against his body in that way, and he reached for her.

"Let's go now," she said, climbing on top of him and unbuttoning his shirt.

"Maybe," he said.

Afterward, they packed their things and she headed up the creek path toward the Willis farm and he went up Town Line Road to the parsonage. He was hoping Mrs. Zubrich had made biscuits when he opened the back door into the kitchen.

Two strange men looked up from the table.

"Run!" Zubrich shouted, but Keith struck the pastor with the butt end of his knife and he fell to the ground. The two men lifted their pistols from the table in unison and pointed them at Harry.

Mrs. Zubrich went to her knees next to her husband and dabbed at the blood on his face before helping him up.

"There's no place to run," Keith said. "Come in and close the door."

Harry raised his hands.

"Don't bother with that," Keith said.

"Don't you hit him again," Harry said.

"Don't you do anything that makes me want to," Keith said. "Now these fine people have already offered up alms for us poor unfortunate war refugees, and we wanted to see what you could add to the cause before we move on to our other business."

"You want my money?" Harry said.

"This jerkwater doesn't raise no idiots." Keith smiled. "I almost didn't bother, but it turns out the good pastor here has accumulated a nice little nest egg. My experience is that Mr. Compson spends other people's money pretty freely, and I'm betting you've done well."

He took a biscuit from the table and slathered jam on it before taking a big bite.

"I'm looking at you guessing you got it buried somewhere nearby. A pipe tobacco tin, maybe?"

"Fuck you." Harry spat, but he jerked back when Keith sent Mrs. Zubrich sprawling.

"That gave me no pleasure," Keith said. "Now this isn't going to work out any other way. You'll take me to the money and dig it up. Me and my boys will head on down to Buffalo. You all get back to your seceding ways like good little Confederates."

Mrs. Zubrich moaned as she climbed to her feet. She was cradling her arm as if it were broken.

Harry clenched his fists over and over again.

"I give you the money, you'll let them go?" he asked.

"As God is my witness," Keith said.

"Let's go," Harry said, opening the door.

He walked through the parsonage garden to the cypress wind break on the far side, listening to the footsteps behind him. He could see their twin shadows stretching long in front of him — his hunched, Keith's tall, with the bowie knife moving in rhythm to their steps. He wanted to jump the Confederate, but wasn't sure what he could do even if he could overpower him. There were still the gunman at the kitchen table.

When they got to the spot in the line of trees, Harry kicked at the fine brown needles that carpeted the ground. He went to his knees and brushed away the dirt from the top of the buried pickle crock. As he lifted the lid and reached for the bundled notes inside, the blade flashed in the sun. He jumped to the side as Keith drove the tip of the bowie knife into the ground where he'd knelt.

Harry scrambled to his feet and felt something drip from his left hand. He looked down to see blood flowing from a gash running the length of his forearm. He couldn't feel his left hand, and it twisted weirdly when he tried to make a fist.

Keith lunged, and Harry jumped back, then took off into the cornfield on the other side of the break.

His head swimming, he stopped to listen, knowing the sounds of bodies passing through the cornfields from countless afternoons chasing Leander and Hans, but all he could hear was the wind through the tall green stalks. He took off his shirt and wrapped his arm in it.

When he heard the shots echo, he screamed into the clear blue sky overhead. By the time he got to the parsonage, Keith and the two others were gone, but he found the Zubrichs in the parlor, slumped together on their couch. He fell to his knees, and struggled not to wretch into the warm blood pooling on the floor.

"We will go west," Katia said. "Ohio."

She held her carpetbag on her knees, swaying as the train rounded a bend.

"I'm going to find them," Harry said.

"You should tell the police," Katia said. "They will handle it."

His arm throbbed and he felt weak. He wished he could just lie down and sleep.

"I am supposed to be the police." He grimaced.

"You bled too much to mess with them," she said. "Let's keep going. I have a little money saved. Enough to start with."

"It's not about the money," he said.

He had barely been able to stand when he got to the Willises' kitchen door. Katia had bandaged the wound, left him in the kitchen for just a minute, then returned with her bag in hand.

"We are not coming back," she announced, and he knew she was right.

She had helped him to the highway where she flagged down a passing wagon that had taken them to Alden. Doc Pride had cleaned and stitched the wound and wrapped the arm again.

"You should rest," he had told him.

"We are not staying here one moment longer than we have to," Katia said, and even the doctor knew not to argue. They boarded the train in Alden.

The line ended at the Exchange Street station and she helped him stand and step off the train. He leaned against an iron post.

"I will find the cheapest way to get us to Ohio," she said, heading for the ticket booth.

Harry grunted and headed for Exchange Street.

She reached for his good arm, but he winced and pulled away.

"You will get yourself killed," she said, struggling to hold onto him and carry her heavy bag.

"I'm not going to let them get away with

it," he said, looking back at her.

He motioned to the luggage check in the station.

"Leave that thing," he said, but she frowned and shook her head.

"We'll go see Compson," he said, exasperated. "We can rest on his boat. It's nice there. He won't let them get away with this. He'll tell us where to find them."

He turned and headed toward the docks. She shouted at his back in German until she finally ran to catch up with him.

"I should have stopped this a long time ago," Harry said. "I shouldn't have run from Keith. I let that big knife scare me. I never should have run."

"You could not have stopped them," Katia said.

"I could have tried," he said.

The midsummer sun baked his back, and he sweated into his shirt. He had felt light-headed since he'd looked down to see the long slice in his arm, seen the muscle and skin and blood opened up to the world like a slaughtered animal.

He ran his hand over the bandage.

Gunshots popped in the distance, echoing on the quiet street.

Harry was used to the city smelling like an unemptied chamber pot, but today there was another smell, a different type of smoke. Gunpowder and wood and something more bitter and ugly.

He stopped himself in the middle of Seneca Street, shaking his head, trying to understand what was wrong.

"It's so quiet," Katia said, coming up beside him. "Is it always this way?"

Harry blinked. That was it. The streets were abandoned. He was missing the throng that greeted him on every trip he'd taken into the city.

A policeman on a horse galloped by.

"There's a riot going on," he shouted. "Down by the canal. Get the hell out of the streets."

Before Katia could say anything, Harry sprinted toward the docks.

There were more guards around the *Abigail* than he'd ever seen before, but the one stationed at the gangplank recognized him and waved him aboard.

Compson glanced at them as they were led onto the top deck, but turned his back to them to keep staring at a red glow to the east. He had a full tumbler of bourbon in his hand.

"That is the spark," he said. "The city will burn tonight. If we do not win on the battlefield, we will help the Union tear itself apart."

Harry blinked. "I'm looking for your men," he said. "Keith and the others. They killed the pastor and his wife. Damn near killed me."

He held up his bandaged arm. "I'm going to take them back to Town Line and string them up at the crossroads."

Compson chuckled. "I doubt you could manage that," he said. "You do not look well, Mr. Strauss. And those three are capable, to say the least. I have many men at my disposal, but I had to search far and wide to find any that would be quite so thorough."

"Where are they?" Harry said.

"I haven't seen them today," Compson said, gesturing toward the red glow. "But your friend Keith has his orders, and that's his handiwork. I have quite an agenda for that trio over the next week or so. They'll be quite busy."

"They're your men," he said. "You need to help me bring them in. You're responsible for what they done."

Compson frowned. "How am I responsible?"

"They're your men."

"Am I responsible for everything you've

ever done? Of course not. But you are as much my man as they."

"I ain't your man," Harry said. "I'm through with you."

"I'm sorry to hear about the pastor and his lovely wife," Compson said. He sipped from the crystal tumbler. "He was a true believer, I'll give him that. Now if you'll excuse me, I think it's prudent to move the *Abigail* across the river. Riots, you know. You can pull the trigger, but you cannot aim."

He gestured to a man standing nearby.

"Show these two to the dock and tell the captain to get us under way." He turned his back on them to watch the fires grow in the city.

They were ushered off the boat, and watched as the boat cast off and headed out of the harbor.

"They'll be down by the canal, where the riots are," Harry said.

"No!" Katia said. "We are getting on a train."

Harry shook his head and headed north.

"I am leaving!" Katia shouted at him.

Harry turned back to her.

"You were right," he shouted. "Damn it, you've been right all along. You've been saying we should go for months. I should have listened. You were right. Tomorrow I will listen to you, and I will do as you say. And I will the next day, too. And the day after that. But tonight, I gotta do this. Don't you understand? The Zubrichs were my friends. I brought Keith and those other two into town. It was me that got them killed. If I don't do something, I ain't no better than Leander Willis."

He pulled away from her and headed north toward the canal.

Katia watched his back, and then rushed to catch up.

"Tomorrow you will listen," she said.

Fire wagons surrounded a burning warehouse near the canal. A dead horse lay in the street, still harnessed to its delivery cart. Men stood in the streets watching the fire. The smell of burning flesh filled the air, and Harry hoped it came from an animal. He found a lead pipe amongst the shards of shattered glass in the street and measured its weight as he would a baseball bat.

At Dug's Dive, the police stood by as half a dozen white men dragged a black man into the streets. As the night grew darker, the mobs split and moved through the streets more freely. Smoke rose over the skyline, and gunfire echoed around them. Harry pulled Katia into an alley as a dozen shouting men streamed by them in a street near the commercial slip.

Harry poked his head back into the street.

"We got thirty of them blocked up in their church," someone shouted. "We're going to burn it to the ground."

"That murdering son of a bitch," Harry said, setting off at a trot behind the man. "That's where he'll be."

Katia followed with her heavy bag.

The burning smell was worse as they headed east. They passed a house collapsed in on itself, its dying flames throwing gruesome light on the surrounding scorched trees.

They followed Broadway east until they came up behind the mob.

Over the line of torches and clubs held aloft, Harry could make out a half dozen black men standing on the steps of the little brick church, shoulder to shoulder, some with pipes or sticks in hand, others empty-handed.

Michigan Street stretched empty between them, covered in shattered glass, shimmering in the torchlight.

Harry pointed to a peg-legged man near the center of the line.

"What the hell is he doing here?" Harry asked.

Katia looked at the line of men.

"There's Palmer, too," she said.

"A reading from the book of Luke." Keith's familiar drawl rang clear in the night.

He sat on Zubrich's old swayback horse in the midst of the Broadway mob, his bowie knife held over his head, flashing red.

" 'I came to bring fire to the earth, and how I wish it were already kindled!' "

He laughed loudly.

"Judgment day is here! The Bible says you must have made good with the Lord by the dawn of that day, but I'm more merciful than your God. I'm going to give all one last chance. Y'all just go back into your church, kneel down in your little pews, and pray for forgiveness for your sins. That way, when I send this purifying fire through, you'll be in my good graces."

"I can't see the other two," Harry said, scanning the mob.

"There's too many of them," Katia said.

The voices shouting at each other across the empty expanse of Michigan Avenue got louder, and a bottle smashed against the brick face of the church.

"I don't care," Harry said. "I'm going after that bastard."

"No!" Katia said, grabbing at his arm, but

Harry pulled away.

"Stay there," Harry said, pointing at an alley. "Don't make a sound."

"You're going to get yourself killed," she shouted, but he ignored her and started toward the mob.

The mob moved into Michigan Street, clubs and torches held overhead. Harry hefted the pipe as best he could and stepped into the street.

The sound of the shot, so close and contained between the tall buildings of Broadway, seemed louder and echoed longer than any he'd ever heard. He fell to the ground instinctively.

"Get down," he shouted, turning toward Katia.

She was already kneeling, open bag in front of her, aiming a pistol at the mob.

The swayback, suddenly riderless, scampered and bucked, knocking two men to the ground.

"Run," someone shouted.

Immediately there were feet and legs around Harry as he tried to climb to his feet. Katia fired again toward the intersection.

Harry lifted his pipe, and ran toward the center of the splintering mob.

He found Keith at the end of a trail of

bloody cobblestones, crawling toward where his knife lay yards away.

Harry kicked him in the face, knocking him onto his back.

Keith's eyes took a minute to focus on his attacker. "You?" he said, coughing up blood.

Joe came up to stand behind Harry.

"Where are the other two?" Harry demanded.

"Weren't you the one telling me you'd wanted the niggers out of there?" Keith asked.

"What the hell are you talking about?" Harry asked.

"Didn't you say you wanted the niggers out of Town Line?" Keith asked again.

Harry kicked him again.

"Or did you come for this?" He reached into his coat pocket, taking out a blood-soaked wad of bills.

"This shinplaster?" He laughed between coughs. "Worthless Confederate script. You couldn't buy a poke from a fifty-cent whore with all this. Compson made a fool of you."

Harry kicked the money and it fluttered into the night.

"Fuck the money," Harry said. "This is about killing the Zubrichs. Where are the other two?"

Keith looked to where Katia stood next to

Harry, the pistol still hanging from her hand. He winced.

"Like I told you, they're after the niggers in Town Line," he said. "And the safe."

"Safe?" Harry blinked.

"My God! Mr. Willis!" Katia gasped. "The farm."

"I'm going after them," Harry said, moving toward the horse.

"No, him," Katia said, pointing at Joe.

Joe looked back, confused.

"Let him go," Katia said. "You can't go back there. You're too weak."

Harry nodded, wrangling the animal. "There's two killers back in Town Line going after Mr. Willis's money," he said, leading the horse over to Joe.

"Leander stole all the money," Joe said, as Harry helped him mount the horse. "There's nothing left."

"That don't matter," Harry said.

Katia handed the pistol up to Joe.

"Take this," she said. "It's Mary's. I took it when I left."

HOMEGUARD

Dear Mary,

Your letters finally found me here, and they mean more to me than I can say. I'm sorry it's taken me so long to respond, and I'm sorry I've worried you for so long.

I'm grateful for all the news clippings you've sent along. I wish that some of it was good.

I'm in Aurora, and there's about ten thousand people here, but nobody can say where this place is. Some say it's in the Nevada territory, others that it's in the state of California.

If a week goes by without someone getting shot, people get worried that things are getting too civilized.

Everything here is brown, but the mountains are pretty. I wish you could see them.

I moved all the way west a few months

ago. Before that, I was in the desert for near on a year, I think. I lost track. I was passing through and found an empty shack next to a spring, and just stayed. It got mighty lonely out there, but the mornings were something to see.

I started a livery. Everyone here is getting ready to strike it rich, but I spend my days shoveling horseshit. The horses don't expect me to talk much, and for that I'm grateful. Most of them haven't seen any kindness for a long time, and there's real pleasure in treating them good.

There's grit in everything here. I wake up and it feels like a layer of dust has settled on my face. I miss green things. I miss the taste of those yellow apples from that twisted old tree behind your barn, and I miss watching the creek swell when it rains.

Even the fish aren't right here. I'd give anything for a brown trout pulled from Cayuga creek.

A while back, a nag came in so badly beaten that I wanted to throttle its owner. I held my hand, but got my wish. He got shot down that night.

Her name is Dusty, and after a lot of work, she's gotten better. She still ain't right in the head and probably never will be, but I can't think of much in my life that's made me happier than watching her spirit come back.

Me and Dusty took a ride down into California a couple weeks back. We kept going until we got to the ocean. There was a mound of something dead there on the rocks. It was the size of man, but it didn't have much shape at all. The sky and the ocean were the same gray and the cold was different than it is back home. Damp and hard.

I sat by the water for a long time. It sounded like the water was alternately shouting and hissing at me. It told me what I needed to know, and I don't aim to see it again. Me and Dusty turned around and came back here.

You'll think I'm crazy, but I miss the snow. If I had anything to my name, I'd surely give it up to see a fresh Town Line snowfall. To wake to that perfect white blanket covering the fields, the whole world made new overnight. It's then that you know God forgives, that there's mercy in this world.

I've taken to using my real name again. They would probably find my history quaint if they knew it. You can write me again here.

Except for you, there's not a human soul in this world I'm much interested in. I wish that you could have seen the things I've seen. You might help me understand what they mean.

YOURS,
CHARLIE

Mary thought she would feel Leander's blows to the door for the rest of her life. She had closed the door and wrapped her arms around herself, collapsing against the solid wood, and had sobbed as each one jolted through her body like a bullet.

Katia came down from her room to stand over Mary, her mouth agape in horror.

"I can't let him in," Mary pled, looking up at her. "Forgive me, I can't."

"You'll burn," Katia hissed, and left her sprawled at the foot of the door.

She heard him climb off the porch and still she lay there, knowing that the house girl was right.

She made her way to her room, but she did not sleep that night.

She was up before dawn, and was pouring herself coffee when Joe found her in the kitchen. They sat together at the kitchen table, and Joe spoke of the day's work, but she could see in his eyes that Leander had found his way down to the men's cabin. Katia came down from her room and announced her presence by slamming the iron skillet onto the stove, and both Mary and Joe left without another word.

Mary went through the day, trying to ignore the goings-on around Leander's presence, Katia's running back and forth to the workmen's cabin, her father following her out there as well, the men's discomfort at dinner as they avoided mentioning the man they were hiding.

Katia disappeared after dinner was on the table, and Mary spent a long evening cleaning up the kitchen.

After she put her father to bed, she slipped out the back door and headed into the woods.

She could hear the men gathered around the fire as she walked the path to the little pond.

Joe was there, as he always seemed to be when she needed him most.

The little cabin was lit from within, but he sat on the ground in front of a fire. She lay on the ground next to him, breathing the applewood smoke and staring into the full moon.

"You couldn't let him in," he said. "He

would ruin you."

"What can I do?" she asked. "What will make him better?"

She curled up and put her head on his lap.

"Closing that door was the hardest thing I ever did." She sobbed. "What could I do?"

He pulled her hair from its bun and ran his fingers through it.

"We'll take care of him," he said. "I'll take care of him."

She cried again, not just for how lost her brother had looked, but also for the kindness of the man that held her then, the forgiveness that allowed him to help someone who had wronged him so badly.

They lay like that until the fire died, then he retrieved the lantern from the cabin and, arm around her, led her back up the path to the back door of the house.

"I'll watch for him," he said.

It did not surprise her that Katia was not in the kitchen when she came downstairs the next morning.

She spent the morning gathering a bushel of tomatoes and several pint baskets of strawberries for the men to take to their families.

She watched as her brother climbed into the wagon with the other men. She wanted to rush out to him, tell him to stay, put him in his bed with toast and tea like she had when he'd been sick as a boy. She wanted to fix him, but she knew that she could not.

Joe stood in the yard, watching as the wagon rolled away until he caught her eye, and motioned that he would ride with them. She nodded, then found her lip quivering again. Twice in three days. She would not survive much longer in this world if she let sentiment rule her. She gritted her teeth and set her mind to work. One of the old sows had gotten too ornery, attacking another's piglets, and she roused her father from the parlor and asked for his help.

Palmer had offered to have one of the men handle any of the slaughterings, but she had raised these animals from nothing more than warm handfuls fresh out of their mother, and she'd not let them see their end by any other hand. Instead, she preferred to take it on when the men were away and the farm was quieter, the animals more calm.

She and her father went out to the pen. He leashed the old sow and led it to the hang, where Mary stuck it. It kicked briefly as it bled out.

They worked as they always had, she scalding and scraping, while he salted the hams and bellies then set them to smoke.

As the afternoon went on, Mary left him to finish stuffing the sausages and took a loin into the kitchen to roast for dinner, but Katia was still not there.

She climbed the back stairs to the girl's room, but as soon as she opened the door, she could see that it had been cleared out. Even the old carpetbag Nathan had given her years before was gone.

Mary slammed the door.

She went down to the kitchen and stoked the cold stove.

In the evening they went onto the front porch with their plates. Her father kept standing, walking the length of the porch.

She listened to the sawing of the cicadas, looking for the courage to tell him that Katia was gone. Instead gunshots echoed up from the crossroads.

"Redcoats," Nathan hissed.

Mary poured him more rum.

Her nostrils were still filled with the smell of smoking hickory and pork fat, but there was something else in the wind, some other fire. There were more shots.

Mary motioned her father back to his chair as she stepped off the porch and out into the center of the quiet highway. A reddish glow lit the southwest sky. She triangulated as flames flicked above the tree line.

"The mill," she muttered, then climbed back onto the porch and rushed her father through the front door. She reached for her pistol, but the peg was empty.

"Goddammit," she hissed and swore at Katia under her breath.

"It's the lobsterbacks," her father said, stomping around the parlor. "They've finally come."

"Please, Father," Mary said, pushing her hair behind her ears. "Please just sit here quietly."

He sat down in the green leather chair and nodded.

She locked the front door and dashed through the house, out the backyard, and through the wheat field toward the mill.

The flames were already towering over the trees, turning the night sky orange and yellow. The waves of heat knocked her to her knees as she ran into the clearing. Coughing, she crawled away and climbed to her feet. She circled around to the creek, dove into the millpond, and swam toward the burning building. She surfaced, gasping, but the hot air seared her lungs. She turned away, fighting for breath as burning cinders rained down around her.

The smoke twisted into a tall column and

flames singed the leaves of the nearby trees. A deck support gave way and the platform fell into the creek, sending sparks and steam into the air.

She looked in the direction of the hamlet and spat. Not one of the farmers had come to help.

She swam to the far bank and watched, helpless, as piece after piece of her father's mill peeled off and fell burning into the water.

Soon, burning timbers floated everywhere in the mill pond.

Another sound penetrated the crackle and groan of the fire.

She cocked her ear, listening.

It was the house bell. Her father was ringing the bell.

She swam across the creek and climbed onto the shore, then tried to run back to the farm, but the brambles and burrs pulled at her wet skirt and slowed her down. Her lungs burned and her eyes teared from the smoke. She could hear the peck of rifles and the thrum of a shotgun and the sound of men shouting.

As she came into the barnyard, she stopped short at the sight of a man writhing on the ground, screaming in pain. Moonlight glistened off the patch of blood on his chest.

He flailed for his rifle, feet away. She crept into the shadow of the barn.

The light of a shotgun blast flashed from the kitchen window, illuminating the yard. A pistol shot answered weakly.

"Son of a bitch, Jesse," the man lying in the yard bellowed. "Get me out of here."

Mary bent lower, but the smoke in her lungs sent her into a coughing fit.

There was a grunt behind her. She whirled around, her hand on the slaughtering knife in her pocket, but it was only the pigs in their pen, woken by the commotion.

"Mary," her father called out. "They damned near got me, but I made 'em pay."

Then there was another sound. Something else, guttural and wild.

She circled around to the cabin, then into the line of poplars where she'd heard the pistol. Every tree frog, every cicada sounded like someone was just behind her, but all she found was a spray of blood on the silvery poplar leaves. She kept circling around the front of the house, and to the side yard, then around toward the barnyard. The man in the yard had stilled, and she crept out into the moonlit yard to take the rifle.

His lifeless eyes stared into the black of the night.

The guttural noise rose again, syncopating oddly with the noise of nighttime insects.

Cradling the dead man's repeater, she circled the house again and again, but there was nothing.

When she finally went inside, the house was dark as pitch and the smell of gunpowder hung in the air. The night wind blew through shattered windows, twisting her mother's drapery into ethereal, dancing shapes. She called for her father and he answered from the parlor.

He sat in the dark, still pointing the shotgun at the moonlit landscape, his face haggard but his eyes ablaze.

"I've been calling the Haudenosaunee," he said.

"I hope they come," she said, biting her lower lip.

"It'll be good to see Chief Parker again."

He sat and waited for his long-dead friends late into the night. She tried to sit with him, but jumped at each creak of the old house. She patrolled from room to room, staring out into the moonlit night. The smell of the still-burning mill mixed with the gunpowder haze that floated through the house. When her father finally started to doze, she took his shotgun and put him to bed.

"They're not coming," he whispered just before he began to snore. "They've left me."

She closed the door behind her. Alone in the empty hallway, she began to shake as the fear of the night took hold of her, but she clenched her teeth until they ached.

She went from room to room, keeping her distance from the windows. Finally, she settled in the parlor, listening through the broken windows, shivering in the night air. The wind kicked up and she nearly fired the rifle three different times at the moving shadows the swaying trees cast in the moonlight.

Finally, she went down into the cellar, pushed away the wardrobe, and crawled onto the pallet that she'd made for Joe years before. She did not find sleep in the dark, but lay there listening to her own breath and the sound of the house around her.

She wasn't sure how long she lay there when she heard the back door creak open and then his voice calling her.

"Joe," she called back, her voice quivering.

There was the pop, step, pop, of him descending the stairs for her, and then he was there.

"You're safe," he said in the dark. "You're safe."

She came out of the tunnel to meet him and collapsed herself into his chest as the fear drained out of her.

"You're safe," he repeated over and over, his voice soothing.

She reached a shaking hand up to his lips to quiet him, and with her other, she took his hand and led him to the pallet where he had lain helpless for weeks.

"I love you," she said as she pulled him down onto her and covered his mouth with hers.

■ ■ ■ ■

1864

■ ■ ■ ■

PHILO PARSONS

Washington, D.C., October 11, 1864

Maj. General John A. Dix,
Commanding at New York:
There is reason to believe that a plot is afoot by persons hostile to the United States, who have found an asylum in Canada, to invade the United States and destroy the city of Buffalo; that they propose to take possession of some of the steamboats on Lake Erie, to surprise Johnson's Island, and set free the prisoners of war confined there, and to proceed with them to attack Buffalo."

— TELEGRAPH FROM
EDWIN STANTON,
U.S. SECRETARY OF WAR, TO BUFFALO

It was near midnight when Yates Bell boarded the *Philo Parsons* at Toledo and paid the captain to stop at Amherstburg during the ferry's circuit around the western end of Lake Erie.

The October night was cold, and Yates went belowdecks to warm himself. A card game had started among the passengers and a skinny man hawked whiskey. He sat on a bench and dozed in the warmth for a while before climbing back onto the deck to wake himself.

Something was wrong with the heavens.

Bands of light gyrated across the northern sky, casting green light on the soft waves of Erie. He stood entranced, imagining that only his hands on the rail kept him from floating into the swirling vault.

The captain came up beside him.

"You don't get the aurora borealis down South, do you?" he asked.

"No. Normally, no," Yates said. "But a few years back they flashed over the battlefield after Fredericksburg, a sign from God that he'd ordained the victory."

The captain took off his cap and scratched his head for a minute, then spit tobacco juice over the gunnel.

"When the lights are strong, they don't even need electricity on the telegraph lines," he said. "They power the lines, instead of the other way around. You can send messages clear across Canada on them. Can you imagine that?"

Yates grunted, not taking his eyes from the sky.

The captain hunkered down, his voice low.

"I have a friend who worked in the telegraph office in Montreal. Whenever the northern lights were dancing, he would always take a few minutes to stop with the dots and dashes, and he'd just leave the circuit open. I was there with him once. I sat and listened and I heard something. I swear I heard a voice in that crackle and buzz. I heard the voice of the lights."

Yates took his eyes from the sky and looked at the browned leather face of the sailor in front of him.

"What did it say?" Yates asked, looking into the man's eyes.

The captain took off his spectacles and polished them with a handkerchief.

"That's the secret I'll take to my grave," the captain said. "But I guaran-goddamn-tee you that it wasn't 'Go out and kill each other.' "

He laughed loudly and nodded at the sky.

"Fools." He laughed, slapping Yates on the back. "Those boys down in Fredericksburg were just plain fools. God drops a dancing curtain of lights on their pointy little heads, and all they want to do is murder. Well, I want nothing to do with it. Just leave me alone out here on my lake with my boat and the borealis."

He turned and walked toward the pilot-house.

"By the way, I came out to tell you that we'll be in Amherstburg in just a few minutes," he said over his shoulder.

Yates watched the man walk away, alternately whistling and laughing into the night.

He had become something of a lake man himself in the year since he'd arrived at Windsor. His beard had grown full and the rest of his face was the same permanent red of the windblown men that tossed their nets into the water each morning. When he wasn't running Confederates across the lake, he poked around on the water, learning the coastline, the hidden coves, the currents. He thought of Scott and Nelda often, and had wondered why he hadn't just bought some nets like the man had told him to.

There was something about time on the water that shifted a man's perspective. He'd felt it himself, and he saw it in the men he ferried in the night.

They'd feel the boat's slow rocking and listen to the quiet lapping of the waves and they would take the drawling sailor as their priest and the sky of stars as their confession booth. As the *Swan* skipped across the water, they would voice their stories of killing and loss, and beg him for solace that he had no idea how to grant.

Sailing in the dark was no easy thing, so Yates would say nothing to his passengers, nodding his grizzled head at them as he guided the boat across the water. When they landed on Canadian soil, he'd put a hand on their shoulders as he guided them out of the boat, and they would thank him as if he'd saved their lives.

With each one of them, he found the war more pointless.

When Compson had finally come to at the western outpost, he immediately sought out Yates.

"At least you still sound like a Southerner," he'd said. He pulled out a tattered Yankee bill and put it on the table. "You'll need to shave and get a decent shirt, at least, before the mission."

Yates had laughed.

Compson, of course, had a grand scheme to change the course of the war. His others had been the talk of the remnants of his men at the outpost. There was the fizzle of a riot in Buffalo, and the torching of an orphanage in New York during the riots there. Even among the ragged criminals of Windsor, that was seen by many as a coward's move. Lately, there'd been talk of a raid on a bank in Vermont. And just a few weeks before, Yates had ferried a friend he'd known back in the John Brown days that talked of a plan to kill the tyrant.

"Why don't you come with me?" he'd said. "You could pass as a gentleman again if you'd clean yourself up. I could use another hand."

Yates had turned down his old friend. If he were honest, he didn't have much taste for killing anymore. The end of the war seemed near, and he didn't place hope in any of these desperate acts to change its course.

And it did need changing. The news had been bad for a long time, but nothing he read in the newspapers convinced Yates that the cause was lost more than Compson's sallow face and the disrepair of the man's clothes.

Yates had almost left after that first meeting.

It wouldn't take much to get the *Swan* north up the Detroit River to Lake Huron. No one would bother him there. He had some money. He could buy a nice cabin and some good nets. Find himself a squaw.

Perhaps it was the other soldiers he ferried. Despite himself, he couldn't help think he'd helped them.

Yates went to the barber and got shaved.

When he arrived back at the boathouse, he found Compson at a table with a pistol and a stack of papers in front of him. The commander pushed the gold pin across the table to him, the three stars of a captaincy in the Confederate Navy.

"You can go home after this," Compson had said.

"What's at home?" Yates said. "The Yankees are at Walnut Grove, and the lawyers won't let me have it."

"They've moved on," Compson said. "It's there, waiting for you. Your birthright."

"That's mighty convenient," Yates said, smirking.

"No, it's not," Compson said. "I wish I was lying, but that battalion just burned Atlanta to the ground and is heading for Savannah as we speak. There's nothing left for the Yankees at Harpers Ferry."

"But there's something else."

He paused, drawing Yates in.

"I found your runaway."

Yates felt the ground shift under him.

He jumped across the table, grabbing Compson by his frayed lapels.

"Son of a bitch. You said he was dead," he growled.

Compson rested his hand on the pistol.

"I spent four goddamned years chasing him, and you knew where he was all this time," Yates said.

"I'm sorry," Compson said. "I swear on my honor I didn't."

"I should kill you," Yates hissed. "Give me one reason I shouldn't."

"He's about to file papers," Compson said. "I'm the only way you can stop him from taking Walnut Grove."

He paused, letting the message sink in.

"You can kill me, but that won't stop Joe from becoming the master of Walnut Grove."

Yates felt like he was adrift on the lake with no shore. He loosened his grip and slumped back in his chair.

"What am I supposed to do?" he asked.

"The *Michigan*," Compson said. "One understaffed Yankee gunboat guarding three thousand Confederate prisoners on Johnson Island."

His tone was that of a grocer trying to sell rotten fruit.

"I have an agent on board who will incapacitate the officers. You and a team of raiders will seize the ship, free our soldiers, and transport them to the Buffalo waterfront. Once there, you'll arm them with the weapons on board and you will turn the *Michigan*'s cannons on the city. The copperheads of Buffalo will rise up and join you, and you will lead the accumulated force, cutting a swath through New York toward Manhattan. Reinforcements will come up through Pennsylvania. On the way, you can stop at a certain little farm outside Buffalo where you will find your slave."

It was so implausible that Yates laughed in Compson's sad face.

"You want me to be the South's John Brown?" he asked. "You know I was at his hanging, right?"

Compson pushed a roll of Union greenbacks across the table.

"Atlanta has fallen," Compson said. "Savannah will be gone soon. You think you can live a life worth anything up here on this lake? You're not a soldier, you've got no status. The Yankees will hang you as a spy when they finally track you down. And they will. You killed a U.S. marshal. That will not be forgotten. There are several other misdeeds around the border that I'm sure you have no alibi for. But do this, and everything you've done will be sanctioned under the cover of war. You'll be a hero."

He paused to let that sink in.

"Or I'll be hanged," Yates said.

"The election is just weeks away. Open another front on the war, and the press and I will handle the rest. Lincoln will be out and McClellan will negotiate."

Yates picked up the roll of money and counted it. Down South, they were using the Confederate bills as tinder. This much Union script could buy half of Alabama.

"Erastus Dratch is your second," Compson said.

"Dratch?" Yates asked. "This really is suicide."

"He's the best we have. He's done more to the Yankees than the Louisiana army, but he's northern born. Richmond wanted your name on these orders. Your men will break into different teams, boarding at separate docks to keep down any suspicion."

"I guess you knew how this would work even before you came here," Yates said. "I wish you could move the Yankees around on the board like you do me."

When the *Philo Parsons* docked, Yates disembarked to meet Dratch on the dock and to help load a crate of weapons, but Dratch lifted it on his own and pushed past him and up the gangplank.

"Out of my way, Your Highness," he sneered.

Others came aboard at Sandwich, then at Malden, and finally at Kelly's Island. At each stop, there were less than Yates had been told to expect and once they were all on board, he came up half a dozen short.

"Where are the others?" he asked after finding Dratch sitting on the crate on the aft deck.

"My lot got themselves some rum and ladies in the tavern last night," Dratch said. "I couldn't speak for the others."

"Sir," Dratch added, fitting as much scorn as possible into one syllable.

"We'll make due with those we have," Yates said. "We'll take the pilothouse once we're on the open water."

Yates pulled his notes out, trying to sort through the substitution of duties as he walked away.

It was a half hour later when he and Dratch pushed into the tiny pilothouse.

"What are you doing?" the captain asked. "You can't be in here."

"We're taking your boat," Yates said. "Just do what I tell you and the *Parsons* will be fine."

Dratch pulled the steam whistle, signaling the raiders to assemble on the aft deck.

Yates went astern to where the crated weapons had been piled, leaving Dratch in charge of the pilothouse. The guns were already being passed around. Yates scrambled to find a pistol, and was strapping on the holster when he heard the gunshot at the pilothouse. He rushed forward again.

The captain lay faceup at the threshold of the pilothouse.

Yates dropped to his knees. The man's blood pooled on the deck, rippling in rhythm to the boat's engine. The green aurora borealis reflected on his spectacles.

"What have you done?" Yates asked. "He's a Canadian civilian. They'll hang us."

"He resisted." Dratch cackled.

Yates put his hand on his holster, but Dratch just smiled and cocked his still-smoking pistol as he walked aft to where the other raiders had assembled the passengers and crew.

Yates climbed to his feet and grasped the wheel of the unpiloted boat in his bloody hands.

"Mr. Bell there just killed the captain," he heard Dratch announce. "The one of you boys that knows how to steer this wreck is the one he is least likely to shoot next. Any takers?"

The brass levers and dials on the helm

meant nothing to him. Yates scanned the horizon, looking into the night for any landmarks he recognized. He turned the *Philo* and aimed it west.

Dratch returned, his pistol leveled at a skinny mate in a worn peacoat with his hands in the air.

"Here's your crew," he said. "Issue your orders."

"Oui?" the man asked.

Yates looked at him, baffled.

"Quel est le cours?"

"Parlez-vous Anglais?" Dratch asked.

"Non."

"He doesn't even speak English," Yates said.

"He's the pilot, the only one who can steer." Dratch smiled with bemusement, then added, "Captain."

"Sandusky?" Yates asked, but the sailor shrugged.

"L'Islande de Johnson près de Sandusky," Dratch said, and pointed him toward the chart table.

The mate stepped over the pool of blood and riffled through cluttered drawers until he found a map to spread on the table.

"They speak that way up here," Dratch said with derision. "How long have you been in this country?"

"Nous aurons besoin de plus de carburant," the mate said. *"Nous ne pouvons arrêter Middle Bass Islande."*

"Oui," Dratch said, nodding.

"What did he say?" Yates asked.

Dratch continued his death's head grin, but said nothing.

Yates pushed past him and out onto the deck.

One of the raiders went from passenger to passenger and had them empty their pockets into a canvas satchel.

"Stop that," Yates ordered, but the thief paid him no mind.

Yates motioned for the raiders to gather, and after Dratch nodded, they formed a circle around him.

Yates looked at his notes and assigned each man's task, explaining the mission to the men.

"Crikes," one of the raiders blurted. "There's fourteen guns on the *Michigan.* You won't get to within a league of that thing before they sink this tub."

"We have an operative on board," Yates said. "He will poison the crew, and signal us with a flare when they are incapacitated."

"Of all the harebrained, idiotic plots," another raider said.

"This can save the Confederacy," Yates

said, not believing it as he said it.

"There ain't going to be no Confederacy," another said. "I'm through. I ain't signing on for any more of this."

Yates wasn't sure how he'd found himself on this boat with these men. Not for the first time since he'd boarded he wished he'd strangled Compson that day and sailed away. But with the captain lying dead on the deck, there was no way but forward for him.

The pack of raiders started to break up, each man grumbling and heading in different directions.

"I'll double your wages," Yates said, pulling the roll of bills from his pocket. "That, and the loot of Buffalo will make you all rich men."

The men did not turn back to him as he'd hoped.

"A flare, huh?" Dratch asked, coming up behind him. "It'll never happen."

"Make certain none of the passengers or crew have weapons," Yates said to him.

"The least of your worries," Dratch said. "You should just kill them now."

"Kill them?" Yates said. "We'll release them at the fort."

"They just witnessed you kill the captain on an international border," Dratch said.

"You really want to set them free?"

"You killed him, not me," Yates said.

"That's not what they think," Dratch said.

The *Philo Parsons* plodded west and south through the day and the raiders found the hawker's whiskey in the cargo hold. Yates ordered them to dump it overboard, but they brought the cask onto the aft deck and drank the afternoon away.

The passengers were crowded on the foredeck, and after seeing Dratch eyeing a pretty young lady, Yates took to standing watch over them himself.

When the *Philo Parson*'s engine idled down and the boat glided toward a small island's dock, Yates scrambled to the pilot-house only to argue fruitlessly with the pilot.

He found Dratch throwing dice with the drunk raiders on the aft deck.

"Why are we stopping?" he demanded. "Order the pilot back underway."

"We need to stop for fuel," Dratch said.

"Fuel? You must be joking," Yates shouted. "Every one of these men will jump ship if we land."

"You don't engender much loyalty, do you, Captain?" Dratch chuckled, then turned and went below. One of the men offered him the dice, and cackled at his back when he walked away.

When the boat reached the dock, Yates put the plank down and ushered the passengers off, followed by Dratch and his pistol.

"Load up on firewood," Dratch shouted at them, motioning at the neatly stacked cords near the dock. "Get it done quick, and I'll leave you here."

Yates stood by the gangplank and watched. Two raiders approached, perfumed in whiskey.

"Get back stern," Yates said, hand on his pistol.

"We're just going to help load," one of them said.

"It's handled," Yates said.

The men disappeared around the cabin and Yates immediately heard splashing in the water on the far side of the boat. He rushed across the boat to see the same two swimming toward shore.

"Son of a bitch," he shouted. He drew his pistol and fired at them, but they turned and waved, laughing as they climbed onto the rocky shore.

He rushed back over to the dock to see another man strolling down the gangway.

"Goddammit," Yates screamed. "Get this thing under way."

He pulled the plank back up himself and rushed to the pilothouse, shouting, "Go!

Go!" at the Frenchman, hoping he at least knew that word.

He heard another raider jump over the rail and into the lake as the steamer lurched into motion. Once the boat was back on the open water, he circled the deck and counted six men, two of them sleeping off the day's whiskey in the fall's fading sun.

They still had not risen by the time the *Michigan* came into view under the harvest moon.

Yates ordered the boat idled, and stood at the prow, spyglass in hand, watching the gunship. He heard the pilot go overboard soon after sunset.

By midnight, the flare still had not come and the *Philo Parsons* rocked adrift and anchorless.

Yates stomped into the midst of his drunken team.

"Goddammit, we're taking it anyway, full steam ahead," he shouted, and fired his pistol into the air.

"Was there supposed to be an element of surprise in all this?" Dratch asked.

"Put that whiskey overboard," Yates yelled. "Take up your rifles."

One of the drunks laughed, and Yates fired in his direction.

"We can shoot this out if you want,"

Dratch said, leveling his own pistol. "We all pretty much know how that'll end. But Compson told me you had a mind to kill some nigger back Buffalo way, and far be it from me to interfere with that kind of work. Why don't you hand me that bundle of notes you've been flashing, take the lifeboat, and paddle your way east?"

USCT

The recruiter looked at the pallid man leaning on his desk for support, and he looked down at the records on his desk.

"There's not a unit that'll take you," he said. "Even your old tent mate wrote a report that called you unfit for duty."

"Maybe the USCT?" Leander asked. "I've got a friend in the 78th."

The recruiter looked over his glasses.

"Why didn't you say so? Sure as shit you can join the colored troops. Damn, they'll give you a commission if you want to mess around with the darkies."

After the muster, the company took the train down to the new state of West Virginia.

The woods felt a lot like Town Line, but there were mountains overlooking the river that made him want to climb to the top every day.

The locals called them hills, but they

seemed like mountains to him. When he had a free day, he'd climb as high as he could go and watch the earth below him.

At first they dug latrines, then they hauled provisions, then they filled in the latrines they had dug and dug new ones.

The work helped him feel strong again.

His CO told him that he might be reassigned to a white unit if he did well, but he squandered that opportunity after being spotted repeatedly in the latrine holes with the colored troops, pick in hand.

He slept well after each day's work, and he woke each morning grateful for the long hours of peace. He had not seen Hans since the opium sweats had ended.

There wasn't a day he didn't want to find a den and feel that bliss again, and he was grateful to spend his days out in a field away from the town. Even in the camp, he could see others in the thrall. He knew he could find some with just a few questions.

He missed his friends, hoping there would come a day when he could think of them without shame.

He understood that the farm belonged to Mary now, but he hoped she might let him have a corner for himself someday. He wanted to make things grow again, to start fresh.

He'd been saving his money as a down payment.

Eventually his unit was moved on to more permanent construction. There was a redoubt on Loudoun Heights and a stone blockhouse at the crest of Maryland Heights. It was not a coincidence that the black troops did the work on everything with the word "heights" in it. The white troops laid the stone, but it was the 78th that hauled it the long miles up from barges on the Shenandoah.

Leander had hoped to lead the unit into combat, but his requisition for rifles was refused. Two of the men deserted the day he announced they would not get weapons, and those that stayed were often AWOL. Still, he kept more than most of the other USCT units.

Lately, even Malcolm had taken to slipping out at night, but unlike the others, he showed no sign of hangovers in the morning, and worked himself to exhaustion each day. Leander did what he could to cover for him. He'd never been worse off than the night Malcolm and the others on the farm had taken him in. When he looked back at it, he still couldn't understand why they had.

He tried not to think of the debts he owed. There weren't enough latrine holes in the

Union Army for him to dig.

More than anything, it was those regrets that kept him from the smoke. He couldn't bear the idea of being that man again.

The summer heat had faded and the leaves had taken a turn from green to red when Malcolm came to him before mess one morning and handed him a calling card with the words MADAME LEVANT, CHARLES TOWN printed on creamy, linen paper.

"Alaura," he said. "I found Alaura."

"What?" Leander asked.

"Joe's sister," Malcolm said. "He's from around here, and I've been out each night looking for her. It's the only thing he ever asked anyone for, help finding his sister."

"You sure it's her?" Leander asked.

"How many black girls you know with one eye green and one eye brown?" Malcolm asked. "I can't break her out myself. I need your help. I see you, I know you've been trying to make things right again. This is your chance. This is how you make it up to Joe."

Nearby Harpers Ferry was occupied by the Union, and its streets were quiet and orderly. But twenty miles to the east, Charles Town had been occupied and abandoned so many times that it had slipped into its own private limbo.

The plantations had been laid to waste and the feed lots and cotton market had closed, and commerce more suited to armies of men had risen in their place.

A women in an alley could be engaged for the price of a newspaper, while the ones that strutted in the satin dresses on the balconies overhead required negotiations with a man stationed on the sidewalk below.

Leander followed Malcolm through the rain-slicked streets and saw the shadowed, below-street entrances where he was sure he could find a bed of filthy satin pillows to lie upon. He saw the glassy-eyed boys, stumbling and falling in the gutters and wished he could pick up each of them, shake them to their senses. As much as the offerings tempted him, they disgusted him more.

Uniformed soldiers stood on corners under gaslights, skirted by the negotiators and their customers. With neither the will nor the means to impede the trade, the Union Army sent them out to ensure that the commerce remained civil and the armed men resolved their conflicts with nothing more than fists.

Leander looked at the calling card again.

Malcolm's face had glowed with pride when he showed it to Leander, but each time Leander asked how he had gotten it, the story had gotten more convoluted, and eventually he gave up on trying to get the real story.

"Are you sure you know where you are going?" he asked.

"It's up here," Malcolm said, leading him through the crowds.

Turning the corner onto Congress Street was like entering another world. The houses were set back from the street, and the lawns were perfect squares of vibrant green under gaslight. The paint was all fresh, and the streets clean.

The single-shot pistol strapped to his calf shifted as he walked. He bent down to tie his shoes, adjusting it when he was sure no one was watching.

The Levant house would not serve the drunkards of Mildred Street, nor would it serve a lowly lieutenant with USCT pinned to his collar. Malcolm's plan required something different, and Leander spent much of his savings on an outfit that would get him into the upscale whorehouse. He could not deny that the tailored clothes brought him a bittersweet pleasure.

Even here, though, he could see the signs of smoke everywhere. The clothing was of a better cut and fabric, but the glaze of the women's eyes and the limpness of their postures spoke of the same affliction that Leander knew so well. He suspected that he read their languid stares differently than the gentlemen that walked the streets around him.

The two of them had plotted their assault on the house carefully. It was Malcolm who had worked through most of the details, scouting the house for an entire night, watching the comings and goings through the brightly lit downstairs parlor and the muted, draped windows of the second floor.

The man at the front door wore a paisley waistcoat, a holster, and a jacket two sizes too small that emphasized the expanse of his shoulders and the bulk of his arms.

"He's not allowed," he said, putting his hand on Malcolm's chest. "No coloreds."

"He's my valet," Leander said. "He takes care of me."

"That's what the girls are for," the doorman replied. "He can wait for you behind the house. There's a bench back there, away from the street. We don't want folks thinking we serve his type."

Malcolm spat at the doorman's feet and dodged as the man half heartedly swiped at him. He laughed over his shoulder as Leander gestured him up the path to the back of the house.

The beveled glass door opened into a room crowded with men in suits and women in silk dressing gowns. A long mahogany bar ran the length of the far wall. As he scouted the faces all around him, a matronly woman approached him and offered her hand.

"Marianne LeSoleil Levant," she said. "Welcome to my house."

"Leander," he said, hesitating to reveal his real name. "Leander Fitch."

"What can we offer you?" the madam asked. A blond girl, no more than twelve, passed them and Levant ran her fingers along the girl's neck. Leander smiled to keep from wincing.

The room was close and stuffy, and he feared he had begun to sweat.

"I'm looking for a black girl with different-colored eyes," he said, his eyes scanning the women as they mingled with the well-dressed men. "A lovely slave woman. I've heard stories about her."

"We don't have any slaves here," Levant said, eyeing him. A suited waiter passed and she snatched a glass of whiskey from his tray and handed it to him. "Here, you look parched. Now, when you finish that, you may go down to George Street for the cheap trade, if that is your taste."

"I misspoke," Leander said, downing the whiskey. "I've heard there are no girls finer than yours, Miss Levant. In particular, a friend mentioned a rather exotic young lady . . ."

"We do have a West African princess of such astonishing beauty that she'll make you long for faraway places, and indeed she has one eye green, the other brown. She is, of course, a bit more than the rest of our girls. Such is the case with royalty."

"Might I meet her?" Leander asked.

"Certainly," Levant said. "Why don't you relax here and I'll bring her to you when she's not indisposed."

The woman flitted away and Leander stepped to the bar.

The wall behind the bar was punctuated by French doors open to the cool night, and he could see Malcolm talking with several other black men gathered in a gazebo. A light rain had started.

Leander took in the overstuffed couches and crystal chandeliers, the dark-wood bar, and leaded glass tumblers in every hand. Looking at the women reminded him too much of Isabel, so he glanced at the clients instead.

He could spot the posture of command evident in his fellow officers, and as the men joked together, he made out the bend and the lilt of the Southern tongue in some of them. The business at hand had caused Yank and Reb to leave their grievances at the door.

He sat on a plush sofa, and two women sat to either side and asked his name. He used a handkerchief to wipe the sweat from his face, and chatted long enough to have two more drinks. He enjoyed how the alcohol made him feel, and that worried him.

"Mr. Fitch," Levant said to him. She motioned toward a woman in a blue silk gown.

Leander could understand why the house billed the woman as a princess. Her long neckline and strong chin gave her a regal bearing and her skin, coffee colored and flawless, glowed in the candlelight, but he could not look away from her eyes.

"My friend Joe told me she was the most beautiful girl in the world," he said. "Said he's missed seeing her for years."

He watched the girl's drug-hazed face closely as he spoke and was rewarded with a flinch of pained recognition at Joe's name.

"She's perfect," he said.

"This way, please," Levant said, leading Leander by the hand.

Leander followed as she led them up the broad marble staircase, down a scarlet carpeted hallway, and into a high-ceilinged room. A canopied bed draped in crimson silk stood on one side of the room.

"If there's anything else you desire, let me know," she said, smiling slyly and brushing her hand across a velvet pull hanging from a bell chain before leaving and pulling the door shut behind her.

Leander lifted his finger to his lips and listened for the sound of the woman's shoes as they made their way back down the heavily carpeted hallway. The princess reached to undo the straps on her dress, but he stopped her, taking her hands in his.

"Alaura?" he asked.

She hesitated, confusion in her face.

"I'm here to take you to Joe," he said.

"Joe's dead," she stammered. "Went up north and got himself killed."

"No, he's not," he said. "I know him. He runs my sister's farm."

The news took a minute to cut through her haze.

"Joe's alive?" she asked.

She sat on the bed and rubbed her face, smearing the powder and paint, transforming her from a princess into a confused girl.

"Where is he?"

"Back at my home. Please, you need to listen. We need to get away," he said.

"Away?" she asked, looking at him blank-faced.

He yanked at the swollen window casement until it opened.

"As soon as we get you out of West Virginia, you won't be a slave anymore," he said. "We just have to get you out of here."

"Yates Bell," she said. "He sold me to these people."

He climbed out onto the porch roof. Still light-headed from the alcohol, he pulled himself up onto the broad roof of the house and crawled across the cypress shakes to the back. He fished a penny from his pocket and threw a strike at Malcolm.

Malcolm tipped a nonexistent cap and made for the front of the house. Leander crawled back onto the porch roof and helped Alaura through the window and onto the rain-slicked shingles.

"He's with me," Leander whispered, pointing Malcolm out to Alaura. "He's a good man. You can trust him."

Alaura nodded.

"Can you run?" he whispered.

She nodded again.

"It's raining, goddammit. Let me in," Malcolm shouted from the street. "It's a goddamn whorehouse, why ain't I good enough for that?"

"Quiet down," the doorman's voice rumbled from the porch below.

"Come over here and make me, hoople-head," Malcolm said. "I've wiped my ass with finer men than you, and I will not be held out here by you."

The doorman's steps creaked on the floorboards of the porch and Malcolm backed away. Leander motioned Alaura to the side of the porch roof where she climbed down and hung by her fingers before dropping into the bushes below. The girls on the porch laughed to see her blue gown billow, but she shushed them with a finger. Leander dropped beside her and took the pistol from its holster.

"Do you know where the courthouse is?" he asked.

She nodded.

"Meet me there," he whispered. "Now, run."

The girl ran north up the street, silk flowing behind her, bare feet slapping the wet cobblestones. Malcolm danced outside the range of the doorman's long arms, throwing wild punches at the air around him.

Leander signaled and he dropped his arms.

"I beg your pardon," Malcolm said, winking at the women on the porch. "I thought you were somebody else."

He turned and sprinted south. The girls giggled as the doorman stood in the rain, befuddled. Leander ran to follow his friend.

The madam stepped onto the porch and pointed at Leander.

"Get him, you idiot. He's taken Alaura," she shouted.

Leander ran up the middle of the cobblestone street, shouting to keep the doorman's attention from the running girl. The chase drew derisive cheers from streetwalkers and soldiers gathered under overhangs and umbrellas. The men waved their hats in the air as if they were watching a horse race or a ball game.

Leander had a vision of standing on third on a spring day with a high blue sky, Harry on the mound and Hans at the plate. His muscles remembered the joy of running home as he sprinted in the fouled streets of the Southern city.

He heard the crack of the bat, and he heard Hans yelling for him to slide home.

His knees buckled and he went down onto the cobblestones, laughing even as the pain of the bullet wound in his back came over him in a wave.

He felt someone pry the pistol from his hand, and heard the snap of the little gun. Malcolm's face appeared in front of his, the same color as the coal-hazed sky.

"Get up," he said. "March, soldier. Let's get out of here."

Leander looked into his friend's black face.

"Home," he said, and his lifeless hand fell to the ground.

LADIES OF THE
NORTH COUNTRY

There had still been leaves on the trees the last time a letter from Leander had arrived for her father. Since then the men had moved back to the city for the winter season, the snow had piled deep on the field, and the knot in Mary's stomach had ossified into a nearly unbearable burden. Even having Joe nearby did nothing to ease her sense of dread.

There had been other letters. One from Katia in Canada. Although the letter was addressed to her father, Mary could see that she expected her to read it to him, and she did.

She told the story of the day the raiders killed the Zubrichs and attacked the house as a way of apology for running out as they did, and said how much she regretted the trouble it had caused them. She wished that both Mary and Nathan had been there when she and Harry had gotten married, and hoped for Nathan's blessing. They invited them to visit in Canada, and made it clear that it was unlikely they'd ever be able to come see them in Town Line.

Nathan said there was only one more border he was willing to cross, but made them a little rocking cradle and sent it to them via Palmer.

Mary tried not to think too much about that day. There'd been too much blood spilled on her farm. There had been a trail of it left behind. Joe had started to follow it, but the buzzards circling a copse of spruce made it clear that he didn't need the pistol he was carrying, instead coming back to the house for a stained canvas tarp to cover their bodies. Mary sent a telegram to the new marshal, but never did hear any more about them.

Out of respect for Hans, she'd gone to see the Zubrichs's funeral behind their little church. None of the Town Line farmers had looked her in the eye, but there seemed more shame than anger in them. She was surprised when Mr. Snyder came up from the crossroads the next day with a cart full of glass panes and went about fixing all the windows broken during the fight. He greeted Nathan as he always had, with a tip of his hat, and never sent a bill.

Fending off the raiders seemed to have cleared the last of her father's cobwebs, and in the weeks after the attack, she took real pleasure in his return to health. He kept pressing to see the mill, and eventually, Joe took him to the ruins. He went for days without speaking again, but eventually Joe asked him for help in fixing the bullet holes in the house.

"Damned lobsterbacks," he'd said, and finally cracked a smile. After that, he was better. He still spoke to her mother, but it seemed more a habit than an affliction.

Without Katia around, Mary found herself cooking and tending her father more, and Joe often helped with the books and the other business of the farm.

She'd always disliked her time in the kitchen, and had found it to be one of the more tedious chores. But now, her father would come and sit at the table and shell peas or husk corn, and then Joe would follow them in and sit at the table and work through this invoice and that, and the three of them would while away the day.

She was alone in the kitchen when she heard the wagon rattle in the snowy driveway and looked out to see Malcolm in the driver's seat next to a black woman weighted under many layers against the winter.

She went out to welcome him and behind the welling in his eyes, Mary saw a sadness that she did not recognize in the big man's face. As he so often had, he stood wordless, but with just a motion, a small movement of his hand toward the pine box in the wagon, he told her that her brother was gone.

Malcolm caught her in his arms and held her as the uncertainty drained from her, leaving a hollow in her chest into which everything seemed to collapse.

She led them into the house and back to the kitchen to sit near the warm stove. She could see by the way the woman held Malcolm by his arm that they were in love.

She brewed a pot of coffee and poured them each a cup before the strange woman broke her silence.

"Is Joe here?" she asked, her voice barely a whisper.

For the first time, Mary looked in the woman's face. There was a hope there, something she thought she would never know again. And there were the eyes, one green and one brown.

Before she could say anything, the popping sound of her father knocking the snow from his boots on the back stoop echoed through the house, followed by the intermingled murmur of his and Joe's voices.

The two men were joking, and as the door opened, Joe's laugh filled the room. The woman rushed to the opening door and leapt into her brother's arms, nearly knocking the one-legged man to the ground.

Mary tried to smile for him when he finally turned to introduce them properly, but he stopped short when he saw her pain.

"We brought Leander home," Malcolm whispered.

Nathan grasped the back of a chair, and Alaura took his arm to steady him.

He looked straight at Malcolm.

"Where's my boy?" he asked.

Malcolm nodded out the window at the wagon.

Mary took her father from Alaura and led him out to the barnyard. He ran his hand over the cheap pine, brushing away the powder of quicklime seeping from the loose joints. Mary lay her face against the snow-speckled wood.

Joe came and moved the wagon to the barn, and Alaura put blankets around Mary and her father, and the two of them sat with Leander and the animals well into the night. When her father finally slumped over, she roused him and took him into the dark house. He shivered under her arm as she led him up the stairs. She added her regret for allowing him to sit in the cold for so long to the others she had spent the day cataloging.

In the morning she lay abed long after sunrise, listening to the murmur of happy voices echoing up from the kitchen. She knew the reunion's joy would be ended the moment they heard her foot on the stairs and she wished she could slip out the door, unnoticed, back to the barn to sit with her brother.

Eventually she heard the back door open and close, and expecting the house was empty, she rose. She checked on her father before going down, and found him sitting in his chair staring into the distance out the window.

"Pine." He spat. "I'll set about making something fitting for him tomorrow. He always liked walnut. I'll make something from walnut."

"Come down," Mary said. "There's work to do."

She helped him stand up, and guided him down the stairs.

Alaura was waiting for them in the kitchen.

"I hope you don't mind," she said, tugging at the floursack apron she wore, a threadbare rag that Katia had nearly worn through. Mary took her hands and nodded, but said nothing.

"Sit," Alaura said. "You have to eat."

She filled bowls with porridge and put them in front of Mary and her father, then sat in the chair across from them.

Mary spooned the warm oats into her mouth.

"You have to know, he died saving me," Alaura said. "He was brave and he came from nowhere and saved me."

Mary got up and took the coffeepot from the stove. She filled their cups, and sat again.

"Tell me," she said. "Tell me everything."

Alaura told of the days after Joe left, and how she'd been sold. Then she told of the night Leander died.

"I went to the courthouse, where Leander told me to go," she said. "I sat there a long time, and I could hear shots and shouting, but I had that poison in me, and I could hardly make anything out. It was maybe an hour I sat there, and I was cold and it was raining, and all I wanted was a warm place where I could have some more of that stuff, and I thought about going back. Then Malcolm came up to me, carrying Mr. Leander over his shoulder.

" 'They're looking for me,' Malcolm had said. 'We've got to go.'

"We had to hide out after that," she said. "We found this burned plantation north of the town, and we hid out in the cellar. We hid out for weeks there. Malcolm, he took care of me. I was sicker than I've been, getting over that stuff. Malcolm, he did what he could, he found some tools and some wood, and he made a casket for Leander. He snuck back to the army camp and he got his uniform and a horse and wagon, and then when I was feeling better, Malcolm waited until there was a rainstorm. He covered me in a tarp, and we set out. It was slow going that night, but nobody was on the road, nobody was looking for us."

A pot of stew was bubbling on the stove and two loaves were in the oven before Mary realized that she and Alaura had been moving around the kitchen, the two of them preparing food together.

"Malcolm," she said. "There's never been a kinder man. You should have seen him worrying over your brother. He went into town and stole that sack of quicklime. I know he hated to do it. He left some coins he had, but he had to take it in the middle of the night. Your brother, he told me Malcolm was a good man and that I could

498

trust him, and he was right."

By the time Joe and Malcolm returned, the three of them were laughing as Alaura told how Malcolm had convinced a Pennsylvania ferryman to give them a free ride as a tribute to Clement Vallandigham.

After the meal, Nathan brought out a jug of late fall applejack, and they sat in the parlor while he and Mary told stories of Leander as a boy.

At the end of the night, Alaura went up the back stairs to Katia's old room, and Joe and Malcolm walked through the night's snowfall to the cabin.

The kitchen was empty when Mary came down in the morning, but Malcolm and Alaura soon came stomping through the back door. As everyone gathered for breakfast, Alaura stood and invited them to ride downtown with them the next day for their wedding.

"This is all so fast," Mary said, after embracing Alaura.

"We've been through so much together," Alaura said.

"I had to see Joe first," Malcolm said. "I had to ask his blessing."

Joe nodded. "He couldn't get the words out fast enough," he said with a chuckle.

In the afternoon, Mary walked down to

the station and wired Father Thomas to make arrangements and spread the word. In the morning, they all walked down the hill and boarded the train.

Downtown, Mary took Alaura shopping for a dress. Afterward, they sat in the lobby of the American Hotel for lunch, ignoring the passersby that stared at the unusual pair.

Sophie had herded together nearly all of the parishioners, and laid out a broom at the church entrance. "Whoever jumps higher rules the house," she said to Mary as the couple held hands and leaped over it together.

Alaura's feet were a good six inches higher, and Malcolm, laughing, demanded a second chance.

Father Thomas ushered the crowd into the little church, and read from his worn Bible. Joe escorted his sister up the aisle and Palmer stood with Malcolm while Mary and Sophie stood beside Alaura.

Afterward, they all sat and watched the newlyweds dance, then the congregation took their turns on the floor. After Mary had danced and Joe had hopped to the sound of a fiddle player, her father motioned for her to take the chair next to him.

"I'm going to stay downtown tonight," he said. "Tomorrow, I'm going to the army to arrange for the funeral. He'll have full honors or there will be hell to pay."

Mary nodded. "I'll send Joe back tonight and you and I can go and see to it."

"No," Nathan said. "You two go back home. I will do this for him."

Nathan watched as Alaura and Malcolm twirled together on the floor, laughing.

"Here's something you don't know," Nathan said. "I almost married another before I met your mother."

Mary choked on her drink.

"I never regretted marrying your mother and I loved her as much as any man could love a woman, but there's still a fondness for Hattie. And some shame."

He reached for his daughter's hand.

"Her real name was Konwanhata, or something like that," he continued. "She let me call her Hattie, because I could never get her real name quite right. I swear to God she changed it every time I got near it just so she could laugh at me."

He chuckled, and she saw a glint in his eye that she did not recognize.

"Her family took me in when I first came west, and her brothers helped me build the barn and the mill. She was a beautiful girl, daughter of the chief. I'd have married her, but I was afraid of what people would say about me."

He rubbed his face, and scratched at his scar.

"I'd come out into the wild to be my own man, and there I was, too much of a coward to marry the woman I loved."

Nathan took his daughter's hand and lifted it to his lips and Mary noticed a glistening in his eyes. Then he rose and hobbled into the fray to take up a little jig among the other dancers.

Afterward, when they walked to the train station, Mary took Joe's arm. She steeled herself for any confrontation that would come of it, but no one seemed to care on the cold Buffalo streets.

It was late when they finally walked up the snowy hill to the dark and cold house. Mary took Joe by the hand, and they climbed the stairs, and he undressed her slowly there in her room. They woke, entwined in the morning light, and together they went down to the kitchen and he sat at the table as she made him coffee and breakfast.

NIAGARA

Harry was warming his feet by the apple-wood fire and watching the orange of the setting sun sparkle on Lake Erie when Champ raised his head and yipped at the yacht plowing through the vast lake's cold water.

He'd come out as he did most evenings, leaving Katia in the house to wash up and put the twins to bed while he had himself a whiskey. She allowed him just the one each night, but he poured the blue Mason jar nearly full and if he'd worked hard that day, she did not object.

He never argued with her. He had stood on the dock the night of the riot and he had promised he would mind her, and he had.

If the girls were asleep and it was warm enough, she'd pour herself a glass, shorter, and come sit with him and watch the sun go down.

It had snowed again that afternoon, adding to the foot or so already on the ground, and he expected that she would stay in the house.

That was fine with him, he liked the quiet. But as much as he liked the hush of a new snowfall, he had to admit that he missed having the pickers around.

When the fruit had started to ripen in the late summer, he and Katia had hired a crew from the same encampment where Palmer and the others had come from. They'd brought their families down to the orchard and set up a camp in a nearby field.

Their Canadians neighbors seemed none too happy with Harry for it, but the way the wives had fussed over the twins had charmed Katia so much that she promised that she'd hire them all back for the spring pruning.

It didn't hurt that they all had been treating her like a hero ever since the night of the riot. He knew better than to argue that things had ended well because of her.

After they'd watched Joe ride the old swayback back toward Town Line, they'd turned back to Keith, only to find that the Confederate had died.

"We need to get you away from here," Palmer said to Katia. "Plenty of people saw you with that gun, and they'll send the police. Or worse. We'll get you over the river as soon as the streets are all cleared. We need to hide you in the meantime."

As Palmer ushered them out of the street, Katia picked up Keith's bag from where it lay beside his corpse and stuffed it into her own carpetbag. After Father Thomas had guided them into a closet-sized hiding space in the labyrinthine cellar, she opened it and found wads of Union currency.

Before Palmer guided them down to the waterfront the next night, they had asked the old black priest to preside over their vows, and he did so right there in the sanctuary.

"My first ceremony with white folks," he said with a smile.

A rowboat ferried them across the river under a starlit sky, and Harry remembered thinking it would have been a beautiful night if he hadn't been so worried about somebody coming after them.

They sent money to Old Man Snyder to pay for proper headstones for the Zubrichs, but they had both agreed never to cross the river again. Katia was worried that the police were looking for her and that she'd end up in the same cell that Joe had occupied.

Harry wanted nothing more to do with

any of it. The war. The Union. The Confederates.

He thought of the way he'd helped turn the Town Line farmers into an angry mob, and he thought of the terrified women and children he'd seen on the streets of Buffalo, and he was ashamed of himself.

Katia had sent a letter of farewell to Nathan, and he had answered, offering his blessing of the marriage. There was a terse note from Mary enclosed as well, offering her sympathy for the loss of their friends the Zubrichs. Harry supposed that was more than he had a right to ask for.

They talked about going farther west, but Katia said there was plenty of good land right there and since she'd never really said the money in the bag was his, too, he didn't argue.

She could not remember much from her early childhood in Germany, but she had dreamed of living on the water ever since the day her father had taken her to swim in Bodensee. She had hired a cab to take them along the Niagara River to look for farms along the banks, but Harry didn't want to have to stare at the Union from his front porch, so they'd agreed to look on the shore of Lake Erie where the water met the horizon.

They bought the orchard a month later from a Confederate deserter. In the end, the call of the man's kin had become too much for him and after a late August cold snap, the Alabamian deserter had been eager to leave before winter set in. Five acres of apple orchards, a tidy little house, and a stretch of rocky lakefront beach with a dock.

"I hear they're giving Confederates free land to raise cotton down in Brazil," he said, counting the bills that Harry had just pushed across the table. "This here will help me buy a breeding couple to get back up and running. My brother's going to meet me there with a few more. We'll have ourselves a plantation in no time."

Harry looked at Katia, his lips pinched together into something like a half scowl and half smile as the Southerner walked out the door of their new home.

Sophie had been there to midwife when the girls, Melinda and Belinda, came into the world. It was early spring, and that night Harry sat by the fire with one in each arm while Katia slept, and he knew that he had done better than he had any right to expect.

That spring he spent hours with the girls in the orchard, the petals falling from the trees and tangling in the little tufts of hair poking out of their bonnets.

He even found himself a puppy, a yellow sheepdog with a white mane and white stripe down his snout. Champ wasn't half as smart as Jep, but he stuck close and had been known to pull up a groundhog every now and then.

When he wasn't pruning trees or tending the garden patch, he took his little skiff onto the lake and pulled chinook from the deep waters. On warm Sundays, they'd take the wagon and ride up to the falls just to feel the earth shaking underfoot and the mist on their faces.

His memories of everything before the orchard felt like a story someone else had told him around a campfire.

Until Champ yipped and Harry looked up to see the *Abigail* sliding across the lake.

He'd seen just about every kind of boat there was on Erie, but the yacht's profile was lower and sleeker than anything else in the water. He didn't need to see the name, but he read it in the evening light anyway. He watched as it skimmed the water in the twilight, the lights in the cabin already ablaze, and he knew he had to do something.

He jumped, spilling his whiskey, and swatted at Champ nipping at his heels as he climbed up the gentle slope to the house.

He banged the door open and rushed into the warm house.

"What?" Katia asked. "What is the matter?"

"The *Abigail,* it's right in front of the house," Harry said, taking his new shotgun from over the mantel. He froze in the middle of the room, his eyes scanning for anything else that might be useful.

The babies, disturbed by the commotion, started to cry, their voices rising in a distinct pitch that made Harry grin.

"What?" she repeated.

"Compson" is all he said, pointing out the window at the lake. "He's right there."

After she saw the boat gliding on the water, she slammed the door and spread herself against it.

"No," she said. "No more killing."

She closed her eyes, and for the first time he could see something in her face like regret for the shots she had fired in the streets of Buffalo.

"No more," she whispered.

He nodded, feeling the cost of his vow to always listen to her was higher than he could ever remember.

"I can't let him just go," Harry said. "Not after everything."

"No more killing," she repeated.

He leaned the shotgun against the wall.

"Okay," he said. "But I'm going after him."

She rolled her eyes.

"In your little boat?"

"Yes," he said.

She rubbed her face with her hands, laughing, and looked up at the ceiling.

"I guess. How much trouble can you get into in that tiny thing anyway?"

She opened the door and he dashed outside and ran down the hill, Champ trailing behind him.

"Don't do anything stupid," she shouted.

He leaped into the skiff, feeling like a little boy. Champ tried to climb in after him, but he pushed the puppy back onto the dock.

"Stay here, watch out for Mother," he said, shoving off.

The yacht had already passed the orchard, but he could still see it and he set his back to the oars. He didn't know what he would do if he caught it, but the smirk the Confederate had given him the night of the riot still haunted him.

Out on the lake, the cold of the water radiated up through the boards of the boat and the soles of his boots and into his feet. The skiff nosed through the occasional paper-thin skim of ice. When the sun dropped below the horizon, the frigid cold of the night came down quickly. Small cabins dotted the shore, their windows yellow against the now-black wall of trees.

Just as the lights of Buffalo came into view, the *Abigail* steered north toward the mouth of the mighty river. The sound of its engine changed, shifting down as the current pulled it forward.

Harry fell in behind it, following the light of the brass lamps that lined the yacht's deck. The current took up the boat and he rested from his rowing.

The *Abigail* kept moving, turning wide around a hook in the shoreline, and he followed.

He heard the encampment before he saw it. The sawing of fiddles, the dull mumble of voices. The sound of men at ease, food and drink in hand. Around the hook the black of the woods opened onto a stone ruin, yellow under lamplights. A long dock extended from a landing on the shore. Two men stood at attention under a lantern on the landing while a third stood at the end of the dock, awaiting the line tossed from the *Abigail*.

Harry jammed an oar into the sandy mud of the bank to hold the skiff out of the circle of light.

"Commander Compson," a loud voice shouted. "Welcome! Bring your whole crew ashore. There's more than enough."

Compson climbed into view, and even across the water, Harry could see the man's bluster had left him. His shoulders slumped and he seemed to shrink next to the boisterousness of the man that greeted him.

"Fresh provisions have been hard to come by," he muttered. "They'd be happy for a good meal, I'm sure. But I don't want to impose."

"Not at all," the other man said, shaking Compson's hand. "We're about to decommission anyway, time to clean out the larder."

"Decommission?" Compson asked, disappointment in his voice.

"Yes," the other man said. "It seems we are closer to the end than the beginning, and there's little reason to keep the men here over winter. It was all for show anyway. If Her Majesty had been serious, they'd surely have rebuilt this old fort. The Yankees burned it fifty years ago, and it's hardly a signal of confidence to leave it in ruins."

"Closer to the end than the beginning," Compson said. "Yes, I suppose so."

Compson motioned and his crew disembarked onto the dock.

"Leave your worries at the water," the host said. "We've roasted a pig and there's plenty of fine Canadian whiskey. I'll leave my man to stand guard."

The smell of roasting pork wafted through the night, and Harry licked his lips even as he shivered in the cold night, watching the band of men climb the stone steps of the ruined fort's embankment. He watched as a bored guard sat on a stool, his back to the water, staring up at the party. Harry stilled himself as if he were perched in the woods waiting on a buck, watching as the guard's head drooped as he drowsed under the glow of a torch. The *Abigail* sat lifeless, rocking quietly in the small waves of the river.

Pulling his oar from the mud of the bank, Harry let the skiff drift until he could reach out and put his hands on the smooth wooden hull. He stood up, guiding his tiny boat to the river side of the yacht. His eyes on the guard the whole time, he floated the skiff to the *Abigail*'s stern, where he tied up to the cleat on the gunnel. Finally, he climbed onto the deck. It took him less than a minute to pull the mooring lines off the dock, setting the *Abigail* adrift.

The whole operation had been silent but for Harry's stifled giggling.

The river pulled the loosed boat toward

its center where the current was swift and irresistible. Harry listened for the sound of the party to fade as he watched the lights of the fort slip out of sight. When he could no longer hear the sound of the gathered men, he burst into loud peals of laughter, stomping his feet.

He ran around the deck, slapping at all the slick wooden surfaces, braying into the night. He wished the whole world could see what he'd just done. He wished that someone was there with him. He wished for Hans and he wished for the others, but most of all, he wished for Leander. Nobody loved a practical joke like Lelo.

"You sons of bitches," he shouted into the wind. "You should have stayed home. We could have had us some fun."

The boat jerked as it slammed a rock and spun around before continuing downstream. Harry checked to make sure his skiff was still there and went belowdecks.

He found a lamp and matches. Shadows jumped to life on the dark-wood walls. He went to the liquor cabinet first, and found a bottle of the bourbon he'd been dreaming of since Compson had poured him his first glass. He was about to take a long plug from the bottle, then stopped, and found one of Compson's cut glass tumblers.

"Here's to you, Commander," he said, holding the full glass aloft. He spat on the polished wood of the desk before taking a big swallow. The liquor spilled as the boat hit another rock.

He could feel the *Abigail* picking up speed. He tried to guess how much time he had, how long the Niagara River really was.

He thought of the bed linens he'd slept on that first night, and ran through the staterooms and tore them off the beds and stuffed them into their pillowcases and tossed them on deck.

Then he remembered Compson's desk drawer of money, and pried open the locked drawers with his knife, tearing through the fine wood. He found a canvas bag and stuffed it full of Confederate script, worth even less now than when he'd fallen for it, and he tossed the full bag up on deck. In the top left drawer he found a little velvet pull-string bag filled with gold coins. He shoved that in his coat pocket.

He opened drawers and cabinets, pulling filigreed shotguns and pistols from display cases, and tossed them clattering onto the deck. He found a cabinet with flags — the stars and bars, the Union Jack, a Confederate battle flag. Giggling between big gulps of bourbon, he stomped back up on deck

515

and hung the American flag on the pole at the fore, and tied the Confederate on the aft railing.

He dove back into the cabin, rifling through Compson's closet, running his hands over the velvet collars and the silk undergarments before he threw it all out onto the deck.

All the time, the boat was alternately spiraling and righting itself into speed. Harry kept falling as the boat shifted, cracking his knee on the deck, and still laughing. On deck, he watched as the black trees of the shore slipped past as if he was on an express train. The shore suddenly looked far away.

He climbed up to the pilothouse, looking at the wheel and the brass controls, but he wasn't sure how they worked. He pushed something forward, and the engine coughed a bit, but it didn't sound right.

The boat jerked again, and he heard a tearing sound unlike any of the others. The yacht started to list.

He looked downriver into the night, but couldn't make anything out. He heard a rushing sound, that same pounding he loved to feel when he Katia brought the babies to the falls. It was distant, but he was sure it was there.

When he went below again, cold water pooled around his feet. He went to the desk for his tumbler of bourbon, but it had fallen to the floor at the last impact and the broken crystal lay at his feet. He opened the cabinet and found another bottle of something, clear and nearly tasteless, but with a kick like a mule. He took it up onto the deck and poured it over the remains of Compson's command. He checked one more time to make sure the skiff was still at the stern, struck a match, and dropped it onto the mound. The whole deck was aflame by the time he untied the skiff.

He knew enough to aim upstream, though it only slowed his speed by a fraction. He rowed frantically, heading toward the Canadian shore. The whole river was lit by the *Abigail*. Bullets popped on board, then something bigger exploded, its boom echoing over the rushing river.

Harry ducked as he rowed. The pounding and hissing was louder now, and he set everything he had to the oars. His hands blistered and the muscles of his arms burned, but he did not stop. As he got closer to the shore, the current slackened and he made out lanterns on the shoreline, the faces of people that had heard the explosions and come to see the burning yacht.

They were shouting at him, but he could not hear what they said for the fury of the rapids.

Harry turned back to see the *Abigail*, its flames as tall as the tree line, suddenly blink out of sight as it went over the lip and into the gorge. He laughed again, loudly, joyously, as he put his back into the oars, and he was still laughing when the nose of the skiff jammed up onto the loamy shore.

He climbed out of the boat, knee-deep in frigid water, and the lights of lanterns rushed down the embankment to him.

A gray-haired man with spectacles and a stocking cap held the light up to Harry's face.

"You alright, young feller?" he asked.

"Do you have a wagon and a mule?" Harry asked.

"Sure."

Harry fished into his pocket and pulled out the velvet bag.

"I'll pay you this to haul me and my skiff back up to my place. It's down on Lake Erie."

The old man emptied the bag onto his palm and used his thumb to count through the glittering coins.

"That's got to be about a hundred dollars," he said.

"Well then, today's your lucky day," Harry said, still laughing.

"You want to come inside and get warm before we go?" the man asked.

"No, thank you, though I'll take a blanket if you have it," Harry said. "I want to get back. My wife is waiting."

■ ■ ■ ■

1865

■ ■ ■ ■

Mary washed the dishes while Nathan and Joe sat at the kitchen table with a skillet of cornbread, a crock of butter, and a pitcher of milk in front of them, haggling over price.

"A quarter acre," Nathan said. "The lawyer will charge more for filing the deed than the property is worth. Let me just give it to you."

"Look here," Joe said, pointing to an ad he'd clipped from the *Courier*. "Lancaster, ten acres, two hundred dollars. This has a pond on it. It's at least forty dollars."

"Pfff," Nathan said. "That ad is for cleared land, with a barn and a house. You're taking about an uncleared plot with no road access. It's a different measure."

"Yes, but this had a house as well."

"Not much of one, and you built it." Nathan laughed. "I shouldn't get paid for that."

Joe kept to his number, while Nathan

cited farm sales from as far as Darien to explain why the number was wrong. Mary could tell by the way her father worked around the price that he was enjoying the negotiation. By the time they finally agreed she was sitting at the table, smiling as she picked at a piece of the bread. Joe, beaming, counted the bills from the worn envelope he used to save his wages, and pushed them across the table.

"It's mine through and through," he said. "Even Mr. Thoreau couldn't say that."

Nathan straightened the bills by tapping them on the oaken tabletop.

"No, he couldn't," he said. "I bet old Henry would be proud to know you."

At Snyder's General Store the next morning, Joe piled a coffeepot, a grinder, and a red wool blanket onto the glass-topped counter. The woman at the till held each bill up to the light and eyed him, but she eventually relented and wrapped the items in brown paper and handed them to him wordlessly.

Mary went to him nearly every day. If it wasn't too cold, they'd walk down to the creek or through the woods. If the wind was blowing they would sit in the tight little cabin, a pot of tea and books shared between them.

Nathan visited sometimes, too. Joe would ask him about the things they sometimes found in the forest, arrowheads and pot-sherds and adzes, and Nathan told him of the Haudenosaunee and showed him a clearing where a longhouse had once sat.

Malcolm had gotten work downtown as a hack-driver, and on Saturdays, Joe walked to the station where he would ride the local downtown and spend the night in the two-room apartment on Michigan Street where he and Alaura lived. In the morning, they'd go to the little church with the rest of the farm's crew. Sunday-night dinner would be back in Town Line with Nathan and Mary, and then back to the pond that night.

Sometimes, after her father had gone to bed, Mary would gather a few things and follow him through the snow-hushed woods to the little cabin.

When sugaring time came, the two of them worked together, going from tree to tree, the only sound the pounding of taps into trunks, the clang of the sap buckets, and Timber's occasional snort.

When Mary deemed the buckets finally full enough to collect, they rode out for the boil.

It was nearly noon before they'd gathered the sap, stoked the fire, and settled onto their stools to watch the wind push the smoke and the steam south over the tops of the trees toward the creek. They sat close and talked of the spring planting as they passed a jar of liquor and warmed their hands by the fire.

She'd felt ill that morning, and she blamed the distraction of her sour stomach when she let a ladleful drip back into the cauldron and found the liquid too viscous and dark to sell for top grade.

"Damn," she said. "It's close to ruined."

"We'll start over," Joe said. "I'll get more wood to stoke the fire."

"I can't bear to just pour it out," Mary said to herself as he headed for the woodpile behind the shack. She was lifting an empty cask from the back of the wagon when Timber whinnied.

"What is it, boy?" she asked. He hoofed the snow and showed her the white of his eye, and she felt a chill colder than she'd expect for the sunny afternoon.

She looked to where she'd left her pistol, but the seat cushion lay in the snow and the bench was empty.

When she felt something stab hard into her lower back, she knew it was the muzzle of her own gun. An arm wrapped around her throat and jerked hard. She stumbled backward, slamming into the body behind her, struggling to gain her feet as the arm choked her and held her up.

The smell of sweat and whiskey filled her nostrils as she tried to break free, but the man had her firm.

Joe came from behind the shack and the sling full of split wood slipped from his hands and tumbled into the snow.

"It's you," the man behind her said. "I finally found you."

She could see terror in Joe's eyes.

"She doesn't mean anything to you, Yates," he said. "Let her go."

"Master," Yates hissed. "You call me Master."

"Never again," Joe said. "I'm a free man."

"You're mine," the man said. "I don't care what any man in Washington says. You're mine."

Anger and despair played across Joe's face.

"Don't do this," Joe said. "The war is over."

"It's not over," Yates said. "Not as long as there's niggers roaming free."

Mary pulled at the arm around her neck, but it held fast. Yates extended his other arm, and she could see her pistol in his hand, aimed at Joe.

"Settle down, missy," he said. He thumbed

back the hammer and swiveled around, putting the weapon out of her reach.

"Just go home," Joe said, stretching his hands out in a plea.

"Four goddamned years I been tracking you,"Yates said. "The last three months hiding out in every goddamned root cellar and cave between here and Ohio. Go home? I'm here to kill you."

"Then take me," Joe said. "Let her go."

Mary plunged her hands into her apron pockets, and gripped the slaughtering knife.

"You can't have it," Yates said. "It's not yours."

"Have what?" Joe asked.

"Walnut Grove," Yates said. "You can't have it."

Joe looked confused. The smell of the burning syrup filled the air.

"It's not yours," Yates said, and Mary realized the man was crying. "It's mine. It's mine."

"Why would it be mine?" Joe asked.

"They say it's yours," he cried. "They say you're my . . ."

Bell gasped, choking on his words.

"They say you're my . . ." he repeated, and he began to sob. His body shook, and each tremor ran through his body and into Mary's. She tried to push herself free, but he ratcheted his arm tighter and slammed her back against his chest. She pulled the knife out of her apron and plunged it into the arm at her throat. It jerked away and she fell forward into the snow.

"Mary!" Joe screamed and ran toward them.

Yates dropped to his knees, raised the pistol with both hands, and pulled the trigger.

Joe fell to his knees, teetering there for a moment before he collapsed forward, his arms outstretched, reaching for her across the snow.

The air rushed from Mary's lungs, her throat constricted, and her mouth opened in a rictus of pain, but her voice was gone.

She lifted the bloody knife from where it had fallen in the snow, jumped to her feet, and turned to attack the Confederate.

Yates Bell stood in front of the sugar fire, rags hanging loose on his emaciated body. His gray face and stringy hair framed dark, sunken eyes and his hand shook as it held her pistol under his chin.

His mouth worked soundlessly for a moment.

". . . my brother," he finally managed to say, and pulled the trigger.

Instinct held the body upright for a long

moment, anguish chiseled on its bloody face, then finally it fell backward into the sugar fire. The tripod collapsed, and scalded syrup poured onto the jerking body, and where it touched the embers, it burst into flame.

Mary scrambled to where Joe lay, and cradled his head in her lap, but by then, he was gone.

INTERREGNUM

She found her father on a Sunday morning, his body cooling but not yet cold under the featherbed. His face was at ease, the bed orderly and neat with no signs of torment or seizures, and she took comfort that his last night had been peaceful.

The hard cold had come again and the ground was too hard for a grave to be dug. Packed in lime and held in a coffin stretched on a pair of sawhorses in the stall next to Timber, Nathan waited for the thaw.

Just the week before, Malcolm and Palmer had pickaxed their way through six feet of frozen ground and they had buried Joe by the pond.

While they had worked, Mary brought Alaura to Joe's cabin, sat her on the steps of the porch, and pushed a wooden box the size of an apple crate across the boards to her.

"Please," she whispered. "Take this from me."

Alaura took off the lid and lifted a scuffed book from the top of bundled papers.

"Thoreau," Mary said. "It was his. You'll find the deed for this place inside. He built it for you. It's yours now."

Alaura flipped through the pages and found the folded document. She ran her finger over the signature at the bottom and nodded, then reached into the box again, bringing out one of the many sheaves of letters. Slowly, she pulled one from its silk-ribboned bundle and opened it to read, but folded it again and offered it to Mary.

"This is addressed to you," she said. "It's yours."

Mary shook her head.

"Take it," she said, her eyes staring at the horizon of snow-laden trees. "Take them all. If I read them again, they will break me forever."

The rest of the winter passed unnoticed. She spent most of her days stitching useless aphorisms into stretched linen and staring into the distance.

The workers insisted they would be back in the early spring, but the time seemed too far away to matter.

When the cold broke, it did so with a torrential downpour. The fields flooded and the last of the mill washed down the creek toward Lake Erie.

Then the letter came. As she often did, she discussed the day's matters with her father as she tended to the animals in the barn.

"Your lawyer, Mr. Ewell, has sent me an offer for the farm. It's a fair one, perhaps more than fair."

She shoveled Timber's stall clean as she talked about the buyer, a captain in the 115th. Then she pulled a stool next to the coffin and sat, her legs splayed out in front of her under the heavy winter skirts. She leaned her head against the polished wood of the coffin.

"You used to get so upset when I talked of leaving," she said, "But I don't know whether it was you or the farm you didn't want me to leave. What would you have me to do now? Should I stay here telling the men how to plow the fields and grit my teeth at the jokes the town will tell behind my back?"

When she felt a welling of tears, she stood quickly, knocking her shoulder on the coffin. The pain focused her on the day's work. She lifted the milk can with her chapped, red hands and left her father alone with the animals.

February had been flooded with different types of letters and telegrams and visitors, men and families with stories of some kindness her father had done them decades earlier that had made all the difference in their lives.

Millard Fillmore sent a basket of Hawaiian fruits unlike anything Mary had ever seen — each the size of a kitten, greenish brown and prickly. She thought of sending them back, but knew her father would be angry at such a mean-spirited gesture. Instead, she gave the whole basket to Doc Pride, who reported they were yellow on the inside, and sweeter than anything he'd ever tasted.

When she heard the first robin of spring, she settled on a day for the funeral, knowing the ground would be soft enough then. She did not make the date public.

The mid-April day broke clear, and she knew her father would have been upset by the waste of a fine spring day on such nonsense. It was a small procession that rode through the crossroads to the cemetery. Malcolm and Alaura brought a wagon full of workers, ready to move back in for the season. Doc Pride tried to guide Mary into his buggy, but she climbed onto Timber and rode through the clear morning to the shady grove of cedars, then stood stone-faced as the casket was lowered. She threw her handful of dirt onto the coffin wordlessly, and everybody hushed, expecting to hear her say her farewells, but she'd been talking with the dead for months and had no interest in doing so for spectators.

Doc Pride stepped forward into the silence.

"You beat me there, old friend," he said. "But I'll join you soon."

And at last Nathan Willis, pioneer, was buried between his long-dead wife and the fresh grave of his son.

The procession went back to the farm, but she broke from it, staying on the old horse and riding through the light of the late afternoon. She wanted to track the old property lines, the ones he'd claimed fifty years earlier. She trailed along the swollen creek, surveying the high-water mark of the March floods, the flotsam scattered on the bank like matches dropped on the kitchen floor.

She passed the foundation of the mill, and ducked under the dislodged bridge at Town Line Road, its supports wrapped with the detritus of the flood. Turning north, she rode along the western line of the barley field, fallow the year before, now silt-covered and ready for wheat. She skirted the crossroads as the sun dropped, and rode up the small embankment of the rail line, a hundred yards from the train station where she could hear a noisy gathering.

The chill of the evening set in and she pulled her new coat tight. She veered farther west, avoiding the crowd, then moved back through the rye field north of the tracks.

She rode on, eastward toward Alden, seeing the house across the field, its windows glowing yellow. The planter's moon rose over the fields Nathan had cleared many decades before. As it grew dark, Timber, too old for much work himself, stumbled in the black loam underfoot.

She'd hoped the house would be empty and quiet when she finally returned, but the windows still blazed candlelight yellow.

Steeling herself for the warm house and the pitying looks, she took her time brushing Timber, putting him up, and filling his oat bucket. The next stall stood empty, the sawhorses vacant now. It seemed like the first time in an eternity when there wasn't someone she loved in that space waiting to be buried.

Finally, she set her jaw and walked up the path to the house.

Alaura met her at the back door, sat her at the kitchen table, and poured her a glass of corn whiskey.

"They killed the president," she said.

In the week that followed, she carried the offer letter with her everywhere she went. Palmer, Malcolm, and Alaura took charge of the farm, directing the crews on where and what to plow and plant. With each passing day, Mary wondered if she was seeing the work done for the last time. She thought of distant San Francisco, a city where people came so quickly that ships had been scuttled in the harbor for lack of crews to sail them back East. She wondered if a lost woman could escape her own heart there.

But she could not sit while the men worked, and after too many idle days, she went out and got behind a mule herself. Returning to the house from a day of planting, she found her father's lawyer sitting in the study with another man. Alaura had set them there with brandies and a plate of cheese and they'd lit cigars.

Mary made a show of closing doors and opening windows to the cool vernal breeze before taking a seat across from them.

"It seems that you may have already purchased the house without my knowledge," she said, her lips pursed.

"I apologize," Ewell replied, putting the smoldering cigar in the ashtray. "Your father was a good friend. I shared many a cigar with him in this room, and sought to remind myself of those happy times. Mary, this is Captain Fletcher Waters."

"Sir," she said, extending her hand, still dirty from the fields.

His suit was of a fine cut, but his face had the lines of a man that had bought it with hard work.

"A pleasure to meet you," he said. He took her hand, and his fingers were callused and rough. He bent over and she thought he would kiss her hand like some dandy, but instead he held it, and turned it gently. "This soil is the color of ashes. I would wager you could grow anything in it."

She tugged her hand away from his grip. "Anything but sugar cane and cotton. Now what are we discussing today?"

"Direct, as I was led to believe," Waters said. "Well, let's get to it. I'd hoped to get a response to my offer for this farm."

"I buried my father a little more than a week ago," Mary said. "It's planting season. Surely four years of war must have taught you a bit of patience. If not, you do not have the makings of a farmer."

Waters smiled at the jibe.

"You are right, of course," the captain said. "I left the cavalry in January. While I was hotfooting around Virginia and Pennsylvania, my beloved wife, a fine woman not blessed with your . . . ah, shall we say 'fortitude,' was not able to keep things running on my farm, and she sold it and moved to town. That news came closer to killing me than any damned Confederate ever did. Many nights I fell asleep to the dream of going home to till soil. I hoped to see the seed in the ground this spring and I'm afraid I've let my eagerness get the better of my decorum."

"The world is tearing itself apart," Mary said. "Decorum seems the least of our problems."

She poured herself a glass of brandy before refilling theirs.

"I appreciate you coming out here, and your offer is fair," she said, after a pause. "I'm not sure what my plans are."

She swallowed the brandy in one motion and lifted the lawyer's cigar from the ashtray and took a long deep draft. She remembered watching the paroxysm that followed Leander's first cigar, but she would have none of it. She exhaled slowly, the smoke curving around her face. She put the cigar back in the tray, straightened herself, and said, "I will have an answer for you within a week."

She turned her back on them, opened the door, and walked out without another word.

Mary Willis rose before dawn, and walked in the chill and still-dark morning across the rye field toward the lonely elm.

The train was scheduled to leave Batavia in the early hours, passing through a half-dozen small towns before stopping in Buffalo where the casket would be displayed. Eventually it would make its way to Springfield, where, like her own father, he would be buried next to his son.

When she made it to the tracks, she stood still, her hands buried deep in her pockets, listening for the whistle in the morning silence.

"I knew you'd be here," a voice said in the dark, and she knew it was Charlie.

He climbed to his feet from where he'd been sitting cross-legged against the tree.

His hair, pulled into a long ponytail, had gone silver, and he was clean shaven. His face was a map of scars and tattoos, a blue wing etched over his right eye, three parallel lines on his left cheek. But the skin was vibrant and smooth, and it seemed that he had shed a year for each that weighed on her.

"You look like some kind of holy man," she said.

He laughed.

"I'm just a farmer," he said, looking across the planted field. "Hoping to work the earth again."

"There's nothing left here," she said.

He looked east along the parallel rails.

"It's only just morning," he said.

"I think I'm ready to light out for distant territories. To see what there is to see," she said. "I have an offer on the farm. A good one."

The train's whistle sounded even as the sun broke, its light whitening the skim of frost on the peaks of the plowed field. Mary could make out a yellow lamp hanging on the front of the engine, its downward cast lighting the sad-eyed portrait mounted there.

"There's nothing left here," she repeated, watching the approaching light.

"I had planned to ask you to marry me that evening downtown long ago," he said. "At the party."

"What?" she asked. The shock was the first thing she'd felt that wasn't pain in as long as she could remember.

"It all seems another world now. Your father had given me his blessing, even planned a public announcement. But you never came," he said.

"Why didn't you just ask?" she said. "I've always been right here."

"I wanted to," he said. "I rode out here through that storm, I had hoped I could ask when we came to this spot that morning."

She managed a smile.

"I make it hard on those around me," she said.

He stepped a little closer.

"I knew then that you loved him," he said, then motioned to her swelling belly. "I'd raise the child as my own."

She wanted to reach out to him, but would not allow herself to.

"All this is yours," he said, looking at the plowed field. "It's sown with the blood of everyone you've ever loved. You'll find nothing more wherever you go. There is a new world all around. You helped make it. You belong here."

The train passed, shaking the ground under their feet. She watched it recede into the west, passing the Town Line station without pause, the light from its red lanterns glinting on the converging tracks.

The quiet of the morning returned.

"We all start over again, today," he said.

She stared, clear-eyed and awake at the broad western horizon and the pink light of the sunrise striking the budding line of trees across the sowed field.

ACKNOWLEDGMENTS

I've had nearly a decade to compile the list of people that helped make this book possible. Nonetheless, someone key will be forgotten. I apologize in advance.

The volunteers, staff, sponsors, and board of the Decatur Book Festival. If Mary Willis came to life today, she would find her happiness amongst you.

Jessica Handler, Joshilyn Jackson, Natasha Trethewey, Joe Borzynski, Karen Abbott, Da Chen, Charles and Katherine Frazier all read this thing when it wasn't very good and helped me see how it could get better. They bought me drinks, commiserated, and encouraged me when I felt hopeless. What a useless mess this thing would be without you all.

When young writers dream of landing an agent, they are dreaming they will land Marly Rusoff. They may not know her name yet, but that's who they want.

If you spend time around authors, you hear a lot of horror stories about the publishing business, but for me, it has been the land of milk and honey. Thanks to Thomas Dunne, for saying yes. To Joan Higgins, Courtney Reed, Claire Leaden, Lisa Bonvissuto, Melissa Bullock-Campion, and the rest of the team at St. Martins. But especially, to Laurie Chittenden, for supervising the train like that long-gone ancestor of yours did for Honest Abe.

But before all of those, at my heart, is Eva. Thanks for being the sensible half.

ABOUT THE AUTHOR

Daren Wang is the Executive Director of the Atlanta Journal-Constitution Decatur Book Festival, the largest independent book festival in the country. Before launching the festival, he had a twenty-year career in public radio, both national and local, with a particular focus on books and authors. Wang has written for the *Atlanta Journal-Constitution*, *Paste* magazine, and *Five Points* magazine, among others. *The Hidden Light of Northern Fires* is his first novel.